THE AFTERLIFE
OF
ALICE WATKINS

BOOK ONE

MATILDA SCOTNEY

The Afterlife of Alice Watkins: Book One
ISBN: 978-0-6483191-0-8

Cover design by Beehive Book Design

Message from the author

Thank you for purchasing The Afterlife of Alice Watkins. The focus of Alice's story is essentially one of second chances, love and discovery. However, some readers have felt confronted by certain themes in the story that deal with inequality and injustice, particularly directed at same-sex and mixed marriages.

I want to assure my readers of my total opposition to the principles of the area in the story, which I named the 'Calamities'. Please understand the inclusion of these themes are not indicative of my personal mindset and are added only for the completeness and balance of Alice's new society. I personally abhor injustice and disrespect towards ***anyone***.

Alice is an uneducated woman who wakes into a society, which like all societies, has flaws. This society challenges her old belief systems in many ways. I placed elements (amongst others less confronting) before her to help her grow, form opinions, banish her ignorance, suffer indignance, develop empathy, know love, question ideologies, and take her place in her new society. I felt these needed to be elements that existed in her previous life, so she had a basis upon which to compare.

Thank you for taking a moment to read this. I hope you enjoy Alice's amazing journey.

Matilda Scotney

For Wyn Howard
A Truly Great Lady

PROLOGUE _

It isn't so hard to start this story because I was there at the beginning. I just didn't know it. Mum and I arrived to collect Grandma to go to the beauty salon and day spa as a treat for her birthday. Grandma didn't answer the door, so mum used her door key while I waited in the car. When I heard mum scream, I ran inside to see what was wrong.

I still remember the terror, not being able to move, my hand lifted to my mouth. Grandma was sitting in her favourite chair, lips as blue as the blue rinse she always put through her white hair, her hands curled in her lap. Her eyes closed.

Mum was yelling at me to get the paramedics as she pulled Grandma to the floor to try to revive her. Mum knew little about first aid, and I was fumbling with the telephone, trying to answer the emergency service operator's questions.

"Is she breathing?" *"No, I don't think so."*

"Is there a pulse?" *"I don't know."*

I whispered each reply as I watched mum pumping Grandma's chest and attempting to breathe air into her and weeping at the same time. I heard the operator say the ambulance would be there soon, but I could only stand in horror, clutching the phone to my ear. It was starting then—Grandma's story. She was already there.

Alice was our grandmother. The mother of adult children and the widow of an ordinary man. Uncomplicated, predictable, commonplace, and unexceptional. I mean no criticism, she was a lovely person, and I adored her, but she was indeed ordinary. To be honest, she was uneducated, never had prospects, married young and was uncomfortable with everybody she perceived to be better than her, you know, people like shopgirls and garbage collectors and people who cleaned houses. Grandma was ill at ease around those folks, and she didn't—couldn't hide it.

And she believed anything anyone told her. For example, her mother insisted shaving made hairs grow back stronger and thicker. The young Alice listened to what she was told, never doubting her mother's skewed logic.

"If God had wanted you to shave, he would have made you hairless."-Alice's mother.

So, Grandma, for all her adult life, spurned razors and sported hairy armpits, even when her little grandson in recent years told her about her chin hairs, she was terrified to shave, preferring instead to keep the hairs she had in preference to getting longer, thicker ones.

She believed all the ads on TV as well because to her,

they were like biblical truths. Often, she would budget to buy this or that brand of soap powder, so her whites would be whiter!

Grandad used to tease her about a time when she read that putting a rice pudding in the oven with the Sunday roast would economise on gas. She did it for ages until someone asked why she always threw the pudding out (no-one in their house ate rice pudding). She was convinced it did something to the gas oven to make it run better (and cheaper). Gullible, Grandad maintained. And he was right, she was.

Grandma was a teenager in the liberal sixties, but she hadn't been liberal herself. Liberal or any of its counterparts never got a foothold in her mother's house, so she never made friends, and the mother carefully nurtured in her daughter zero ambition and few social skills.

"Girls whose hormones are triggered by kissing and dirty words are not nice girls."-Alice's mother.

Ted, her mother's handyman, kissed Alice when no-one was looking. No hormones got triggered, so Grandma supposed she was "nice." In truth, she had no idea what a "triggered hormone" might even feel like. Ted was her first and only boyfriend, and at seventeen, she married him.

Since the age of thirty, Grandma had the same hairstyle as her mother and over the years, as the mousy tones of her hair grew to a salty white, chose a blue rinse, the same as her mother. She even held her teacup like her mother, laid out the house the same way and often caught herself dishing out old wives' tales for advice, just like her mother. And she still didn't understand why the rice pudding story made people laugh.

As the years rolled by, she became all that her mother had insisted on and, without considering it, supposed it would be that way with her own daughter when she got old. Generations of hairy armpits and blue rinses, but her daughter (my mother), Michelle, rebelled and shaved her armpits. And her legs and somewhere else that shocked Grandma!

But now Grandma had sprouted chin hairs, her wee grandson Toby pointed them out in a loud voice, "Grandma, you got a beard!"

She got up to look at herself in the mirror, pushing the small, accusing body with the probing fingers from her lap to see for herself how much more she was becoming her mother. She wasn't sure she wanted them removed, but Michelle had other ideas. Grandma didn't have original thoughts, never really needing them because everyone else did her thinking for her; her mum, her husband, and then after he died, Michelle, her eldest child, made the decisions. And Michelle had now decreed her mother needed these particular hairs dealt with even if the underarm ones stayed put.

Grandma didn't understand the goings-on of beauty salons or day spas, only knew Michelle liked them and that they did "things," but she was suspicious and anxious about what those "things" might be, despite her daughter seeming to enjoy the experience thoroughly. Michelle, at forty-one years of age, had been going to the beautician all her adult life.

As Grandma's sixty-fifth birthday approached, a visit to the salon and day spa was organised, where our hairy grandma would lose her chin hairs and have her first facial and massage.

"Facial?" she said, her eyes wide with the enormity of it all. *"Where they peel your skin off?"*

She had read about facials in a magazine and hadn't grasped the concept and now, with the expectation of having one herself, suffered no small measure of anxiety. Still, Grandma would not dare challenge her daughter and, in the end, tried to accept my reassurances.

After the salon, Mum decided Grandma would be off to the hairdressers to update her hairstyle and get foils. "Foils" baffled Grandma, but Michelle organised it with no thought of asking if all this beauty therapy was welcome. Grandma told me privately that she always thought her blue rinse smart and stylish and that she would miss it. I tried to tell my mum, but she ignored me because she wanted Grandma to have all these things done, insisting she would love the results.

So, that was my grandma. I've told you something about her, so you might understand how her extraordinary experiences changed her and shaped the woman she became. What comes next is her own remarkable story, entrusted to me so many years ago, and though we were close, I wasn't part of what happened or part of where she went, only that she asked me to write it down for her. "Like a novel," she said. "No-one will believe it anyway," were her exact words.

It's her story until it's finished, and as you will see, "finished" means something that had a beginning, a middle and a conclusion. You can decide for yourself where the unremarkable, homely, getting-on-in-years, Alice Watkins's story started, middled, and ended. Or even if it has not yet begun.

Eliza Campbell (Alice's granddaughter)
Sydney NSW – 19th August 2103

CHAPTER ONE _

Alice Watkins seldom bothered with the mirror, but that morning, she screwed up her face to check out the wrinkles that had been her constant companions for many years. She'd lived behind this face for almost sixty-five years, a face that at one time had been smooth and unlined. Now, deep creases etched both sides of her nose and mouth, but their presence didn't trouble her. The wrinkles were welcome to make their home in her face because, after all, that's what happens when you get old. Alice accepted such things.

She thrust up her chin, inspecting the hairs that were due to be waxed off that day and ran an arthritic finger over her neck and jaw, the bristly sensation reminding her of the stubble on her late husband's face when he hadn't shaved.

Alice Watkins suffered not a skerrick of vanity. Still, Toby thought facial hair on his grandma so hilarious; she wondered if others found them entertaining. Perhaps people at the shop were snickering and pointing at the bearded lady. Hence, she kept her head down since Toby drew her attention to them, knowing all the while, no-one would bother paying her any mind.

"Why would anyone be watching you, Alice Watkins? What's so special about you?"-Alice's mother.

Alice's sixty-fifth birthday was on Saturday, and a special family dinner arranged to mark the occasion. Michelle decided it was too much to pack into one day and arranged for the three of them, herself, Eliza, and Alice, to visit the day spa a few days before.

Alice didn't know what went on in a day spa, but Michelle waved away her concerns, explaining that the ladies there would wax off Alice's chin hairs, put hot stones on her back, give her an "all over massage" and do "stuff" to her face to relax the wrinkles. It would be a wonderful experience, Michelle promised, but it didn't sound wonderful to Alice, even though she didn't dare argue and only hoped the day spa ladies wouldn't make her take off her bra and knickers.

On that day, the pre-birthday, chin-hair-gone day, blue rinse gone day, Alice lingered at the hall mirror. She didn't want to forget what it looked like to grow old gracefully as her mother's God intended and feared she might not recognise the new image that would look back at her when she arrived home.

So, what if she came back all fresh and tarted up? Who would see it? Who would care? Alice didn't, but if it gave Michelle pleasure to take her to this place, she would go obediently and not complain.

Turning away, she checked her watch. There were

still a few minutes before Michelle and Eliza were due to arrive, so she eased herself into the somewhat saggy-seated, worse-for-wear old chair facing the window. Folding her hands in her lap, she allowed her mind to wander as she strained her ears a smidgeon to hear if Michelle's far-too-large four-wheel drive had turned up the street. She thought about the new baby Michelle was due to have in a month and marvelled, not for the first time, how she fitted that enormous baby bump behind the steering wheel.

Michelle had to drop the other children off at school first, but Eliza, now aged sixteen, had finished for the year, her exams over. Alice loved that Eliza was going with them, even though she couldn't imagine what Eliza might need at a day spa. As beautiful as a model, bright, happy and the apple of her grandma's eye, she would easily get a job in an insurance firm or a department store that one! Alice's heart filled with pride at the thought of her granddaughter's future success.

Sammy, the big tabby cat with one tooth, jumped on Alice's lap. It was only eight-thirty, but the day had already warmed, and through the open window, she could hear the city waking up in the distance. Sammy's fat tummy was cosy and rumbly—he wouldn't recognise her when she got home. She tickled his ears and watched the rogue branch of the frangipani tree tapping against the window. What on earth possessed her to plant the blasted thing so close to the house? She must cut it back again before it broke the windowpane—it had only been a few weeks since she last went out to it with her secateurs.

Alice felt warm and sleepy; it would be so easy to close her eyes and doze. The day spa might be nice, she thought, trying to reconcile herself to going and hoping that keeping her bra and knickers on wouldn't be an issue. Eliza said they had gowns, but that knowledge hadn't been enough to reassure her.

If her mother had still been alive, she'd have pursed her lips and told Ted, and Ted would have said the day spa was "a bloody waste of money," and Alice wouldn't have gone. Now, she could do as she pleased, no mother, no Ted. If she wanted, she could take the chin hairs off with a razor, even pull them out by the roots, although that might make them grow back thicker, darker, stronger, despite Michelle assuring her that was an old wives' tale and that waxing made them finer and less noticeable when they regrew. Even so, the idea of defying her deceased mother and husband still caused Alice considerable anxiety.

And so, Alice's small, simple life and thoughts sat with her in the chair with Sammy. The rhythmic tapping of the branch lulled her, and she thought she heard Michelle's car pull into the driveway, but her eyelids felt heavy, and it wasn't easy to stir herself to get up to answer the door. And why suddenly, was it night?

CHAPTER TWO _

Alice tried to open her eyes, but her eyelids were too heavy. From somewhere around her, an unfamiliar scent wafted into her nostrils, and she heard an irritating knocking sound at the door. Odd? Michelle had a key. Why not just let herself in? Alice's legs had gone to sleep; the pins and needles were so intense she tried to hoist herself into a position to get her blood flowing and to push Sammy off her lap. But he wasn't there. Alice supposed he jumped off while she slept, preferring to sit in his special spot on the floor where the sun came through the window.

She made to sit up, certain now she was awake, but her body wouldn't co-operate. Either way, she was conscious of being in an odd place, somewhere between sleeping and waking. Her vision, good for someone of nearly sixty-five and only a bit hazy when watching TV, was more clouded as she attempted to focus. She couldn't tell if her eyes were open or closed, it all seemed so bright, and she couldn't make out any forms through the brightness.

Alice's legs lay straight out in front of her, just like in bed, and as the sensation returned, she could feel the soft touch of a light blanket on her feet. Strange, she'd been sitting in a chair, with Sammy, waiting for Michelle and Eliza. Now, she was in a bed, under a blanket and unable to move.

Years of no excitement and not a single adrenalin rush took their toll. Alice lay dazed, paralysed, and confused, hoping someone would come and tell her how she came to be here. There was always someone who knew best, but where on earth was she? Not in her chair, that much was certain, so there was nothing to do but wait, and as she waited, she ticked off her most recent memories, playing them around and around in her head. Michelle, Eliza, chin hairs, day spa, the branch on the tree; she made a mental checklist to tick off each one. Tick. Tick. But the memories wouldn't hold still long enough for her to arrange them into any order.

Alice delved further back to capture the events and put them into a proper sequence. She'd been standing in front of the hall mirror; then she sat in the chair where she must have dozed off with Sammy while waiting for Michelle and Eliza. The same scenario played out over and over, with little details being added and subtracted, and now and then, she tried to see through the fog, each time giving up because she could only make out vague shapes and colours. A sudden, terrifying thought came to her about Ted, how he'd felt when he had his stroke.

"Can't see too well," he told her when it first happened, his voice slurred and tired. "Like someone's tied me up in blankets."

Can't see and tied up in blankets? Although she had little imagination for imagery, this must have been what it was like for Ted, and that could only mean one thing; the same thing had happened to her, and she was going through what he had gone through. A stroke. It would be the only explanation, but Ted died, leaving Alice a widow at fifty-seven years old. She wasn't ready to die, and she didn't want a stroke. She tried to cry out, to call for help, but her motionless body thwarted all her attempts to attract attention.

"I've had a stroke, and I'm in St Marys Hospital." Alice tried hard to say it aloud, but no sound came, just a jumbled rattle of words that crashed about in her throat. She thought of Michelle and Eliza's worry when they came to collect her for the day spa. They would have found her unconscious in the chair and would be dreadfully upset. Only, Alice didn't remember them arriving, just her chin hairs, sitting with the cat, the noisy branch and then, here.

Ted had been looked after at St Mary's Hospital during his illness, and knowing she was there too steadied her a little, giving her much needed comfort. She would have good care here, and she must place herself in their hands, then she would get better. It wasn't their fault Ted died.

But Alice didn't remember having a headache or tiredness like Ted suffered in the weeks leading to his stroke. It must have been sudden because now, she couldn't move a muscle, and there were no warning signs.

There was no way of Alice knowing how long she

waited before a figure came into view. A figure with a kind, smiling, blurry face. The figure leaned over and spoke, but the sound of the person's voice made Alice's ears ring, a ringing when she breathed in and a different ring when she breathed out. She tried focusing again, but it was all so noisy and difficult and frightening. Alice felt pressure on her arm, reassuring pressure, the kind person was trying to help, but the confusion lingered.

"Don't try to speak." Alice battled to make out the words that combined with the ringing. It was a pleasant voice, a woman's voice, confirming to Alice that she must be in St Mary's because everyone was nice there.

Even a simple soul needs answers, and Alice wanted to know what had happened. And she wanted Michelle. The vet placed Sammy on a special diet only the day before, and she planned to tell her about it on the way to the day spa. Now, Michelle would be looking after Sammy and might give him the wrong things to eat. He had only one tooth, so his food needed to be soft.

Alice tried once more to rouse herself, but there was no point. Her arms and legs remained limp and useless. She was locked into her body, and she was frightened, her fear causing a solitary tear to roll down her cheek, a tear seen by the kind lady in the room who gently wiped it away.

As the kind lady dried her tear, a man appeared at the side of the bed. His face came close to Alice. He smiled and looked into her eyes, lifting her eyelids like she'd seen the doctors do to Ted. She peered up at the man, trying to make out his face, hoping her eyes would communicate her fear. If he were a doctor, he would know why she was here, but when she tried to ask, she only managed a few grunts and some aimless twitching of her arms, then that awful ringing sound when the man spoke. Bewildered and exhausted, she gave up, and the man placed his hands on her shoulders.

"Try not to struggle," he said, but his voice was indistinct because of the ringing, and she found it hard to make out what he was saying. "You are still uncoordinated. It will take a little time before you learn to use your senses again."

Alice was aware of the touch of his hand and the lady who touched her arm; that's a good sign, isn't it? But without warning, a sudden coolness swept over her body, and as the man and woman drifted away, she glimpsed a third person, a pale, white-haired young man, gazing at her over the doctor's shoulder.

Alice always slept well. Her mother said she could sleep on the edge of a razor blade, and this place was no different. When she woke again, in what she assumed was the next morning, her vision had improved enough to question if it was morning at all because no sunshine came into the room. Ted's room at the hospital had been bright and sunny and even had a view of the gardens from his window. Maybe this was intensive care? Though it didn't seem as if there were other patients or lots of machines.

Michelle would have been in to visit, and Steven

might even be on his way from the oil rig—Michelle would have told her brother about the stroke. By now, she would also have found the new diet food for Sammy in the cupboard under the sink.

With her improved vision, Alice established she was not alone. A tall woman with clear, olive skin, dark hair, and a blue dress stood in front of a desk. She looked neat and efficient. Alice thought she might be a hospital cleaner or orderly because lots of them came from overseas, the Philippines or Spain or somewhere—she didn't know, but often, their English wasn't very good. Alice tried to speak, but her voice was weak and distant, and it took a supreme effort to get any sound out, having to employ her whole body in forming the words, with even her bottom cheeks getting involved. Every word she spoke got squeezed out from heaven knows where, but with uncharacteristic perseverance, she attracted the woman's attention.

"Can you get the nurse, please?"

Her voice, a low, hoarse whisper, sounded hollow and clattering to Alice, and the short sentence took an eternity to produce. Still, the woman came close and listened patiently, from Alice's first squeaky syllable right through to the equally squeaky conclusion. She placed her ear close to Alice's mouth, and Alice realised it was the same kind face she had seen before. She was happy to see the face again and grateful for the woman's patience while she stumbled and stammered through her words. When she finished, the woman smiled.

"I'm your appointed carer. You can call me Kelly,"

the woman told her. Alice liked her smile. "I'll provide anything you need or want and be with you at all times." She patted Alice's hand, sending pins and needles shooting along her arm. The woman's voice was educated and unaccented, but "appointed carer" meant nothing to Alice. Nurse would have made far more sense.

"Are you a nurse?" Alice squeezed out more words. She thought she spoke clearly, but her rasping, hollow speech must be garbled from the stroke as Kelly appeared not to understand.

"I care for you, your health, well-being and rehabilitation," Kelly said, speaking slowly and distinctly, so her patient would understand.

Alice tried the question again. What she said, despite its raspiness, sounded okay to her. Perhaps the woman didn't understand English as well as she spoke it.

"Am I in St Mary's Hospital?"

The lady in blue, Kelly, shook her head and took Alice's hand.

"I know you have many questions. Dr Grossmith will answer them for you, but you've been here a long time, and it might be a while before you make sense of your surroundings."

A long time? Alice heard her, but it made no sense. If she'd been in the hospital a long time, she would have known. It begged the scratchy-sounding, bottom-clenching challenge to produce a question. Two questions.

"How long? And where are Michelle and Eliza?"

Kelly shook her head again to show she didn't

understand.

Alice remembered a story in a magazine at the hairdressers, about a woman in a coma who woke up speaking French. She hadn't believed it, but this Kelly didn't understand even simple questions. Alice knew Michelle was a French name, so this lady would at least understand that, but she didn't; instead, Alice saw her reach above the bed, then she gave her hand a gentle squeeze.

"I've called Dr Grossmith for you. He's far better equipped for questions than I am."

Yes, perhaps the doctor would understand. With a closer look and better eyesight, Alice saw that Kelly was young and slim with large brown eyes set underneath perfect, arched eyebrows. She had a flawless complexion, and there was not a single hair out of place. With an air of efficiency and dedication, something in her demeanour suggested to Alice she took that efficiency and dedication to a higher level than even the kind nurses at St Mary's Hospital.

So, with no answers, no imagination and little education, and waiting for Dr Grossmith, Alice formulated a different idea; not a stroke but an accident in that far-too-large car that Michelle drove. She couldn't remember an accident; though she had heard sometimes, people wipe out the memory of such things.

If so, Michelle and Eliza would have been in the car too. Michelle was eight months pregnant, the baby due in December. Dear God, where were they?

CHAPTER THREE _

Dr Grossmith arrived around the time Alice worked out the new reason for being in intensive care, the stroke idea now abandoned. Sitting beside her on the bed, Dr Grossmith smiled and patted her hand, just like Kelly did, sending the same pins and needles cascading up and down her arm. Alice recalled the doctors and nurses patting Ted's hand; sometimes, it meant bad news, but not this time.

"Good morning! It's good to see you wide awake! I can finally introduce myself to you. I'm Dr Grossmith; I understand you are asking questions?" His smile was so enormous, Alice thought he would hug her! She had a good view of him now, older, white hair, grey eyes. Tall for a man of his age and dressed in a grey uniform.

"Now," he continued, "I will try to answer your questions. Take your time." He had a kind voice, and he seemed so pleased to see her, he couldn't stop grinning. Alice attempted to smile back.

"Good, good! Facial muscles are working well. Now, you must work hard to recover your memories; that will take some rehabilitation, my dear. Only baby steps for now."

"Where are Michelle and Eliza?" Alice spoke slowly, and as Kelly had before, the doctor waited for her to gather the words.

When she finished, Kelly and Dr Grossmith looked at each other. This time, there could be no doubt they understood. Alice was positive she wasn't speaking French. She didn't know any French words anyway, except for the name Michelle.

"I'm sorry," Dr Grossmith said. "I'm not aware of either Michelle or Eliza—you are the only one."

"The only one?" What did that mean? The only one of *what?* The only one who *survived?* It couldn't be! Alice wouldn't believe it. She wanted to gag from sheer terror but had to control the alarm and get answers.

Alice's voice came out strained and hesitant, "Michelle is my daughter." Each word was formed with painstaking effort, an effort that demanded rest after every one or two words, but Alice needed to know what had happened. Thankfully, her audience was patient and respectful. "She's eight months pregnant, and Eliza is my granddaughter. She's sixteen. Were they in the accident? Did they go to a different hospital?"

Dr Grossmith's brow creased into a concerned frown, and he glanced at Kelly, who made a small movement of her shoulders to show she didn't understand either. The doctor shook his head and stroked his chin. Alice had seen doctors on the TV do this when considering a diagnosis, but when he next spoke, he avoided answering the question.

"Your memory processes need to settle down a little more, my dear," he said. "This isn't a hospital, but a specialised facility. There's nothing wrong with you now. You had several tumours and an aneurysm. There is no evidence you were involved in an accident."

Alice didn't wish to question her betters, but all this felt wrong.

"You understand me, don't you?" she asked, her voice plaintive and shaky with tears. Why couldn't they answer her questions? They were just confusing her even more. It was as if they should be saying all this to someone else.

Dr Grossmith nodded, "Yes, my dear, every word, you speak very well, considering."

They watched her confusion, trying to get answers, make sense of the situation. How lonely and frightening it must be to have been through so much with still so much of the unknown ahead. Her first words perplexed them both. It would be natural for her to question her surroundings, but to ask for specific people and not to have any memories they could verify was unexpected. Still, with no precedence, no criteria against which to compare, they had no choice but to follow their instincts. This woman, this situation, was unique.

Too weak to sob, Alice felt the tears running down her face. Kelly took Dr Grossmith's place and sat on the bed to comfort her, massaging her hands until the pins and needles and tears settled. Dr Grossmith stepped back to allow Kelly to soothe her.

"Early days," Dr Grossmith whispered to Kelly, then smiled at Alice as he made to leave the room. Kelly responded with a nod, looked at Alice, then back to him.

"I'll look after her."

Alice didn't see the exchange because she'd dwindled back into familiar confusion. Every cell in her body got caught up in the turmoil as she changed her mind again about what had put her here. Not a stroke or a coma but still in her chair, with Sammy, waiting for Michelle and Eliza, dozing and having a fantastic dream.

Alice knew sometimes people woke up in dreams. She once read it in a magazine at the hairdressers. That must be it. It all made such sense now. She hadn't been ill; this must all be a vivid dream. Grateful for the comfort this realisation gave her, she relaxed and enjoyed the gentle massage, glad the explanation was so simple. Now, it was only a matter of waiting until she woke properly. She allowed herself to drift, secure in the knowledge she would wake in her chair, go to the day spa and have her chin hairs and armpits waxed—no, not her armpits, and definitely not the other unmentionable place. She decided she would keep her knickers on, regardless.

To her dismay, there was no morning sun when she woke. Still trapped in the dream, she had no more control over her body than earlier. She felt vulnerable here, with people who said things she didn't understand.

Alice knew dreaming time differed from waking time, so a long time might only be moments, and she tried to take comfort from that, plus the fact that now her vision had cleared, she could see better than she ever could when she was awake in her real life. As a bonus, she could swivel her head a little to inspect her room.

It was an odd room, with walls made of smooth glass she couldn't see through. There were no corners to speak of, and in one place, part of the wall curved inwards, like an inside-out bubble. She had difficulty inclining her head around fully because of the stiffness, but there weren't any tables or pictures or windows she could see. Kelly, who always managed to be there when Alice was "awake", worked quietly in front of a glass panel. She turned to see Alice watching her.

"Hello, sleepyhead," she said, seating herself beside Alice and fiddling with a few shiny objects on a table near the head of the bed. "How are you this morning?"

Alice thought she nodded, but she wasn't sure; whatever the action, Kelly grinned and helped her sit up.

"I've tied all this up out of the way," she said, reaching over to smooth Alice's hair. "It's grown long, way past your waist! We can sort it out when you are up and about."

Alice had never been allowed long hair. Her mother insisted on it being short, so she didn't get lice, but she always longed for long, black swingy hair. In her dream, it would seem she had given herself her wish.

Dr Grossmith's face appeared behind Kelly, breaking into a broad grin at seeing Alice sitting up in bed.

"Well, how is our patient today?" he took Kelly's place beside Alice.

"More relaxed, Dr Grossmith," Kelly looked to Alice for confirmation, and Alice nodded a little. Happy with that, Kelly went off to busy herself, although just where Alice couldn't see, and she took the opportunity to ask questions of Dr Grossmith.

"I would like to know where I am, Doctor, and why. I don't want to hold you up," Alice heard her voice gathering strength. "I'm sure you're very busy." Yes, her voice was clearer, and she took far less time to say what she wanted.

"You're not holding me up at all!" Dr Grossmith leaned a little closer and whispered, "You are my favourite patient!" Then he sat up again with a grin, hoping he had reassured her about bothering him. He had, but she was still waiting for him to answer the question.

"As to where you are, this place, my dear, as we said a few days ago…"

"A few days ago?" Alice echoed, flummoxed—dreams don't go on for "a few days". She was only snoozing in a chair—she can't possibly be still dreaming.

"Ah! I see the time difference is puzzling," Dr Grossmith crossed his legs and folded his hands over his knee.

"I'm sorry for interrupting you, Doctor," Alice said, quick to apologise, "but you said, 'a few days ago,' yet it seems like only yesterday you were last here."

He nodded. Speak in simple terms. Baby steps for him too, he thought as he reminded himself of her specialness. She had no equivalent in the known universe. She *was* the unknown.

"Well, it's true you sleep for extended periods, but these are becoming shorter, and soon, I'm confident you will be back into a more natural rhythm. We believe it to be an after-effect of your suspension, but as your situation is unparalleled, it's all supposition. As to why you are here, when you woke from stasis, most of the medical issues we expected were somehow resolved."

He waited, in the hope his words might prompt a reaction, but when none was forthcoming, he continued, "We undertook several procedures to restore you to full health, and as time passed, you became less dependent on life support, but you didn't recover as anticipated and your body gave no clues on how we should proceed. We had no choice but to monitor and observe and hope we were doing the right thing."

Dr Grossmith was wasting his time expecting her to react. Alice had taken to watching his mouth move because he wasn't making any sense. *What on earth was he talking about?*

And it was manifestly plain to him he'd only confused her further.

"You've been here with us for a long time," he said, hoping a different approach might work. "Although you have been free of the Extended Life Support Prosthesis for four years, you never showed any awareness of your surroundings until a month ago." He grimaced and pursed his lips, wondering if his context might be perplexing to an already clouded mind.

But he knew no other description. The ELSP was the whole life support system used for the most critical patients until they recovered at least basic, independent functioning. She was on it for six years before weaning onto partial support.

It meant nothing to Alice.

Life Prosthesis? *What was that?* Alice moved her head from side to side, only managing enough movement to signify she didn't understand. How, she asked herself again, is it possible for anyone to have a dream with words and things and ideas of which they had no waking knowledge and had never read about in a magazine?

"You're shaking your head; you don't understand? You don't remember?"

Alice made the same movement again, only stronger this time, and Dr Grossmith realised she'd agreed to both of his comments. She neither understood nor remembered.

"Perhaps if we get you up and about, you may make better sense of it all. Tomorrow, we'll check on your reflexes in readiness for walking. If all is well, we'll get you moving." He knew none of this was guaranteed to make a difference. "Your confusion is understandable," he said, "this is a whole new world for us both, but you are doing remarkably well. We are very pleased with your progress."

Progress? The stroke? They said she hadn't been in

an accident. Maybe the dream. Do dreams progress?

And then, if she wasn't confused enough, before her eyes, after smiling and making a funny little bowing movement towards her, Dr Grossmith disappeared, as if by magic, through the curved, inside-out bubble in the wall. Alice didn't understand technology, but she was sure no machine existed which made people disappear, and there was no way she could dream up such a thing.

What if she never woke up and only stayed here like this? She supposed she might be hearing the doctors in St Mary's talking about her in real life, and what they were saying was filtering through to here, but it wouldn't explain how Dr Grossmith, a real live person, could vanish into thin air.

And where were Michelle and Eliza?

She attempted to conjure them up, but nothing happened, then focused on the indentation in the wall where Dr Grossmith disappeared and imagined Michelle coming through, again, nothing. Perhaps if she called her name.

"Michelle?"

Kelly came over, "Did you say something?"

Alice nodded, "Yes, Michelle, my daughter."

"Your daughter?" Kelly pulled up a high stool and sat next to Alice's bed, her face so kind and friendly, it made Alice glad Kelly was her nurse and would be with her all the time.

"Sometimes," Kelly told Alice, "we've found in people who suffered brain damage, memories surface which don't belong to them, but are echoes of things they have seen or read about. Michelle may be someone from your past."

Alice appreciated Kelly's kindness, but she'd got it wrong.

"Michelle's my daughter. Why isn't she here in my dream?"

"Do you believe you are dreaming?" Kelly seemed surprised.

"Yes, no, I don't know," Alice said. "I believe I've had a stroke or ameerism...that thing Dr Grossmith said I had and I'm in a coma, in St Mary's and I'm dreaming. Or I'm asleep in my chair and dreaming there."

Kelly couldn't even begin to imagine how perplexing it must be for her patient, and she had nothing to offer that might help. She lifted the covers from Alice's bed.

"Things will become clearer, I promise. Now, I want to prepare your limbs for your first steps on your own. You've been out of the land of the living far too long."

Kelly moved Alice's body with skill and patience, and in such a way, Alice felt the life flooding back to her limbs. Kelly explained all the instruments and lights as she touched the various parts of Alice's body needed for this exercise. Alice understood none of the explanations but loved feeling so invigorated. Was this how a hot stone massage feels? If so, Alice liked it!

"Why didn't we do this before, Kelly? It's wonderful!" Alice rewarded Kelly with the brightest smile her out-of-practise face could muster.

"We did, many, many times, you've just forgotten," Kelly laughed as she worked. "Dr Grossmith and your other Kelly's have been doing this for years. If we hadn't, your muscles would have wasted, and your nerves rendered unresponsive. That would have been a sad state of affairs and one we worked hard to avoid, but that you feel wonderful is a good sign." Kelly hugged Alice before settling her back on the pillow. But Alice's joy dissipated quickly into the familiar confusion. *Doing it for years? Why didn't she remember any of it?*

CHAPTER FOUR _

As always, Alice had no idea of how long she had slept, but this time, when she opened her eyes, a tall, stern man bent over her, peering into her face. Without a word or any form of greeting, he passed a small box across her body and, every so often, held it up to view, then returned to his examination. Dr Grossmith and Kelly were there, observing. Alice didn't know who this elegant man with a moustache might be, taller than Dr Grossmith and dressed similarly; he had neither friendly face nor manner. Alice decided he bore a remarkable resemblance to a prune.

"Are you breathless?" the man did not introduce himself before placing a white pencil-shaped object over her chest. He must be a doctor, Alice thought. A very senior doctor.

She shook her head.

"Any discomfort?"

"No, doctor," she mumbled, it would be impolite not to answer. Years of indoctrination still rear their head in dreams, it would seem. "I'm alright, a bit stiff. I have a touch of arthritis."

The tall man raised an eyebrow and said "Ah-ha," like old Mr Sykes who lived down near the railway, one eyebrow always down and the other hidden under a cap pulled over his brow and who only spoke a couple of words like "ah-ha," and "one-one," and "hello." He always said "hello" to Alice, but she never replied because she feared him.

"Well," the tall man said, at last, straightening and turning to Dr Grossmith, his eyebrow remaining raised. "At least her language is standard English-based."

Alice was too afraid to comment. This doctor looked grand and important, grander and more important even than Dr Grossmith, but why the remark about her speaking English? She couldn't speak any other language.

"I'm Dr Clere," the tall man turned back to Alice, placing his hand on his chest by way of introduction. "I have been overseeing your recovery, at least regarding your heart, kidneys and liver. You'll be pleased to know they are in perfect working order." Dr Clere's speech was clipped and lacking in any warmth or kindness.

Alice felt it essential she must be polite and answer. If he was a doctor leaking into her dream from the hospital, he might think her rude.

"Thank you for taking such good care of me. Dr Grossmith told me I'm cured."

"My colleague refers to the tumours. I refer to the heart and kidneys and that part of the liver which required regrowth. These organs are mature and functioning and subject to the usual rules of maintaining one's health."

Dr Grossmith raised his hands to stop his colleague from continuing.

"Our patient has suffered some confusion of thought, Dr Clere. I have not yet informed her of this part of her treatment."

"Oh?" Dr Clere was most put out at not having either this information or his significant role conveyed to the patient but pleased to explain to Alice his contribution as he launched into a self-congratulatory speech on the wonders of his treatment.

His explanation got lost in the fog of her uneducated brain. She had never heard words and phrases such as cell engineering, cell coaxing, organoids, support scaffolds, in situ and the biological complexity of reprogramming and regrowing cells given her physical condition and how he prevailed against considerable odds. It was all foreign to Alice, but she did marvel he could say all that without scarcely pausing for breath.

Disregarding her expression of undisguised bewilderment, Dr Clere assumed his account was reaching the mark, so he continued, full of self-importance and pride in his abilities, pausing only once for effect. Dr Grossmith took that moment to point out that although Alice was listening, she understood not a single word.

Dr Clere conceded grudgingly with a slight bow that perhaps he had been a little enthusiastic in expounding the appeal of cytotechnology.

"Well, Dr Langley, you and your fellow researchers

were foremost in the study of cytology in your time. Indeed, portions of your research are still relevant today. You have received a new heart, new kidneys and a small section of the liver. We placed neurological stents...," Dr Grossmith laid a hand on Dr Clere's arm lest he continued to confound the patient. Dr Clere turned to him, then to Alice, who was busy trying to find this Dr Langley, even though she could see no-one else in the room.

"I apologise," Dr Clere said. "I realise this must be a little overwhelming, and of course, the details can wait. It is enough you are recovering."

"I have a new heart, new kidneys and a piece of my liver?" she asked.

"That is correct, Dr Langley," Dr Clere acknowledged, "and I also understand you are asking questions about your surroundings. That's good. We also have many questions, but—" he glanced at Dr Grossmith, "those questions can wait. For now, I'm content you have made such remarkable strides in your recovery. We can learn much from you."

"I still don't know where I am," Alice whispered.

There were four important people in this room, Dr Grossmith, Dr Clere, Kelly and another doctor, Dr Langley, who Alice couldn't see. Alice felt overwhelmed and shrank down into her bed, plucking at her blanket. Kelly moved to stand beside her, creating a silent barrier between Alice and Dr Clere. Her patient needed compassion and understanding, and Dr Clere was a supercilious oaf with a habit of being overbearing. He chose not to address Alice's petition, just offered a declaration of his own.

"You've been asleep for a long time, Dr Langley, but now, you are awake. Properly awake."

Alice did not believe herself to be awake. If this was as awake as she would ever be, she didn't want it. She wanted her old life, not locked into her body with only dream people around. She wanted her grandchildren and Michelle and Steven.

Dr Clere scrutinised her for a moment longer before deciding he had no further reason to be here or participate in this conversation. With one small, unsmiling bow that took in Alice, Kelly, Dr Grossmith and the unseen Dr Langley, he collected his equipment and vanished through the wall. Dr Grossmith raised his eyebrows and grinned at Kelly in a shared understanding of Dr Clere's poorly cultivated bedside manner. A disappearance through the wall was now accepted by Alice as a natural element of her dream, even though Dr Clere said she was "properly" awake.

"How did they know I had this anee—anjee—thing you said," she asked Dr Grossmith as he sat beside her, performing tasks with instruments she didn't understand but trusted him with.

"An aneurysm."

"Yes, I don't even know what an anjerism is. Did Michelle and Eliza find me? They were taking me to the day spa. It's my birthday on Saturday. I'll be sixty-five."

Dr Grossmith stopped what he was doing. He was

unprepared for this. Even after having devoted almost his whole career to this extraordinary woman, he assumed, dreamed even, that if she ever awoke, she would be the person she'd been before. Her identity was well-established, and though he anticipated a degree of disorientation and therefore could accept her somewhat rambling questions, her references to Michelle and Eliza puzzled him. There must be reasons for her behaving this way. Her previous KELA carers told him that once or twice, during many of their movement and stimulation sessions, she had rambled about a Michelle and a new baby that was coming.

Dr Grossmith had a custom of contorting his face and rubbing his hands together when pressed; he was doing it now under Alice's not-so-patient gaze. He realised he was taking too long to reply, but these responses required careful thought. His answers needed to be measured, so he decided to play along to some extent without blundering in with replies that might confound. It was essential to speak in a manner not meant to patronise but as if talking to a child, or as he believed, a patient suffering from amnesia. He did his best, but the explanation, when it came, still proved too technical and terrifying for Alice, and he had no more luck in helping her understand than Clere had, even in using what he considered the most straightforward language.

"The aneurysm had a role in a much wider problem. You had a tumour in your brain, here," he showed her on his own head the general area. "The tumour spread into your spine, and from my understanding, at the time of your preservation, it would have been inoperable.

"We know at one time, tumours were also present in the liver, kidneys and lungs, but some unknown factor, possibly the preservation fluid, reversed their growth. There are no signs of any active cancerous lesions anywhere in your body now. Our doctors here repaired the aneurysm."

"I have cancer?" Alice understood that at least, but she hadn't known—she had been so well. To discover now she was so desperately ill made little sense.

"You *had* cancer," Dr Grossmith emphasised. "You don't now. Nor an aneurysm. Apart from needing therapy to help you walk, you are, at least physically, in excellent health."

Dr Grossmith must be wrong.

"I have never been sick in my life, doctor," Alice said, thinking about how she felt as she sat in her old chair. "I didn't know cancer could be sudden. I was going out for my birthday, and I felt fine. I must have collapsed, and Michelle and Eliza found me when they came to collect me."

Dr Grossmith shook his head, "The Chinese military found you. In a cavern at the base of a mountain, placed there by your uncle to protect the sarcophagus."

This was extraordinary! Steven went on a school trip to China years ago. That must be creeping into the dream. She knew the cancer word though and dreaming or not; it scared her. People died of cancer. Now she was being told she'd had it all over her body, and that was why she'd been so sick. And all without her knowledge. How could that be?

Alice took a deep breath and offered what she thought explained her presence in this place. Why she would ever dream about cancer was beyond her comprehension.

"I'm in the hospital and in a coma," Alice said, "like my husband Ted before he died, and I can hear what the doctors are saying, but my brain is mixing it all together."

Dr Grossmith listened to her explanation. He would give her as much time as she needed. He'd already devoted forty years of his life to her; he could afford to be patient.

"This isn't a dream, but these times awake do tire you; do you wish to sleep?"

"Only because I might wake up properly next time, Doctor." Alice lifted her hand and gestured feebly around the room, "And not in this strange dream with words and—" she pointed to the wall where people disappeared, "amazing things, but I'm not tired, it seems as soon as anyone mentions sleep, I do it anyway."

"That, my dear Alexis," Dr Grossmith said as he stood, "is because your body knows best."

As the familiar coolness swept over her, Alice thought she saw concern mixed with the kindness in Dr Grossmith's face, and how curious? He called her Alexis.

The next time Alice opened her eyes, she was fully awake

and moving well. Her breathing had become easier, and her sense of touch returned to such a degree she could appreciate the softness of the blanket draped across her— such a lovely fabric, so light and perfect for a blanket for Michelle's new baby. Alice made a mental note to pop down to the fabric shop and get some when she got home from the hospital. And her vision was so clear! She always hated wearing glasses, so maybe strokes, anjerisms, whatever, had an upside.

"Nurse?"

As always, Kelly was at her side almost as soon as she spoke.

"Call me Kelly, or even Ann. That's my name."

"My mother taught me to respect nurses and doctors and give them their proper titles."

Kelly laughed. "Well, your mother was right to teach you respect, we value it in our society, but Kelly is my title."

"I have never heard of a Kelly. Is it something to do with caring? Ted only died seven years ago, and you were still all called nurses then."

Kelly hesitated. "I can answer the first part of that question. In a manner of speaking, you are correct; a Kelly is something to do with caring. It's an acronym. Kelly's receive cells from their patient's brain stem; those cells are programmed to respond to the patient's requirements. The implants attune me to your needs."

"Isn't that what happened to me, an acronym?"

Kelly giggled a little, "No, you had an aneurysm. An acronym is...," Kelly saw that Alice had already assumed a blank expression. "Never mind. KELA means Keller Engineering Life Aide. Keller Engineering pioneered the procedure. They called us KELAs for years, but we ended up known affectionately as Kelly's. We work for up to a year with our patient after implantation. At the end of that time, any stem cells are removed, and we resume our normal lives until reassignment. It only happens three times over a six-year period."

There was no way of Alice knowing about such a procedure in her waking life, but then neither would she have considered such a thing as the materialisation of Dr Clere and Dr Grossmith through the wall at that moment. It was all imagination, and Alice left it at that, preferring to believe her mind was performing oddly and filtering real events into a dream state and then changing them to the fantastic. Alice wondered if her life had become so ordinary, her mind was taking a bit of leeway to sharpen things up, but she suspected she would never be the same once she was back home. She might even watch science fiction on the TV, but for now, she would reassure herself that she was being cared for, that Michelle had discovered Sammy's new diet, and she and Eliza were regularly visiting. Steven might have called in too and knowing him, brought grapes because it wouldn't occur to him she couldn't eat yet.

But that brought her to wonder for a moment how they fed her because she didn't feel thirsty or hungry. She felt around her tummy for any telltale equipment or tubes, but there was nothing there. Neither was there a roll of fat

39

around her middle, but somehow, she failed to notice.

CHAPTER FIVE _

Alice felt comfortable with Kelly and Dr Grossmith but wary of Dr Clere, who, although appearing interested in her welfare, possessed a far less friendly manner than Dr Grossmith, making it difficult for her to respond to him. Besides, she didn't believe his story about her heart.

Dr Grossmith always greeted Alice as if she were indeed his special patient, and she looked forward to his visits. This morning, Dr Clere once again forgot his manners and failed to acknowledge Alice before starting his probing around her face and chest with the little white pencil thingy. He peered into her eyes, gazing first into one, then the other, his prune face set with concentration. He declared her fit to begin.

Alice looked at each person in the room. *Begin what?* Dr Grossmith folded back her lovely blanket and smiled his encouragement.

"Today is a celebration," he explained. "Each time we got you up and moving before, you needed full neuromechanical aids. Now, because you are alert and responsive, we can assess your balance and possibly scale your walking aids right back to a simple calliper."

"You want me to walk, Dr Grossmith?"

"If you are up to it, but if you become unsteady or anxious, you can stop and try again when you feel ready."

Get out of bed? Anxious? Alice was all for it. Without another word, she swept her legs over the side of the bed and planted her feet on the floor. She stood tall, with one hand just touching Kelly's arm to maintain her balance. The two doctors looked stunned.

"That was unexpected," Dr Grossmith murmured to an equally surprised Dr Clere.

"Well, I didn't need to ask twice, did I, my dear?" Dr Grossmith couldn't help himself. He beamed with pride and pointed to Alice's hand, "Now, let go of Kelly's arm and see if you can take a few steps unaided. We won't let you fall."

Alice had no intention of falling, and even though the first step threatened her equilibrium somewhat, she recovered herself, holding up her hand to make sure Kelly didn't rush to help. The second step was slow but easier; the third and fourth steps—felt wonderful! She was walking again! Alice looked up, her frown of concentration giving way to a huge smile! She reached the wall and, taking great care, turned and began the return journey to her bed, but as she moved forward, it wasn't so easy anymore— maybe that touch of arthritis in her hips was causing a little stiffness because she couldn't keep her co-ordination. She reached out to Kelly for assistance, who only offered her hand in token support. By the time Alice reached the bed, she had adopted a more shuffling gait but determined she would stay upright and willed her back to be strong and sure.

She flopped onto the bed, triumphant! Nothing would diminish this achievement, not even Dr Clere's prune face expression and grudging admiration.

"It appears your faith is rewarded, Grossmith."

But Dr Grossmith wasn't listening. He had waited for this moment for decades, and now it had arrived, he was bursting with pride and entirely focused on Alice's achievement. Kelly pointed out that Dr Clere had spoken, so he turned, catching the echo of his colleague's words.

"I'm most relieved that it has, Dr Clere, but your skill has been a significant factor in her recovery."

Dr Clere inclined his head to accept the recognition, then inclined it again towards Alice with a curt, "I look forward to hearing of your progress, Dr Langley."

But she wasn't ready enough with her thanks. Dr Clere had already vanished through the wall.

Dr Grossmith turned his attention back to Alice. This was a proud moment for him, having watched over her sarcophagus for so many years, almost reliving his sense of awe and privilege when he witnessed her awakening ten years ago. Now, hearing her speak and seeing her walk was the fulfilment of his life's dream. And there she sat, smiling, proud and happy, unaware of what her accomplishment in this room today represented. In danger of becoming emotional, he cleared his throat noisily before speaking.

"Well, you did all that with very little help."

"I did, didn't I?" Alice was too pleased with herself to notice any wavering in his voice. "I don't want to be in the hospital forever, Dr Grossmith. I promise I'll do everything you tell me to help me get better."

"Then you will be out of here and getting back to normal life in no time. How does that sound?" He helped her settle back into bed—he knew it wasn't necessary, but the time fast approached when she would no longer need him or his help.

"That sounds wonderful, Dr Grossmith, but I still have questions," she shifted over to make room for him to sit beside her on the bed. "Can you spare me a few moments?"

"We can talk for a while." There was no urgency to leave. "Later, Kelly is taking you for a walk on the station. We'll use a calliper, only as a precaution."

The station? Alice wondered if, in real life, they were transferring her to a different hospital, but then, it would be by ambulance, not by train? She wasn't that good at walking yet.

Before Dr Grossmith agreed to answer any questions, he needed to tell Alice the story of a woman called Alexis Langley. Alice listened, but the big words he used left her behind in the opening paragraph. He explained he was both a medical doctor and an anthropologist who studied ancient plastination techniques and cryopreservation to help him with his work on an important project.

He told her that this project didn't have the advantage of previous studies. There were no precedents, no other specimens, no-one with experience to assist, and he had to deal with many differing opinions from the scientific community.

The project's subject, a woman—Alexis Langley, had many years before been desperately ill. Her uncle preserved her hoping one day, sometime in the future, when medicine had advanced, she might be revived.

Dr Grossmith explained that Alexis had been in a sarcophagus for many years, not preserved after her death in the usual manner of cryopreservation, a method that invariably failed, but while alive, sometime in the days or hours before the terminal disease claimed her life. The preservation method had defied analysis through the years, and Alexis Langley remained suspended, sleeping, safe in her impenetrable shroud.

The early scientific teams uncovered documents and data relating to her illness, written by her uncle, in the cavern where Alexis was found. While this information appeared authentic, no-one, not even the great scientific minds through the ages ever penetrated or even obtained a sample of the shell which encased her. Neither had they discovered the secret of the fluid in which she slept. At first, they thought she might be a remarkably well-preserved corpse, but over time, as technology advanced, they detected brain activity. With that came the realisation she was a perfectly preserved, living, human female.

The recounting of the story reminded Dr Grossmith of the contempt he faced when he suggested that, due to the fact the anticipated term of her preservation had not been documented, she was where her uncle intended. She would, as Sleeping Beauty in the fairy story, one day awaken from her long sleep unaided. This suggestion coined the phrase, Sleeping Beauty Phenomenon, taking over from the project's previous cold, scientific title.

Alice didn't know what to say. The story appeared to hold great relevance to Dr Grossmith, but she wished she understood its significance and why he'd told her.

"That's an amazing story, Dr Grossmith," she said, impressed he could remember such detail without referring to a book. "But you used words I didn't understand, so I did get a little lost, I'm sorry. I'm not sure why you even told me about this poor lady. It sounds like a terrible thing to have happened. I've heard of people being frozen after they died, but I didn't know what they called it. Cryo…?"

"Cryopreservation. Cryogenics," Grossmith finished her question with a couple of suggestions of his own. "The science has had many labels over the years, and it was big business during the twentieth and twenty-first centuries, people became wealthy by offering an immortality service, but there have been no successful revivals from any of these techniques."

"Do you remember that you called *me* Alexis one time?" That was the name of the lady in the story.

"Yes, I remember, because the story I told you," he felt almost as if he dared not say it, dared not confirm to her the truth—the truth about her. "*You* are Alexis Langley."

Alice would have laughed had she not seen the respect in Dr Grossmith's eyes. Dr Clere had said "Dr Langley" earlier, but Alice thought he'd just made a mistake. Now, Dr Grossmith was insisting this story was about her. She lifted her hand, her fingers outstretched, in an unmistakable "STOP". This is all nonsense anyway, she decided, with words she had never heard before and had no use for. May as well nip it in the bud right now.

"My name is *Alice Watkins*," she said, drawing out each word for emphasis.

Dr Grossmith smiled, "Your name, my dear, is Alexis Langley, Dr Alexis Langley."

She shook her head, her lips firm. She didn't know Alexis Langley, and she also knew for certain she wasn't a doctor; she had far too little education. There was nothing left but to tell him her version of her life.

He listened, but his own confusion grew as she related what sounded like a categorically dull existence. Her assertion she knew nothing of Alexis Langley, save what she learned from his account, gave room for disquiet.

"You'll remember in time, I'm sure," he tried to calm her anxiety, realising his reassurances were as much for his benefit as for hers. "We had no way of knowing your memory would be so disrupted, but I assure you, when you do remember, you will take your place in the world again." He hoped with all his heart that would be the case.

"I have a place in the world, Doctor," Alice said. "A

nice place. It's as a grandmother to five grandchildren, looking after the cat and being a mum to Michelle and Steven, that is my place in the world, and I'm content with it." Alice made sure she spoke with respect; she would not forget her manners, Dr Grossmith was a nice man, an important man, but now, as she was progressing, she needed him to listen.

He decided he would indulge those glimpses into a past she believed to be hers. They may be a pathway to uncovering her true memories, and there was no time like the present to start that recovery.

"Tell me again the last thing you remember?"

"If you think it will help, Doctor. I was waiting for Michelle to drop the children off at school before coming to collect me to go out for my birthday. I'm turning sixty-five."

Alice had the sequence of events sorted now. Her mind clear on the facts.

"Do you remember the date?"

"Of course, November first was the day I was going out. My birthday is on November fourth.

She noticed his eyebrows twitch ever so slightly.

"A birthday is a significant event?"

"Yes, I told you; my sixty-fifth birthday."

Dr Grossmith commented to Kelly, who handed him a large cloth.

"Your sixty-fifth birthday? Would you mind describing yourself—your appearance?"

Alice thought it an odd request. She was right in

front of them. Couldn't they see for themselves? But she would do as they asked and describe what she saw the last time she looked in a mirror.

"I'm short. I have white hair, with a perm and a blue rinse. I am a little overweight, not too much, though," she added, "and I have chin hairs now as well."

Dr Grossmith made no reply, but with a flick of his wrist, the cloth opened into a large rectangle. Kelly indicated to Alice to get out of bed and stand up. Alice obeyed, and without a word, Dr Grossmith manoeuvred the cloth rectangle to position it in front of her. It looked like a full-length mirror, hanging in the air without wires to hold it up. Perfectly lit, it afforded the viewer the most accurate of reflections.

But Alice's reflection was not as she expected—that of an old lady with a few wrinkles and chin hair—off to the beauty salon. In this mirror, her reflection had changed— the image of a much younger woman stared back at her— a young woman with a small, neat nose, well-defined, arched eyebrows and a mouth that curled softly in a puzzled smile. She was taller than Alice, and had she been less pale, Alice would have thought her beautiful.

The woman's hair, red to the point of carroty, bore no resemblance to the shiny locks Alice dreamed of. It looked more like the colour of a faded carrot, the one that got left in the bottom of the fridge for too long and lost its vibrancy. Her hair was tied back, and little wispy curls framed the forehead. She looked to be around thirty, and Alice had never seen her before in her life. A pale, frail figure she didn't recognise, wearing a long grey shift, hanging loosely on a too slender frame. As Alice gazed at her, the woman gazed back, her green eyes shining with a radiance that contrasted starkly with her otherwise pallid features.

Alice pointed to the image and turned to Dr Grossmith; her finger still poked in accusation towards the mystery woman.

"That's not me," she said, "that mirror has made a mistake."

"It is you," Dr Grossmith countered, standing next to her, so their reflections stood side by side. She could see he was exactly as he appeared. "This is what you looked like when they found you," he indicated to the mirror, "except you had no hair, and this is what you look like now. We expected you to start ageing when the sarcophagus opened ten years ago, but you didn't; that process only began in the last year."

"That can't be me," she protested. "There is no way I can change from being an old, wrinkled person into a pretty young girl, plus I don't know anyone in the family who has ginger hair—so that is not me."

Kelly and Dr Grossmith could see she believed it to be a prank. Alice took one last look at the mirror and sat back on the bed, unsure she could endure any more of this. She'd done so well today, but the sense of achievement was disappearing as quick as a doctor through a wall.

Dr Grossmith saw the barriers going up and wished he could leave her be, but a few things needed clarification.

Now she had returned fully to a conscious state, and despite her memory loss, new systems and protocols needed to be put in place to protect and educate her.

"You mention children?" Dr Grossmith said, trying to coax, but Alice folded her arms and didn't answer. "You are convinced you have children and grandchildren?"

What's the point, Alice thought, don't argue, go along with it, so she nodded, looking at both Dr Grossmith and Kelly.

"You must know I do, Doctor," she sighed. "My daughter will be shocked to know what has happened to me. I don't even understand what happened myself, but she will come looking for me."

"You've never had children," Kelly said, knowing somehow she was delivering bad news, so she came to sit with Alice, placing her hand on her shoulder, hoping she could offer a measure of comfort.

"I have two." They would not dissuade Alice. She knew precisely how many children she had.

"According to our information and our physical examinations," Dr Grossmith put his hand up to his chin, "you have never conceived. We retrieved the data your chip contained; it remained intact and functioning throughout your stasis, so for a primitive device, it was remarkably durable. The data from this chip, including the date it was inserted into your spine, left us in no doubt about who you are. No doubt at all. When the sarcophagus opened, you were in immediate danger and required a life prosthesis. This prosthesis gives us a full picture of your past and present health. My dear, you have never been pregnant."

Alice's simple mind was reeling. *Chip? Sarcophagus?* Words to boggle and bewilder. She closed her eyes and took a deep breath, wanting to sleep again so she could disappear, for whenever she slept, there would be the chance of waking up in her real life. Even though Dr Grossmith saw her weariness, he made no move to leave.

"I don't know what you mean by 'chip'?" she said, at last. They meant this news for someone else, a clear case of mistaken identity and Alice said so.

But Kelly and Dr Grossmith stayed resolute, assuring her she was Dr Alexis Langley, just as they said and that this was a challenge for them too. There was no manual for a human body surviving centuries of preservation. Dr Grossmith tried to explain that to the still uncharacteristically belligerent and unresponsive Alice that he had only his instincts, his patience and his faith plus a hell of a lot of luck. So far, she was a success, the only one of her kind.

When she didn't respond to his words, he wondered, whose success? He only watched over her and stayed close during those last years of her long sleep. Her awakening had been orchestrated by a power or science over which he had neither control nor knowledge. He vowed to answer her questions wherever he could and, in so doing, possibly gain an insight into this unique wonder with the defiant expression, seated on the bed in front of him.

"Everyone is microchipped at birth." He would use

common terms where he could, even though he knew he had a habit of straying into technical jargon. "All biological data is stored within the chip, at least in the ones we have today. The chip we found inserted in you was ancient technology, only recording DNA, drug use and certain medical conditions."

"People don't get microchipped." Alice thought it was a ridiculous part of any dream, almost as ridiculous as someone capable of growing a heart and kidneys and a liver.

"I microchipped Sammy," she thought out loud, talk of microchips reminding her of her little furry companion. "Michelle had him done."

"Is Sammy someone else you remember?"

She nodded. "My cat."

"You gave your cat a human name?" Dr Grossmith and Kelly looked at each other.

Alice shrugged. All her cats had human names.

"The various governments have microchipped humans since before you were born," Dr Grossmith smiled, at least she was speaking to them again, "and we still call it microchipping. The technology would be unrecognisable to the scientists of your day, but microchipping it has remained. I suspect no-one ever found a better word for it!"

He thought it amusing. Alice didn't, and her expression abruptly halted his mirth. He gave full attention to her serious and angry gaze.

"I don't know anything about this. You're talking

nonsense."

Alice lay on her bed and turned her back to them, disregarding manners and wishing they would leave her alone. Dr Grossmith watched her for a moment; maybe he'd gone too far, now might be a good time to leave. Other questions would have to wait. He'd only confounded her again, which hadn't been his intention, and he stood to leave.

"I am eager to learn about you and for you to learn about us." He leaned across to make sure she was listening, "But I didn't mean to upset you. We can talk more later. If you think of anything you wish to ask, I will do my best to answer. Kelly will take you for a walk soon; moving around more will help, I'm sure."

Alice didn't acknowledge him as he left. None of this made any sense, not even for a dream. Why would anyone dream words of which you had never heard? She kept her face turned away from Kelly, who eventually wheedled her way back into Alice's good books with kindness and gentle persuasion.

CHAPTER SIX _

Later, Kelly stood with Alice beside the bed. Looking around, it occurred to Alice she no longer wanted to be in this room. Dr Grossmith was right, moving about might help. She felt a mite suffocated in here, and some fresh air would be nice.

Standing still, she lifted her arms to allow Kelly to place a clean shift over her head and tie a belt around her waist. She placed little slippers on Alice's feet, then brushed her hair and tied it up again. Alice remained unmoving, like a small child being dressed for a first outing after an illness. She hated this no-choice dream, wishing she would hurry and wake up—she might look young again, but *red hair? Really?* Alice had told them her real name, but they only knew her as this Alexis Langley. Alice knew no-one called Langley. They must have her mixed up with another patient, which would mean she didn't have cancer, and they had made a terrible mistake. She looked down at Kelly, busy on one knee, adjusting a metallic band around Alice's hips. The band had lights which Kelly poked and manipulated until the band contracted to give Alice a snug fit.

"Why do I need this?" Alice asked, reaching down to touch the belt.

"You've worn it many times before," Kelly said as she stood. "The full kit takes over the mechanism of movement. Like this one, the partial kit acts as a support and records muscle strength and neurological response. Previously, we also used the upper body component because, much of the time, you were in a semi-catatonic state. Even though you are awake now, there may be a few problems with spatial awareness, which could cause balance issues. Those few steps earlier were not enough for us to evaluate how much your equilibrium is affected. This device, this calliper, will be a better indicator. Don't worry, lots of people wear these after the procedures you've had. It will keep you steady, and you can walk at your own pace with complete stability."

Alice smiled her thanks. Of course, she would need this contraption. Why hadn't she thought to ask for one? It was a dream, after all. Nothing short of the fantastic here.

With Kelly's encouragement, Alice took a few bold steps forward, the calliper supported her back and legs, and she felt her confidence increasing. Still, she stopped in front of the indentation in the wall where Dr Grossman did his vanishing acts.

"How do you go through it?"

"Just carry on walking."

"But it's glass."

"You'll see, go on."

Alice did as she was told and found herself on the other side. She looked back.

"How…?" Alice checked herself to make sure all of her had arrived. She couldn't see inside her room, and the glass-like wall didn't look as though anyone had just walked through it.

Kelly laughed and pointed to a large black frame.

"That's the portal entry. See those lights on that side panel? To get inside the room, the forcefield needs to be deactivated. Look, I'll show you."

Kelly waved her hand over a point of light, and with a twisting motion, the portal opened to reveal the interior. She took Alice's hand and waved it over the light again, and the portal closed.

"That's amazing!" Alice was genuinely impressed.

"These are one-way portals, Alice, that means we only need controls to enter as they are never locked from the inside. Now, we have an appointment. Let's get going."

But Alice couldn't get going. After her initial astonishment at her ability to walk through a wall, she quickly realised, with some alarm, that passing outside her room were four lanes of people, two lanes going one way and two going another. Each direction had a lane for normal walking plus a moving walkway for anyone in a hurry. A few people had callipers. Others wore the same colour clothing as Kelly and Dr Grossmith.

She grabbed Kelly's arm; going out for fresh air didn't seem quite so inviting.

"Can we go back inside, please?" she begged. In answer, Kelly placed her arm on Alice's back, and with a smile, helped her move forward.

The calliper gave Alice a rhythm for her walking. If she concentrated, she could ignore the people moving along the corridor. All along the walls, she saw the black outlined portal entries with people stepping in and out. It was hectic, and she didn't like it. She asked Kelly where they were going.

"To see Principal Hardy," Kelly told her, "the commander of this facility. You'll like him, Dr Langley; not only is he delightful, he's an amazing historian. He'll be able to clear up a few things for you."

"My name's Alice Watkins, not Dr Langley. Will I be going back to the glass room?"

"As it happens, no, we've arranged quarters for you. I'll be staying with you, for now at least. You still need observation, but your own quarters will give you more freedom, that is if you wish."

Alice didn't care for the word "freedom" with the implication she wasn't free, but if this were a dream, it would end sooner or later. She noted Kelly hadn't commented when she corrected her on the use of her name.

Dr Grossmith fell into step beside them, putting one hand under Alice's elbow. She didn't need the support but appreciated his care, feeling entirely secure in the calliper and a little guilty about her earlier rudeness. He had her best interests at heart, even if he talked nonsense most of the time.

With Alice between them, Kelly and Dr Grossmith stopped at one of the portals. Letting go of Alice's arm, he waved his hand over the panel and stepped through, followed by Alice and Kelly both together.

On the other side of the portal was William Shakespeare. In this dream, he wore a greyish tunic with matching trousers and sat on a fancy plastic chair. He stood as they entered.

This was a much larger room than Alice's and, like hers, had no flowers or ornaments, only an enormous picture of space and a planet with rings around it; a picture so big, it took up an entire wall. The opposite wall contained glass shelves, covered with books, and stretching right across one large, curved area—Alice had never seen so many books except at the local library.

Mr Shakespeare reached out and took her hand, making a small movement with his head and shoulders, the same as Dr Grossmith did. Like bowing.

"Alice?"

She wondered if she should curtsy.

"Good day, Mr Shakespeare," she said humbly, not knowing how to address someone so famous, and she cast her gaze downwards to her feet, not wishing to meet the great man's eyes. What a privilege—she was willing to bet he didn't pop up in many dreams. Michelle and Steven had both participated in his plays at school, so Alice knew what he looked like. There was a pause, then Mr Shakespeare guffawed with laughter, the joke lost on Kelly and Dr Grossmith, but as soon as he started laughing, Alice realised her error—this was Principal Hardy, not William Shakespeare.

"William Shakespeare, the ancient playwright," he explained, lifting his hands, palms up before realising he was the only one laughing. He sobered up at the sight of blank looks.

"Well, it was a long time ago. Come and sit here, Alice," he said, his grin lingering under his moustache. He held out one of the super-expensive-looking plastic chairs.

"Alice and I can chat alone," Principal Hardy told Kelly and Dr Grossmith, inviting them both to leave, but Dr Grossmith hesitated, glancing across to Alice.

"If I have any concerns, Grossmith, I will call you at once."

Dr Grossmith made that same movement with his head and shoulders. "Very good, Principal Hardy—we will go for morning tea and return presently."

His words jogged a memory of a ritual she loved. Morning tea. Two biscuits, bread and butter and a pot of English Breakfast, Sammy on her knee.

The smiling man with whiskers changed chairs and sat down on the opposite side of the desk. Alice watched him, still feeling foolish at her mistake, but his smile seemed friendly, and she decided he was a nice man and would forgive her, even though he did look like Shakespeare. Under the circumstances, what was she supposed to think? She waited for him to speak, not wanting to make a fool of herself again. He steepled his fingers and raised his eyebrows, elbows on his desk.

"So. Alice Watkins?"

Alice nodded.

"You mistook me for William Shakespeare, and I laughed. I'm so sorry, most ungracious of me."

Alice shifted uncomfortably, wishing he hadn't mentioned it.

"Well, sir, you look like him. Both my children were in Shakespeare's plays at school."

He nodded as if he understood, then reached over and spoke to a tall oblong on his table and asked for morning tea. Then he settled back.

"I'm Principal Hardy, but I enjoyed being William Shakespeare for a while. Were you acquainted with him?"

"Of course not." What an odd question. "He's been dead for hundreds of years, sir."

"Definitely not alive then?"

Alice frowned; that's a peculiar thing to say.

"I don't think anyone can live that long," Alice said.

"Quite—and Alice, how long have you been alive?"

"Oh, well, sir, I'll be sixty-five on Saturday, at least that's what I thought until Dr Grossmith told me I'd been ill for a long time, so I'm confused about what day it is."

"Do you feel well, Alice? Are you able to make sense of your surroundings?"

"I feel well, thank you, sir, and no, I can't make sense of my surroundings. They told me I was almost dead, but

I hadn't been ill, at least not that I can recall, and now, I think I might be dreaming."

A man brought the tea. Alice hadn't eaten or drunk anything in all these days, but with the sight of a teapot, she fancied a cup of tea might be welcome. She was a great one for spilling tea in company. Posh teacups made her nervous, ever since she broke one of her grandmother's good china cups as a child, remembering only too well the awful repercussions. It was a relief to see the trolley, without wheels and floating on its own, carried only small, very manageable cups

Principal Hardy filled one for her but didn't add the hoped-for sugar and milk. Hot and sweet; that's how Alice liked her tea, but it didn't matter because the tea was such a surprise. Purple and fragrant and unlike any tea she had ever seen, she gazed at the floral-scented steam, spiralling upwards.

"I've never seen tea this colour before," she looked up, and Principal Hardy saw in her expression, the lack of sophistication reported to him by Jim Grossmith.

"You have had it, but it isn't likely you would remember. It's very pleasant, and while I realise it would be customary in your time to have a biscuit or cake with your tea, I was only able to persuade Dr Grossmith and Kelly Ann to let you have fluids. Any solid food is to be offered only under their strict supervision."

"I haven't had any food, at least I don't think so."

"You have, but again, you wouldn't remember. The food for our rehabilitation patients is not in the least memorable, and you've suffered significant memory loss."

He raised his teacup in a toast and sipped, nodding his agreement to the cup's contents and watched as Alice took a sip. It was *gorgeous!!* Alice wanted a whole pot. Hang the biscuits. A sweet, tingling sensation covered her mouth and lips, as though she had been desperately thirsty, and suddenly, that thirst was quenched. She hadn't *felt* thirsty, but the experience brought a huge smile and gasp of delight. Principal Hardy enjoyed her reaction.

"I knew you'd like it. It's a favourite of mine and one of the few teas you didn't refuse when you came off the ELSP—the life prosthesis. I congratulate myself on my excellent taste in teas! I assumed it was a popular drink in your time—a very long time ago?" he added cautiously, waiting to see if she picked up his last comment.

Alice licked her lips and saw with disappointment she had emptied the cup in one gulp. How embarrassing. She hoped he didn't think her rude, but he took the cup from her and refilled it without comment. This time, she showed more moderation and instead allowed herself a moment to marvel a little more at the vivid colour of the liquid. Then she looked up at him. She'd heard him.

"How long, Principal Hardy? How long is a 'very long time'? Kelly and Dr Grossmith are kind, but all they say is that I have been here 'a very long time' or that I have been sick for 'a very long time'."

Principal Hardy had to be careful with his words. Grossmith had reported, and he recognised this now, that far from the educated scientist they understood her to be, she appeared simple and uninformed, with a curious insistence she was someone else—this Alice Watkins. He wondered if this could be an effect or result of the preservation or aneurysm, but she showed no signs of brain damage. He would be cautious and gentle but wouldn't answer her question just yet; instead, he had one of his own.

"Dr Grossmith has reported you believe you are dreaming. What if I said that is not the case?"

"If I'm not dreaming, then what Dr Grossmith said, that I had cancer and a brain anjanism must be true, but I've never been sick, and I don't know the person I look like now."

Principal Hardy knew she showed no recognition of herself in the image definer. He decided to explore some of the memories she claimed to be hers.

"I understand you were waiting for your daughter to arrive to celebrate your sixty-third birthday. Remind me of the date?"

"My birthday is on November fourth, and I was nearly sixty-five, not sixty-three. It was three days before, and I was waiting for Michelle to arrive. I thought I heard her car in the driveway."

A lucid and pointed contradiction, he noted.

"Dr Grossmith told you, according to our investigations, you've never had a child?"

"Yes, he did, but he also showed me a magic mirror that made me young and pretty, so it's hard to believe anything that's happening. I don't even believe in you…sir."

Principal Hardy smiled at her definition of an accessory that, for him, was an everyday part of life. To someone who had never seen one, an image definer doubtless would seem like a magic mirror.

"An image definer. It's more accurate than any 'mirror'. The reflection given is an exact definition of you."

"I've never heard of anything like that."

"They were invented after you went into stasis."

"I'm not sure I know what stasis is. Do I call you 'Principal', like School Principal? Is stasis when people die and get frozen?"

"Yes, that's right. I'm always called Principal Hardy. You don't need to say 'sir'."

"Thank you, Principal Hardy, so when did I nearly die?"

"According to your chip…"

"I don't understand that either— 'chip', my cat was microchipped. They don't microchip people, sorry." She'd interrupted him.

"Never interrupt your betters, Alice. You have nothing of importance to add to any conversation."– Alice's mother.

Alice had been pregnant with Michelle when her mother made that statement. Far too old for her mother to tell her what to do, but she remembered the humiliation because they were visiting relatives at the time. She withdrew into silence. Principal Hardy saw the sudden change as she gazed into her empty cup, and he lifted the pot in an invitation for more. Alice declined with a small self-conscious shake of her head. He took her cup and came around to perch himself on the edge of the desk. He folded his arms.

"The government extended microchipping to humans in 2078, Alice. A breakthrough in the technology allowed for global positioning to be applied to those with a criminal record. It also allowed for specific aspects of a person's medical and biological history, DNA and such like, to be recorded. Microchipping helped reduce crime and disease. We are still microchipped, but it's much more advanced now. Your chip recorded a cellular degradation, which could be dated, so we knew how old you were when you first became ill. This chip, of a primitive design but manufactured to a high standard, functioned throughout your stasis." Alice failed to see why he seemed so impressed.

"What does that mean?"

"A microchip can only record living data. If a body is deceased, the chip degrades."

"Dr Grossmith told me. I wasn't dead."

"Yes, the remarkable thing with your stasis is that you weren't preserved after death as in all other cases of which we are aware but underwent an unknown procedure in the days or hours prior." He waited, hoping the significance of what he said might spark some memory, a glimmer or splinter of remembrance. But there was nothing.

"Dr Grossmith told me the story, Principal Hardy," Alice said. "He thinks it's about me, but he's wrong."

Hardy sighed inwardly. He was trying his best not to be too technical. There had to be a simpler language, a less confusing way to draw her out.

"Do you remember what you did for a living?"

"Nothing," she stated. That *was* what she did. Nothing.

Her reply was unexpected, but he kept his expression neutral.

"Then, tell me what you were doing in the moments before you—before you fell asleep?"

"Well, do you mean before Michelle was due to arrive?"

"If that's the only thing you can remember."

So, she told him the same story she told the doctor and nurse.

When she finished, he poured her more tea without asking. Her third cup of this purple glory was every bit as delicious as the first, and she wondered why it hadn't gone cold in the pot.

Principal Hardy agreed with Grossmith; she wasn't what they anticipated. Deliberately bypassing the registry that contained better historical images but might have been too advanced for her, he walked to the bookcase and selected a book, a picture book, much like a child would read. He showed it to Alice, who recognised one or two pictures of a bus, another of a train and random images of clothing that looked like the outfits she wore when she was a teenager. She pointed out the things she recognised.

Principal Hardy closed the book and turned away,

placing it carefully on the table. He joined his hands behind his back. Alice stayed quiet in case he was considering things of importance. It would be better to let him speak first.

"This is puzzling," she heard him say, not sure if he was addressing her or talking to himself. He walked slowly over to the picture of the planet and stars and stood, gazing at it in silence before returning to his chair. "These seem to be personal memories, but..." Principal Hardy tapped his finger against his lips.

"Alice, what was happening in the world to the best of your recollection? There might be something that will help me piece things back together for you."

"I don't know," which was true enough. Alice knew little. "There was a global warning," she shrugged. And a sale at the shoe shop. Brussels sprouts at the supermarket for less than three dollars. Petrol was cheap too, Michelle had said so, but these nuggets of information might bore such an important man, so she left them out.

"Do you mean global warming?"

"I suppose," she shook her head and shrugged again. "They're only words; I don't understand what any of it means; I didn't have much schooling, Principal Hardy. Global warning—warming, has something to do with earthquakes and tidal waves, I think."

"What else do you remember? Can you tell me something about the community in which you lived?"

So, the Brussels sprouts and petrol stories got an airing as he studied her and smiled encouragement while she described her small world to him. The shops, the weather, the trains, buses, Michelle's too large four-wheel-drive car, her widow's pension. She shrugged again when she finished. She was in the presence of greatness, and shrugging was not polite, but it didn't matter because she was dreaming. She could be as rude as she liked, then corrected herself. Rudeness is uncalled for. You shouldn't imagine rudeness.

"I wonder, if, like me, you are a historian," he said when she finished relating these small events to him. "What you are describing belongs in the early twenty-first century. Alice, these can't be your memories."

"But you said I was Alice Watkins."

He held up his hand. "I acknowledged the identity you have adopted for yourself. I may have been wrong, but I don't suppose our little conversation here today would have gone nearly as well had I insisted upon addressing you as Dr Langley."

"I *am* Alice Watkins, Principal Hardy."

"I know you believe that."

He had no wish to denigrate nor devalue her account of her history, not while she held so fast to those memories. She may be taking comfort from them, and he had no desire to cause her distress, but facts are facts.

"These memories, these depictions of that time, to my knowledge, are accurate, with the only explanation being you absorbed and retained them through a study of history. You couldn't have been there, but after your long sleep, these have surfaced and emerged as your own. The personal references, I can't explain."

"I remember them, Principal Hardy," Alice would not back down on this; he was questioning her existence, "because I was there, well, not actually there for earthquakes, but I read the newspaper sometimes."

"Newspapers haven't existed since at least 2028."

Alice looked at him, at the book on the table, the books on the wall, the space picture. He was sincere, but he didn't believe in Alice Watkins. No-one believed in Alice Watkins. She had taken her place beside the tooth fairy, a figment of the imagination.

"Did I really have an angelism?"

He nodded and didn't correct her.

"Dr Grossmith and Dr Clere, did they experiment on me like in the war, and that's the reason I'm here?"

"Dr Grossmith and Dr Clere are no longer medical doctors in the usual context from your time—their careers have progressed on a different path, but I *am* a medical doctor and closely associated with your recovery. I repaired your aneurysm. I can assure you we would never harm anyone."

"They said they saved my life and put things inside me, transplants—I'm not sure. I know sometimes people can get a heart from someone who died. Dr Clere tried to tell me about it, but I didn't understand what he was saying."

"Most of your internal organs had failed. You couldn't have survived without the bio..." Hardy decided it might be prudent to rethink his explanation. Alice hadn't understood Dr Clere, no point in making matters worse, "…the new organs. Nothing was transplanted. Your new organs are natural. Regrown. Dr Clere is foremost in…" he searched for a word or phrase she might understand that would encompass everything Dr Clere meant to the scientific community,

"…there is no-one better than he to help patients like you."

"I thought he was a doctor, same as in a hospital. What other sorts of doctors are there?"

"Many kinds, you will learn about them in time, but Dr Clere has saved countless lives with his techniques. Dr Grossmith is very interested in ancient people, but he also has an interest in how people were frozen to preserve them. He has devoted a good portion of his career to the study of your case." He was glad to have skirted words such as forensic anthropologist and cytogeneticist.

"Only me? Why was I so special?"

"Nothing special about you, Alice. Don't go getting ideas above your station."- Alice's mother.

"There has never been anyone like you," Principal Hardy told her. "Dr Grossmith has been beside you, watched over you and protected you for forty years."

No-one like her? Dr Grossmith had said she was the only one, his favourite patient, and now she was being told she took up forty years of his career. How long had she been asleep before that? She could ask Principal Hardy, but he might try to sidestep.

A movement on the space picture drew her attention. She didn't react to the realisation it wasn't a picture at all, that the massive planet with rings and the little ships moving around were real, going about their business outside the window, in space. The sight represented just another fantastic aspect of the dream, so she may as well ask.

"Principal Hardy, how long was I asleep?"

He had no way of knowing how she might receive this information. Had she woken with her memories intact, she would have been excited, enthusiastic, animated and bombarding them all with questions, eagerly embracing her new world of technology and medical advancement. Now, he faced a woman diminished by life, not edified, uneducated, and not well-informed. But whatever he had hoped for, it was still her life and her history. And she should know the truth.

"Four hundred years."

She studied him for a moment, then looked back at the window and wondered how they got that giant planet so close to Earth?

Kelly arrived, and the interview ended. Principal Hardy helped her to stand.

"You'll be here for a while longer, so we can spend more time together. I very much enjoyed our visit today."

"Thank you for the tea, Principal Hardy."

Kelly adjusted the calliper for walking, but Alice asked her to wait.

"Principal Hardy, you believe I'm this lady, Alexis Langley?"

"Yes," he inclined his head in agreement. "You are

absolutely who we say you are."

"Would you like to know what I think?"

He nodded, a puzzled smile causing his moustache to curl downward at the tips.

"I think you got the labels mixed up."

CHAPTER SEVEN _

After a brief stop at the hospital room where Kelly spoke with Principal Hardy and Dr Grossmith on an odd-looking glass panel with red and green lines, Kelly took Alice to a large area she called a "mess". Rather than messy, to Alice, it was neat and tidy, and she would have been proud to have kept her home to this standard. The "mess" had views of the big planet, a view Alice ignored, choosing instead to check out her surroundings, pleasantly set out like the cafés she went to with Michelle. Alice felt a sudden wave of longing for her family; sitting here in the "mess" reminded her of some lovely outings she'd had with them. A waiter placed a soft white cake on the table, alongside a pot of the lovely purple tea, complete with cups like the ones in Principal Hardy's office. All very manageable.

Kelly cut the cake into four pieces, just big enough for a mouthful of each portion. They looked like solid rice flour. "Do you recognise these at all, Dr Langley?"

"I seem to recall but can't fix a time and place. I'm sorry, Kelly."

"Please don't apologise, Dr Langley. These pastes give complete nutrition. Four pieces are enough for one day."

"Can you call me Alice? It's strange being called Dr Langley. I'm not a doctor."

Kelly wasn't sure. "I'm required to address you by your proper title, Dr Langley, but I suppose I could call you Alice when we're alone."

"That's nice of you, thank you, Kelly. It makes me feel better."

"Good. In that case, perhaps you should ask Dr Grossmith to call you Alice as well. Maybe that's how they pronounced Alexis in your time, with a silent 'x'. Who knows?"

It sounded plausible to Alice, and when, directed by Kelly, she lifted a piece of the cake to her mouth, she allowed herself to believe, for the first time, things might turn out okay.

Kelly recorded her observations on Alice's cake-eating, checking for swallowing and fussing around with various small instruments. Alice saw that a few of the other people in the mess were eating white cakes too. It could have been a hospital dining room anywhere if you ignored the thumping great planet outside the window. A view of the stars and a pot of tea. What a lovely way to while away an hour or so.

Kelly saw her passing glance towards the viewport and took it as a cue to acquaint Alice with her new surroundings. She told her about Saturn Station, the medical facilities and research programs, about her work here and how she loved returning to Earth whenever she could. Alice listened, but Kelly's explanation confirmed to her that all of this could only be in her imagination. Saturn Station? But then, where else would she be in a dream that gave her carroty hair four hundred years into the future?

She suddenly turned to Kelly, interrupting her in mid-sentence, as if she had not heard a single word.

"Dr Clere must be a molecular physiologist."

Kelly paused. Alice seemed different. "Yes, amongst other things."

"He regrew my heart?"

"Yes, your heart, part of your liver and your kidneys."

Alice was thinking, her gaze leaving Kelly and wandering back to the viewport.

"Forgive me, it's hazy," Alice smiled as she looked back at Kelly. "I seem to remember an organisation, a team, something to do with cellular...no, it's gone."

Kelly watched and waited for another question. She had sensed the shift herself and for a few seconds, felt out of time, lost.

"Am I dreaming?" Alice had changed back.

"No." Kelly rapidly collected her thoughts.

"How do you know?"

"Because I just monitored where that nutrition cake went and what it's doing on your insides, and Alice, no-one ever dreams about opening their bowels."

Going for a poo was unmentionable. It hadn't

occurred to Alice that all this time, somehow, she had to be going to the lavatory! How couldn't she have known?

"I don't know. I don't feel as if..." Alice was appalled, with no way to conceal her embarrassment from Kelly.

"Don't worry," she patted Alice's hand. "Privacy in such matters is safeguarded. But now, with no form of prosthesis to extract and process all eliminations, you'll get the normal bodily urges and functions like the rest of us. Come on; I'll show you to your new quarters."

Alice walked alongside Kelly. Although she had only been walking since this morning, it seemed a good deal longer. She said as much.

"That's because you've been walking for the last year," Kelly smiled. "But always in the full calliper. We aren't going to take any chances for no other reason than you believe you can do it."

"Walking for a year? Why can't I remember?"

"It takes years for hearts to grow, and attaching them once again takes many surgeries. When you woke from stasis, we placed you on the life prosthesis. Even after Dr Clere grew your organs and they became fully functional, you stayed in a semi-catatonic state, despite having normal neurological responses and bodily functions. Well, normal apart from the fact you weren't ageing. You continued to challenge medical reasoning, but Dr Grossmith decided to proceed as if you *were* awake. And that meant getting you moving."

"If I'm dreaming, I can understand that my daughter's not here. I don't always dream of my family."

"You aren't dreaming."

"Then, I'm dead."

"You aren't dead either, or dying, not anymore."

"I was once dying, and now I'm alive?"

Alice didn't expect answers to these questions; she only made these statements to help her sift through the vast amount of information she received that morning.

"Yes, in a manner of speaking."

"How old was I when I died?"

"Twenty-nine, but you weren't dead."

"I'm almost sixty-five."

"You were twenty-nine and close to death when your uncle placed you in stasis."

"No, I'm almost sixty-five."

"No, you were born in the year 2098."

"I was born in 1951."

"2098, we retrieved the information from your chip."

"I microchipped my cat."

"Yes, I know."

"I mean, only dogs and cats were microchipped."

"Principal Hardy summarised his conversation with you."

Alice stopped walking, stepping to the side to let other people pass. Kelly stood beside her and waited. Any information could mean a breakthrough.

"I worked in a bakery as a casual before I got married, then I never worked again."

"You were a scientist. Several university records from your time have survived, so we referenced you. If we are to go by the information found, you were a biochemist and part of a research team studying cellular and molecular biology. There was no personal data about where you lived and so forth."

"The records must be wrong, Kelly. I don't even know what a biochemist is, and those other things, I have no idea what they are."

"They're not wrong, and in the mess, you asked if Dr Clere was a molecular physiologist."

"I don't remember," Alice had a vague recollection of a conversation she overheard in the mess, but it was indistinct. "Tell me about Alexis again."

"After you're settled in, I'll tell you about Alexis."

"Okay." Alice allowed Kelly to lead her back onto the walkway.

Alice's new quarters turned out to be like a room in a posh hotel, and Alice felt very undeserving of the luxury. Kelly, who appeared immune to the surroundings, busily checked the equipment in the room. She looked up, amused by Alice's wide-eyed appreciation.

"Principal Hardy wanted you to have one of the nicest rooms, Alice because you still have a few months here. He told me to make sure you're comfortable."

"This isn't just comfortable, Kelly; this is like a hotel. One I could never afford, I might add."

"Well, you deserve it. Now, I'll show you around. This portal here leads to the washer."

Alice went inside. There were no windows, and the walls had the sheen of stainless steel. Alice recognised at once a piece of equipment jutting out from the wall. A toilet. At the sight of it, all the tea she had drunk that morning made its presence felt. She looked at Kelly.

"Sit on it," Kelly instructed. "It will take care of cleaning you up afterwards."

Alice made to sit down, then realised Kelly was still there. Kelly smiled and stepped outside. Considerable progress today, she thought, her patient could do this safely on her own, and she waited until Alice appeared at the portal, wearing a happy smile. Who would have thought doing a pee by yourself would be a cause to celebrate!

"That's a milestone, Alice."

"I won't ask how I did it while I was asleep."

"The life prosthesis takes care of all bodily functions until you're weaned. Now, you place any soiled garments here." Kelly showed her an area on the wall that curved out like a sink.

"Who washes them?"

"No-one. See this little package?"

Alice took the little gel-like pack from Kelly.

"Place it here." Kelly showed her a narrow shelf, and Alice placed the gel-pack as instructed. Kelly put a jacket in the curved area next to the gel-pack then waved her hand over a circular light on the wall. The gel pillow and the jacket disappeared with a whoosh.

"Oh." Alice was stunned and reached out a hand to touch the empty space the jacket left behind.

"It will be on this shelf here," Kelly showed her a flat area, "in an hour or so."

"Is it ironed as well?"

"That's not a word I'm familiar with, Alice, but it will be ready to hang in the closet. Here is the shower; it starts automatically as soon as you are inside. You put the gel here," she showed Alice another shelf outside the shower, "it will wash and moisturise your skin and hair. See these two panels here? They'll dry you."

"Is that water in the little package?"

"It's water-based and condensed for use on starships and space stations."

Kelly made no further explanation, and Alice was glad, she wouldn't have understood, anyway. Kelly continued the tour of the washer.

"This little basin here has measured water if you want it, and these little fibrelettes are for wiping your hands."

The washer was a very comprehensive room; a person only needed to strip off and go to the toilet, shower and get the washing done in one place. She grinned to herself as she thought of the outside toilet they had when she was a child. It wouldn't work on a space station!

The tour concluded in the bedroom where Alice found a bed the size of those she'd seen on the high street, big enough to get as far away from Ted as possible without sleeping on the floor, but far too expensive for their budget and probably too large for their little double bedroom. The linen was fresh and crisp with a coverlet in the same dull grey as most of the station's fabrics. Kelly had a separate, smaller room off to one side.

Across a long bench, a glass panel, covered in red and green lines like the one in the hospital room, hung in the air. Beside it, a drinks dispenser, which Kelly tried to show her how to use. Alice was mystified by the lack of buttons or switches and asked too many questions. No, Kelly told her, you don't put milk in coffee, and you don't sweeten it either; it's served as it is, and would she like to try?

Alice had a weakness for coffee, although, like tea, she always had it with milk and sugar. Chocolate was another weakness. She loved chocolate. The local café Michelle took her to always sprinkled chocolate on the coffee. It was heavenly.

But again, she didn't miss the milk and sugar. This coffee was like no coffee she had ever tasted. Sweet and smooth, it needed nothing sprinkled on top. Her delight was unmistakable, so Kelly poured one for herself and sent Alice to sit in one of the luxurious chairs.

"You asked me about Alexis. As a story, there's only what Dr Grossmith told you earlier. The historical and medical data is available, but that needs to wait until you learn how to use the registry," Kelly pointed to the glass panel above the bench.

"Just tell me the story again, if that's okay, Kelly. I don't mind if you repeat what Dr Grossmith said. I'm just trying to get things clear in my head."

"Very well. The information we can verify tells us you were born in 2098 and, according to cell degradation, you fell victim to a life-threatening disease around 2125. Records left by your uncle gave us the diagnosis; an aneurysm, along with multiple tumours throughout your body, specifically, a brain tumour, secondary to a larger primary tumour on the liver. From the detailed medical records kept with your sarcophagus—your stasis capsule, conventional medicine had no effect. In short, your condition was incurable. The disease progressed at a torrid pace, but no-one knows when or where you were treated. It would appear your uncle left the information in the hope someone in the future could cure you."

"What happened then?"

"Your uncle didn't leave any data about how he preserved you, and we have never discovered the formula. The experts all agree he waited until the eleventh hour before he acted. No-one knows why he waited or how he developed the technology. It's unknown, completely unknown." Kelly shook her head and spread her hands to emphasise the mystery.

Alice had never been interested in technology. Even using a microwave oven scared her. Technology had not been part of her world, and she knew nothing of biochemistry. She couldn't spell it or explain it. She had never heard of microchipping humans or had any concept of a future self born in 2098 or ever considered a future that contained the year 2125.

Kelly saw Alice's concentration had wandered. She was looking out the window. Kelly told Alice the proper term was viewport, but to Alice, it looked and acted like a window. Any enormous pane of glass that a person could see through was a window as far as Alice was concerned. They had so many fancy words here for everyday items.

Kelly sensed how difficult this must be; removed from your own time, learning all the new technology. Alice needed a friend, and one day, in the not-too-distant future, she would return to Earth, and Kelly wouldn't be there for her. She puzzled for a moment about the incident in the mess when Alice was…different. It was only a moment, and it passed so quickly. She would tell Dr Grossmith and Principal Hardy at the first opportunity.

Alice gestured with a sideways nod towards the view outside.

"And that's Saturn out there?"

"Yes, Alice, that's Saturn."

Alice studied the planet from her seat. Saturn. Saturn had rings; she knew that much.

"It's beautiful. How did we get here? I remember man going to the moon."

"That's when it all started..." And Kelly told her about the progress of space travel through the twenty-first century and the terrible plague which wiped out much of Earth's population. She told her of the A'khet, gentle beings from another world who, with their kindness, saved

Earth by sharing their knowledge. From this act of altruism, humanity was transported from a dark age to a new world of peace and harmony.

"When did the A'khet arrive?" Alice saw no reason to be surprised at the presence of aliens. It was a reasonable question given the subject of the dream.

"We're not sure," Kelly said. "Some say during your lifetime, but there is no exact date. We believe well before they revealed themselves. The plague was a space-borne virus; they knew of it, how it behaved but couldn't offer a cure; they helped us rebuild when it was over."

"That would have been in my great-grandchildren's lifetime."

Kelly smiled. "Those memories again."

Alice gazed in silence at mighty Saturn, then down at her slender, fair hands wrapped around the coffee cup, and felt the steady beat of her regrown heart. She contemplated her new kidneys and liver and wondered how she could dream so vividly, given she didn't follow science fiction, besides knowing someone in one show had funny ears.

There was sadness in her reply. "These are the only memories I have."

CHAPTER EIGHT _

A few months later, Alice still hadn't fully overcome her feelings of unworthiness regarding the degree of luxury in her new quarters. Each time she met with Principal Hardy after moving from her hospital room, she took special care to thank him for his generosity and the obvious expense he had gone to. He chuckled and told her money didn't exist in this society and that she deserved only the best, so it amused him when, even after his explanations, Alice was still thanking him for his kindness.

Over time, the few station staff involved in her care, particularly those not aware of her history, became accustomed to calling her Alice. Although she had not yet shown herself as the rational, brilliant scientist Dr Grossmith and Principal Hardy believed her to be; they warmed to the gentle, kind, curious and easily discombobulated young woman they were now coming to know.

Kelly remained with her as promised, supervising and fussing despite Alice carrying out most tasks alone.

Sudden dizzy spells and episodes of coolness and low temperatures had previously slowed her progress. Now, with Alice so excited about becoming independent, walking, eating and moving around the station, Kelly knew the time was fast approaching when Alice would no longer need such specialised care.

Alice sometimes stood gazing into space through the huge windows—the viewports. The imposing planet hanging outside, which at first made her feel small and inconsequential, was now an object of wonder and fascination, as she quickly came to appreciate its beauty and presence. At other times, it served as a reminder of how incredible her life had become.

Alice asked Kelly to give a broad outline on how to use the registry. Kelly told her that throughout known space and all over Earth, the registry served as both a communications device and research tool, holding calendars, diaries, world events and local news, educational programs and a myriad of other information for the user's convenience. The registry was a transparent glass rectangle, suspended, without supports, over a flat box, which Kelly called a "responder".

Kelly instructed Alice how to communicate with the registry. First, she had to tell the responder what she required. The topic and associated folders would then appear in list form; the more specific she could be, the shorter the list. Kelly suggested Alice ask the registry a question.

"What do I say?"

"It has a lot of information. You can ask whatever you wish. Say 'Registry' before your first question."

"Okay. Registry—umm… kittens."

The references appeared—960,000,000 of them. Five were highlighted.

"How would I know which one to choose?"

"We would seldom offer the registry such broad parameters, Alice. You didn't ask a question, just offered it a word. See how this image is slightly forward of the screen?"

"I see it."

"Display," Kelly said and instantly, the kitten enlarged and hovered in front of them, like a photograph that could be seen from all sides.

"End," Kelly commanded the kitten, and it disappeared back into the screen.

"Does that work with everything?"

"Yes, except if you are linking in the communications section, but usually, we use the registry for specific research. Let's try kittens again but give the registry more information. Ask it about a kitten's diet."

"Registry, what should I feed a kitten?"

Another picture of a kitten appeared along with text highlighting a kitten's proper diet and exercise requirements.

"It will give you the most recent research Alice. The problem you may face is that a registry on a space station like this is designed for staff with years of education behind them, who would know to control the exact parameters or even quote the precise reference to display. You only need to say 'Registry' at the beginning of the session."

"Would it matter if I didn't learn how to use it?"

"Yes, because they are in use every day on Earth, it's how we communicate over distances. Don't worry; you'll get the hang of it."

Alice could see mastery over the registry would take time and patience and far more knowledge and education than she currently possessed.

In contrast to her abilities with the registry, Alice's recovery was nothing short of remarkable. The fainting spells and temperature dips eased, and she passed all medical checks with flying colours. From time to time, she attempted the registry alone but always ended up frustrated. She was far happier learning from Dr Grossmith and Kelly and going to the station library where she could ask as many questions as she liked. Eventually, it became apparent to both Dr Grossmith and Principal Hardy—and the realisation hit them hard—Alice was outgrowing Saturn Station. It was time to send her home.

Dr Clere and Dr Grossmith sat opposite Principal Hardy, who, in Dr Clere's opinion, took a far too laissez-faire approach to the subject's recovery. Their attitude irritated him. Dr Grossmith, in his usual mode as Alice's protector, was incensed, and Principal Hardy was trying to diffuse the simmering tensions.

"Her memories will return in time, gentlemen," he said. "There's no hurry. No reason to pressure her."

James Grossmith concurred, grateful for the support, but Clere found their subjectivity disturbing and alienating. They had no business becoming emotional about Dr Langley.

"In allowing her to return to Earth, we are about to pass up an extraordinary opportunity to study a human body that has survived for almost four hundred years!" Clere was emphatic and animated, his face red, highlighting his frustration. "We've suffered decaying corpses—pieces of meat preserved by primitive cryogenic processes, which have yielded, what? Nothing of importance, but here; *living* tissue, a breathing, functioning model to promote scientific advancement. She must remain where we can study her." He pounded his palm with his fist. This conversation—no, this argument, had been going on for weeks, and he had to make them see their lack of vision.

"You forget we didn't revive her, Larry." James Grossmith would not turn Alice over to Clere and his team for experimentation. "She came out of her stasis without our help, and we applied a life prosthesis in the same way we would, had she been a victim of illness or accident in our own time. Would you take away the independence of one of those patients?"

"She isn't one of 'those patients' Jim. She's in an altogether different category. Don't you see? We are presented with an incredible opportunity!"

Jim Grossmith couldn't even fathom why they were having this discussion, yet again. "She isn't in a different category, Larry. She was ill, in a coma, she woke up, and we treated her the same as any patient. There are no mandates on how long a person can remain comatose."

Clere turned to Hardy; it would be impossible to convince the sentimental Grossmith.

"You are both simplistic in your attitude towards her. In a controlled environment, she will regain her memory."

"Are you saying her uncle preserved her, not to be cured, not to resume her life, a productive life, but for us to use as an experiment?" Hardy shook his head. "You haven't petitioned convincingly, Larry. I don't see what there is to study. Physiologically, anatomically, she's no different from any other human, so from that perspective, she can tell us nothing we don't already know."

Principal Hardy respected Dr Clere but found him hard to like, and having developed a friendship with Alice in the preceding months, on this matter, he stood with Jim Grossmith. He would not randomly turn her over to the Molecular Physiology Team to live her life under a microscope. And all for no good reason.

"That is where you are wrong," Clere jabbed his forefinger towards them both. "She carries the secret of that suspension fluid—a liquid, both life-giving and curative. The sarcophagus defied any attempts at penetration or analysis through the centuries and then, at the precise moment she woke, the liquid disappeared.

Poof!" he said as he flung his hands upwards in his frustration and to underscore the irony of the situation.

"Exactly, Larry," Abel Hardy continued to be the voice of reason. "The liquid is gone. It's been ten years. There's no residue, no signature, no structure we can analyse. It is no more."

Lawrence Clere sat down and folded his arms.

Principal Hardy tried to placate him. "It is possible that our technology isn't advanced enough to detect traces of the fluid in Alice. Now, it may develop to that point in the future, but we can't keep her here hoping that such technology turns up in her lifetime. She's ageing naturally now."

"Yes," Clere leaned forward, "and that is precious time we are letting slip by." He tapped his finger on Principal Hardy's desk. "If we can't study the preservation, we must turn our investigation to her memories. Put aside all that Alice Watkins nonsense and help her find her true identity. She may well remember the formula."

Jim Grossmith would resist this with his last breath.

"That's if she had any involvement in its composition," he could hear the anger in his own voice. "You are making a huge assumption, Clere. She was terminally ill. Her brain would not have been functioning to any practical capacity. It's possible, probable even she is unaware of the formula, and that would mean it died with her uncle."

There followed an awkward silence. As expected, Larry Clere was the first to break it. He pointed a finger at

Dr Grossmith.

"I blame you for this, Grossmith. You should have been more prepared. You were the one who always insisted she would wake naturally."

Principal Hardy stepped in on the defence.

"There's no way Jim or any of us could have known the fluid would dematerialise in such a manner. It's a mystery—one I believe we must live with."

"Then use drugs to encourage her memory." Clere stood, his left hand clenched, waving it at his colleagues. "Hypnotics to stimulate her cerebral cortex and hippocampus, psychotropic agents and stimuli and failing those, I have a theory where modification of a KELA procedure would force her to remember."

Jim Grossmith was incredulous, and his anger finally spilt over. He stood and faced Clere, no longer a colleague but an opponent, an adversary.

"How can you propose that?" he hissed. "I know your theory on KELA. You developed it solely in response to Alice with no concern for how it might affect her. She's remarkable, a miracle, and she deserves to live a normal life! What you propose is preposterous. Inhumane. She might lose all sense of identity!"

"What identity?" Clere raised his eyebrows, unmoved by his colleague's outburst, his voice dripping with sarcasm. "Of Alice Watkins? She isn't her, anyway. If she loses that memory, what of it? It isn't what she will lose that interests me; it is what we will gain. She was preserved for hundreds of years in that—that fluid! A fluid that not only sustained her life but cured her of disease. There are cancers today we cannot cure. She holds a key! Can't you see that?"

Hardy saw all this turning into a circular and progressively heated argument, one that would get them nowhere.

"Psychology isn't a valid form of medicine, Larry," he said. "It hasn't been practised for years, and you have no expertise in the techniques. How often have you had cause to use the drugs of which you speak?"

Clere was silent, fuming.

"I'll take that as 'never'. What about you, Jim?"

"Yes, twice, after a military accident in the Andromeda corridor. Just after I graduated."

Hardy nodded. He had never used such techniques or drugs on any of his patients.

"We were never able to analyse the fluid, Larry," Hardy said. "Even if a molecule had been left, there's no guarantee we would have ever discovered its secrets. How do we know the cancers she suffered were of the type we couldn't cure?"

"No," Clere didn't like his deficiencies pointed out, but much was at stake here, so he would try reasoning, "but as an alternative to the Life Prosthesis."

Jim Grossmith saw that potential, but it would not be at Alice's expense. He looked to Principal Hardy, although he doubted he would actually consider Clere's proposal.

"It would be inhumane to keep her as a specimen,

Larry," Principal Hardy's word was final. "She's learning, socialising, albeit only with Jim and Kelly and the library staff, but she is adapting and rehabilitating. I note you have not even spoken to her in many weeks. The life to which she is entitled must be expanded and not taken from her. I'm sorry, Larry, you have not placed a convincing argument before me; therefore, the plan remains. She will return to Earth on the Significator."

"Her life belongs to science," Clere dismissed the principal's remark with a wave of his hand, a breach of protocol Hardy ignored.

Dr Clere acknowledged neither of his colleagues as he turned on his heel and stormed through the portal.

They watched him go. Lawrence Clere, all charm when he was getting his way, receiving accolades, having his ego stroked, struck out like a wounded bear if opposed.

With Clere gone, Jim Grossmith aired a few concerns of his own regarding Alice.

"If she continues to insist she's Alice Watkins, do you think she will keep that persona?" he put the question to Principal Hardy. "To fully heal and integrate, perhaps she needs to be who she really is. I disagree with his proposals, but Clere might have a point."

"Why? Because that is who we have told her she must be? You know her, Jim, Alexis Langley isn't going to happen anytime soon, for now, we have Alice Watkins."

"I'm worried about what the future holds for her."

Alice's going away represented a sense of grief for which Jim Grossmith wasn't prepared, and Larry Clere's persistence worried him. Hardy's view, just to leave her be for now, let her get back to Earth and be normal for a while in the protection of the Tabernacle, seemed sensible.

"What about the Moses pathogens, Jim?" Principal Hardy opened the registry. "Is there any reason to believe she's not protected?" Alice had received all the required immunisations, he had checked and rechecked this information many times and didn't need to do it again, but he wasn't taking any chances.

"I've never mentioned the Moses pathogens to her," Dr Grossmith said, "besides, I think they're irrelevant. Now she's immunised, she's no more likely to be infected than any of us. Clere has used the threat of the pathogens as a reason to keep her here."

Principal Hardy nodded. "Off the record, Jim, do you remember in the history, the original custodians of the sarcophagus approached A'khet about Alice when she first went to the Bell Institute?"

Dr Grossmith did remember. He even asked them himself in recent years.

"Alice calls all this science fiction, Abel," he said, "I don't know if A'khet have ever seen this method of preservation before; if they have, they didn't communicate it to me when I asked them. I can't even remember what they said."

Principal Hardy steepled his hands and tapped his forefingers on his lips.

"*Alice* is science fiction to *us*; we never dreamed of a technology we couldn't decipher. If A'khet doesn't know, then we, years behind them in understanding such mysteries, don't stand a chance. Still, we both agree, do we not," he continued, "that neither of us understands her references to this Alice Watkins and that she doesn't even recognise her own face?"

Dr Grossmith conceded that was the case. "We can only take solace in the fact that she uses the name Watkins, her uncle's surname," he said. "Somewhere inside her mind, she recognises that at least."

Principal Hardy agreed. "That's true, and for now, it's all we have. We'll be patient, and though I agree her memories are perplexing, the mists will clear in time. I wish I understood how she gained such extraordinary insight into the century from which she claims to come; her explanation and details are uncannily accurate. I almost believe something more is going on here."

And somehow, he had a sneaking suspicion that the "something more" involved the A'khet.

CHAPTER NINE _

A few hours after the intense debate in his office, Principal Hardy linked through to the guest quarters. Kelly's face came into view.

"Principal Hardy."

"Kelly Ann," he said, using her proper title and name. "Has Alice had her afternoon tea?"

"We're just leaving for the mess, Principal Hardy."

"I'll escort her today, Kelly. There are one or two matters I need to discuss with her."

"Of course, she'll enjoy a visit with you."

Despite him receiving regular updates about Alice, they told him little of her emotional state. He found spending time with her allowed far more insight into his unusual guest than any progress report.

Alice was delighted to see him. She'd been on several outings to the mess with Principal Hardy over the weeks. He was a busy man, and she felt honoured he made time for her.

"Good afternoon, Alice."

"Principal Hardy." Alice had been learning how to respond to greetings in this society and where Principal Hardy was concerned, she no longer felt the urge to curtsy.

"Today, we're going to the officer's dining room for tea. I may find some different morsels to tempt you."

"I don't need tempting, Principal Hardy," Alice confessed. "The food is delicious. I haven't found a single thing I don't like. I even liked those little semolina cakes Kelly gave me to see if I could swallow."

"Well, you would be in the minority. They're not manufactured for their palatability."

"That makes them sound awful, but I liked them."

Alice intrigued Hardy, her humility and gratitude were refreshing, and she took simple pleasure in such ordinary activities. He understood why Jim Grossmith was so protective of her. She was an infant. Changing. Learning. Growing.

Alice always had a store of questions about the station, the planets, himself, but today, he had to inform her that her time on the station was ending, that soon, she would leave these familiar surroundings and return to Earth.

"Are you happy here, Alice?" he asked when she at last allowed him to steer the conversation.

"It's all I have for the moment, Principal Hardy; I'm safe here. I've even got used to Saturn outside the window," she pointed to the viewport.

"Do you still believe you're dreaming?"

"You ask me that every time and yes, I suppose I

do."

"Have I asked you before if it's a pleasant dream?"

Alice thought about it. No, he hadn't asked her that.

"It's not a bad dream if that's what you mean. I only know you, Kelly, Dr Grossmith, the library staff and Dr Clere, and I don't see him. I'm fine if it's a dream. If it were real life, I would feel confined and somehow…" she looked around her before returning to him, "…without purpose."

"Alice, we plan to return you to Earth. You are ready to leave the station and broaden your world."

He'd been worried the news would upset her, but she only smiled.

"Whatever you say, Principal Hardy. I suppose even fantastic dreams like this move along."

"I often reminisce about our first meeting Alice, when you said we had the labels mixed up?"

She remembered. She still believed it.

"I don't think we did," Hardy said, "but Dr Clere believes you should be studied, that we should use techniques and drugs to help you recover your memories."

"I don't need help to recover memories."

"Dr Clere appears to be unable to separate you, as a person, from a cryogenic specimen. He views you in the same light and proposes more study."

She was silent. Perhaps deep down, the news of her leaving made her anxious, but when she spoke, he didn't hear concern in her voice. If anything, he heard…*disdain?*

"Dr Clere views things through a narrow scientific

lens, Principal Hardy," Alice made strong eye contact. "To apply known scientific paradigms to a situation beyond his, yours, and if I may say so, any of your scientist's comprehension is a pointless exercise."

Principal Hardy maintained his composure in the face of this change. It could be pivotal.

"Why do you say that?"

"What would be his theoretical positioning? Where would he begin? From my understanding, all that could be done has been done, and all known scientific approaches are now exhausted. My uncle preserved me, Principal Hardy, so that I would live. *That* is where the conundrum resides."

He nodded. "And he saw this outcome?"

"I doubt it; how could he? But don't look to science for answers. Therein lies a blank wall. I see this as posturing by Dr Clere, and his attitude is disappointing."

"So, you formally reject any further scientific study?"

She picked up her cup, her expression blank.

"I'm sorry, Principal Hardy, I was away with the fairies. Paradigms? I'm not sure what that means."

Remarkable! *This* is what they expected! No-one had mixed up the labels! And he would not be advising Clere of this conversation.

"It is I who should apologise, Alice," Hardy said, the moment over. "I went off on a tangent about Dr Clere."

"Dr Clere is a prune," she said and returned to her tea, acknowledging the steward who refilled her cup.

Principal Hardy found it almost impossible to

contain his excitement. He had seen a glimpse, a potential, like the one reported by Kelly, and he'd learned from it. They needn't explore these momentary insights, at least for now. Alexis Langley had survived. Whether conscious or instinctive, he wasn't sure, but as a doctor, he knew the human body had a surprising capacity to heal itself. Alice only needed time, and her memories would surface. He became even more resolute in his decision about Clere's proposal.

A day later, Dr Grossmith and Dr Clere were again in Principal Hardy's office.

"Larry, you're not to pursue her. Jim can follow her up and report back to you if there are any problems."

"That's taking things too far, *Principal* Hardy!"

"Nevertheless, *as* your principal, you are still under my command here on this station. You are to leave her alone."

"I will send my concerns to Principal Katya at the Tabernacle."

"I've already contacted her. These are her words to you, Larry—Dr Clere. Leave her be unless authorised otherwise. Principal Katya is preparing orders as we speak."

Lawrence Clere, grim, unsmiling and heartily dissatisfied at this turn of events, knew that Principal Hardy's word was the law here on Saturn Station. He decided not to argue the point but wait until he could make the proposal to the World Principal herself. If anyone would see reason, it would be her.

As they turned to leave, Principal Hardy stopped Dr Grossmith, allowing the disgruntled Dr Clere to exit alone.

"Wait a moment Jim. I'd like to talk to you. That first time I spoke to Alice, she told me she had a theory."

"About what?"

"About how she arrived here. She says we mixed up the labels."

Grossmith grinned. "I see, in that she is Alice Watkins, somehow preserved, changed in appearance and age and that the history we found with her relates to someone else? Yes, that sounds like Alice, but if that's the case, how do we explain the data recovered from the chip?"

"I know it's impossible." Principal Hardy was eager to tell him of his conversation with Alice. "Do you recall Kelly's experience of clarity with Alice?"

Grossmith had read and reread Kelly's account of the incident, "Fleeting at best. It could have been random."

"You know you don't believe that, Jim. Alice takes too simple a view of things to drop surprises on us, but I also had a similar experience yesterday. I told her about leaving the station and, as an afterthought, about Clere's views on further study."

"Didn't that worry her?"

"No, on the contrary, she struck me as irritated by Clere's intentions. She countered his ideas, spoke as a scientist; confident, articulate and incisive. Her demeanour, speech, even the way she held my gaze, was not the Alice we know. The moment passed as quickly as it had begun, but it was certainly not random. It was focused and on point. I've recorded my observations and encoded them to your personal file."

"Why didn't you tell me straight away?"

"I hesitated just in case it *was* random, but I realised at the time and became more convinced since that her journey is one we can't direct. Alice might be thirty or so and new to our society, but there is little difference between her and a newborn baby. What do we do when a new baby comes into the world?"

"We educate the child, nurture it, love it and encourage its growth?"

"Exactly. That will be our research but at a distance. Give her a life, a family. I will suggest this to Principal Katya—hopefully, she may find a close enough DNA match, and we'll see where that takes us. We'll keep in touch, and as time goes by, observe her milestones and enjoy watching her grow, as friends. In time, I'm certain she will recover her true self."

"I rather like Alice Watkins," Dr Grossmith said quietly. He and Alice had become good friends. Her origins and all their old theories and expectations didn't seem so important.

"I like her too," Hardy agreed, "but we only see one side of Alexis Langley's personality. She is a beautiful, gentle soul, but I would like to think she will eventually have all aspects of herself available to her, and we should do all in our power to ensure that happens."

"Clere wouldn't agree with any of this."

"He doesn't have to agree. The Significator will arrive in proximal space within the month. When that ship leaves Saturn Station, Alice will be on board. I've arranged for one of Clere's former patients, Educator Sebel, to meet with Alice. I will brief her on the circumstances. She is also returning to Earth, and though a little younger than Alice, I suspect, given her personality, they may become friends. She will be able to provide Alice with both companionship and tuition."

"It will be hard to let Alice go, but I confess to being relieved, Hardy. She deserves a good life. Meanwhile, I'll make sure she gets an Eduction chip inserted."

"This can be the only course of action, Jim. In a nurturing and loving environment, she may just remember her true identity."

CHAPTER TEN _

"Kelly, I've never asked, when do you sleep?" Alice had dressed in one of the too-flimsy nightgowns Kelly had given her, much skimpier and more revealing than anything she'd ever worn before and made of the same lovely fabric she intended to buy for the new baby's blanket.

"When you sleep, Alice," Kelly replied.

"What if something happens while I'm sleeping?"

"I'd know, don't worry, I'll be here."

"Does everyone who gets defrosted get a personal carer?"

"Not everyone, Alice, only people with extended rehabilitation, and you weren't defrosted."

"How long am I going to have this rehabilitation?"

"As long as it takes."

Alice learned something new every hour. New things to add to her amazing dream, if indeed it was a dream. Whatever, she was fine with it. She was happy here, and although she didn't know why, liked the normality her life had taken on now everything felt less foreign.

"Why do you only sleep when I do?" Alice stayed on topic.

"Not all the time, Alice, if I did that, nothing would get done!"

Alice smiled, and that always pleased Kelly.

"But how do you know when I need you?"

It was like answering a child with never-ending questions.

"I told you, I have your cells co-written into my system, and my body clock corresponds with yours."

Alice had forgotten. Cells and programming. She should remember such a simple thing.

"What about when I go back to Earth?"

"The cells will be removed, and I will return to my normal work and life until I get another KELA assignment, although none will be as amazing as you!"

Alice couldn't imagine life without Kelly, "Who will look after me?"

"You can already look after yourself, Alice. You're quite independent. Don't worry, on Earth, you will have capable and caring people to guide and support you, but you don't need looking after."

Alice was standing at the viewport. She didn't know precisely how far apart Earth and Saturn were, but the simple act of being able to wash and dress herself here might not mean the same thing as starting a whole new life on an Earth she hadn't seen for centuries.

Alice felt like a queen in her new quarters. She even liked the funny shower with water in a packet that washed and moisturised her skin and the little peppermint-flavoured wafers that cleaned her teeth. Every night, she had hot chocolate in a pretty mug, just like she always had in her old life. Even in the future, bedtime rituals were the same and always at bedtime, Alice thought of her family.

It was her memories of Eliza that started the tears. Her granddaughter wouldn't know her in this dream, she looked so different, and the new baby when it came, may never know his or her grandma. Alice wondered if Eliza did well in her exams or if she had a boyfriend by now. She wished she could see her again.

Sometimes, Alice thought maybe she *had* died. Whether she'd gone to heaven or hell, only time would tell, but this was a nice place meanwhile. She enjoyed meeting up with Principal Hardy, having a cup of tea with him, chatting with Dr Grossmith, and going to the mess to eat proper food, much of which she didn't recognise but liked. And most of all, she liked the warm friendship developing between her and Kelly. She tried to make this her last thought. A lovely thought to drop off to sleep with.

But Alice's body was changing. One morning, she woke, startled by the artificial light from the station's day/night system. Kelly was already by Alice's bed.

"Did your alarm clock go off too early?" Alice said, peering through a haze. It felt like the first morning she found herself here, and it took a moment for the fog to clear.

Kelly laughed. "No! You woke with a start!"

"Did I? Oh, okay. I was dreaming. I thought I saw a young man with white hair."

Alice rubbed her eyes. Her mouth tasted terrible, and she needed to pee. Sliding out of bed, she looked for her slippers, but they were next to her bed at home, so, barefoot, she stepped through the washer portal. This morning, she felt stiff and sore, her tummy ached, and her brain felt foggy.

"Kelly? What year is this?" she called out, standing in the shower and blinking to wake herself up. Alice had been giving thought to the fact that in all these weeks, no-one mentioned the date. "It hasn't occurred to me to ask."

"The year is 2513. We're on the twenty-eighth day of the first quarter."

"2513? That's impossible." Alice's face twisted up in concentration as if trying to grasp all the years between her birthday and now. She'd bypassed Christmas.

As she dressed, she tried to get her head around the missing years. When she first moved to her new quarters, Kelly gave her sleeveless, grey shift-like tunics to wear. They were tidy enough but plain and uninspiring and shorter than she would normally wear, so she wore trousers underneath, with no bra or knickers, leaving Alice feeling a little exposed. As she was deliberating about the year, lack of a bra and more importantly, the lack of knickers, Dr Grossmith chose that moment to step through the portal, unannounced.

"Dr Grossmith," Kelly acknowledged him as

protocols demanded, then reproached him with a grin. "You really should buzz in, Doctor."

Alice thought so too but wouldn't have dared say so. Fortunately, she was almost dressed.

"I'm here to see my patient." He looked chastened, seeing Alice quickly sliding into her slacks, and Alice felt sorry for him getting told off. "I should have buzzed. I'm sorry." He bowed a little and left the room. Alice and Kelly looked at each other and burst out laughing. The portal buzzer sounded, and Dr Grossmith was invited in.

"Good morning, Alice. I thought to take you outside after breakfast."

Alice looked out the window—going out there didn't appeal. Out there was outer space. She pointed to the viewport.

Dr Grossmith laughed loudly and placed his hands on her arms

"On a shuttle, Alice! It's exciting. Don't worry; I'm not planning a spacewalk! Trust me; you will enjoy it."

Exciting? Out there? She trusted him, so she would go. Her tummy fluttered. Nerves? Probably hunger.

"Why do I never see Dr Clere?" she asked as they travelled on the walkway. She'd discarded the calliper weeks ago, and she walked as well as she ever had. Better even. "He seems to have disappeared," she said, peering across to someone vanishing through a portal.

"Dr Clere's work is finished now you are resuming

your life. He will conduct one more examination before you leave and after that, keep in close contact with me to ensure your heart and other organs stay healthy."

The first part about Clere finishing his work was a lie, but Dr Grossmith saw no reason to add that Dr Clere's own heart was made of stone and that his interest in Alice was far less vested in her internal affairs than keeping her in a laboratory. He'd known Larry Clere for years and always found him to be a self-congratulatory, pompous ass. Recent events confirmed his diagnosis.

A sudden fog came over Alice, and she retreated to a listening place, with no control over her voice, "Thank you for all you have done. I'm sorry I haven't regained my memory. It must be frustrating for you to have invested so much, for so little return."

Dr Grossmith didn't notice the brief change in her pattern of speech. "Don't worry, Alice; it may take a long time. That you are alive and going home is reward enough."

"How did I get preserved, Dr Grossmith? Please explain it again." They sat at their favourite table in the mess, and Alice fell back into familiar, ignorant territory. She knew she'd somehow been preserved; it was the how that interested her—boiled with sugar perhaps. Vinegar?

He wished she'd asked him something else. The weather patterns on the moons of Saturn, the composition of the rings, anything but this. It was easy to confound and confuse Alice, but he would stick to his promise; that when she asked questions, he would answer as directly as he could.

"A preservation technique that appears to have died with the creator of its formula and technique, I'm afraid. After your removal from the mountain vault, no-one could gain access to the preservation fluid to analyse its composition. When the sarcophagus opened, with no interference from us, we still couldn't examine it."

"Why not?"

"It doesn't exist."

He expected her to ask why, but she didn't.

"Did they find anyone else with me?"

He wanted to tell her everything, the whole story, not leave out a single detail, in the hope it would dislodge a memory and give an answer that would satisfy Clere enough to ensure he left her alone. But she'd moved on, so he reined himself in to provide an answer to this much simpler query.

"A few human heads and tissue samples," he said, "but there appears to have been no effort to preserve them in the way you were preserved, nor by employing either primitive or known cryogenic applications. They looked like specimens, with evidence of cell manipulation in one or two but far too degraded to be of any use."

Alice had made a point of reading about cryogenics and bombarded Kelly with questions, but it still made no sense.

"And they found me in China?" Alice asked between bites of Petit Pan Au Chocolate, a new and delicious discovery.

"Well, yes, that is what they called it then. It's

Principality 4 now. The moment you woke, the fluid evaporated; it vanished before my eyes. No residue, no signature, no trace, as if it hadn't existed. I was the only one present."

"Can you tell me anything about the people with me in the chamber?"

"No, no records relating to them at all and they were only heads, no bodies."

As he spoke and listened to her occasional reply, he wondered about the labels being mixed up. Could that have happened? What about those moments of clarity witnessed by Kelly and Hardy? Her chamber and the sarcophagus were clearly marked, her chip in place, but if someone else got there before? Could they have missed something of importance? And what about her assertion she was a mother to—who did she say? Yes, Michelle.

She was asking him about chips.

"Chips?" he said, his expression blank, still off somewhere with Alice's sarcophagus.

"Yes, chips."

"Chips—your chip gave us personal history, your birth date, the state of your health but little else."

Alice sipped her coffee and studied him. Her green eyes held only the question. He'd spoken of this many times, but it was clear she hadn't retained the information.

"The sarcophagus was impenetrable. Hammers in the early days, lasers, even weapons didn't so much as scratch the surface. And you were suspended within it. By the time you arrived at the Bell Institute, about eighty years after your discovery, they still believed you to be a perfectly preserved corpse. That's why they tried to open the sarcophagus, believing you were dead. Technology hadn't advanced to the stage where they could detect you were alive."

He wondered why she had asked about the preservation. He could see from her expression she was no closer to believing any of it. Soon, she would leave, and he needed to help her understand something of her origins. She waited for him to continue, and he would tell her the story as often as she wanted to hear it, adding in tiny snippets of extra information each time.

"I became a consultant to the project forty years ago, some one-hundred-and-fifty years after the discovery that you were living and almost three hundred and fifty years after your preservation. In the centuries before my involvement, and although the sarcophagus yielded none of its secrets, scientific instrumentation did at least detect rudimentary brain activity. The neurological sequences proved indecipherable but were too organised to be random. In short, we don't know what kept you alive or how. There can be no conclusion other than specific, unknown factors within the fluid-filled, glass-like sarcophagus, somehow sustained your life."

"How did I get out?"

"As technology developed, we found that you had a heartbeat, though it was slow and irregular, and although preserved, your kidneys and liver weren't functioning. The other organs seemed intact, and apart from their dormancy, seemed to be normal healthy tissue. To grow a new heart, Dr Clere required tissue samples and of course, to achieve that, he would have to access your body, but the sarcophagus, as I said, could not be penetrated. Around fourteen years ago, one of our technicians noticed hair growth over the top of your scalp, a few months later, fingernails. It was extraordinary, Alice. Just before the sarcophagus opened, your hair covered your body like a shroud from just four years of growth, and you were barely visible. Around that time, your internal organs showed signs of necrosis."

"What's that?"

"Dying. Specifically, the death of tissue."

"So, to save me, you had to pop the blister."

"What an intriguing analogy, Alice. Well, yes, I suppose the capsule did look like a blister," he angled his head. This might be a good time for a little digging. "Do you remember any of this?"

Alice shook her head. She didn't believe it either. Not really.

"We didn't 'pop' it as you say; we were never able to penetrate any part of it. When you woke, the fluid vanished, leaving you lying in a primitive polymer shell. This shell had somehow been encased along with you in the sarcophagus. It was only the fluid and the sarcophagus that dissipated the instant you woke."

How often had he relived that day? A day that started like any other, three years following the project's removal to Saturn Station. He was in her room, carrying out the solitary task of routine checks on life signs and equipment function; once completed, as he always did, he sat down to record his findings on the registry. Identical readings to the day before, and the day before that, besides the tissue decay, which appeared to have accelerated.

He'd stopped to deliberate on his concerns, at first ignoring the eerie tingling that started at the base of his spine, but as the tingling became more intense, he became aware of a presence behind him. He remembered sitting up straight, all senses attuned, and he turned slowly towards the centre of the room where Alexis Langley lay enshrined.

It was opening. Without a sound, the uppermost chamber of the sarcophagus had parted. She lay still and pale, silent and serene. Transfixed, he watched the sarcophagus lift, centre itself and rejoin to form a canopy, hovering over her while the fluid, instead of rushing like water bursting from a broken jug, continued to ripple and cradle her within its depths. Slowly, her body moved upwards and, for a moment, floated, her shroud of hair falling away from her face while gently, the fluid supported her descent into the shell-like remnant of the sarcophagus. No equipment sounded, no distant everyday noise from elsewhere on the station. There was no sound at all, save that of his own heart beating.

He didn't even try to move; such was the impossibility of the moment; such was the incomprehensibility of the scene he witnessed. The room was still. Hushed. Suspended in time. An eternity.

The peace exploded when the canopy suddenly

shattered, sending him scrambling for cover. The shimmering liquid slipped from around her and joined with the shards of the sarcophagus before vanishing into nothingness, leaving her abandoned in the shallow capsule. He had enough presence of mind to slap the visual beam on the registry as he dived for the floor and, in doing so, preserved the final image of the disappearance of both sarcophagus and fluid.

He later learned her awakening and the subsequent disappearance of the fluid took less than twenty seconds. As the only witness, he filed a report that, given the image recorded, suitably satisfied and astonished the Tabernacle, but he never told another living soul what he saw in the room that day. Not because he didn't wish to, but because when he tried, his tongue stilled, and his jaw would not move. He tried recording it in the written word, a skill possessed by only a few in society, but with each attempt, his fingers refused to move the pen.

Alice watched him while his thoughts dwelt in the past. He could not tell her of them.

"Then you struggled to breathe, and we were all galvanised into action," he finished quickly when he saw she was watching him.

"I suppose it would have been no loss even if you had been able to penetrate the shell before that, seeing I was dead already."

"I disagree; it *would* have been a loss, a great loss," he held up his hands as though measuring the extent. "Alice," he clasped his hands over hers, she saw his wonderment and awe, "you are one of a kind; there are no others."

Alice did not share his wonder. It was too unbelievable, no matter how often she heard the story. She took her hand away and picked up her tea.

"If we had lost you," his voice an urgent, emphatic whisper, "we would have lost part of our history." Then he realised what she had said before. "And you weren't dead."

"Near enough," she pointed out. "I can't fill in the gaps, Dr Grossmith; I'm not part of your history. If anything, I appear to be part of your future."

He raised an eyebrow at the sudden variation in her tone and speech. Was he going to witness an episode of elucidation?

But then she shrugged the shrug her mother would have thought disrespectful and sat back, speaking in the words of Alice Watkins.

"You don't know how I'll turn out, really, you don't. You don't even know if I'll survive."

"No, Alice, we don't, but you are neither an experiment nor a curiosity. You are a wonder."

"What about my appearance?"

"Alice, your looks are the same as before your stasis, although you do look healthier!"

"I don't recognise myself."

"I realise that, but the woman in that sarcophagus is the woman who is sitting before me."

"Dr Clere replaced most of my insides."

"He grew them, Alice. They are entirely yours. The scientist who placed you in that chamber; he took the chances."

"How?"

"By preserving you in a living state. No technology, not historical nor current, was ever successful in that. Your uncle either had a vision or help. You were the original Sleeping Beauty."

She doubted that. The original only slept for one hundred years and woke up looking like she did when she first got into bed. Alice was an old lady dozing in a chair.

Dr Grossmith was proud of her and didn't treat her as a curiosity. No-one here behaved as if they were curious about her. Only a select few knew the truth anyway, and those who did treated her with kindness and respect. As for Dr Grossmith, she considered him a friend.

"Would it be alright if I asked for more pastries?".

"Yes, Alice," he said with a sigh. "It would be fine."

CHAPTER ELEVEN _

The shuttle landing bay was like many of the rooms on the station, glass-walled with portals and a view out to Saturn, the only difference being the presence of a complicated-looking metal door. The pilot was waiting and, on seeing them, bowed and released the door by flicking his finger against a series of lights. The door slid away in four parts, up, down and side to side, to reveal what looked like the inside of a small car, with a driver's seat, passenger seats and controls but no steering wheel. Beyond the shuttle, through its viewports, Saturn glowed, looking bigger and brighter than it did from inside the station.

This would be what Dr Grossmith called "going out", buzzing about in a tiny vehicle in space. Unsure whether to be overwhelmed or terrified, Alice settled for both and held on to Dr Grossmith for support, hoping he would reconsider.

"Is it safe?" She didn't want to look out the bay door. There looked to be a sheer drop through eternity on her side.

"Perfectly safe, Alice. There hasn't been a shuttle accident in twenty years."

"Oh dear, maybe they're overdue for one."

"Don't worry; these little shuttles are very robust and manoeuvrable. I guarantee you will think differently at the end of this trip. Besides, we use shuttles all the time on Earth to get around."

Councilman Chen, the pilot, fitted pleasantly into the role of proud tour guide, flying the shuttle around the station so Alice could see it from all angles. It was big, bigger than any machine Alice ever imagined and shone like silver in the light reflected from Saturn. Not at all like the bleak and dark experience of space Alice had expected, and Dr Grossmith was right, anxiety gave way to awe as the shuttle moved to a distance where Alice had a complete view of the station.

Within a graceful form not unlike a wind spinner, the station had a central solid core and a platform around the lower third. The exterior reminded Alice of Steven's gyroscope toy from when he was little, which made shapes like this. On the platform, a ship, larger than the shuttle, glowed blue; a supply ship preparing to leave, Councilman Chen told her, enjoying imparting his knowledge to someone he was sure knew nothing of space.

He spoke with much enthusiasm about the use of the minerals found in Saturn's icy rings, their composition and importance in engineering and medicine. Alice heard about asteroids and black holes and the technology that advanced space travel. He pointed out a few of the moons of Saturn and named them all. Though informative and knowledgeable, his narrative was lost on Alice, but she didn't care; the sheer scope of a project that could create a place to live in space enthralled her.

After they thanked and farewelled Councilman Chen, an animated Alice chattered about the tour with Dr Grossmith all the way back to her quarters. Once inside, after Kelly made them coffee, Alice recounted the whole experience again, missing out the big words which Dr Grossmith kindly inserted for her. Once Alice had brought her excitement under control, he produced a tiny tube from his pocket.

"I'm going to place this little chip here, Alice," Dr Grossmith indicated to a spot on the inside of her arm.

"Will it hurt?"

"No, but it will clear away the fogginess you suffer at times and help make sense of much of what you heard today. This chip, an Eduction chip, will help you to absorb information and bring clarity. We use them often; they're harmless and biodegradable. You are keen to learn; your experience today has shown that, let's make sure we give you every opportunity."

He put the point of the tube on her skin, and a little dot appeared.

"There. Now, when the Eduction chip kicks in, we can expect lots of questions."

Alice's high spirits over her fantastic morning out on the shuttle were settling, and as Dr Grossmith left, a curious sense of gloom descended, a kind of anticlimax.

Her bursts of bravado and confidence were more sustained now, but in the last two days, she was aware of tears being close to the surface, perhaps due to a realisation this wasn't a dream and the knowledge that soon, she was to leave this place. Kelly sensed her mood and lay on the bed beside her and held her as she cried.

Alice had hoped Kelly might go with her to Earth, and the coming separation was disquieting. She knew everyone acted in her best interests; that was one constant in her real life and this dream; she always did as she was told.

On Earth, her experiences might be as strange as her experiences here, so she decided she must learn as much as possible. To do that, she must persevere in learning how to use the registry. Alice discovered a child's lesson program, too advanced for her, which worked on the assumption that the user already knew something of Earth's society. Alice cried to Kelly that the Eduction chip wasn't working and faced with her frustration, Kelly explained that while the chip would help Alice prepare questions concisely and aid retention of knowledge, it wouldn't stop her from being impatient.

"Once those questions are answered, Alice," she said, "once the information is received in here," she tapped Alice gently on the head, "loud and clear, the chip allows rapid extraction from your memory engrams. But it doesn't happen overnight."

Alice understood. The chip wouldn't do all the work, so she selected a few words and phrases and later tried them out on Kelly so she could explain them in a language Alice understood. On the evening of her trip to the outside, she sat at the registry.

"What are the Loyalties, Kelly?"

"That's where most of the population live."

"And the Calamities?"

"Those who don't conform to social conventions live there."

"Where will I live?"

"That will be Principal Katya's decision."

The image of a lady, perhaps a little older than Alice, around seventy or so, showed on the registry screen. She had white hair and looked sprightly and efficient. Principal Katya.

"Is she special?" Alice liked the look of her.

"Yes, she is World Principal, each principality, countries in your time, has a principal. Each starship has a principal. Each station has a principal."

"Like Principal Hardy?"

"Yes, that's right."

"Do they live normal lives, have wives, husbands and children?"

"Of course, but starship principals and crew tend towards a single life. Principal Katya isn't military, but she is unmarried."

Alice mostly understood. Principals get married and do what ordinary people do, but they're like royalty.

"What about people who aren't principals?"

"They live, love, marry and have children too. We

are all given wonderful and varied opportunities."

"Did the plague kill lots of people?"

"Yes, it took two-thirds of the world's population over its three waves. It didn't discriminate."

"How could the world recover?"

"It didn't take them all at once, Alice. People were born during and between waves. The plague started in 2026, and each wave lasted around six years before subsiding. There were still deaths from other diseases apart from the plague. It's a long time ago, centuries."

2026, Alice paused. That would be in her lifetime and the kids and grandkids. It would affect them. She thought of Eliza's asthma; Marianne caught lots of colds, then there were the twins, Jack and Peter, and little Toby and the new baby. Steven hadn't married, choosing instead to work and build up wealth. That might be a blessing if this plague was going to happen.

"Store up your questions," Kelly said. "I understand an educator is to be assigned. You'll receive lots of answers, but then you'll discover more questions."

But Alice felt a twinge of uncharacteristic curiosity. There *were* a lot of questions rattling around inside her head. If only, when she asked them, the answers made sense. She needed to navigate the complexities and gain a deeper understanding, but by the next day, twenty-four hours after receiving the chip and mulling over what she had learned, she found the fog clearing, just as Dr Grossmith promised.

Alice hadn't been given any definite time for when she would be leaving. In the meantime, she stayed with her routines and did her best not to overthink the changes to come. She still slept well, and her few tears at night had almost ceased. Although now independent of Kelly, she was still relieved when Principal Hardy told her Kelly could stay until they decided on a date for Alice's departure.

Most mornings, Alice had breakfast with Dr Grossmith, who answered her questions, usually of a general nature, comprising such everyday information as what people ate on Earth, did they still have cows, etc.? He held a secret disappointment the questions were not more complex, given the insertion of the Eduction chip, but at least she was learning.

The questions of her origins were not revisited, and he asked himself once or twice whether he cared if she rediscovered herself. He'd discussed this with Abel Hardy. They agreed it didn't matter one jot if she remained Alice Watkins and never recovered her memories. She would have every opportunity to fulfil any potential, regardless.

Dr Grossmith researched the term "housewife" Alice used to describe herself, and the modern explanation, "a married servant in ancient times, used for reproduction and domestic duties", horrified him. He couldn't envision Alice in that role. He was pleasantly surprised when, at breakfast one morning, she asked him a sensible question. She had been on a foray into the education programs.

"The A'khet, Dr Grossmith. What do you know about them?"

"They're rumoured to have been on Earth for centuries, Alice. The A'khet themselves are vague about when they arrived, but without their help in rebuilding, the effects of the last wave of plague may have seen the end of humankind as we know it. Later, the A'khet gave us the ability to travel in space."

"What do they look like? I've only seen humans here on the station. Are they green?"

"No!" he laughed, "they're humanoid, shorter than us and telepathic. They communicate through touch, but they can speak if needed. A'khet are a gentle species with a philosophy that every event is guided according to the will of a higher power."

"Like God?"

"Well, I can't say, I'm not a follower of religious doctrine, but A'khet believes the universe is, at all times, subject to an unknown, unseen, great and mysterious authority."

They were in space; there had to be aliens. Alice didn't believe in gods or aliens.

"Are there many of them on Earth?"

"A number, no-one knows how many, but you needn't be afraid of them."

But to Alice, many things were alien to her. She had become accustomed to different food, different drinks, technology and, from what the registry showed her, species of plants on Earth she had never seen in her lifetime, but there were no pictures of the A'khet. She hoped she wouldn't ever have to meet one.

"What sort of people live in the Calamities?"

"Anyone entering into a marriage which doesn't conform to our society's conventions."

"I saw that on the registry. I couldn't make head nor tail of it. How do you determine what is outside your conventions?"

"Homosexual marriages, mixed-race and other marriages where the scale has been disregarded in favour of choice."

Alice wished she hadn't asked. She might be brighter with this chip in her arm, but she still got easily embarrassed by certain words.

"What's wrong with a mixed-race marriage? Where I come from, they happen all the time."

"Not in our society, Alice. We take a different standpoint on such things. Marriage between males and females of the same ethnic origin, from a similar cultural and educational background preserves culture and ethnicity. Marriage between those of the same sex cannot produce a child. We consider their union unnatural, so a couple choosing this path is assigned to the Calamities."

"But if they aren't hurting anyone," Alice suggested. She hadn't had opinions on this subject before, but these methods sounded harsh.

"The world has changed in the last four hundred years, Alice. Around the time you were born, it was in a precarious state, and for the one hundred or so years before your birth, some world religions actively demonstrated against what they saw as globalised moral decay. Others took the view, for society to grow, it was essential to be more inclusive of minority groups such as homosexuals. The government didn't separate church and state, and eventually, anarchy reigned. At times, I'm surprised humanity survived."

"I'm not," Alice said.

"You aren't?" Progress. Communication. Debate. She's thinking. Grossmith inclined his head to show his interest in her opinion.

"No, humankind has managed to recover from a whole variety of disasters. It's in our nature to survive. You can't blame people who thought differently for the government's failures."

"Well, put that way, I am inclined to agree, Alice. According to his notes, your uncle believed the world to be in a parlous state and removed himself from it. Where he removed himself to, we have no idea. I'm not sure he shared your faith in human nature."

"Do you know, Dr Grossmith, everyone refers to him as 'your uncle'. Would you believe no-one has ever said his name? I couldn't look him up on the registry because I didn't know it, so I tried checking the Sleeping Beauty Phenomenon, I thought it would be there, but the registry denied me access."

"His name was Martin Watkins."

Her name. Alice thought it over, but as always, didn't react.

"How did you find out his name?"

"From the records in the chamber. We don't know his full credentials, though we were able to glean limited information from history. He graduated high school at fourteen and studied physics at university, but the trail ends there, so we haven't been able to work out his interest in human preservation techniques. We can only gather he had significantly advanced scientific ability from a young age. A university in his homeland makes mention of him taking a lecturing post around 2090, but it seems he disappeared around that time."

"Obviously, he didn't disappear altogether, Dr Grossmith, if he preserved me in the fluid."

"Clearly, because you and he found each other. We believe he raised you after you were orphaned in 2103. Beyond that, information is scant, and we certainly don't know why he left you and the tissue samples buried in rock. It was lucky they found you, Alice, but we don't know what became of him," Dr Grossmith concluded, shaking his head.

"He has the same name as me, but you still say I'm Alexis Langley."

"We know you are Alexis Langley, that is irrefutable, and we know that you are related to him, not only by his references to you as 'niece' in the recordings he left but because you are his sister's daughter, and we can trace your birth. Unfortunately, records extending further back can be unreliable. He also refers to you as Alexis. That's why we believe you have somehow integrated his name, Watkins, into your memory and made it your own. Alice is not dissimilar to Alexis, and perhaps the 'x' is silent."

To his surprise, she asked for no further information about her time in the chamber, nor her family, only held his gaze for a moment before sighing, a sigh which he took as a sign she found his explanation once again, too fantastic.

"You were telling me about the Calamities." Alice returned to questions about the society she would soon join.

"Most principalities have them for any couple who wishes to engage in an unholy alliance. In the Calamities, they can do so without affecting normal society."

"Unholy?" What an awful adjective. Alice frowned.

"It's just a word, Alice," he assured her, "with possibly a different meaning today than in your time. It's not religious nor associated with any deity. To us, it means a marriage or partnership that does not conform to societal norms."

"What about disabled children?"

"There aren't any. No-one can be born with a disability."

Alice didn't need the Eduction chip to understand the implications of that statement.

"What about human rights?"

"I would have to refer back to your time to answer that. Criminals and drug addicts could breed unimpeded, is that right?"

"Yes."

"So, would you agree that a child born into such an environment and nurtured by the criminal element of society would exhibit an inclination to adopt the same antisocial lifestyle as the parents, given the example set?"

"You mean children follow in the footsteps of their parents?"

"That is what I mean. When microchipping became widespread and compulsory, it also became illegal for anyone who had a history of drug abuse, alcohol abuse, child abuse or any form of criminality to procreate. The government of the day removed that right to protect society."

"How could you police something like that?"

"By licencing procreation. The chip allowed tracing the movements of an individual. Eventually, all microchips placed in women were equipped with bio-programming to prevent pregnancy. It's deactivated upon marriage and with the permission of the principal. Hence, lower birth rates, safe, happy childhoods and no crime." Simple, his smile and expression told her. Society sorted.

"Safe and happy if you are what your society decides is normal." While Alice agreed to some extent about the criminal part, there didn't seem to be much compassion for those who made mistakes then changed their ways, with judgement harsh and final. Alice wondered about the tolerance of such a society.

"Yes," Dr Grossmith said, not catching the scepticism in Alice's voice. "And if you aren't, then largely you can be helped if you wish. If you refuse help, then you are consigned to the Calamities. Those in the Calamities do not reproduce. Single people seldom go there to live, usually just those in disloyal partnerships who wish to live in a married association."

"There must be a lot of unhappy people there."

"You'll be surprised. There are boundaries, but the Calamities are as beautiful as anywhere on Earth. Your birthplace has one."

"I'm from Australia."

"Yes, I know. Principality 19."

Just a number now. Alexis Langley must have been Australian too. "There are lots of deserts and spiders and snakes in Australia. Not all of it is a good place to live." Where Alice lived in her little unit outside Brisbane was nice enough, though.

"It sustains its population well."

"A big population?"

"Not really," he said. "Over the centuries, your homeland has become a seat of learning. It has many universities and aptitude hubs, with much of it dedicated to mineral and climate research. The Calamities are separate from the mainland, and they're beautiful. I've been there."

"I need proper education, Dr Grossmith," she decided, very sensibly, he thought. "I don't yet have a context for all this knowledge. Kelly helps me with the registry, and I sometimes go to the library, but I need a formal education. Kelly told me you've assigned me a real teacher?"

Alice's display of insight delighted Dr Grossmith. He noted and recorded all these little milestones.

"We hope to ease you into society," he told her, "but at your pace. An educator will accompany you to Earth. She's also a patient on the station, and you will meet her soon."

"Will I be going to the Calamities when I get to Earth?" Alice didn't see herself fitting the mould, so they might put her with all the other misfits.

"Of course not! There's no reason. You're going to have a home in the Loyalties and, in time, possible reintegration into your old or even a new career, but we must take things as they come, as you are ready to accept new things into your life. And I must clear up a misconception, Alice, those who live in the Calamities work in their professions and enjoy all the comforts loyal citizens enjoy. They are only forbidden to live and travel with their partners within the Loyalties, and they can't have children."

Alice thought it unfair on the face of it but felt unsure she was qualified to offer an opinion.

"I won't pretend to understand completely, Dr Grossmith," she admitted. "And I don't remember having a career to be reintegrated into."

"I know you don't at present. But we'll see. And don't worry about the Calamities."

"It seems people are sent to the Calamities because your government doesn't like what they do. It sounds like punishment or prison."

Dr Grossmith shook his head.

"In your world, Alice, people who didn't conform went to prison. We don't have prisons. In our world, there is no prejudice; everyone can learn and grow. People are what they are; there are no circumstances to dictate who gets on in life and who does not, even in the Calamities. Everyone is equal, but unlike in your time, no-one lives in poverty, no-one is unemployed or homeless, and every citizen on Earth has rights. I think you will find it a pleasant and refreshing surprise and quite different from what I understand was the bleakness of your time."

I liked it fine, Alice thought. My life wasn't bleak. I had everything I wanted. But a tiny, irritating voice niggled. *Did you? Did you really?* She ignored it.

"Are we definitely going to Earth?"

"Yes, Alice. *You* are going to Earth. Principal Hardy feels the time is right, and I agree with him, but I admit, I will greatly miss our morning conversations."

Alice had become fond of him. She would miss their conversations too.

"It's big, isn't it?" she said, her voice becoming distant, turning her head toward the viewport, towards space.

"What is?"

"My new world."

"Yes, Alice, it is big. Much bigger than ever imagined in your time."

My time, she thought, or Alexis's time?

CHAPTER TWELVE _

Alice made a habit of sitting on the observation deck after breakfast. She and Dr Grossmith spoke of so many things; she rather enjoyed sifting through the remnants of what she remembered while watching the comings and goings of patients and crew.

Alice found the politics of Earth's society a little confusing but discovered a certain pleasure in unravelling the conundrums placed before her. Unused as she was to exploring ideas or making considerations and reaching conclusions, she liked having a mind of her own at last.

No date for her leaving had been advised, but she sensed it would be soon, and Alice recognised her leaving would be an enormous wrench for Dr Grossmith. His dedication to the Sleeping Beauty Phenomenon had caused him to pursue little of a life outside his work. He'd made tremendous sacrifices on her behalf, even though he never said as much but told her, often and with pride, the impact she made on the scientific world. He told her about her transfer to Saturn Station when her hair started growing and how Principal Katya gave dispensation to his theory that she might wake without interference years before showing signs of reviving.

Removing her to Saturn had been his idea to protect her from a bug, Alice forgot its name, which could interfere with the growth of new organs, and in answer to her completely unrelated question one time, he told her no; he hadn't married. He liked to tell her that his favourite memory was of his wonderment when she finally woke and of his enormous relief on her successful weaning from life support.

Alice felt no connection to Alexis Langley, but she did feel enormous gratitude to Dr Grossmith for his kindness and care. Alice imagined he behaved as a father, had she ever known one, interested, supportive and patient. She supposed even in an impossible dream, you can still feel gratitude, but no matter how often he said it, she still didn't believe she was Alexis Langley.

One evening, in her quarters, Alice pored over the registry, Eduction chip or no, she still had problems working the display command. She was allowed only restricted access to the full registry, and consequently, much of what she saw gave incomplete explanations. While she assumed it was to stop her from getting overloaded, she found this "surfing the net" dull. It was beyond her comprehension why Eliza found it so much fun.

Alice had hoped to expand more on what to expect

on Earth. Or what on earth to expect? But eventually, she wearied of the registry and turned to Kelly.

"What's your story, Kelly?"

Kelly was working with her own portable registry, not needed here now save as a companion for Alice and didn't mind engaging in conversation.

"No story, Alice. I'm a medical technician; only a few of us are compatible with KELA technology. That's why I'm assigned to you."

"How old are you, if you don't mind me asking?"

"Thirty."

"Do you have a family?"

Kelly's face broke into a big smile.

"I have a husband, Paul, assigned to one of the minor principality ships, the Argos. He'll be arriving here in about two months, and we're returning to Earth to start a family. I told you this before, Alice."

"I'm sorry. I forgot," Alice tried to recall asking. "I don't remember you telling me at all, but it's wonderful!"

"It *is* wonderful. You are my second KELA implant, and there won't be another, seeing as Paul and I have decided to have a baby. It's been fantastic, but I'll be happy to return to Earth. Paul is due to take up a lecturing position in geology at the university in Principality 11, so I might work in a City Infirmary, at least until a baby is on the way."

"Won't you both miss working in space?"

"Not too much," Kelly confessed. "We're both homebodies, and Paul's not military. He's a civilian on secondment who prefers solid ground beneath his feet."

Alice dreamed of Earth that night. All evening, Kelly entertained her with stories about home and what it would be like when she and her husband were together again. Alice built up a picture in her mind of a beautiful green Earth where every element and aspect of life existed in harmony, a place where children could play outside without fear and parents were assured of their child's success. Kelly's Earth sounded like heaven.

It wasn't the Earth Alice saw in her dream. Yes, there were lush, green pastures filled with happy and contented families. But she also had glimpses of barren patches of land, where sad-faced people looked through high fences at the green and glorious place on the other side, their hands gripping tightly to the bars that separated them. A sign, roughly tacked to the fence, read "Calamities".

As Alice viewed the scene from her dreamlike state, a youthful man appeared and stood beside her. She turned to see who her companion could be. He shone with beauty, his face so noble, so gentle, she couldn't tear her eyes from him, feeling she could gaze at him for eternity. His hair shone the purest of white, and many colours and shapes, in constant motion, surrounded him. But he did not speak.

Alice didn't mind the morning/night routine, but there were no clocks with dials or numbers. It occurred to her she hadn't seen a clock and had never asked about days or hours. Alice measured time in breakfast, morning tea, lunch, afternoon tea and dinner and someone usually came to fetch or send her where she needed to go.

There must be proper time and days, so she went to the library to ask about clocks or what method they used to tell the time. But the library steward brought her a new friend, Educator Sebel, one of Dr Clere's patients and who, like Alice, was returning to Earth. Taller than Alice by a few inches, with brown eyes full of sparkle and mischief, Educator Sebel had the cheekiest smile! Her blonde hair, tied over her right ear, fell in a cascade of messy curls over her shoulder. Educator Sebel's stunning figure was shown off to advantage in the most beautiful maroon and one-piece cream uniform. Alice loved the colour. Grey was the permeating colour on the station, apart from an occasional green tunic and, as Alice learned later, the colour of the uniform signified designation. Maroon signified Educator.

Bubbly, bright and friendly, and despite the usual formality of greeting, Alice quickly found Educator Sebel's warmth and friendliness matched her physical beauty.

"Dr Langley, I couldn't be happier!" Educator Sebel whispered following completion of the usual formalities of introduction. "I know you're classified, but I've been stuck here for weeks and feel like bouncing off the walls! I almost kissed Principal Hardy when he told me about you!"

"That would have surprised him," Alice grinned.

"More likely given him a heart attack!" Educator Sebel laughed back. "Then Dr Clere would have had to have grown a new one for him!"

They giggled, and Alice couldn't stop smiling at her good fortune in meeting this lively, happy girl. Educator Sebel showed Alice to a registry console.

"Did he tell you everything?" Alice wasn't sure how much Educator Sebel knew. "I mean *everything?*"

"Do you mean the part where you got chased up a tree by a bear?"

Stunned, Alice replied, "I've never been chased up a tree by a bear."

"Of course you haven't! I'm teasing. You were suspended in time for four hundred years, and now, you have amnesia. The bear would have been a lot easier to explain." She gave Alice a bright smile before laughing.

"You seem to be taking all of this in your stride, Educator Sebel."

"Dr Langley, you are a part of history, but me? I think I'm hilarious, so I add humour to all situations. These are unusual circumstances, and they could be overwhelming, but I decided I would treat you as a contemporary first and a student second."

Educator Sebel pulled a face and rolled her eyes before whispering, "I will admit I spent a good half hour with my mouth wide open in Principal Hardy's office! He smiled a lot and brought coffee. Imagine, coffee with a Principal! Now, *that* overawed me, I can tell you!" Then she assumed a matter-of-fact expression and shrugged, "But then I thought, meh, it'll be fine, she's four hundred years old, no match for me! They all want you to be as prepared as possible for your return to society. Count on me."

"I will, but would you call me Alice? I'm not comfortable with Dr Langley."

"Sure, and when we're alone, you can call me Amelia. Dr Grossmith told me you used another name. I must address you by your title and surname in company, and you will need to call me 'Educator Sebel'. Social etiquette is important to our society, but I'll teach you all you need to know."

Alice nodded. It was vital for her to learn these things. Although she'd become accustomed to the bowing and formality, she didn't want to let herself down.

"Manners maketh the man Alice. People will judge me by your manners. Mind them!"-Alice's mother.

A silver band around Amelia's arm drew Alice's attention. She had so many questions; this might be a good place to start.

"It denotes rank," Amelia told her, running a practised hand over the registry and bringing up several uniforms and rank insignias. "All professions attract rank. In education, we wear this colour uniform, and we are all titled 'Educator'. The silver band signifies that I'm a three-year graduate. At five years, the band will be blue. After that, I'm eligible to be promoted to Statesman."

"I've only seen people in grey here, like those," Alice pointed to the library staff, "but none of them has bands like this, and apart from Principal Hardy, they're all called 'doctor' or 'Kelly'."

"Isn't Principal Hardy a hoot?!" Amelia exclaimed. "I love him! He looked after me after Dr Clere did his part."

"Me too, for a while," Alice said. "He said there are lots of different kinds of doctors."

"Well, yes, there are. But 'doctor' is the title given to a science graduate. It doesn't matter whether you are a medical doctor, a physicist, a cosmologist, a linguist; all these, and more, come under the umbrella of the sciences. Principal Hardy is a medical doctor. In time, he advanced to statesman and then to principal. Principal outranks statesman and doctor. If he's in uniform, you can see he wears a gold band."

"I've seen it, but isn't being a doctor the most important thing anyone could be?"

"It's important, but being a principal doesn't stop you from doing what you do; it just gives you more responsibility, and it's a command post, even as a civilian."

"Dr Clere is still Dr Clere, and Dr Grossmith is still a doctor. Why aren't they statesmen? Is it because they aren't as young as Principal Hardy?"

"Not everyone wants a promotion." Amelia showed her, on the registry, the level of responsibility given to a principal. "Dr Clere serves the world best in his capacity; his work gives him a special responsibility. Dr Grossmith though, hmm," she thought for a moment. "I'm not sure. I know little about him, apart from what's on the registry. We can look him up if you like?"

Alice stopped her with a shake of her head. She'd looked already, and the text spoke only of his tenure with the Sleeping Beauty Phenomenon. Besides, she wanted to know more about Dr Clere.

"How did you find Dr Clere? I'm a little afraid of him."

"I swear he has never found out how to smile," Amelia declared but then conceded his abilities were truly amazing, pointing a finger at herself and then Alice. "Look at us, testaments to a great man!"

"Oh yes, and I'm grateful—" To acknowledge Dr Clere's skills was only proper, "but is he the only one who can do those things?"

"No," Amelia said brightly, not minding Alice flitting from subject to subject. "There's a whole team, but he pioneered the techniques used today, and while he's here, we use him. When he retires, the torch will pass to someone else. But he is rather a misery guts." She pulled a funny face, making her cheeks sink in, and her lips thrust outwards, setting off Alice in a fit of giggling. It wasn't hard to see that fun was one of Amelia's great motivators.

"Did you have something serious, Amelia, with your health that required you to be here?"

"Pretty serious, but I expect to pick up where I left off!" Amelia replied without hesitation.

Alice didn't doubt it, but with Amelia offering no further information, she didn't press. They'd only just met, after all.

Amelia explained things in such a coherent and light-hearted manner, by the end of the day, Alice suspected she had soaked up a whole year's worth of lessons, and the time had flown. Amelia had such a spark for life, Alice found it amazing that anyone, after major surgery, could be so lively and enthusiastic.

"How can I learn so much in one day?" Alice asked her, feeling admiration for her new teacher and a sense of achievement for herself. "I only did the basics of formal education, and I was hopeless at school, but I can remember almost everything you told me today even though I can't vouch I'll recall any of it tomorrow! But thank you anyway."

"It's your Eduction chip," Amelia grinned. "Not the perfect solution for memory loss, but it helps. And of course, I'm an awesome teacher! The chip will dissolve by the time we get to Earth, but you'll have developed good learning habits by then."

"You people like your chips."

"They're useful tools. Particularly when we need to fast track information."

"Do you know when we're leaving for Earth?"

"Not exactly, Alice. The Significator is due anytime. It's up to Principal Hardy. He may send us on one of the smaller ships, or he may treat us to a ride on the largest ship in the fleet!"

As the lessons for the day ended, Alice remembered her question about clocks. Amelia showed her how to use the chronometer and reminder on the registry and arranged for them to meet the next day before parting ways at the library portal. Amelia stressed to Alice she must take time to absorb the day's lessons and bring any questions to the library in the morning. Alice thanked her again and returned to her quarters wearing a smile so big, her cheeks ached.

Kelly was waiting for Alice as she stepped through the portal. "You've met Amelia Sebel. Isn't she fabulous?"

"Actually…" Alice couldn't argue because educator Sebel *was* fabulous, and her bubbliness and enthusiasm were highly contagious. Alice began to laugh. She clasped her arms around herself, then flung them out wide to embrace her happiness. Kelly laughed with her.

"I haven't felt energy like this since…" Alice said, lifting her hands to her face to touch her smooth, young-again skin. She held her hands out in front, turning them over to look at the slender fingers. She was renewed. How had she never appreciated her youth when she had it? What did they say? Youth is wasted on the young? But now…

"You have a new body Alice," Kelly smiled. "It's yours. Enjoy it."

CHAPTER THIRTEEN _

Alice spent part of the following day with Amelia in the library, flitting from subject to subject, as she had the day before. Her new teacher appreciated her pupil hadn't had the benefit of being born into her society, so considerable catching up was needed. Often, the two strayed from the lesson to chat about other things, which, while fascinating, didn't form part of Alice's education, and Amelia gained a sense Alice might soon be more in need of a friend than a teacher.

Dr Grossmith came to the library to check on her, and Alice practised her newfound knowledge of formal and informal greetings on him, pleased and proud when he complimented her on her progress. Amelia tested her on her knowledge of the principalities, and Alice paid careful attention to Amelia's lesson on the seat of government, the Tabernacle.

Alice couldn't wait to share all she learned with Kelly back at their quarters, but on her return, later that day, she found Kelly laying out unfamiliar clothing on the bed.

"Who's that for, Kelly?"

"You, Alice. You're having dinner with Principal Hardy and the senior statesmen from the Significator."

"The Significator? Isn't that the big spaceship that's due here soon?" Alice looked at the dress and then to Kelly in dismay. This was not good. No-one mentioned meeting important people.

Kelly leaned up from her task to point to the viewport. The Significator took up most of the view, and just a quick peep was enough to panic Alice. She didn't want to have dinner with grand, educated people who worked on enormous starships. She would make a fool of herself like she always did in company, and she felt some of her old insecurities resurrecting themselves.

The day's fun and knowledge vanished as her level of anxiety grew. This was a huge and confronting development for her.

"What is it, Alice?"

"I can't go to dinner with Principal Hardy and people from that ship! I wouldn't know what to say. I don't want to meet senior people!" Alice paced and wrung her hands.

"You go to breakfast with Dr Grossmith." Principal Hardy asked Kelly to soothe Alice if she showed concern, "He's a senior member of staff."

"But Dr Grossmith is my friend," Alice reasoned.

"What about Principal Hardy? He's the most important man on this station, in high standing with the World Principal herself. You aren't afraid of him, are you?"

Alice wasn't afraid of Principal Hardy, she didn't even consider his rank, and she counted him as a friend too.

"And you won't have to say much," Kelly said, making another attempt to soothe Alice's fears. "As you know, Principal Hardy likes to talk. You only have to remember your protocol rules."

Rules? Oh, dear, this wasn't helping Alice's nerves.

Kelly sent Alice into the washer, and while Alice cleaned and moisturised, Kelly tested her on the social protocols she needed to observe when meeting statesmen and principals. In her panic, Alice found she could remember nothing Amelia told her about protocols. She'd get in a muddle and look like an idiot. Alice started to cry, her sobs turning her fair skin red; stepping out of the shower, she grabbed a handful of fibrelettes and wept, her tears soaking through the thin cloth onto her hands.

A few minutes later, after Kelly cooled off the red blotches left on Alice's face from the bout of weeping and her nose no longer a bright red beacon, she sat in front of the image definer. Kelly stood behind her, going through protocols again while tidying her hair. Alice tried to calm herself and remember the rules.

"I say 'Statesman' or 'Principal' and then their name," she said. "I hope I don't get flustered. I've only practised on Dr Grossmith and Principal Hardy. These senior officers, Kelly, are they men or women?"

"Men in this case. You'll be fine, and if you forget what to do, Principal Hardy is there to help."

"Why does he want me to go? Why didn't he ask me if I wanted to first?"

"I don't know, Alice. Maybe because you'll face many new situations when you get back to Earth, situations that might test you, and you can't avoid meeting people. It may be his thinking that at least here, under his supervision, he can ease you into more complex social situations. There's some virtue in that."

"I don't see it."

"If he'd asked you first, would you have said 'yes'?"

"Yes."

"Why, if you hate the idea so much?"

"Because he's done so much for me, and to say no would be ungrateful."

"If he'd told you earlier, you would have had more time to agonise about going, and you do agonise, don't you?"

"Yes, I do. I'm a worrywart. Will they call me 'Alice'?" Alice was watching Kelly's reflection behind her, brushing her hair. It seemed her hair would be loose tonight. Kelly slipped so easily back into the role of carer.

"No, Alice, they'll call you Dr Langley."

"But I'm Alice Watkins."

"Only with your friends, anywhere else—" Kelly waved the hairbrush around, "—you are Dr Langley."

Kelly stopped for a moment, not wanting to add to Alice's misery.

"It won't be so bad, Alice. Principal Hardy is well able for the military types. He won't allow anyone or anything to overwhelm you. You may even enjoy yourself."

"Military? I thought there wasn't any war?" Amelia mentioned military when they talked about rank but didn't elaborate.

"It's only a term, Alice, from way back. Starship personnel are always military."

Alice appreciated Kelly's efforts at soothing her fears, but she was more anxious at the prospect of this dinner party than finding herself on a space station next to Saturn. In fact, Saturn felt quite homely now.

Kelly feared using a term like "military" might have made things worse, so she decided it might be prudent to keep quiet. Alice put the new, straight green dress over her head, and Kelly tied a gold belt around her waist. Alice stepped into matching trousers, and Kelly found earrings that stuck to Alice's ears without clips, laughing when Alice mentioned they stuck like glue, not knowing what glue might be. She placed a delicate chain around her neck but, though Alice thought it too much, didn't like to refuse. Kelly finished the ordinary outfit with a shawl in the same green with a contrasting ribbon at the hem.

"It's got a hood Alice, against the coolness of the station if you're late back," Kelly told her.

Alice didn't like the clothing. With the hood up, she looked like Maid Marion. It was all the same, green dress, green slacks, green cloak. Green, but she supposed it was a change from the colourless grey. But then, she'd been colourless all her life, apart from the blue rinse. She envied the glorious maroon of Amelia's uniform.

"I need the toilet," Alice said suddenly, turning away and overcome by a desperate need to be alone. She handed the shawl to Kelly and headed toward the washer. To Kelly, the rooms where one performed bodily functions were always called washers, but now, accustomed to Alice's verbal mannerisms, understood what she meant by "toilet".

In the washer, Alice stood in horror. There was blood on the inside of her thigh, only a trickle, but blood even so. A period. No wonder she'd been so emotional these past few days. Taking a handful of the soft fibrelettes that served as general wipes, she tucked them between her legs only to find she couldn't walk normally. She needed knickers, and she needed them now.

Wiping herself, she went back to her room. Kelly had nursed her, cared for her and probably had been involved with all sorts of personal things, but this bleeding, Alice didn't know if it happened before, and she couldn't share it, not now. She forced her voice to sound casual,

"Kelly, I really would like some, um, knickers. You know, something to put here…" She outlined the area she wanted covering.

Kelly understood. "I know what they are. Panties. But they're not hygienic Alice; you're far better off without them."

Alice never discussed periods, believing them to be an unmentionable bodily function. She was relieved when, just after she turned fifty-two, they stopped, but even now, although she couldn't have had one for hundreds of years, she couldn't talk about them.

Alice might have to beg. "I've tried to do without, but Kelly, I feel a little…bare without them."

"Give me a moment. I'll be back." Kelly disappeared through the portal, leaving Alice to ponder the foolishness of giving herself dream periods. She always hated them, then again, she hadn't liked ginger hair either, and now, she rather liked her hair, but she would never like periods. Hopefully, Kelly would locate some knickers, particularly when they didn't seem to be a popular item. While she waited, Alice looked at herself in the image definer, twisting a little this way and that.

She looked so much better than she did a few months ago. Since being able to eat, she'd even put on a little weight, no longer looking as gaunt as the first time she saw her reflection. She didn't like wearing grey all the time, at least tonight she'd get to wear green, and it set her to wondering what colours would be available on Earth, red with a bit of luck. Pink hopefully as well. Alice liked pink, but it might clash with red hair.

Kelly came back with brief grey knickers. Tiny and economical with fabric, they would never have fit her mother's standards of decency, but they would serve the purpose. If Kelly felt surprised when Alice disappeared back to the toilet to put them on, she didn't comment. A few of the fibrelettes folded into the crotch of the panties did the trick, and Alice breathed a sigh of relief. Now she just had to get through this evening.

CHAPTER FOURTEEN _

The shuttle from the Principality ship Significator docked at the station just before twenty hundred hours. A hail from Principal Hardy lit up the registry communications visual as the three senior officers readied themselves to disembark. The most senior officer answered.

"Principal Hardy."

"Principal Ryan."

"Problem, Hardy?"

"My apologies, Ryan, I've been detained and won't be joining you this evening."

"That's a pity, Hardy. We'll go back to the ship." Principal Ryan sat down again, prepared to leave.

"I realise that would serve you very well, Ryan—"

Principal Ryan made no secret of his dislike for social events.

"—but this time, I want you to go ahead without me. I'm sending a patient to meet with you, Dr Langley, a young woman who suffered a catastrophic brain injury. She's been on the station for more than ten years."

"Ten years?" Principal Hardy could see second officer Statesman Hennessey's expression of surprise behind Ryan's shoulder.

"Yes, Statesman Hennessey, ten years," Hardy reiterated. "She requires extensive rehabilitation. I planned to escort her this evening myself, an experiment, to ease her back into social situations, if you will. She has almost complete memory impairment and is confused about her identity, but she is pleasant and gracious in company."

"I doubt we're your best choice for such an undertaking, Hardy," Principal Ryan said with ill-concealed irritation; Hardy was crossing a line here. "Can't you 'ease her into social situations,' with your own officers? Surely that would be more appropriate? We've just returned from a year in threshold space and not inclined to entertain."

"Even so, Ryan, you are here now, and I would like you to disembark. Don't ask her about her illness and if she asks questions of you, keep your answers simple and to the point. She doesn't need 'entertaining' but will need an escort, so send one of your officers to collect her from her quarters. Keep the evening short, around one hour, and I must stress, she needs to feel at ease, so Ryan, when I say send one of your officers to collect her, I mean send Patrick. Hardy out."

Principal Ryan looked up from the registry as his second officer shook his head. He was with Principal Ryan on this.

"We walked into a trap," he grumbled.

"It's his call," Ryan made an impatient flick at the

registry to shut it down, resigned to stay. "He's the principal on this station; that's why he delayed contacting us until we docked so that we would be under his command."

They both turned their attention to Statesman Patrick, the Significators First Officer. His superior officer slapped him on the shoulder as they left the shuttle, "Looks like you just volunteered."

The portal buzzer sounded right on time. Alice sat on the bed, dressed up in her shawl, wishing it was big enough to make her disappear. Kelly jumped up to answer, but the man waiting for admission was not Principal Hardy.

Immaculately uniformed in a lighter shade of grey than those on the station, he was possibly in his early thirties, well over six feet, with dark hair that framed a face more handsome than any face Alice could ever have imagined. The cuffs of his jacket, circled with purple braid, showed his seniority, but Alice was so busy holding her breath, she forgot how senior.

With a small bow to Kelly and offering Principal Hardy's apologies, the spectacular-looking young man turned his attention to Alice and his mouth parted into a glorious, lopsided grin. With a quick nod to Kelly, he approached Alice and spoke through his beautiful smile with a voice clear and precise and with an accent Alice couldn't place.

"Dr Langley," the disarming grin did not leave his

lips. "I am Statesman Patrick."

His eyes were the most extraordinary shade of blue, and she studied him for a second before dropping her gaze in embarrassment. A Statesman? Not a King or a Prince? Alice had such an urge to curtsy. He was just so... well, grand!

"My goodness, young man—oh, I mean," Alice heard herself babbling. She struggled to remember the protocols. "Yes, of course, Statesman Patrick." How on earth does one so old and foolish make a good impression in the presence of perfection? But the young man simply waited as she collected her thoughts.

Kelly watched, amused. This wasn't the first time she'd seen Statesman Patrick turn a woman to jelly.

"I didn't realise this was so formal," Alice glanced across at Kelly, feeling inadequate in such company and suspecting her fears about the evening were about to be realised.

"Not formal at all, Dr Langley, I assure you," Statesman Patrick didn't lose his grin nor take his eyes from her face, "but overwrought military protocols dictate an officer's dress code for any social event. Your outfit is most appropriate. A credit to your carer."

He turned to Kelly to acknowledge her efforts. He must be around Steven's age, Alice thought, wishing Steven had taken more care with his speech and manners.

Statesman Patrick tucked Alice's hand through his arm and guided her through the portal. Alice glanced back at Kelly, trying to communicate her terror, but Kelly paid no attention. Statesman Patrick was a perfect choice to set Alice at ease once she got over the initial reaction of meeting him, but Kelly still felt Principal Hardy had thrown Alice to the wolves, and hoped for Alice's sake, he'd made the right decision.

Alice tried to stay calm. She listened to Statesman Patrick's explanation that Principal Hardy was detained and wouldn't be attending, advising a personal apology would be forthcoming at the next opportunity. In his absence, Principal Hardy asked for an officer from the Significator to escort her to dinner. That happy task fell to him, Statesman Patrick added with a smile.

Statesman Patrick walked at the pace Alice set. Her fear slowed her, and she wished she could ask him to take her back to her quarters. But that would be rude. She thought about the fibrelettes stuffed in her panties. What if one fell out? What if they all fell out?

This was such an ordeal; Alice found it hard to concentrate. Statesman Patrick made general comments about Saturn Station, the planet, Principal Hardy, and appeared not to notice her awkwardness. Alice mustered a quiet "yes" or a nod in agreement here and there, but untroubled by her responses and obviously adept at answering his own questions, Statesman Patrick even laughed at his own answers. Alice was sure he would think her stupid, this incredible young man.

Ill-equipped for this, Alice's private response was to

be cross with Principal Hardy for placing her in such a situation. And what was she thinking, noticing that Statesman Patrick was so handsome? Feeling sick with nerves, shyness and bewilderment, she prayed the evening would hurry and be over quickly.

CHAPTER FIFTEEN _

Alice imagined and feared a large dinner table with lots of people standing around and going by Statesman Patrick's appearance, all grander and far more refined than she. Historically, Alice suffered nerves when eating in company and invariably would slop something or make a noise with a drink or choke on food, so a dinner party was the stuff of nightmares. She found social jaunts to cafés with Michelle for cake and coffee and breakfast or tea with Dr Grossmith or Principal Hardy simple and manageable.

Stopping at a portal, Statesman Patrick turned and smiled that smile.

"We're here. Ready?"

She raised her eyes but still felt too shy to look right at him.

"I'm a little nervous, Statesman Patrick."

"Don't be." He dropped his voice to a whisper and leaned towards her ear, "Statesman Hennessey is an old woman and Principal Ryan, well, Principal Ryan is just stuffy." He stressed the 's' of stuffy and wrinkled up his nose. Alice had to smile. Such a nice young man. His mum and dad must be so proud.

But it wasn't a party. The table, quite as large as Alice pictured, was only set for four places, away from the portal entry. It appeared the waiters already knew Principal Hardy wasn't coming. Two men stood at the far end, absorbed in conversation. With their attention on things away from the portal, they didn't appear to notice when their colleague, Alice at his side, stepped through.

As his colleague's attention appeared diverted, Statesman Patrick asked her to wait. Happy to oblige, Alice took a deep breath, shaking her head gently to dispel her anxiety. She watched Patrick as he walked away, making idle note his hair was tied back in a ponytail and how his jacket emphasised his slimness.

One of the men was similar in height to Statesman Patrick, the other, easily half a head taller. Alice thought them pleasant looking, without the spectacular good looks of their counterpart, broader in the shoulders and with heavier physiques but their manner of dress was every bit as immaculate as Statesman Patrick. The shorter man, with hair a similar colour to Alice, had the same purple braid on his cuffs. The taller man's jacket was edged with gold braid. His hair was fair, past his collar, with a hint of grey. Everything about him was large, and his presence so commanding, Alice decided this must be Principal Ryan. She swallowed hard because, really, he just looked big and scary.

The man with the red hair also had a ponytail like

Statesman Patrick. Alice had always thought only yobbos and bikies wore their hair in that manner, but these men couldn't be yobbos or hooligans, they drove a starship, but they all needed a good haircut.

The two men looked up as Statesman Patrick approached and gave him their full attention before looking over at Alice. Neither man smiled, giving Alice the distinct impression that her presence here was little more than a chore. They waited until Statesman Patrick drew her into their midst before acknowledging her with a slight movement forward of the head and shoulders. Statesman Patrick introduced her as Dr Langley.

Alice had not met military people before, either in real life or in this one. She had been correct in her assumption the big-faced man was Principal Ryan. Along with Statesman Patrick's description of stuffy, Alice added a sour and bored expression. Still, she would be polite, and in response to his bow, smiled a nervous acknowledgement, reminded of how she felt when she first met Principal Hardy.

The red-haired man, Statesman Hennessy, held a chair and invited her to be seated. She sat opposite Statesman Patrick, next to Statesman Hennessy, with Principal Ryan at the head of the table. These titles were tedious. She would much rather say "Patrick", or "Ryan" or "Hennessey", but it occurred to her they probably weren't their first names. She wasn't likely to say anything, anyway.

Briefly, the men spoke amongst themselves. Amelia

had mentioned the Principality ship Significator was returning from a year in deep space, "threshold space" to give it its proper name, so Alice wondered if they were tired and just wanted to go home. But Alice didn't mind silences. She wasn't awkward with them because it meant no-one was listening to her or asking her questions.

The steward poured water into glasses and served something Alice had never seen on the station; a small brown roll, in the shape of a little sausage, with a tiny dish of clear fluid. Alice loved sausages and hoped, despite the odd appearance, it would be like the sausages she got from the butcher's shop. Patrick commented to Statesman Hennessey, dipped the roll in the liquid and put the whole thing in his mouth, winking at Alice and pointing his fork in her direction.

It would be safe to follow his lead; he knew the technique. Alice inspected the roll, dipped it into the liquid and put the whole thing in her mouth. It tasted fine for a second, sweet and fishy, but then the burning started, her eyes watered, and her throat turned to fire. Her nose and eyes streamed, and she couldn't see for tears. Gasping, she reached for what she desperately hoped was the glass of water but not quick enough, she coughed and spluttered most of the roll into her hands. She regained control in time to see Statesman Patrick laughing. Principal Ryan shushed him and got up to help her with fibrelettes to wipe her hands and give her the water while Statesman Hennessey patted her on the back.

Is there a stronger word than mortification? Alice

doubted it. Right now, she might have to invent one. She closed her eyes and willed herself not to run from the room.

"I'm afraid Statesman Patrick is not a good example of table manners, Dr Langley." Alice opened her eyes in time to see Principal Ryan send a stern and withering look towards Statesman Patrick.

"What?" Patrick pulled an innocent face, "it's the only way to eat them. They're disgusting without the firewater. I'm sorry, Dr Langley, I had no idea you hadn't had them. They're standard fare on Saturn Station—possibly not for patients."

"Why do you have them then?" Hennessey cut in, "I swear you'd eat anything put in front of you."

Patrick gave a playful smile in response, and Principal Ryan returned to his seat, waving away Alice's mumbled thanks. The steward brought her a scented fibrelette to clean up her hands, after which she found a neutral spot on the wall opposite to gaze at, hoping her lack of refinement had had enough of an airing for one night.

"So, Dr Langley. Saturn Station!" Patrick never stopped smiling that dazzling smile. "Have you had a trip through the rings yet? It's spectacular. Research within them has brought to light remarkable data, even discoveries, many of them since you became a patient here."

He had lovely teeth, not like Ted's, dirty brown from smoking. Alice had hated them.

She had to answer, so far, she'd stayed out of the conversation, and already her nightmare had come true with the roll. There must be something sensible to say, an answer that might suit. They were watching her, and she wished she was invisible.

Putting on a brave face, she tried to smile. It's not easy, trying to hide the fact you're an idiot—no point in pretending. Eduction chips did a lot of things, but they wouldn't turn you into the life of the party. She opened her mouth to speak, hoping, by some miracle, something intelligible might tumble out. If not, she hoped they would be as accepting of her as they were the roll incident.

To her amazement, the miracle did tumble out.

"I haven't been through the rings, Statesman Patrick," she said, "but I would be fascinated. In my time, space travel was in its infancy. The space program, restarted in the mid-twenty-first- century with much fanfare, was abandoned almost as quickly in the wake of the plague. Not enough that our planet was infected; better not contaminate the entire universe! We didn't know how the virus might behave in space."

The men agreed.

Alice had heard herself. *What?* What on earth was she talking about? She wasn't even there in the mid-twenty-first century, and her only knowledge of a plague was what Kelly and Amelia told her. But the confusion didn't end there. She spoke with confidence, looking across at Statesman Patrick, and this time, he saw something else in her eyes. Something that hadn't been there earlier.

"Statesman Patrick, what is your role on the Significator?"

"Just 'Statesman', Dr Langley, now we are introduced, it's only when you speak of me to someone else, would you say, 'Statesman Patrick'."

"There are many protocols I haven't yet mastered."

"I'm sure society hasn't changed too much, Dr Langley," Principal Ryan said. "Social mores and protocols have, I'm pleased to report, remained constant over the years. You might draw comfort from that."

She fancied he would be a stickler for mores and protocols. She inclined her head a little, deferring to him. Alice still didn't know where she was in all this. Somewhere in the topmost corner of the room, it seemed, watching her body make sense of the conversation.

"Dr Langley asked you a question about your role here, Patrick." Hennessey looked at Alice and then back to Patrick.

"Of course, I apologise. I'm an engineer, Dr Langley."

"I was told by—" Alice's voice continued, "—please excuse me, I'm not sure who, that a scientific background was a prerequisite for working aboard the starships. Isn't engineering a separate discipline from science? Or has that changed?"

"Yes, my branch of engineering and metallurgy concerns space venturing vehicles only. It's still considered a science."

"So, you make the engines go, Statesman?" It

sounded like a phrase Alice might use, understanding and interpreting things in the simplest of terms.

"I suppose I do, Dr Langley," he waggled his eyebrows. Principal Ryan leaned back and passed his hand over his mouth. From her hiding place, Alice swore she saw him sigh.

"And you, Statesman Hennessey?" she said, turning her attention to the man on her right.

"I'm an anthropologist and phonetician, Dr Langley. I also specialise in ancient dialects."

"Is there a need for linguistics experts in the military?"

"I'm a civilian, but yes, linguistics play an important role in contacting other species."

Whatever was driving Alice then directed its attention to Principal Ryan, but his expression made it plain he would answer no questions about himself or his role, and he glanced away. Well, Alice supposed from her corner, he's the one in charge.

"And you travel to other planets?" Alice's intelligent other self, noted Principal Ryan's silence, so she took care to include the other two men in the question. "I understand there's a race of beings now settled on Earth. Have you encountered many other species?" As these were general comments, Principal Ryan felt more inclined to respond; he didn't like personal enquiries. His role on the ship should be evident.

"As I am sure you're aware, we've just returned from a mission," he said. "The A'khet gave us co-ordinates of two inhabited planets, both these planets are in close proximity, and both are civilisations the A'khet visited before they arrived on Earth. The system is relatively near to ours, so it was expected the mission would take only a year." He was matter-of-fact about meeting beings from other worlds, as if it happened every day. If it didn't excite him, it excited Alice's other self.

"My goodness, how thrilling! Were you welcomed?" Alice felt a surge in her chest. She had no control over it. She listened, riveted. Her fascination must have reached as far as her face because Patrick laughed when he saw her expression.

"Not the last ones!!"

Principal Ryan held up his hand.

"Patrick, Dr Langley won't be interested…"

"Come on, Ryan," Patrick turned his eager face to Alice. "It's a great story."

Before Principal Ryan could say another word, Patrick launched into the tale about how, upon reaching the coordinates given by the A'khet, a landing party was dispatched. Patrick wasn't part of the landing party, but he would have loved to have seen it, he declared, laughing as he went along, caught up in his own amusement.

It was impossible not to smile, even when Patrick ignored Principal Ryan's unspoken order to silence.

"The inhabitants chased them with sticks and whips!" Patrick stopped just short of acting it out with his cutlery. "We all blamed Hennessey because he couldn't speak the language or decipher any dialect. It was a miracle they made it out at all!"

Principal Ryan listened, his expression unreadable. He clearly knew Patrick well, but Hennessey's face was like thunder. Principal Ryan didn't let Patrick continue. He held up his hand again and this time, silenced him.

"Patrick has somewhat condensed the story for dramatic effect, Dr Langley." Principal Ryan turned his unsmiling face towards Patrick, who allowed him to take over the story with a more reasonable and measured but somewhat less humorous recounting.

"The A'khet, as you know, are a telepathic race, an obvious advantage, as they prepared the inhabitants of the planet..." He looked over at Patrick, who was going too long without speaking, and without invitation, chimed in, "...that they were arriving and were friendly," he added, helping the story move along.

Statesman Hennessey nodded, agreeing. "They're a tribal society with little technology and no space travel, although they did have a rudimentary grasp of engineering and industry, in short, an evolving and developing civilisation."

But Patrick couldn't help himself. The story wasn't heading quickly enough to the punch line.

"They landed a tube in the bushes, Dr Langley, made their way to one of the groups and announced their arrival."

"It wasn't like that, Patrick," Hennessey turned to Alice.

"We landed the tube where they wouldn't find it, in

THE AFTERLIFE OF ALICE WATKINS: BOOK ONE

the belief that seeing such advanced technology might cause fear or panic." Even Alice, in her limited understanding, saw how that might happen.

Then Principal Ryan took back the story.

"We did approach the tribe, Dr Langley. We tried to dress like the A'khet, to be more recognisable. Statesman Hennessy has extraordinary linguistic skills—" From the corner of her eye, Alice saw Patrick bite his lip against a retort, Principal Ryan saw it too and ignored it.

"—except he isn't telepathic. The key to A'khet's success with these people is their ability to reassure, to mollify. Humans don't have that ability..."

"So, they chased them with those sticks and whips, and they had to run!" Patrick interrupted again, "sticks that burned like hell if they touched you!"

Principal Ryan glanced at Patrick, then turned back to Alice with a look that showed a certain amount of long-suffering.

"Statesman Patrick believes a diplomatic solution would have taken the form of landing the tube and charming them into accepting our overtures of friendship," Principal Ryan concluded with a trace of sarcasm.

"Or talked so much they begged for mercy," Hennessey murmured, his sarcasm a little less restrained.

Patrick looked over and beamed at her; this time, she met his eyes. Yes, charm. A skill he had in abundance.

"Well, Principal Ryan," she said, bringing the conversation back on track. "Thank you for that amazing account. I can't speak for the people you visited, but I

171

understand a little about strangeness. I remember none of this technology," Alice-not being-Alice gestured to the registry, "and I know of no-one able to relate a story such as the one you have. Every day, I'm presented with new and unfamiliar concepts which baffle and bewilder me. Even though I'm human, your manners, your dress, your society, they're all strange to me. I can imagine how those people felt; hiding the tube, and I don't even know what that is, might have been the least frightening part of your arrival there. Perhaps a member of the A'khet should go with you, or you should present yourselves as you are, with less elaborate planning or trickery."

Principal Ryan disagreed with this young woman with amnesia. She remembered nothing of space travel, meeting or intermingling with people from other worlds, and she'd been ill for a decade. He wondered what branch of science gave her the title of doctor and had to remind himself he was only doing this for Hardy's sake.

"I agree we got it wrong, Dr Langley. We're not so experienced. The two societies, the A'khet called them 'Baru', meaning 'double' in their language, appear to have a common ancestry. Of course, we don't know how they came to be related, as neither race possesses the ability to travel in space. We have restricted travel to their system. Their origins will remain a mystery, I believe, as both civilisations rejected any form of contact with humans."

"The A'khet won't travel in space again, Dr Langley," Hennessey told her, "they refuse to join missions or be separated from one another. We can't insist they join us. We respect their privacy."

"So, why do you want to meet these other species? Travel to distant planets? Isn't there enough on Earth that warrants your attention?"

"It's called exploration, Dr Langley," Principal Ryan's voice took on a tone that Alice recognised in Amelia when she was firmly in the role of educator. "And exploration can mean a simple study of the composition of a mineral or examining the complexity of a microcosm. In a larger sense, the universe is purely that, something we need to understand, to explore. It's far too large for us to place under a microscope in a laboratory. So, we go out there, travel amongst it, endeavour to unravel its mysteries."

Alice fell to silence. Inexplicably, and with no knowledge as to why such a thought might come to her, she considered that, when exploring a bacterium, she would essentially view it from the outside. Microscopes and Petri dishes and chemicals might aid further exploration, but how much more satisfying to unravel its marvels by *being part of it?* And at that moment, she came down from the corner of the room.

What was that conversation about? There was a vague, rattling sensation inside her head. She looked at the safe spot on the wall and realised that all three men were still watching her. Was there a question? Who asked it?

"You want to meet our neighbours," she said. It sounded good.

Hennessey gave a small laugh. "That's a good way of

putting it, Dr Langley. Yes, we want to meet our neighbours."

Bake them a cake, thought Alice.

Alice didn't choke, cough, splutter or do any other things to embarrass herself for the rest of the meal, and afterwards, the steward brought them Alice's favourite coffee.

The men were talking, their voices in the background as she sipped. She'd asked sensible questions, hadn't she? If only she could remember. What did they discuss? Other worlds? That rang a bell, but the more she tried, the more the memory faded. She looked across at Patrick, and seeing her, he smiled. It would be nice to have him as a friend, along with Kelly and Amelia.

"Dr Langley," Statesman Hennessey addressed her. "We've been advised not to tire you with questions, but to be away from Earth for so long a period, you must be glad to be returning."

"I don't remember Earth at all. None of it," she said, not wanting to get into a discussion about time periods.

"Once you're home, you'll remember. It's a beautiful place," Patrick said. "The most beautiful in the galaxy."

"You've only seen four others, Patrick," Hennessey pointed out.

"Yes, but of those four, Earth is the most diverse."

The two Statesman started a good-natured argument on the virtues of Earth, and Alice found herself intrigued by the camaraderie existing between the three men, even with poker-faced Principal Ryan acting as a quiet referee.

She was on the periphery of their conversation now, they sometimes acknowledged her, but mainly they were happy just for her to listen in. She made a mental note to ask Amelia about the military's protocols because the rules seemed pretty relaxed tonight.

But protocols were again sharply observed when Principal Ryan rose to his feet at a lull in the conversation between Patrick and Hennessey. The other two men also stood and Alice, not knowing what to do, stood as well.

Principal Ryan bowed to Alice.

"It's been a pleasure to meet you, Dr Langley. Please forgive our lapse of professionalism this evening. We've been away for a long time, and my colleagues have gained a habit of arguing. A habit, it would seem, they brought with them to this table. Patrick, please escort Dr Langley to her quarters. We'll wait for you on the shuttle."

Hennessey also made his customary bow, and Alice supposed Principal Ryan dismissed her as Patrick steered her towards the portal.

"That was a sudden ending, Statesman," she said as they entered the walkway. He placed the shawl around her shoulders.

"Always is with Principal Ryan," he chuckled. "Ryan doesn't allow himself much leisure time. Most passing ships get dinner with Principal Hardy. Refusal isn't an option, and Ryan is the only one who'll wheedle out of it if he can. He never stays for long."

"Oh, I thought he'd just stopped enjoying himself."

Patrick stopped to laugh, and then placing his hands

on her shoulders, turned her towards him. Was this protocol? He was dazzling. Stop it, she told herself. But she still looked up at him.

"Principal Ryan does not *enjoy* himself," he told her, looking serious and grinning at the same time. "He never removes himself from his role. If you encounter him again, expect courtesy but not friendship. As for me…" he raised an eyebrow at her, making her smile.

On the short walk back, Patrick regaled her with non-stop chatter about space stations, space travel and Earth. Alice hoped this wouldn't be the last time she would see him because, like Amelia, he was warm and friendly, but it wasn't likely they would meet again. He works in space, she thought, more than a little disappointed, and space is a big place.

When they arrived at her quarters, Alice thanked him for his kindness. His easygoing attitude to the proceedings made all the difference, even if he laughed at the roll incident.

"Statesman Patrick…?"

"Dr Langley?" He smiled and inclined his head.

"Thank you for your kindness this evening. I'm sure it's obvious I'm not comfortable in company."

"You are most welcome. I hope we meet again." This time, instead of bowing, Patrick gave a little salute and walked away, throwing an easy-going and non-protocol smile over his shoulder as he left.

CHAPTER SIXTEEN _

Alice waited until Patrick was out of sight before activating the portal. Kelly looked up from the registry as Alice entered.

"Well?" she said, giving Alice her full attention. Alice sat on the bed. Somewhere, during dinner, her terror subsided, leaving, in its place, only a tiny smidgeon of social anxiety. It felt good; like progress, not a perfect performance, she decided, but getting there, and maybe not the time to tell Kelly about the roll incident.

"Statesman Patrick is very nice. Principal Ryan, civil, doesn't smile much, and I don't think overly pleased with me being there because, after coffee, he got to his feet and announced it was time to leave! Statesman Hennessey, well, he got friendlier as the evening went on."

Kelly nodded. "Statesmen Hennessey married a girl from my principality. I was at school with her. He acts a little superior for me, but his wife's a delight. He's recalled to Earth because she had a baby while he was away on this assignment."

"Oh? Statesman Hennessey's married? Is Patrick married?"

Kelly grinned; Patrick always made an impression. "No, but isn't he amazing? He served on the Inquisitor when I did my space year. The girls all swooned for him."

A sudden faraway expression passed over Kelly's face, and she sighed.

"And?" Alice prompted, wondering if something had transpired between the two.

"And nothing." Kelly shrugged. "The sigh was for my husband. It's been ages since I saw him last."

Alice hugged her. For the first time, it was Alice doing the comforting. Kelly had become a good friend, and Alice didn't know what she would do without her.

Later, Alice stood in the washer and inspected the panties for blood. There didn't seem to be much more, and the fibrelettes had contained it well. The panties were unstained, so she disposed of the used fibrelettes, realising she would have to use the panties again and ask Kelly for more in the morning. If this happened again next month, there might be no one to ask. The possibility bothered her. Where on Earth would she get sanitary towels? Did they have supermarkets?

After showering and tucking more fibrelettes into the panties, she returned to her room.

"Would you like a store of panties?" Kelly asked, not realising the immeasurable relief her question provided.

"Yes, please, Kelly. I would."

"Good, I got more while you were out."

"Thank you, Kelly."

Panties concerns relieved for now, Alice turned her attention to the viewport and the Significator.

"Kelly, will I be returning to Earth on that ship?"

"I'm not sure, Alice. I expect you'll find out tomorrow when you have lunch with Dr Grossmith and Principal Hardy."

"What if I don't want to go to Earth and I want to stay here with you?"

Kelly shook her head. "Alice, let's be honest, you no longer need me, and though it doesn't feel like it yet, you're going home. There's peace on Earth, and everyone is happy and content."

"You sound like a Christmas Carol."

Kelly looked puzzled. "A Christmas Carol?" she laughed. "What's that?"

"Nothing," Alice said. "A memory."

"Alice, you won't be able to go back to those people you believe you remember. Never. That place, that time, doesn't exist."

Alice pointed to her chest. "They exist here, Kelly. Michelle, Steven, my grandchildren. Sometimes…" she knew Kelly didn't understand.

"…it's just sometimes," she repeated, "I hear myself speaking strangely; it happened again tonight. I say words I don't understand, talk of things I don't even know exist, and I have no control over what I'm saying. Then, in an instant, I'm myself again, and everything becomes vague. By tomorrow morning, I won't remember any of it."

She took Kelly's hands and held them tight. Kelly looked down, surprised at Alice's strength and the firmness of her grasp. Alice's lovely green eyes were wide and serious.

"I am, or I used to be Alice Watkins," she said. "That's who I remember. When I talk sense, is it Alexis Langley? Is she in here?" Alice let go of Kelly's hands to tap her fingers hard against her temple. Kelly was reminded of the moment of lucidity she witnessed in the mess months ago. She didn't have answers, only the truth as she understood it.

"You are Alexis Langley," Kelly responded. "What we don't know is how, or when, accurate memories will emerge. Many of them might be frightening and strange, while others may be comforting and reassuring, or you might experience a sudden clarity where it all makes perfect sense. As to why you adopted the identity of Alice Watkins, I'm at a loss; there could be a million explanations."

Alice had to accept it because she had no answers either, and once Kelly had gone to bed, she stayed awake, staring into the darkness. After a while, her thoughts strayed to the delightful young man she'd met earlier. Then she dismissed them and turned over. She was old enough to be his mother.

During the night, Alice dreamed again of the youth with the snow-white hair. He stood a little distance from the bed, and again, she couldn't stop looking at him, he burned so brightly, and she propped herself up on her elbow to get a better look at his face, a face glowing with gentleness. As her dream vision faded, he bent towards her with a smile. When she woke, despite the memory of him remaining vivid, Alice dismissed it as part of a dream. Another dream. A different dream.

Statesman Patrick arrived back at the shuttle a few minutes after leaving Alice.

"I wonder what Hardy thought he was going to achieve by that?" Hennessey unwittingly expressed Principal Ryan's private thoughts, "And how can someone not know about A'khet?"

Patrick got into his seat, weighing up the somewhat fragile but lovely redhead he'd met that evening. "Don't be too harsh; she was pleasant enough, and it wasn't so bad. I wonder how old she is? She must be a lot older than she looks."

"I wondered about that," Hennessey took his seat beside his colleague. "To be titled 'doctor', she has to be a science graduate."

"Well, no-one gets that title until at least twenty-five, then taking into consideration her internship and her time here. She'd be at least thirty-six."

"She doesn't look it," Hennessey said. "We should have asked her."

Principal Ryan glared at them, impatient to leave. "I don't care if she's ninety. I don't know what Hardy's playing at, but I'm far more interested in releasing these docking clamps and getting out of here before he finds us another babysitting job."

CHAPTER SEVENTEEN _

"You did *what!!* Are you out of your mind, Hardy? Sending her to dinner alone—with—*those* three!" Dr Grossmith was not a happy man. He crossed and uncrossed his legs before getting out of his chair to stalk around the room, only stopping to glare at the Significator through the viewport.

"Calm yourself, Jim," Principal Hardy soothed. He'd expected his little enterprise to ruffle Grossmith's feathers, but he didn't anticipate an explosion. "I planned to go, but instead, I conducted a little experiment—to see how she handled it. We can't mollycoddle her forever."

"But it was too elaborate, and without consulting me? I could have predicted the outcome!"

"I knew you would have argued against it. Come and sit down."

Dr Grossmith, glowering, retook his seat.

"She's fine," Hardy said. "I talked with her this morning."

"Fine? Truthfully? Huh! I doubt it."

"I told them nothing of her history, Jim, only that she has been here for ten years following a catastrophic brain injury. Ryan and Hennessey engage little in idle conversation, but Patrick is outgoing and friendly, a perfect foil for the other two. I don't believe she found it too demanding."

"I met Ryan once or twice, Hennessey, never," Jim Grossmith complained, "but Abel, Patrick is a playboy, the female crew transferring across to the Significator are all hoping he'll notice them."

Principal Hardy might have laughed if his friend wasn't so stirred up.

"I don't think Patrick had that effect on Alice. She told me he was a polite and pleasant young man, very well brought up and even remarked on how proud his parents must be. Jim, Alice sees herself as a woman in her sixties. I doubt he or anyone is capable of charming her."

"She *isn't* a woman in her sixties, Abel, and don't tell me Patrick wouldn't have noticed how attractive she is. *And* he has been away a year!"

"I'm just saying, don't be too concerned," Abel Hardy kept his voice level and calm. He understood Grossmith's feelings of protectiveness. He had those feelings himself towards Alice, but she was leaving the nest, and of the two, he was the more willing to let her try her wings. There would be other tests, and many of those in conditions where they would have no control. Alice must determine her path. He just gave her a little practise and encouragement.

"The trip to Earth will only take a few days, Jim. I will advise Principal Ryan about his new passenger and release the last ten years reports to him. He can tell his officers as much or as little as he thinks fit. When they get to Earth, she will go to the Tabernacle. She might then choose to tell people about her history. If she does, she must deal with the fallout, good or bad. Principal Katya will guide her."

Dr Grossmith tapped the palms of his hand on his knees and took a deep breath as if these actions might make this easier. He'd watched over her for so long, and now, taking her first steps into a new world, it would be unreasonable for him to put up barriers. If he did, he'd be no better than Larry Clere.

"Did the Tabernacle respond to your request to find Alice's relatives?"

"Yes, but Principal Katya has reserved the right to speak of this to Alice herself. When we see Alice for lunch today, we'll inform her she and Educator Sebel are to leave on the Significator on its return to Earth."

"Yes, of course. I assume you sent Principal Katya the supplementary reports documenting Alice's belief she isn't Alexis Langley?"

"I did, but I won't send those to the Significator. It won't interest Principal Ryan. I'll give him some background on the subject, just enough to inform. Besides, she'll be spending most of her time with Educator Sebel. If she meets up with Statesman Patrick, the worst that can happen is that she asks him to call her Alice. He knows she has amnesia. I think he'll be professional, and it's a short trip home."

Dr Grossmith stood to leave, and Principal Hardy placed a friendly hand on his shoulder.

"Don't worry, Jim," he said. "This is the beginning for Alice, not the end, and Principal Katya will look out for her."

"I wish it weren't so soon," Grossmith said, not attempting to keep the sadness from his voice, "or that I could ask for more time."

"More time for Alice, or more time for you?"

He didn't answer. Hardy was right; the time had come for her to leave.

"But what will you do, Jim? Now Alice is on her way?" Principal Hardy walked to the portal with him.

"There are more reports to complete and the transfer of the Sleeping Beauty project to document," Dr Grossmith said without enthusiasm, "then I'll retire and go to live with my brother. I've taken two extensions to retirement and had no plans beyond seeing her revived. Maybe, I didn't believe it would ever happen."

"And now it has; it's harder than you imagined?"

"She's like my daughter, Hardy." Then, bowing, he offered a polite and formal, "Principal Hardy," before stepping through the portal.

"*Daughter?*" He had no idea Grossmith felt that way. If so, this would be harder on his old friend than he imagined. He returned to his desk and flicked on the registry to send a link to the Significator. Now he had to spill the beans to Principal Ryan.

Ryan's response was immediate.

"Principal Hardy."

"Principal Ryan."

"Problem, Hardy? You're showing a personal channel."

"No, Ryan, no problem. I wondered how last night went, you know, the dinner?"

"Fine."

"How did you find your guest?"

"Fine." Principal Ryan was a master at impassive expression, and Hardy well aware of his extraordinary endurance for conversations where he offered only monosyllabic replies.

" 'Fine' is all you have to say?"

Ryan opened his hands to express both his bewilderment and disinterest at the line of questioning.

"A secure channel to ask me about a trivial event which I had consigned to history, Hardy? Why?"

"Were you not even a little intrigued why I set you, of all people, such a task?"

"Not in the least. Perhaps you simply don't like me."

"I need to tell you who you entertained last night."

"I know—you told me. Dr Langley. Though none of us knows why you chose us to entertain her."

"Then I'll clear that up for you—she is Dr Alexis Langley."

Principal Ryan leaned back, elbows resting on the arms of the chair, his hands clasped over his chest as if settling in for a discussion.

"Are you going to give me a clue, Hardy?"

"You don't need a clue, Ryan; you just need to access your memory banks. How many Dr Alexis Langley's have you heard of?"

"Only one."

"That one."

Principal Hardy didn't expect this revelation to move Ryan but, he hoped, maybe, just maybe, this time, there would be a response. He respected Principal Ryan. He was a big man, with a big view of the universe but also taciturn and aloof, with a reputation of being punctilious and conservative as a commander. Principal Hardy once met Ryan's happy-go-lucky family and had been left to wonder how they could have ever begotten such a solitary son.

He still waited, though, to see if this momentous disclosure would finally break the drought. It didn't, and for a moment, in the ensuing silence, he wondered if Ryan had heard him because he saw not a flicker, not a hint, to suggest Ryan found the information astounding or astonishing.

"I suggest you read these files," Hardy stated, yielding to the fact that trying to engage Ryan in further discussion was a pointless exercise, and he might as well say what he had to say and leave it at that. "I'm also transmitting orders for Dr Langley's transfer to your care aboard the Significator. I arranged dinner for her to meet you and your senior officers. She is to travel to Earth with you."

"Since when do you issue orders on my ship, Hardy?"

"Since today, when the Tabernacle transferred temporary control of the Sleeping Beauty Phenomenon from me to you for the duration of the voyage."

"I hope you don't expect me to entertain her again?"

"I wouldn't ask such a thing of you personally, Ryan, she might throw herself out the nearest airlock. Give her reasonable access on the ship, the same as any guest, but she shouldn't wander alone. Educator Sebel, a former patient here will accompany her as teacher and companion. If you have any of your sleep-inducing concerts on the officers' decks, perhaps you or Patrick might accompany her?"

"Guests are Patrick's territory, not mine."

"It's a comfort to hear you say that, Ryan."

"The files and orders are through," Ryan looked down and away from the registry. "We are to deliver your patient to Principal Katya."

"Correct. Please remember, Dr Langley has suffered substantial memory loss, to the extent she denies the truth of who she is. Except for occasional moments of clarity, she mostly thinks of herself as an elderly woman from the twenty-first century."

"Fortunately, that isn't my problem."

"You're a hard man, Ryan. I'll keep in touch. Hardy

out."

The screen darkened, and as Ryan leaned over to flick off the registry, his face broke into a huge grin.

"Holy *shit*!" he exclaimed, his deep blue eyes widening with admiration. "Grossmith did it!"

"*Alexis* Langley? I don't believe it." Patrick's handsome face was incredulous in the light of these revelations. Principal Ryan had summoned his first and second officers to apprise them of their prospective cargo.

The records took Ryan many hours to read, a few references he remembered from school, but he'd found the more recent information fascinating. It was easy to predict how his two most senior officers would respond.

"The records are available to read on your personal files," he informed them. "It seems Grossmith's theory she would wake spontaneously proved sound."

Hennessey was in disbelief. "I remember Grossmith's paper on her from university. His dedication and certainty she would wake on her own, without help, was impressive."

"I remember reading it," Patrick added, trying to get his head around the fact that the evening before, he had escorted a four-hundred-year-old woman to dinner. "Ryan, that paper could only have been written a few years before all this happened. Why did they keep the details of her relocation to Saturn station so quiet?"

"Read the file for details, Patrick," Ryan said, "but

to summarise, the body showed signs of change. Where there had been only unusual but consistent brain activity, there was also hair and nail growth. Grossmith was sure the sarcophagus acted like a shell, a chicken's egg, if you recall his analogy, and in time, would open, leaving the body susceptible to pathogens that hadn't existed in her time. In the belief her awakening was imminent, he wanted to ensure a sterile environment. They have that on the station."

"I bet Principal Katya had a hand in agreeing to that move," Patrick said.

Hennessey nodded, "I bet she did, but what if Dr Langley *had* been subjected to the Moses Pathogens? Her internal organs would never have regrown, and those four hundred years would have been for nothing. That would have been such a loss. What was it that deteriorated? Heart? I can't remember."

"It's on file, Hennessey," Principal Ryan told him. "You can learn all you need about the ten years since she woke."

"I feel as if I'm prying, Ryan. She's walking and talking and breathing, and we're all delving into her private business. It doesn't seem right."

"I can't believe we were working out how old she was and came up with thirty-seven," Patrick laughed at the irony. "We were out by about four hundred years. I thought she looked good even for thirty-seven."

But Principal Ryan wasn't in the mood for speculation. If they wanted answers, they would have to read up on her themselves.

"Dr Langley is transferring to the Significator. She'll have clearance for guest deck and amenities, but she is not to be left alone. A third-year Educator has been assigned as her companion, but Hardy suggested I give Dr Langley access to the officers' entertainment decks. I'm amenable to that, provided Patrick is with her at all times."

Lost in thought, Patrick gave Ryan a blank look.

"Is that a problem, Patrick?"

"No, Ryan, it's fine. I'm sorry, but it's an unusual situation. I assume I can't ask questions of her?"

"She has amnesia, and she gets confused, so none of us can ask questions. You need only keep her amused and away from the general crew. She ceases to be our problem once we get to space dock. I'll inform this Educator of the plan. For now, Dr Langley's circumstances are classified."

Once outside the briefing room, the two men looked at each other, still in wonder at what they had just heard. Hennessey spoke first.

"Hardy said 'Dr Langley' before the dinner, not for one second did I put two and two together."

"Why would you?" Patrick was also trying to make sense of it. "I'd only ever heard her referred to as the Sleeping Beauty Phenomenon, I must have been at university before I even knew she had a name, and I didn't give it much thought."

"How come Ryan's so blasé about her? She is science at its most impressive, and in many ways, as remarkable as the Knowledge given to us by the A'khet."

Patrick had known Ryan since childhood and felt he had some authority to speak on the man. "He plays his cards close to his chest, Hennessey, and he is a scientist. I bet he stayed up all night reading about her. He's had that same attitude since we were kids!"

"If you say so, but this isn't an elaborate hoax, is it, Patrick?" a tiny note of suspicion creeping into Hennessey's voice.

Patrick had to grin at that. "With Ryan involved? Not likely. He's incapable of deception."

Principal Ryan's link through to Saturn Station was redirected to the gymnasium. The steward stressed to Educator Sebel it would be inadvisable to suggest to Principal Ryan she would call him back after she had finished and urged her to take the call in all haste. She arrived at the registry red-faced and sweating with a towel over her shoulders.

After the usual greeting protocols, he came to the point, offering no apology for disturbing her workout or her leisure.

"You are due on the Principality ship Significator the day after tomorrow. I presume you are aware?"

Amelia nodded. "Yes, Principal Ryan."

"You are cleared for blue and yellow zones only, Educator Sebel, but you also have restricted access to the guest deck, namely Dr Langley's stateroom, the observation deck and the dining facilities. Dr Langley is not permitted outside the guest deck except in the company of a senior officer. If you have concerns or queries, address them to Statesman Patrick."

"Yes, Principal Ryan, I will."

"Good day, Educator Sebel. Ryan out."

Amelia pulled a face at the console as his image faded.

"Arrogant bastard," she said out loud, and with the image of Principal Ryan still in her head, she returned to her punchbag and bashed the hell out of it.

During lunch, Dr Grossmith and Principal Hardy undertook the painful task of informing Alice that she was leaving for Earth on the Significator. She tried to stay calm, but the emotion of finally knowing got the better of her, and she broke down, right there in the mess hall, with both men trying to comfort her and drawing attention from a steward who brought fibrelettes to mop up her tears.

"I'll have no-one," she wailed.

Principal Hardy tried to soothe her. "You'll have Educator Sebel. And you met Statesman Patrick; you said he was nice."

"And Statesman Hennessey and Principal Ryan," Dr Grossmith added, even though he realised, as soon as the words left his lips, that probably wasn't terribly reassuring. Hardy's sudden glance suggested he didn't think so either.

"You'll stay with Principal Katya at the Tabernacle," Principal Hardy allowed her to cry into his shirt. "She's kept a close eye on the events of the last forty years. She's a lovely person, Alice, and so excited to meet you at last."

Dr Grossmith agreed. "Principal Katya and I are old friends. She is much loved, and you and she will get along well. You can rely on her to help you with your integration back into Earth's society. There's nothing to fear, Alice, I promise you."

"And you can contact us here on the station whenever you want," Principal Hardy assured her. "You will have your own registry and complete privacy at the Tabernacle."

Alice stopped crying. What purpose did it serve, anyway? She was going even though Saturn Station had become her home, with Principal Hardy and Dr Grossmith and Kelly. Now, she would leave in less than forty-eight hours. Outside the viewport, the Significator waited, and Alice shivered. She had to go on that enormous ship. Even the thought of seeing Statesman Patrick again didn't diminish her sense of loss.

CHAPTER EIGHTEEN _

"You have exceeded our expectations, Dr Langley," Dr Clere stated his findings, his face as sour as his manner was brisk, before turning back to his case of instruments. He'd resented Hardy's absurd insistence she need not return to the infirmary for her review because of her current emotional fragility. Whoever heard of house calls on a space station? What utter nonsense. As ordered, he attended her quarters to examine her one final time before she left, arrogant and firm in his belief the time would come when Principal Katya, as World Principal, would approve his research over Hardy's short-sightedness. Then all this Alice Watkins nonsense would be forgotten. When Kelly admitted him to Alice's room, he was surprised to see Dr Grossmith also present. Bowing stiffly, he decided he would not make waves, at least for now.

Alice heard the anger in his voice and saw his mouth twitching; something had upset him. Even her exceeding his expectations didn't seem to make him any happier.

"As of this moment, Dr Langley, I am no longer

involved in your care," Dr Clere continued. "Dr Grossmith will carry out any further examinations, either remotely or when he returns to Earth in the next few months."

Dr Grossmith returning to Earth soon? Alice peered round Dr Clere to give Dr Grossmith an approving grin. Clere saw it and sneered. What a waste of time, he thought to himself, nurturing her delusions.

"However," Dr Clere turned his stern gaze to Dr Grossmith, "I doubt he will have anything untoward to report, at least not regarding your internal workings."

Alice meant to thank him for everything he had done, but by the time she'd sorted out the words, he'd left the room.

Dr Grossmith knew even after all these weeks; Larry Clere was still angry at the outcome of the conversation with Principal Hardy, anger compounded now that Alice was leaving the station. Clere would have taken the view that not being allowed to carry out his examination without him being present and in his infirmary represented further insult.

"Do you have questions, Alice?" he said.

"I wanted to thank Dr Clere, but I expect he's still upset I haven't got my memory back."

"Don't mind him. He's pompous and self-opinionated, but he has a right to be proud of what he did for you. He's composed a paper and plans to publish when you're declassified."

"When will that be?"

"When you decide, Alice, but I recommend waiting

until you return to Earth and then telling only a select few as you get to know them."

"Alright. Does everyone at the Tabernacle know? Besides Principal Katya, I mean?"

He shook his head. "Just Principal Katya and her two chief statesmen. You'll learn to judge for yourself whom you can trust. Our society is far removed from the world of your time, and I know you will make many friends. Your history will take second place to their regard and respect for you."

"You say lovely things, Dr Grossmith. I'll miss you."

"I'm also returning to Earth in a few weeks, Alice. We'll see each other, I promise."

She squeezed his hand.

"There is something, though. What if I get travel sick on the spaceship? I'll die of embarrassment. And don't people float around?"

"You won't get sick, I can assure you, and you won't notice the movement. The ships are equipped with artificial gravity, the same as here, so you won't be floating around. Once you arrive in space dock, you will go by shuttle to the surface."

Two mornings later, Dr Grossmith, Principal Hardy and Kelly waved Alice and Amelia goodbye. Alice promised herself she would not cry at the farewell, but of course, she did. Amelia held her tight and walked her to the shuttle. Alice didn't want to look at the Significator looming outside, but it filled just about every viewport, and she couldn't avoid it. Her friends stood at the viewport as the shuttle banked and turned, and she watched them until they were out of sight.

***

The shuttle that took Alice on her tour outside Saturn Station was the same one that ferried them across to the Significator. It seemed such a short distance between the two. Alice could have walked.

"Isn't she magnificent?" the pilot called over his shoulder.

Yes, Alice agreed, magnificent. Amelia had told her that the starships were principalities in their own right, and Alice had no difficulty believing it. Close to, Alice estimated this one to be the size of a city.

The Significator's forward section was an oval disc, indented in the centre with a gentle, sloping hollow as if someone had pressed down a thumb to create a shallow dish. The rear of the disc rose high into a narrow tower, making Alice think of the skyscrapers she'd seen in magazines about America. The topmost part of the tower bent slightly towards the ship's front like a scorpion's tail. The young pilot pointed out the fairings, the communications array and other structures to his passengers. Rather than trying to educate them, Alice could tell it was his way of voicing his amazement at the scale of the vessel, making sure the whole ship was burned into his memory. All over, pinpoints of lights twinkled, which Alice guessed were viewports.

The pilot rotated the shuttle and flew along the

length of the Significator and around into the docking bay.

Alice looked down at her hands. Fists clenched and knuckles white; the ship represented the immensity of what lay ahead for her, and she felt like a little speck of frightened dust.

CHAPTER NINETEEN _

Alice expected the docking bay to be a place of industry and mayhem, but instead, she found it quiet and ordered. A few people working inside glanced up as their shuttle passed through the forcefield but returned to their tasks without sparing them a thought. A few minutes later, a separate shuttle, with different markings to the station shuttle, landed on the other side of the bay. Several uniformed personnel disembarked along with their pilot. Alice had seen the shuttle leave the station when she looked back, and Amelia told her it belonged to the principality ship, carrying station personnel returning to Earth aboard the Significator. A few loud greetings came from the docking bay staff, shattering the initial quiet, and laughter rang around the high ceilings and walls.

Alice wanted to shut her eyes and ears against the sudden, intrusive clatter and held onto Amelia like a limpet, ensuring she couldn't leave her side.

A tall, slender youth, dressed in a pale blue uniform and aged about nineteen, met them as they exited the bay, ahead of the noisy, happy group. He bowed to Alice.

"Dr Langley, welcome to the Significator. I'm Tyro Drake; I'm here to show you to your quarters." Then he turned to Amelia. "Educator Sebel."

He lifted his arm out to the side and invited them to follow him.

"Tyro? His first name?" Alice whispered to Amelia.

"A title," she whispered back. "It's like a novice or learner. He's doing aptitudes."

"He knew who we were."

"That's his job."

The portals, placed at intervals on either side of the walkways, did not indicate their purpose or who was in residence. Tyro Drake deactivated one of the unmarked portals and stood back to let them pass through, following just in time to see Alice gaping open-mouthed at the luxury of the beautiful apartment awaiting her. He waited, without a word, as she composed herself.

"This is beautiful, Tyro Drake, thank you."

He put her bag on a table, but to her dismay, he kept Amelia's bag in his hand and walked back to the portal, making it clear Alice would not be sharing.

"Where are you taking Amelia, I mean, Educator Sebel?"

"Educator Sebel has quarters on crew decks, nearby." Tyro Drake pointed to the registry. "You can call each other any time you wish."

Alice wasn't sure about this arrangement, but Amelia plastered on a bright smile. She didn't need to be a genius to know Alice's thoughts.

"I'll come right back. Must be morning teatime!"

Alice had overlooked the fact that they would consider Amelia as part of the organisation, even though she wasn't military. To Alice, it highlighted her lack of a "place". She hadn't found her "place" yet, but she had this splendid room all to herself. She could do this. She could be alone.

As expected, the viewport took up an entire wall, but Saturn Station wasn't visible from this side of the ship; there was only a view of Saturn itself. She sauntered over to look out.

Saturn. Sometimes, back on the station, she thought she could reach out and touch the rings, though she knew that it was a long way away from the station despite its immensity. Only now, faced with the prospect of never seeing it again, did she truly appreciate its majesty and presence. How silly, she thought, to feel sad about a planet.

Her new bed was large and luxurious, so large even Kelly couldn't have called it a bunk. The washer was identical in layout to her other washer, complete with the gel pillows for washing. An entertainment registry panel, like the one in her quarters on Saturn Station that she never got around to using, hovered over a long desk. A regular registry panel hovered alongside, quite unlike the registry she had learned to use before. She didn't recognise this configuration. As she analysed its technology by poking around, the communication panel lit and taken unawares; she waved her hands around madly for a second or two before it came to life. Alice was clueless about how she activated it, but Amelia's delighted face came into view.

"Wow! These crew quarters. I don't think I'll ever want to leave."

Alice agreed. "It's five-star luxury." Five-star meant nothing to Amelia, but she gathered it was Alice's way of being impressed.

"I'm coming back. See you in a second."

The screen flicked off with no help from Alice; far more sophisticated than those on the station where both parties had to end a link. By the time Alice worked out the difference in technology and found the beam that activated the communication link, Amelia arrived at the portal.

"I thought we might have coffee here," Alice pointed at a drinks dispenser. "It's not like the one in my other quarters, and I don't know how to work it."

"I've got one too. All you need do is this..."

Amelia made a flicking movement over a small panel on the side, and the dispenser woke. Alice tried the flick, but nothing happened, must be a knack, so she tried a wave; that worked, so she did the same thing with the entertainment registry, and that too came to life. She waved her hand again, and it went dark, then waved her hand once more and back on it came. Then she waved it dark again.

Amelia watched as Alice amused herself. Like a little child, she thought. How would life on Earth be for her? She had already decided to remain friends with her unusual and interesting student.

Alice saw Amelia watching her and suffered a moment of feeling foolish. She must have looked daft playing with the registry like that.

"Shall we find the mess and let them make us tea?" she suggested.

"They're called dining rooms and pasticiums on the starships," Amelia said as they left Alice's stateroom. "There are pasticiums on Earth too. You'll love them! I love them!"

Alice grinned. "You love a lot of things, Amelia. I'd only just got used to 'mess'."

"I know I do," Amelia admitted, "but they don't have messes on these ships. Pasticiums are where you get cake and coffee on Earth. If you want a meal, you go to a restaurant or dining hall. Unless you can cook."

"We had restaurants."

"Did you? Tell me about them."

"I've never been to one. I've only been to cafés. Pasticiums."

Alice chatted about the coffee shops she visited with Michelle, taking care not to mention her daughter's name or be too time-specific and hoping her descriptions weren't too old-fashioned for Amelia to understand. Then, trying to find the pasticium, Amelia saw the zone lines change from the guest habitat red zone to green. She looked around. She hadn't yet mentioned the restrictions to Alice.

"We need to go back the way we came and ask for directions," she said, stopping Alice from walking further.

They turned and retraced their steps until, to Alice's delight, she saw Statesman Patrick coming towards them on the walkway. Dressed in overalls and looking more like a plumber than a high-ranking officer, Alice thought he would have turned heads even if he'd been wearing a sack. *Stop it*, she told herself.

"Dr Langley. What a pleasure. I was on my way to your stateroom to welcome you aboard."

Alice remembered the protocols, but she was already smiling anyway.

"Statesman Patrick, it's nice to see you again."

He snapped a glance across to Amelia and waited for the introduction, but when Alice hesitated about what she should do next, Patrick helped her out.

"Educator Sebel." He bowed to Amelia.

"Statesman Patrick," Amelia responded. Alice took a second to realise it wasn't how the introduction should have gone, but no-one appeared troubled at her lapse.

Patrick turned his attention back to Alice.

"Well, Dr Langley, I've been looking forward to seeing you again. Tyro Drake reported your safe arrival, and I thought to contact you to inform you I am assigned as your escort and protector for the trip. You may contact me if you have any requirements or wish to attend events your companion doesn't have permission to attend."

Amelia used Patrick's inattention to mouth at Alice behind his back.

"You know him?"

Alice stifled a grin. "Protector, Statesman Patrick?

Protection from what?"

He didn't skip a beat. "Space dragons. Monsters. I've no idea. But if you need protecting, just call, and I will ensure it is I who rescues you."

"I wouldn't want to put you to trouble."

"No trouble, it would be my pleasure."

"Well, Statesman Patrick," Amelia smiled and turned on her charm, drawing his attention away from Alice. "It seems we need you to rescue us now. We're lost."

"Are you indeed? I expect you are looking for morning tea if I am not mistaken?"

"You are not mistaken, Statesman."

"Then, I will escort you."

Patrick did not comment on them being so close to a restricted area, although Amelia was sure he would be aware of her orders. He showed them to the pasticium but declined to stay, insisting he was there only to help two lovely damsels in distress.

"He's *gorgeous*!!" Amelia sighed as soon as Patrick was out of earshot. "Wherever did you meet him? And a military statesman, my goodness!"

"A couple of nights ago," Alice said. "I didn't see you yesterday to tell you. Principal Hardy wanted me to go to dinner and meet the pilots or whatever they are, of this ship. But he couldn't go, so Statesman Patrick took me instead. I met the principal and one of the other officers. They weren't as friendly or nice as Statesman Patrick."

"You're so lucky. That's what you get for being a heroine. And he seems interested in you."

"I expect Principal Hardy has told them everything, and I doubt Statesman Patrick gives me a second thought."

The guest deck pasticium, small and cosy and with a more modest viewport, was a far cry from the bustle of the 'mess' on the station. Saturn Station was visible through the viewport, where all her friends, save Amelia, remained. Fearing the sight might reduce her to tears, Alice changed seats, so the view of the station was behind her; she then distracted herself by asking Amelia to run through Earth's society and the statesman, principal, title thing she found so tedious.

"Earth's culture is one of respect for rank and achievement, Alice. Whatever your designation, that is your title. As you know, I'm Educator Sebel. Statesman Patrick's title would have corresponded with whatever he did before he became a statesman."

"An engineer."

"Engineer Patrick in that case. Engineering is a scientific qualification, but we don't call them 'doctor'. Elevation to statesman overrules all other titles as does the title of principal."

Amelia nibbled her biscuit, anticipating more questions.

"What would they do if I asked them to call me Alice?"

"They'd say 'no'. Such familiarity is disrespectful unless you are on close terms, and even then, they might not because, frankly, it's not your name."

Alice let it pass. "Is Patrick, Statesman Patrick's first

name?"

Amelia shook her head. "No, that's his family name. They don't go by their first name unless, as I said, you're on close terms with them. Until then, they're 'Statesman' and whatever their family name is or just 'Statesman' if you are addressing them directly after being introduced."

Alice listened and learned, wanting to know if, on Earth, would things be different?

Amelia said no, the same. "As a rule, you should address everyone by their title and family name, but when you have your circle of friends, all that gets dropped. The formality is only for strangers or in work conditions. If your husband is an educator, you wouldn't address him as Educator while you are having sex." She popped the last of her biscuit in her mouth and cocked her head to one side, munching away.

Alice's eyes widened, and her jaw dropped. Amelia gave her a crooked smile, and they both burst out laughing. Alice had never laughed at the word 'sex' before, but she giggled like a naughty teenager for a moment or two more before Amelia once again became the instructor and Alice, the willing learner.

CHAPTER TWENTY _

"How long will it take to get to Earth?" Alice asked Amelia.

Having found a signpost to point the way to the guest observation deck, the two women looked out across the panorama of space. They'd departed Saturn Station, but Alice couldn't detect any sensation of movement.

"Maybe a week at this speed," Amelia estimated.

"This speed? A tortoise could overtake us at this speed!"

"There aren't any tortoises in space, Alice. Lots on earth, though, and we're moving very fast, but nowhere near the ships true capabilities."

"How fast is very fast?"

Statesman Hennessey joined them, dressed like a plumber, just as Patrick had been earlier, though not possessed of the same glory, and answered Alice's question before Amelia had the chance to speak.

"At present, Dr Langley, we are travelling at around 2,500 kilometres per second. And Educator Sebel is correct; compared to the speed at which this ship is capable, we are literally crawling. We never engage Magnitude within proximal space, so the journey takes longer."

"Statesman Hennessey," Alice smiled a greeting, once again completely forgetting to introduce Amelia. Still, he acknowledged them both, having already assumed Dr Langley's companion, dressed in the requisite maroon, must be Educator Sebel.

"How far are we from Earth, Statesman?" Alice could see no planets outside the observation deck viewport.

"Planet to planet, the distance can change in a day, Dr Langley. At this point, we're around 1.2 billion kilometres from space dock." He looked towards the viewport, unaware of how cryptic his answer sounded to Alice. "Alas, for me, it will be a long time before I'm out here again."

He seemed more affable away from the formality of the dinner.

"I heard your wife had a baby, Statesman. Congratulations. What a wonderful coming home present." Kelly had told Alice the baby was about three months old.

"The best, thank you. I'm delighted. Working in space is exciting and a challenge, but I'm more than content to be going home to my wife and child."

"You're a civilian, Statesman Hennessey?" Amelia asked.

"Yes, Educator Sebel, Statesman Junnot had been assigned to this role but met with an unfortunate accident only weeks before departure. As the only other linguistician available with experience of deep space travel, the Tabernacle appointed me; not an opportune time as I had recently married, but the mission couldn't be delayed after so much time invested."

"You have a new position on Earth?"

"At the Bell Institute for the next five years. My focus will be anthropology." He turned back to Alice. "I note you're cleared for the officers' observation deck, Dr Langley?"

Amelia guessed he knew Principal Ryan had put her in her place, and the knowledge irked her.

"Statesman Patrick will escort you there if you wish. The view from here is limited, but from the officer's deck, you can also see the length of the ship. It's a wonderful sight."

"I don't have clearance for the officers' decks, Alice." Amelia folded her hands behind her back and lifted her chin, hoping Statesman Hennessey would notice her display of defiance and suggest to the principal such sanctions were a little extreme. But the meaning of her gesture was lost on Alice.

"Oh, are there many places we can't go?"

"Without clearance, yes," Statesman Hennessey said. "Most particularly, the forward disc."

"Is there something there we shouldn't see?"

"The engines," Amelia declared. "And the bridge."

"Yes, in part. Engineering is Statesman Patrick's realm." Hennessey paused, noting Educator Sebel's attitude, though he didn't know what he'd said to make her bristle in such a way. Alice still didn't see Amelia's irritation.

"We met Statesman Patrick earlier today when we got lost. He showed us to the...to the...?"

Alice looked at Amelia for help.

"...pasticium."

"Yes, pasticium. He was very nice and kind."

"Statesman Patrick has a cheerful disposition. Sometimes, irritatingly so. Now, if you will excuse me, I'm just passing through." Statesman Hennessey smiled, and Alice understood he meant no criticism of Patrick.

They watched him leave.

"How did you know he was a civilian?"

"He doesn't wear a military insignia on his uniform."

"An insignia?"

"Yes, next time you see a military... oh, here's one, excuse me, Councilman, I'm Educator Sebel, this is Dr Langley."

"Councilman Stewart," the woman inclined her head in greeting.

"Councilman Stewart, Dr Langley and I were discussing insignias. May I?"

Amelia pointed out the badge embroidered onto the shoulder of Councilman Stewart's uniform, blue and gold chevrons set in a narrow cord circle. Alice remembered them from her first lesson with Amelia.

"Thank you, Councilman."

Councilman Stewart inclined her head again. "Pleasure."

"I hadn't noticed that on Patrick." Alice only remembered the purple braid.

"I wouldn't notice it on Patrick. How would anyone take their eyes off that face! Or that body!"

"Amelia! You're shocking! Hennessey seemed much nicer today."

"Pleasant enough, yes."

"I thought him a bit of a sourpuss at the dinner. I might have to revise my opinion."

"Well, maybe he doesn't like formal get-togethers. I hear Principal Ryan doesn't either."

"He didn't seem too keen the other evening. What did Statesman Hennessey mean? I can go to other places with an officer but not with you?" Alice wasn't keen on exploring the ship without Amelia.

"Principal Ryan placed restrictions on me," Amelia said. "What does he think I'm going to get up to? It's because I'm only a third-year educator and rank too low, but under the circumstances, he's unreasonable." She pulled a face. "You aren't allowed on my deck or any general crew areas. If you're with an officer, Statesman Patrick, I suppose, you can go anywhere he chooses," then, with a naughty grin, she added, knowing her next words would shock Alice, "even his quarters!"

Alice and Amelia spent a couple of enjoyable days at the registry in Alice's stateroom, indulging in chocolate, drinking coffee and, at other times, exploring the guest habitat deck, an area large enough for Alice not to consider what lay in the rest of the ship. Patrick checked in on her once or twice via the registry and on one occasion, accompanied them both to the pasticium, charming them with his humour and stories.

Alice had always enjoyed a nap in the early afternoons, and even in her new life, the habit continued. Here, it was more comfortable napping almost nude, wearing only her camisole and panties. She kept the portal locked to stop anyone from entering unannounced.

One afternoon, the communication registry sounded and woke her from a deep sleep. Still groggy, Alice wandered over to the registry and passed her hand over the panel. Statesman Patrick greeted her with a smile. She rubbed her eyes.

"Oh, Statesman Patrick."

"Did I wake you?"

"No, I…" She couldn't think up an excuse for her confusion.

"You have an imprint of your hand on your cheek. You *were* sleeping. I'm so sorry."

"Oh, well, yes, I have a nanna nap each afternoon."

"A nanna nap?"

"Yes, it's a nap old people take." She glanced down at herself, realising with horror, she only had on her panties and a tiny vest.

He saw her alarm. "What is it? Are you alright?"

"Umm...on these things, do you just see my face?"

"Yes, and your shoulders, why?"

"Nothing. Nothing at all." Thank goodness, that could have been highly embarrassing!

"What I can I do for you, Statesman?"

"I thought we might have dinner tonight?"

Dinner? Have dinner? Alice was speechless. A date? What should she say? Old ladies don't go out on dates. But she's young again. Oh, dear, what to say. She wanted to go, but what if she made a fool of herself? How should she answer? She was all in a dither.

"Us? Alone?" she blurted out.

"Yes," but he didn't notice her panicky confusion. "I thought you might enjoy the cabaret in the officers' dining room, rather what serves as a cabaret. It's just background music, really, but we could go to the officers' observation deck afterwards. The views are more spectacular than in the guest area. Whatever you would like, Dr Langley."

"It sounds nice." *Control yourself, Alice Watkins, keep your voice steady.* She took a deep breath. "I would like to go to dinner with you, Statesman, but I had already arranged to have dinner with Educator Sebel here. Should we ask her? Would she be allowed if she is with you?"

She imagined he sounded disappointed, but he didn't say Amelia wasn't welcome. Instead, he offered to call her to suggest it and collect them both at nineteen hundred hours.

A date! What would her mother say? She spent the afternoon awash with excitement and nerves. Alice Watkins had a date! Statesman Patrick invited her out!

As the time for her dinner date approached, Alice wondered why she hadn't heard from Amelia. Perhaps she wasn't going to come tonight? The thought of spending time alone with Patrick filled Alice's tummy with butterflies, and she was surprised she wasn't floating around the room. For most of the afternoon since Patrick woke her, she'd been deliberating what to wear. Kelly had left the earrings and the belt in her case, insisting they brightened up the drabness of the clothing and to keep them until she found more beautiful things to wear when she arrived back home. The comm. registry flashed, and Amelia appeared, her face festooned with knowing smiles.

"You got an invitation, didn't you? From a gorgeous statesman?

"Well, aren't we all going?"

"Not me! I'm not going to be a gooseberry. You go with him and have a great time."

"But what about you?"

"I'll see you for breakfast…maybe."

Alice pursed her lips, but Amelia only giggled at Alice's unspoken admonishment.

"Don't worry about me," she said. "I know two of the crew members on board. They suggested meeting up for dinner, but I told them we had plans, but now, I'll go. Statesman Patrick left me a message, but I didn't call back."

"Are you sure?"

"Of course, don't you want to spend a couple of

hours with Mr Dreamy?"

"It's not like that, Amelia."

"And it won't be either if I tag along."

Alice hesitated.

"What's wrong?"

"I'm nervous."

"Gosh, so would I be, going out with him. But you still gotta do it. Forget the nerves; you can have those anytime, but a hunk like that and a statesman as well! What are you wearing?"

"Grey. It's all I have, but I have got a chain belt and a gold necklace and earrings."

"Good. Do you want makeup? I have some."

"I've never worn it. My mother wouldn't let me."

"Your mother?" Amelia had to think about that one. "Well, she's not here to know. I'll be there in a sec."

Amelia could turn her hand to many things, and one of them was applying makeup, arriving with an array of gel colours and tiny lighted tubes that changed colour when applied to the skin. When she finished, Alice stood in front of the image definer, and despite reflecting an overall impression of grey just as she predicted, her pinker lips and the green shading to her eyes brightened and lifted her complexion. She was pleased with the result.

"I like it. I wish I'd discovered it before."

"It suits you, and you only have a little on. It's designed to enhance, not hide. Shows how pretty you are."

Alice looked back at her reflection. Pretty? Even as a young woman, Alice had been small and mousey, then when old age crept up, she'd got white hair and wrinkles. There had been chin hairs too. Yes, Toby said chin hairs. She paused, looking at her reflection and waited for the pain of remembrance to begin. This time, it didn't come.

Precisely at nineteen hundred hours, the portal buzzer sounded, and Amelia released the door. Statesman Patrick, out of uniform in a blue shirt that matched his eyes and wearing casual slacks, was dressed to impress. His hair, even though he'd tied it back, was softer and less regimented than when on duty, and he topped off the vision with his glorious smile, even while he made polite effort to hide his disappointment at seeing Amelia. She turned to wink at Alice before making cheeky wide eyes at her.

"Educator Sebel," Patrick gave a stiff bow.

"Statesman Patrick. Please forgive me; I must decline your invitation. I have a prior engagement. I'm sure you'll take good care of Dr Langley."

Patrick was not in the least upset at her having a prior engagement. Educator Sebel could have whatever she wished, provided it meant having Alice all to himself. He didn't fool Amelia; she knew his type. Patrick turned his attention to Alice.

"Dr Langley. You are beautiful."

"Thank you, Statesman." Alice's reply was gracious and proper, and she hid her shyness at his compliment well. As he took her hand to lead her through the portal, Alice resolved she would take Amelia's advice and leave her anxieties in her quarters for the next few hours.

CHAPTER TWENTY-ONE _

The officers' dining room looked like the officers' mess on the station, only larger and busier. Patrick led Alice to a table by the viewport, away from the bustle in the centre of the room. Once seated, she had a favour to ask of Statesman Patrick.

"Would you do something for me, Statesman?"

"Of course, if it's in my power. Outer space can be a bit limiting, though."

Alice was unaware he was as dazzled by her as she had been by him the first time they met. Meeting her on the station, finding her lost in the corridor on her first day onboard, knowing her history, everything about her intrigued him.

"Would you call me 'Alice' instead of Dr Langley?"

"Alice?" he looked baffled. "Alice? Why?"

She told him why, at least in part.

"For some reason, I only ever remember being called Alice. I don't remember being Dr Langley, and it feels strange when people call me by that name."

MATILDA SCOTNEY

He thought for a moment. "I'm aware of your history Dr Langley…Alice. On this ship, other than myself, only Principal Ryan and Statesman Hennessey have been appraised of the events of the last fourteen or so years. Educator Sebel knows, of course. I haven't read the reports fully but, Principal Ryan tells me you have amnesia."

"So I'm told, but it doesn't feel like it to me."

"Well, I'll call you Alice when we're alone, like this," and, on impulse, touched her hand. She was so surprised at the pressure of his fingers that she didn't think to pull away. For a nanosecond, she compared him with Ted. There'd been no-one before Ted and no-one since. In all honesty, she couldn't have cared less if there'd not been any Ted between those two points, except for the kids, of course.

Patrick, realising he'd breached protocol, was the first to withdraw his hand. Always drawn to beautiful women, this woman was bound up in mystery and classifications, and under both the Tabernacle's and his protection while she was on board. That meant off-limits. Not that he paid much attention to restrictions of that kind.

The steward brought a clear, red liquid, which Alice called wine, but the steward quickly informed her, rather tartly, alcohol is *never* served on starships. Alice thought it a sensible rule. What if you were drunk and driving a starship? It didn't bear thinking about. You might crash into Mars.

Amused by Alice's changing faces as she tasted the drink and examined the edible floral concoction the steward placed before her, Patrick was reminded of the time he first learned of her at school. He'd paid little attention back then. At university, the study of cryogenics was mandatory, but the subject, lumped in with other ancient and obscure sciences, gave no weight to her uniqueness. He mostly forgot about her as the years passed. What was the analogy Ryan used during their debriefing? That was it, like Carter, the archaeologist, finding Tutankhamen's sarcophagus and discovering, far from being mummified, what was inside was alive and breathing. True and living history!

He hadn't expected this when he met her. Hadn't expected her to be so lovely, so sweet. As a scientist, her history and awakening fascinated him, that she survived was astonishing, that she was so beautiful, mesmerising. She looked up and smiled, clearly fascinated by the intensity of colour and variety of dishes served.

"We have a hydroponics deck for fresh food, Alice. Fresh and preserved food is combined to offer diversity. Even though the portions appear small, they meet all our nutritional needs. They look good too!"

"It does look good," she looked up. "It's not laced with firewater, is it?"

"No, I promise," he grinned.

"Thank you, Statesman."

"Well, *Alice*. You can drop the Statesman part. Just Patrick."

"Oh, okay, if you won't get into trouble."

He grinned again. "Just don't say it in front of Ryan

or Hennessey."

"I promise. Amelia told me your surname was Patrick, so why can't I call you by your first name?"

He took a second to own up. "Because it's Carmichael."

"Carmichael?"

"Yes, awful, isn't it? No-one uses it. It's my mother's family name. It doesn't work as a Christian name, but it's a custom in her family that the women always name their firstborn son, Carmichael. My mother calls me Michael, but everyone else, when I'm not being Statesman, calls me Patrick."

"Michael is a lovely name," Alice said, "and Carmichael is very solid. I think it sounds fine."

"Solid? That settles it. It's official. I *hate* it! Just Patrick, or I will call you Dr Langley forevermore. Hennessey is the same, he hates his first name, so everyone calls him Hennessey."

"What is it?" then she reconsidered. "Perhaps you shouldn't tell me. It might upset him."

But Patrick was not so sensitive about revealing his colleague's name.

"It's Lester, which is almost as bad as Carmichael. The only one of us three command officers with a normal name is Ryan, and he's so used to being called Principal Ryan, or Principal, or just Ryan, he probably doesn't remember it!"

Alice laughed. "A normal name? I suppose you're going to tell me?"

"Noah."

"That's appropriate. Noah in charge of a big ship."

"Biblical Noah—from the ancient text?"

She nodded.

"I never made that connection," he said. "He doesn't answer to Noah, anyway."

Patrick was so easy to be with that there was no place for nerves or unease. Alice forgot her social ineptness in her other life and laughed at his silly stories, his candid observations of life in space, and his extraordinary wit. But when she asked him about his home, he became reflective.

One of the small principalities in the northern hemisphere, he told her—called Ireland centuries ago. He loved that name. It sounded so musical. Had she heard of it? Alice told him she had and could even picture it on a map. Knowing now where he came from, she immediately placed his accent.

Patrick was a poet. Never at a loss for words or the ability to communicate his thoughts, he built up a picture of a beautiful Earth, where animals and people and cultures lived without fear or oppression. It was clear to Alice; Patrick loved his home. His soft, dreamy rendition of an old Irish poem, which he recited in clear and unbroken Gaelic, his expressions changing with the lilt and rise of the verse and entirely from memory, captivated and enchanted Alice.

But in contrast, when he spoke about the engines of this great ship, he became animated, enthusiastic, his eyes bright and wide as he gesticulated about their size and speed. He laughed as he told her of all the things that can go wrong during the development of the components, then dropping his voice to speak with reverence and pride of their ultimate success.

"I don't understand anything about engines, Patrick," Alice admitted. "I can't imagine anything so large it would power a ship of this size."

"They're not so large, Alice. A'khet provided us with an organic material that powered their own ship. This material, this Substance, is the power. A'khet have a sacred name for it, but when they offered it to us, they called it 'Substance', a rather ordinary title for an extraordinary element. We don't know where A'khet sources it.

"Our challenge was to build a container to house Substance. Over the years, they carried out many tests, but each time, it burst through the housing as we reached light speed. For reasons we don't understand, A'khet didn't need to contain Substance on their ship. We only know that with our technology, it becomes unstable unless it's sheathed. A'khet tried to help, but they aren't engineers. We had no choice but to develop a method of containment."

"What happened?"

"Over time, we developed materials containing widely available minerals, usually noble metals, which work well but unfortunately, only for limited periods. Eventually, A'khet identified that we needed to understand and harness the harmonics to fuse Substance with our technology. They selected a few people, not at random—those who had distinguished themselves and whom A'khet trusted and gave them what we call today, Knowledge. Without it, regardless of all the components being in place and all the theories, the engines won't work to any great effect. The coalition of the two technologies made space travel possible but initially, difficult and lengthy until the advent of Knowledge."

"And your family? They were involved in these trials?"

"Yes, my great-great-grandfather created a housing, a Gravidarum, able to diffuse the intensity or magnitude of Substance into three other chambers. These are the portage cylinders, and though we could use it for speed, it still didn't give us the ability to sustain essential systems such as gravity, temperature, light and so on, over a long period, even for a crew of a dozen. On this ship, those systems are maintained as a byproduct of the joining of Substance and the Gravidarum."

Prompted by her evident and genuine interest, he continued.

"My great-grandfather then took up the torch and, in time, found that by manipulating the minerals in a particular way, all Substance within the portage cylinders remained stable. As the ships approached light speed, Substance lifted and floated inside the portage. It became stable, and the Gravidarum stopped the portage cylinders fracturing. It all led to the engines we use now, allowing us to travel at considerable speed over considerable distances while sustaining all the systems we need. I use the term 'engine' loosely, Alice, because really, it's a complex merger of technology, organics and harmonics, and I gave you the simple version," he laughed. "It's more complicated, but I don't want to fry your brain!"

Alice found it amazing. Complicated, mystifying, but amazing.

"So, space travel is relatively new?"

"Of the exploratory kind we undertake, yes, but humans have been in space for hundreds of years, tinkering around." His gaze wandered to the darkness of space beyond the viewport and then back to her when she asked,

"And you have no idea what this Substance is?"

"No. It's organic, that much we know, possibly brought with A'khet from their planet of origin. Even those with Knowledge only know as much about its composition as our scientists do. I can tell you about the everyday minerals used in the Gravidarum, gold, rhodium, osmium, iridium, but Substance is another matter, so to speak."

"Do you have it? This Knowledge?"

"Yes, I do, and my father and grandmother and great-grandfather and his father before him. Way back, another ancestor had a form of Knowledge that didn't relate to engineering, but none of us knows anything about it. Few are granted Knowledge, possibly half a dozen or so. Two of us are military, but all are engineers."

"Sounds like a big responsibility."

"It is. But I'm sure I'm giving you more information than you need!"

"I'm afraid I found even your easy version of your engines a little too involved for me. How long can you be away from Earth for, with these engines?"

"We were away a year each on our last two missions," Patrick told her, "and now we'll have a few months back at space dock to upgrade the Gravidarum. I've designed several modifications to increase longevity; in theory, the engines would keep going forever because Substance appears to be indestructible and has never shown signs of decay. At one time, because of its durability, it was thought A'khet Substance might have been used in the manufacture of your sarcophagus, but it was just a theory and never proven. So even though we have this wonderful gift where we can move amongst the stars, our technology limits us, that and perhaps, our courage."

"Courage?"

"Yes, to simply point to the first star and fly on until morning. Long-range communication is an issue, so we're caught up with having to come back to Earth, file our reports, catch up with family. Principal Ryan would stay out in space forever, on his own, cataloguing planets and star systems, investigating nebulae and discovering black holes. I see the appeal of longer missions, but I do not share Ryan's disposition. He tends towards the solitary. Hennessey has a baby now, so his career as an explorer is pretty much over."

"He's excited about the baby. I met him on the observation deck."

Patrick couldn't fathom such a thing as being excited

about a baby. He would take Alice's word for it and change the subject back to technology.

"I'd like to show you the engines. I'm proud of them. Would you think me self-indulgent?"

"Not at all, but I'm hopeless with mechanical things. I don't even own a computer. I can't work out how to use them."

"A computer?" he stood and held her chair for her. "Why would you own a computer?"

"Perhaps that explanation may have to wait for another time. Let's go look at your engines."

The engine room was in the centremost part of the forward disc, and they passed through dozens of portals to get to their destination. A few crewmen glanced up with curiosity at the sight of their senior officer escorting a civilian in a restricted area, but their interest was fleeting and after taking in the unexpected sight, went back to their tasks. Patrick did not introduce her to the crew; he just led her to a single, narrow portal and invited her to step through with him.

The structures Patrick called engines were little more than three long cylinders, stretching into the distance, two below and one sitting above. If she stood in one cylinder, the uppermost part would touch the top of her head. If she raised her arms, she would reach the sides. There were no visible signs of technology within the tube. The shining interior reflected the only source of illumination in the room, a row of soft lights across the floor in front of the cylinders. The cylinders were contained within a large ring, set within a series of smaller rings around the outer cylinders. Narrow bars entered and exited almost like a latticework binding the rings together. It was huge. This was the Gravidarum. Alice knew that without Patrick having to tell her.

Near the mouth of each cylinder, a much smaller tube, not suspended by wires or any structure visible to Alice, silently rotated, bathed in a barely perceptible light, light not reflected from the floor. From where she stood, the smaller cylinder looked to Alice like the middle of a toilet roll wrapped in sandpaper, a simple structure devoid of beauty or elegance, it emitted a soothing radiance that held her spellbound, purple to blue and back to purple. And the song, the chiming? Soft on the ear. D major, perhaps? As the chiming changed to a rhythmic chanting, she felt as if her ribs had opened like fingers to receive the music into her heart. Tilting back her head, Alice closed her eyes, the colours and sounds perfusing through her mind and body, bringing eternity within her reach.

Patrick walked on ahead, chattering on about angstroms and parsecs before noticing she wasn't following him. He stopped his bright chatter and turned to see her face inclined upwards towards the Gravidarum.

"Alice?" She didn't answer.

"Alice? Are you alright?" He retraced his steps.

She turned then and opened her eyes, her lips curled into a small quizzical smile. She lifted her arm to point towards the cylinder.

"I know this."

Patrick stood, bewildered, and though he knew he shouldn't be touching her in sight of his crew, placed his arm around her to steer her from the engine room.

"*I know this,*" she had said. How could she know this? Any of it? He glanced back at the Gravidarum to see what secrets they might have imparted, but they were silent, as they should be.

The moment in the engine room apparently forgotten, she thanked him for the evening all the way to her stateroom. At the same time, he relegated the incident to something he would consider later.

"Patrick…"

"I know," he laughed, " 'Thank you, Patrick, for a lovely evening'. You've told me ten times!"

"Well, it *was* lovely."

"We have a couple of evenings left before we get to space dock. We'll do this again."

He put on his gorgeous smile, kissed her hand and left her to watch him walk away before she opened the portal. He certainly knew how to make an entrance! And an exit!

Alice stood at the image definer. No longer the image of an ageing Brisbane widow, this was the image of an attractive young woman. To where Alice Watkin's face and body had gone, she had no idea, and she didn't care. She liked this image much, much more. And Patrick had told her she was beautiful.

CHAPTER TWENTY-TWO _

Amelia amused herself the night before so much she missed breakfast, not linking via the registry with Alice until much later in the morning, half asleep and full of apologies.

"I'm so sorry. I spent the whole night talking! Can you imagine that?"

Alice could imagine.

"I didn't get to bed until dawn," Amelia peered at her from the comm. screen, bleary-eyed.

"Dawn?" Alice hadn't realised. "We have dawn here?"

"Well, just before lights up anyhow. I am so *tired!*"

Alice grinned. "Serves you right."

"How did your night go?"

"It was...lovely."

"What time did it end?"

"At a decent hour!"

"Just asking. I'll be there for lunch. What are you doing now?"

"Accessing the information registry. My educator has a hangover, so she can't come and help me with my lessons," Alice took the opportunity to poke some fun at her teacher.

"We're on a starship, can't be a hangover, more of a sleepover. Keep with the registry and store up the questions. We can go over them after lunch."

The communication screen flicked off, and Alice turned her attention to the information section. A light blinked in the bottom right corner. She hadn't noticed it before; Amelia always sat directly in front of the registry during lessons. A word blinked in rhythm with the light.

"Command."

On Saturn Station, Alice used the voice responder on the registry with varying success, but she had never seen one of these icons. It was listening and waiting for her to speak, blinking and listening, listening and blinking. Alice was unsure, so she stared at it as if it might do something other than blink and listen.

She said the first thing that came into her head, a computer word she'd heard Eliza use, bending towards the light and raising her voice as if the registry were deaf.

"Goggle."

The computer showed her a pair of ancient-looking eye coverings. She wasn't sure what Goggle did, anyway. Perhaps a word from this time might work, something she'd heard mentioned but didn't understand. The listening light blinked and waited.

"Sarcophagus."

A list appeared, and there, an entry entitled:

"Sarcophagus images. (Fragment-public domain/educational). Human preservation specimen (Sleeping Beauty Phenomenon (colloq.), Sarc & Darwin et al.). Research documentation dated: May 2318 (closed file– clearance code essential). Property; Bell Institute. Archived. 2497/4th quarter."

Several images, captured from a distance, showed the cave's interior, the chamber where they found her. Alice tried to read the date on the first slide, but the numbers had degraded. It looked like 11/2206 though she couldn't be sure. If she had been preserved in 2127 and Dr Grossmith said the Chinese military found her around eighty years later, then these were old images, original images and taken at the time of her discovery.

Held fast by morbid curiosity, she watched as each picture drifted in eerie slow motion across the registry, mostly showing containers and the grotesque image of a withered head. Bright lamps had been installed in the cave for illumination, and positioned in the centre of the cavern was a long glass-like receptacle. At this distance and with the image's inferior quality, it wasn't easy to gain an appreciation for its contents. It occurred to Alice that in the long years she was in there, undiscovered, it would have been cold and silent. She shivered but didn't turn away.

One image stayed longer on the screen; the camera or whatever device took the pictures had moved alongside the receptacle. Instinctively, Alice's hand rose to touch the image with her fingertips, and as she made contact, there followed a deep and profound sadness.

The pictures resumed their gradual progress, ensuring each feature of the cavern was covered. The camera swept in close on the final image to view the glass container from above. Alice couldn't get a good view because of the reflection of the lights on the glass. Alice leaned forward and peered at the image, just making out the sickeningly pale, hairless, corpse-like figure lying within.

Alice's eyes widened in horror, and her breath felt as if it had been sucked from her body. She leapt to her feet, almost knocking over her chair in her haste. She'd dared to ask the registry, and now, it had given her the shocking answer. A sarcophagus was a coffin, and Alice found herself staring down at her own grave.

Unnerved, she passed her hand over the access panel, backing away as the register went dark, but the listening light still blinked. Sitting on the bed, she tried to slow her breathing but couldn't settle. Shocked, she needed Amelia but felt too menaced by the registry to call her, and she had no idea where crew decks were, even if she'd been permitted to go there.

Desperate for a distraction and the need to do something, anything while the shock and horror of those images passed away, she decided the observation deck might just offer a place of safety.

Rushing through the portal, she ran straight into Patrick's arms.

"You're in a hurry, trying to avoid me?"

"No, no...not at all. In fact," Alice stammered, relieved to see a friendly face, "if you have some free time, I can't think of anyone I would rather have bumped into."

Patrick, secretly thrilled at her evident relief in seeing him, held her steady longer than needed. In his head, he appreciated he was already breaching one directive or other, but she looked pale and anxious; something had occurred to bring on such distress.

"Yes, a few minutes. Where were you headed?"

"I was on my way to the observation deck. I had a fright and just wanted to...I'm not sure..."

"Get away from what frightened you?" he offered, at a loss to guess what one might find in a guest room that would be so upsetting. Not much of anything happens on starships in proximal space. She shook her head,

"At least not be in the same room with it."

Patrick took her to the highest point of the tower, many levels above Alice's stateroom, where the officer's observation platform opened out, affording a spectacular view of the ship. The entire area was equipped for comfort and relaxation. Once there, he showed her to a private area, away from the few other officers socialising and enjoying coffee.

"Tell me what happened."

"I can't tell you how happy I am to see you, Patrick." Alice still felt too breathless and anxious to worry if she sounded gushing.

"I'm glad I can be of help. What upset you?"

"I told you last night I'm not good with computers,

but that didn't stop me fiddling with the registry in my room. It's different from the ones on the station, but I worked out how to use it."

"And that was frightening…?"

"Not really," she shook her head. "I felt quite proud of myself. At my age, computers are…" trailing off to study his young face. She might need to keep that information to herself for now. It would be nonsense to him.

"I didn't understand many of the big, scientific words I heard on Saturn Station, but Dr Grossmith placed a chip here—" she showed him the blue dot on her arm "—to help me learn."

"Eduction chip," he'd seen them before, even had one himself once.

"Yes, so I asked the computer a word I remembered from my conversations with him to learn more. I've heard this word a few times, but I didn't know its significance. I'm sure it will be clear to you why I thought of it."

"What was the word?"

"Sarcophagus."

Her anxiety made sense to him now.

"And the registry showed you a sarcophagus or…something more…personal and disturbing?"

"It showed the cave where they found me. There were images, distant images as though someone took the pictures from a doorway. I couldn't see too much at first, but then the last image went really close, looking from above. I saw myself inside, and it felt as if I was staring at myself in a coffin." She thought about the image and shuddered. "Patrick, I was viewing my own grave. I was looking into my coffin."

Alice trembled. How had she ended up in that terrible place, in a glass coffin? Dr Grossmith described it, but she never believed it. Now, she'd seen it for herself. Whether Alice Watkins or Alexis Langley had awakened, she didn't know, but wasn't it impossible to be both?

Patrick would have responded to her trembling by holding her had they been in a less public place. Instead, he sat as close to her as protocols allowed, and Alice was grateful for his nearness.

With Alice settling and Patrick needing to return to his duties, he offered to fetch Educator Sebel to look after her.

"Thank you, Patrick. She's coming to collect me for lunch. I think I'll be fine now."

Only agreeing to leave her if she wouldn't be alone, Patrick walked with her to her stateroom and instructed her not to go to that segment of the registry again, suggesting instead researching her family tree might be less stressful. It may even prompt a few happier memories. He cautioned her not to do it alone.

"Let Educator Sebel help. There are safeguards in place to protect confidentiality, so you only get general information. When you have your own registry, you can search for anything you wish."

"Thank you, Patrick," she said, then remembered he was outside her stateroom when she bumped into him. "I didn't ask you why you came to see me earlier."

"I forgot! Do you like music?"

"I—I'm not sure," she thought of the Saturday morning radio program she used to listen to while doing the housework, the only time she listened to music at home. "I don't know anything about music."

"Well, you are in for a treat. Tonight, we have an assembly for senior staff, after which we are to have a soiree. Principal Ryan plays the oboe, you know."

"I didn't know."

"Well, he does. He plays at the concerts because he has no choice, but he doesn't consider himself a performer. I hoped you'd come with me."

"I would love to, Patrick, but you must forgive my ignorance. I've never been to a concert."

"Light entertainment is just what you need after your upset."

He saw her inside the portal before bowing and smiling that wonderful smile. He was popping up just when she needed him, but she didn't mind, didn't mind one bit. What a wonderful new experience, to have friends.

Amelia had spied them together as she came to collect Alice for lunch and quickly scurried back to the crew quarters to wait until she was sure it would be safe to return. She refused to eat any lunch until Alice told her the juicy details of her unplanned meeting with the devilishly handsome Statesman Patrick.

"Nothing juicy, Amelia. He came to ask me to a concert this evening, but I had an upset, and he took me to the observation deck then sat with me till I settled down. He walked with me back to my room."

"What upset you?" Amelia changed seats to sit close to Alice, putting her arm around her shoulders, her beautiful face creasing into a frown as she forgot all about Statesman Patrick.

Alice related the story of the chamber, unable to repeat the 's' word and struggling to hold back tears. Amelia squeezed her hand to reassure her throughout the retelling and felt terrible for leaving her friend alone this morning. She doubted she was a substitute for Statesman Patrick but happy he turned up when he did.

"Amelia, what does 'colloq' mean? The registry said, 'The Sleeping Beauty Phenomenon' (colloq)." Alice couldn't remember all the words listed.

"It means colloquialism. The project had another name, a scientific title, the name escapes me, but Sleeping Beauty was coined when Dr Grossmith likened you to the fairy tale, appropriate seeing how you turned out."

Amelia lied about not knowing the project's name, but the title involved impersonal terms such as specimen, biological material, properties. Cold, unfriendly terms she would never apply to a warm and sweet individual like Alice.

"Patrick suggested we find my ancestors."

"We'll do it after lunch. It's a lot of fun, though records as far back as you will be sparse, I imagine."

"What if we don't find anyone? I don't even know who I am."

"Maybe it will give you a nudge."

In Alice's room, Amelia woke up the registry, but Alice sat on the bed, unwilling to look in case she saw an image that would upset her.

Amelia turned to her. "Give me a name."

"Robert Redford."

Amelia repeated the name, and a grainy image appeared.

"Wow! Is he your ancestor? He's gorgeous!"

"No, he's a celebrity," she grinned at Amelia's look of surprise.

"A celebrity? Not many of those around, so why did you say his name?"

"Because it frightens me to see Alexis Langley, and it frightens me to see Alice Watkins. If she even exists."

"Do you want me to stop?"

Alice wavered. "I'm not sure."

"Ok, let's try Alexis Langley, 2123."

The registry responded immediately.

Alexis Langley would have been twenty-five then. From where she sat, Alice saw the image appear. Amelia moved aside and invited Alice to get a better look.

"Here you are."

Curiosity moved Alice from the bed. The woman on the registry was younger than she, her hair shorter, and she wore a blue check blouse with a sweater tied over her shoulders. She was clad in white slacks and sandals.

The blue sky hinted of summer, and the woman, standing on old, worn steps, smiled downwards towards the camera. She seemed happy.

"Why didn't Dr Grossmith show me this?"

"He showed you your reflection in the image definer, didn't he?"

Alice was silent.

"It was this person…?"

Alice's expression was answer enough.

"You?" Amelia pointed out gently.

Alice took stock of the young red-headed woman. It was her, or at least, someone who looked the same as she did now.

"Ask about Martin Watkins."

Amelia obliged. "Martin Watkins."

And another image appeared. An older man, around fifty, Alice guessed, an older version of Steven.

"He looks like my son."

Amelia grimaced and flicked at the registry to put it to sleep.

"Maybe this wasn't such a good idea."

Alice disagreed.

"For a moment, Amelia, I thought I might piece things together. It's gone now, but…I'm glad we did this."

As usual, Alice wanted to nap in the afternoon. Amelia promised to catch up for breakfast the next morning to hear the news from the concert and offering to return if

Alice needed help with make-up.

Alone in her stateroom, Alice sifted through the events of the day, and even though she felt sleepy, her nanna nap evaded her. Her gaze kept wandering to the registry. Inside lay images of people from her past, Alexis Langley's past and possibly, even people who knew Alice Watkins, but all of them, Alice's and Alexis's family, would be long gone now. She no longer wanted the registry in here, a machine that contained pictures of dead people and worse, the image of her in a glass coffin.

CHAPTER TWENTY-THREE _

Alice wanted to dress nicely for the concert, but only owning dull grey shifts and slacks made her envy the deep maroon of Amelia's uniform even more. She longed for the day when she could have more variety in her wardrobe, a lack that never bothered her in her other life. Amelia had her off-duty clothes with her but being more endowed in the bosom area than Alice, her clothes weren't of any help, only offering a few accessories and a small jacket for Alice to use. She'd borrowed one or two pieces of jewellery from Amelia but, never having developed fashion sense, took a chance on what might look nice, deciding on green earrings and a green necklace and leaving off the gold belt. Although she feared she might overdo the makeup, she applied it sparingly as Amelia had shown her, and the subtle results were rather pleasing.

It was only after dressing she noticed the green shift Kelly gave her back on Saturn Station. Green would look nicer than grey. In a second, Alice pulled off the grey shift and replaced it with the green. It was just as plain as the others, but with the gold belt and hemline just above her knee, it was a definite improvement. In a moment of uncharacteristic daring, she discarded the slacks, leaving her legs bare and slipped into Amelia's gold sandals, making a dramatic statement to an ordinary outfit.

Patrick arrived, in uniform, to escort her to the assembly. Alice wondered if she would ever get over his good looks; he seemed more handsome each time she saw him. She invited him into her stateroom, hoping he might be able to shut down the registry. He advised her, no, not possible, but should he arrange for it be covered? She thanked him but told him not to worry. He thought she was alluding to her bad experience earlier, and in part, he was correct. But it wasn't that alone; she didn't want it knowing more about her than she did. The flashing light had taken on a sinister presence in her head, and irrationally, felt it was like an eye, watching her. She found it annoying the damn thing had to stay, but she only had to endure it for a couple more days.

She smiled at him as they left her quarters.

"I'm looking forward to this evening, Patrick. I had a trying day."

He looked down at her, he heard what she said, but any answer fled as he studied her face, upturned to him. *'Green,'* he thought, *'she's wearing green. It matches her eyes.'*

Alice gave him a puzzled smile, expecting him to comment, and realising he might be making her uncomfortable; he quickly composed himself.

"As a senior officer, I must attend these functions,

but thankfully, they are of short duration. I'll confess the concerts are sometimes too long."

"You said I'd enjoy it!"

"I lied. I didn't want you to refuse!"

Patrick always found something amusing to say and was always so kind and attentive, she didn't need to be afraid if he were by her side, but this time, unlike the dinner with Ryan, Patrick and Hennessey, many more people were in attendance. Alice tried not to count them. No tables or seats were available, and everyone stood in two's or three's or moved as individuals from group to group. She held Patrick's arm tight.

"Nervous?" he whispered, leaning a little closer, close enough for her to catch a hint of cologne or aftershave. Ted wore nothing like that; he had a name for men who wore 'perfume'.

"I'm afraid so."

"Well, you said you were nervous before the dinner on the station, and then you sparkled. I expect more of the same."

Alice had a vague recollection she made intelligent conversation after the firewater roll episode but didn't remember a single thing she said and certainly didn't remember sparkling.

Patrick introduced Alice as Dr Langley to a few of the people present, but thankfully, not one of them attempted small talk or questioned her presence on the ship. Principal Ryan stood with Statesman Hennessey, positioned as when she first met them, half-turned to each other and in deep conversation. Patrick drew their attention, and Principal Ryan, unsmiling, bowed to Alice. This time, Hennessey linked his bow to a grin.

"Are you being well looked after, Dr Langley?" Principal Ryan asked, more out of duty, she thought, than interest. He glanced at Patrick as he spoke, but Alice still hadn't learned to read expressions.

"Yes, thank you, Principal Ryan. Statesman Patrick has been kindness itself."

Principal Ryan was a towering figure, and to be honest, he scared her, but he wouldn't intimidate her into forgetting her manners.

"I understand that you are playing the—er," good heavens, she'd forgotten, "flute for us this evening."

"Oboe, Dr Langley," he corrected her, "and I apologise in advance; I am an amateur. There are many more accomplished musicians than I onboard, but they are mainly strings; we have only one pianist of merit who accompanies each performer. I hope you enjoy the concert." His gaze lingered for a moment before his attention turned to the other officers who joined the party.

Alice suspected the crew members were accustomed to Principal Ryan's dismissive manner. When his contribution to the conversation ended, he moved on. She resolved not to take it as a personal slight.

"Don't mind him," Hennessey said under his breath when Principal Ryan was out of earshot. "He hates performing and only does it because he's the only other instrumentalist apart from strings and piano and someone more important than him found out he can play. Ryan attends these functions under sufferance. He would rather be somewhere, anywhere in space than here. His whole life is out there." Hennessey made a vague gesture toward the viewport.

"Why doesn't he just say 'no' to performing?" From a shy person's perspective, Alice saw no point in putting yourself through such an ordeal.

"He can't," Patrick said. "Ryan can be brusque in his manner, but he's not one to discourage morale. We're in space for extended periods, and the recitals are an outlet for musical talent on board. Our guests requested a final performance tonight, and he had no choice but to agree. He started these soirees for the officers and crew, so he has to take part, regardless of how he feels although being the star attraction wasn't on the agenda." The two officers grinned at each other. "Now he's stuck with it."

Alice was fearful Principal Ryan would overhear, "We shouldn't talk about him."

"I only said he didn't like performing. That's common knowledge," Hennessey snorted. "Trust Patrick to fill in the gaps."

Alice thought the assembly served no other purpose than as a get-together with speeches made by grand people in uniform. Still, as she'd never attended a gathering like this before, she had no criteria by which to judge. It wasn't the same as Michelle's barbeques, which were more a free-for-all with kids running in and out and heaps of laughter. She always relegated herself to the kitchen with the washing up to avoid mingling with guests, but here, there didn't appear to be a kitchen. Patrick would like Michelle's barbeques, she thought, he'd be right at home.

The stewards moved amongst them with little bits to eat on trays, but Alice couldn't imagine the implications of eating standing up, so she declined, only accepting a sparkling drink in a fancy wide glass without even questioning what it might be. Sweet and cold, it reminded her of lemonade. She loved lemonade and gasped at her first sip, drawing attention from both Patrick and Hennessey. Patrick laughed.

"Have you had this before?"

"Yes! It's lemonade! Michelle keeps a few bottles in the fridge for the kids. They love it!"

So delighted was she with a familiar flavour, Alice paid no attention to what she said. Hennessey cast a look towards Patrick, who merely shrugged, both assuming a stray memory had surfaced.

Although Alice loved lemonade, too much of it irritated her bladder and made her want to pee, not something she wanted to admit to Patrick, so when offered another, she declined, although she would have cheerfully drunk a few more. Maybe back in her stateroom, she could get a steward to bring some, now she knew it existed.

Principal Ryan and his two officers paid close attention to the speakers and at times, murmured between themselves. Patrick kept an eye on Alice to make sure she was handling the evening well. To her surprise, she understood a few of the topics covered.

The man and woman speaking wore mustard colour uniforms. During lulls, Alice asked in a low whisper to Patrick what the uniforms meant.

"They're environmentalists," he whispered back. "This presentation is for them to give an overview of the report they will present to the Tabernacle. They've been studying the effects an artificial environment might have on the human body over an extended period, particularly in the context of space travel. This summary is for the benefit of officers and councilmen who aren't recipients of the initial report."

"Do you say 'Environmentalist' and then their name?"

"No, you address them as 'doctor', same as you," and he returned his attention to the speaker.

Alice looked around the room. She wasn't a doctor; she was a fraud. As Principal Ryan moved away, she reached up to hold Patrick's arm. It comforted her to have him here, and he smiled, holding her hand against the crook of his elbow. Amelia had told her holding his arm this way was permissible as an invited non-military guest. Alice remembered that Steven did the same thing at Michelle's wedding when the crowds became too much for her.

The concert took place in the auditorium following the assembly. The seats, set along tiered semicircular rows between aisles, led down towards a stage, with a piano on a raised platform.

For Alice, the perspective of looking down at performers and not up at them as the audience did at the school concerts appeared skewed to Alice, only having been to the children's plays in the school hall.

While she tried to sort it out, Patrick told her that there were entertainment facilities, a health club and spa on this deck. A spa! Alice thought about chin hairs and the hot stone massage scheduled for Saturday, before all this. She frowned.

"You are a funny thing tonight," Patrick showed her to their seats. "Excited about lemonade one moment and lost in thought the next. Why are you frowning, beautiful lady?" He smoothed his thumb over her hand, making sure no-one saw such an intimate gesture, then smiled and held her gaze with his glorious blue eyes.

"A memory. A memory I'm not supposed to have."

"No-one can tell you not to have a memory, Alice. Memories are yours."

"Not this one," she said as the lights dimmed; the soiree was about to begin.

Alice had seen violins before, but never so many and with such different sizes. Of the ten instruments carried onto the stage, some were so large, the people playing them had to sit down and rest them between their legs. Fascinated, she looked to Patrick for an explanation.

"Cellos," he said.

Cellos, she echoed to herself—she'd heard of cellos.

The lights from above the violinists and cellists cast

a soft glow, and the sound of the strings filled the auditorium, rich and haunting. The simple joy of listening brought to Alice an incredible hush and peace that she wanted to last forever. When the music finished, she realised she had been holding her breath, then joined in with the enthusiastic applause.

"Oh, Patrick!" she cried, and without thinking, grabbed his hand and squeezed, barely able to stay in her seat. "It's so beautiful!"

"Principal Ryan is next," he whispered, leaning towards her and indicating to the side of the stage.

Alice returned her gaze to the proceedings below, her eyes shining with expectation.

A young woman stepped up to the piano and with a bow of acknowledgement to the ripple of applause, seated herself at the piano. Principal Ryan entered from the side, expressionless as usual, unsmiling as usual. With no acknowledgement to the audience, he lifted the instrument to his lips with a nod to the lady at the piano and began to play. Only seconds into the music, Alice again became enraptured with the sound. Music, so new to her. What an incredible experience, a thing of beauty that might have coloured her grey life had she known. This wasn't the radio playing in the background on Saturday mornings; this was real. The sound filled the surrounding air, and Alice closed her eyes as the music transported her. She didn't know if Principal Ryan played well, but the sound soared and resonated right through to her core, leaving her with a sense of weightlessness and purity.

With each movement throughout the concerto playing below, Alice's body swayed gently. Her breathing became deeper or shallower as the mood dictated. At times, in her happiness, she placed a hand on Patrick's knee or his arm, not conscious of her actions. As she applauded, she turned to him, sheer delight making her eyes sparkle. It mattered little to her that Principal Ryan gave only the slightest hint of acknowledgement to the audience before walking from the stage. Alice knew nothing of the technicalities but believed he played beautifully, that the piano player played beautifully and only knew that everything she heard was magical. Agog with anticipation, she waited for the next performance. Again, the hush settled upon her. Spellbound, Patrick decided, as he took a moment to glance across and enjoy her pleasure in an event that, for him, was routinely dull and boring.

The pianist remained onstage after Principal Ryan left. The young woman played, but it was not the gentle music of the strings or the different cascades, and mood changes and tempo heard with Principal Ryan. This music clattered along like a steam train, so fast it confused Alice and jangled around her head. Keys were banged and played with such harshness, Alice couldn't take her eyes off the pianist. She didn't like it. When it was over, she forgot her manners and didn't applaud.

"The Pizzicato Polka. Not to your taste?" Patrick asked, surprised at her sudden change in appreciation and disappointed the spell was broken.

"More like the Bang and Crash Polka," Alice half

turned, pouting and screwing up her face in displeasure, then, as she turned back to the stage, startled him by adding, "Some people don't get Strauss."

He touched her arm, and from over her shoulder, she threw him a quizzical smile.

"I thought you didn't know anything about music?"

"I don't," she shot back, her voice bright, grinning again as the strings re-entered, her odd comment of a moment ago, forgotten.

And there she was, lost in the music, back under its spell, even laughing with pleasure at the end of the piece and forgiving the pianist for her rendition of the Pizzicato Polka. Patrick knew Councilman Ellis, the pianist, and knew she always finished a concert with a ballad composed by a more modern composer. In this, the girl redeemed herself to Alice, who loved the softness and emotion and the further surprise of her singing, in the loveliest of voices, a sweet and pretty melody which settled Alice back into her dreamy state.

Later, as the last performer left the stage, Alice clasped her hands together. "I loved it. *I loved it!*" the pure joy on her face making Patrick laugh, but she was too caught up in the moment to see herself as amusing.

"I've never been to a real concert. I loved it!" then, controlling her excitement, added, "Thank you, Patrick."

"I hoped you would," he said, drawing her to her feet. "We have these events from time to time. Sometimes, they're open to the whole crew and are quite popular, less of the highbrow stuff. Principal Ryan doesn't play at those."

"Well," she said, still experiencing a little of the euphoria. "I thought he played well."

"He does. But it's a talent he doesn't share too often."

"Perhaps he lacks confidence."

"*Confidence?* Principal Ryan?" Patrick burst into laughter. Alice looked on, surprised, not sure how such a comment engendered such mirth.

"Will you tell him," Patrick said after a moment, still laughing as they left the auditorium, "or shall I?"

CHAPTER TWENTY-FOUR _

"Would you care to go to the officer's observation lounge?" Patrick wasn't ready for the evening to end. Alice, still feeling the effects of the concert, was of a like mind.

"Oh, yes!" then, deciding she sounded too eager, modified her tone. "The view is amazing there."

For a while, they sat in silence. The observation lounge, only one deck above the auditorium, was deserted. Alice found it soothing, sitting here with Patrick, looking out into space, music in her head.

Patrick spoke first.

"We only have one more full day before we arrive in space dock."

She didn't look directly at him but peeped with her peripheral vision. He seemed relaxed, long legs straight out and crossed at the ankles, his left arm over the back of the seat behind her and his other arm stretched out over the seat the other side, his jacket undone.

"What does that mean?" She wasn't sure how this might play out but felt a nagging sense of foreboding.

Patrick had become her friend. She parted company with Kelly and Dr Grossmith and Principal Hardy and now, maybe Patrick too.

"It means I may not see you again before we dock."

"What about when we get back home?"

"Well," he straightened up with a grin and twisted round to face her. He hoped she might say that.

"If you wish, I'll come to see you when you're settled. I have to stay on board for a while to supervise the engine and Gravidarum refit."

"Settled where?"

"I don't know yet. Principal Hardy is making those arrangements."

"And didn't involve me?" she exclaimed. "What am I? Six years old? He told me I would be going to the Tabernacle."

"You *are* going to the Tabernacle, Alice, but you won't stay there forever." He hesitated. "You believe they're taking away your right to choose for yourself?"

"Don't you?"

Possibly, he thought. "Ok, if you had the choice, where would you go?"

Alice didn't have a clue. Earth was all new to her now, so she had no answer.

"Precisely, but you will first go to Principal Katya. She has a conference with Principal Ryan, Principal Hardy and Dr Grossmith scheduled for tomorrow. You are far too special to leave to your own devices."

Even after centuries, everyone still knew better than

she did.

"Wherever you are staying when we get home," Patrick promised. "I will visit. There are some amazing places and wonderful sights, and I'd love to show you around."

"I want you to visit, Patrick. I'll be disappointed if you don't, but aren't you going away on this ship again?"

"Not for a few months. I come and go while we're in dock, so I can see you often, wherever you are."

She nodded without speaking. She didn't want Patrick going anywhere. He made her feel safe, like when Kelly tucked her into bed during those first few weeks when she wasn't ready to face an unfamiliar world alone.

Later, Patrick took her back to her stateroom, filling her head with anecdotes of Hennessey and Ryan and other crew members. He was so funny and charming and likeable; she suspected he got along with everyone. And he's handsome, she reminded herself. Can't forget, handsome.

When they reached the portal, he released the portal control without asking and stepped through with her. Once inside, he pulled her close. She heard his heart beating as her head rested on his chest. She had expected this and feared it.

Placing his hands on her shoulders, he set her back from him and ever so gently cupped her face in his hands before lightly placing his mouth against hers. As their lips touched, she resisted an old, inbred urge to pull away. Instead, she kept her face still, breathing in the scent of him, trying to concentrate on the sensation of his tongue touching the inside of her top lip.

He kissed her eyelids and the tip of her nose before placing his hand behind her head and holding her again to his chest. He smelled wonderful, nothing like Ted's tobacco and sweat stench. She curled her arms around his back and leaned against him, wishing she knew how to respond. Was this how it should be? To be held in the arms of the kindest, the sweetest man she had ever met?

"I'm sorry if I don't get to see you before you leave," he murmured gently, lifting her face and stroking her cheek and looking deep into her eyes. "I'll be on duty from now on, but you can contact me if you need. I hope that's okay."

Not okay, she thought but smiled anyway, no point in making it complicated. She didn't own him. He released her and kissed her gently once more before he left.

Patrick headed straight to the bridge. Principal Ryan, engaged in dialogue with the bridge crew and communication engineers, acknowledged him without even a glance.

"Patrick."

"Ryan," Patrick replied, not bothering to look over to see if whatever they were deliberating on required his involvement. Instead, he gazed out the forward viewport.

After a moment, Ryan joined him, interrupting Patrick's thoughts of Alice.

"I hate those bloody concerts," Principal Ryan ran

his hands through his hair. "I swear they are becoming duller. I'm leaving my oboe at home next time."

"You implemented them, Ryan; you only have yourself to blame. Besides, it wasn't dull."

"It was the same program we did a month ago, Patrick."

"I didn't mean the music, Ryan. Alice was so taken with it; she was a pleasure to watch. Interestingly, she said she knew nothing about music, but I believe she does. She thought you played beautifully."

"In that case, she's right; she doesn't know anything about music. I'm mediocre at best. Why do you call her, Alice?"

"You are too modest, Ryan. Besides, it was the first time she'd heard one of our concerts. She asked me to call her Alice."

"Keep it professional, Patrick," Ryan had nothing else to say on the Dr Langley subject. "We need to modify the senior staff concerts for the next trip if we are to continue using them as entertainment for the crew. At least we won't have to have those goddamn awful assemblies while we're away."

"Shall I make sure any new crew members play something other than violins?" Patrick suggested, even though musicality was not criteria for service on a principality ship.

"Agreed," Ryan turned to leave. "Now I'm off to get some exorcise."

"Exorcise, Ryan? Don't you mean exercise?" Ryan

was a midnight gym junkie.

"I've been playing host to those environmentalists for the past year. Call it whatever you like."

Patrick watched him leave. Rare for Ryan to make a funny.

Back in her quarters, Alice took off her earrings and looked at herself in the image definer. There were changes all the time, in her hair, her skin and tonight, her eyes. She liked her eyes, liked the green, her old ones were brown and dull, but these eyes were wide and alive. She thought how it felt to be in Patrick's arms, his kiss and the light touch of his tongue over the inside of her lip. Ted seldom kissed her, and when he did, she always shrank away, something she knew she almost did this evening. Habit, she supposed, her mother's warnings of triggering hormones must still have an effect, but Ted's kisses disgusted and terrified her, knowing what would follow and naturally, she thought all kisses would be like Ted's.

But Patrick's kiss wasn't disgusting. His kiss was sweet and light and gentle. So why, oh why, didn't she feel anything? Was she so old now, there was no possibility of any hormones getting triggered?

The link sounded. It was from Amelia.

"Well?"

"Well, nothing."

"*Nothing?*"

"He kissed me, that's all." Alice wanted to play down

the situation until she sorted out her feelings about it.

"You have all the luck!"

"It was just a kiss. What did you do?"

"I spent the evening in the dining hall with a couple of off-duty stewards. They were both educators before they retired, so we had a lot in common."

"How does that work? Why aren't they educators still instead of stewards? Seems a backwards step."

"Ask me in the morning. I'll be there bright and early."

As the screen flicked off, Alice stood in a daydream. What a day. She needed sleep but first, a shower. Standing in the gel flow, she let her mind wander to the concert, humming a few of the tunes, then she stopped. Alice Watkins didn't hum, she whistled a little, but she didn't hum. Stepping out of the washer, she leaned close to the image definer; pursing her lips, she blew. Nothing. Alexis Langley's lips did not whistle.

But she remembered that one tune, the one played with all that noisy energy. What was it, pomp om pom...? Alice tried to conjure up the sounds. She woke up the registry, but it was already listening.

Pom pom pomp om. She hummed a few bars, and the music to Pizzicato Polka floated into view; the registry then sounded out a piano rendition.

Satisfied, she walked over to the bed, pulled the green shift over her head and, without waiting to put on her beloved knickers, stepped barefoot through the portal.

The auditorium on the officer's deck was in darkness, and the sensor lights lit her way as she descended towards the podium. The bright downlight appeared when she stepped onto the stage, bathing the piano in a golden glow. A grand piano. Alice circled it reverently. It had been years since she had played a grand. She ran her fingers lightly over its contours before reaching the curve of the well, where she stopped and lifted the lid. Small points of light sparkled where she expected to see hammers and felts, but no matter.

She called softly, "Eeh Aaw," then smiled as the piano made a soft echo in reply. She made her way slowly around to the keyboard and sat down.

The keys were the same as any piano, so she pressed one or two to test the tone, trying to remember the noisy melody. She played a few more keys as a hologram appeared at eye level. The Pizzicato Polka. She peered at the music, struggling to transpose the notes to the keyboard. The result was cacophony.

"Five and five, Alexis. Remember, five times right hand and five times left hand. You are trying to train your brain to at least have some idea of where your fingers need to go. Then put them together. Try again."-Miss Rowan, Piano Teacher of Alexis Langley, aged ten.

So, five times she tried the polka with her right hand, and five times with the left, as she had been taught all those years ago, then put them together. This time, it made sense, but it was difficult to get her fingers moving. Her joints seemed stiff and rusty.

There was a piece she liked; what was it called? She had a hazy recollection; how did it go? Ah! She pom-pom pommed at the piano, and the music appeared. To A Wild Rose. Yes, that's it. She didn't rush this time. Five times on the right hand, five on the left and from somewhere, long-buried, surged forth all she needed to play this much-loved piece she knew so well. This piece was Uncle Martin's favourite. The notes returned so easily; she barely even had to look up at the music that appeared as a hologram above the piano.

Absorbed in her playing, Alice didn't notice the figure standing at the top of the steps. He'd heard the music as he passed by and wondered why Councilman Ellis had stayed so late. Entering the auditorium, he quickly recognised his error but stood for a moment before taking the nearest seat, careful not to disturb or distract her. Pulling his left ankle up comfortably onto his right knee, he placed his left hand over his calf and leaned his elbow on the side of the seat, resting his cheek against the back of his other hand. And listened.

Alice was oblivious to her audience. The piano registry gave her a few more suggestions as she pom pommed her way through, but she was keen to try the polka again, and this time, her hands flew more surely. Although she hadn't touched a piano in centuries, she brought more animation and joy to the piece than Councilman Ellis had done with weeks of practice. A fact not lost on her lone spectator. She sat back, satisfied, and folded her hands in her lap.

As the last few notes of the polka died away, he stood to leave, not needing her to learn he'd been listening to her performance. It would seem, rather than her knowing little of music, she knew a great deal. Still, he hesitated; she only had access to these decks in the company of a senior officer, protocol demanded he should remind her, even if no harm was done. After a moment's deliberation, he walked down the steps towards the podium. Of course, he could speak to her. He was the Principal of this ship.

"Well played."

Alice spun around, her face contorting in surprise and her eyes widening in recognition. She shrunk away, her back against the piano, grateful for its support to stop her sliding to the floor in embarrassment.

"Principal Ryan!"

Seeing him standing in front of her, Alice thought her heart would stop. "I am so sorry. I thought…" But Alice couldn't think. Confusion set in, and with it, the inability to fathom why she was here, not wearing shoes or knickers? She felt weak.

He stepped forward to steady her, but she clung to the piano and only glanced down at his hands, reaching out, ready to catch her if she should fall. Alice had no intention of that happening. She slid her back around the well of the piano.

"I startled you, I'm sorry, Dr Langley, but there is no

need to apologise," he withdrew his offer of support and placed a hand on the piano, hoping a step back may calm her. "The piano is for everyone's enjoyment. I'm surprised to find you here alone, that's all. Statesman Patrick told me you know nothing of music."

Alice was too terrified to respond. Why was he saying these things? What was she doing here?

"I—I don't remember."

"You were playing the piano, Dr Langley." Principal Ryan didn't understand why she should be so frightened. Perhaps a compliment might help. "Most accomplished."

Alice looked at the keys, gleaming in the light, then returned her horrified gaze to Principal Ryan, her hands still gripping the piano behind her, wanting to run and wishing Patrick was here to protect her. She didn't even know how she got here in the first place, but she needed to calm herself. Principal Ryan had been so polite when she choked on the firewater roll; he would forgive her now. She took a deep breath.

"I'm not sure what I'm doing here. Please excuse me, Principal Ryan; I would like to go to my room."

He held out his arm again.

"You're unsteady. Shall I escort you?"

She shook her head vigorously.

"No—no, thank you, I'm fine."

Alice wasn't fine. She backed away until she reached the steps, then turned and fled up the stairs.

Ryan watched her run up the steps, exiting through the foyer at the uppermost level, the sensor lights fading as she departed, but he didn't move even after she was out of sight.

What the hell was all that?

But it wasn't just the exchange that bewildered him. As he spoke to her, he'd suddenly become aware of how small and light she was, how her hair gleamed red and gold in the glow from the downlight, her eyes—incredibly green, fixed on him with fear. When he first entered the auditorium, it was not just her playing, not just her technique, but the emotional depth which had attracted him, but now... He pressed a few keys as his thoughts dwelt upon the last few moments. Then, closing the piano lid, he turned smartly and strode back the way he came, leaving the auditorium in darkness.

CHAPTER TWENTY-FIVE _

Amelia sounded the portal buzzer early the next morning. Alice had only just dressed, not understanding why she felt half-asleep. Amelia had Tyro Drake in tow, laden with half a dozen bound volumes while she brought breakfast on a hovering trolley. It was easy enough to see Amelia had Tyro Drake twisted around her little finger because she needed only to point towards the table. Without a word, he deposited the volumes, looking up to see if she had another command. She shepherded him back through the portal.

"We'll call you if we need you."

Alice watched him leave.

"He seems smitten."

Amelia agreed. "Yes, much like a pet. He is only nineteen and still being educated. Too young for me, but he likes to be useful. What do you think of these?" she held up a volume. "They're transpositions of books from your time. I got them from the library. I thought we could see if they help your memory, but more importantly, I brought…Tah dah!"

"What are they?"

"Cream cheese bagels," Amelia expected Alice to be over-the-moon with excitement, but instead, her expression was somewhat deflating.

"I don't know what a bagel is, Amelia."

"Didn't they have them in your time?"

"Possibly, but I never had one. It looks like a bread roll." Alice picked one up.

"Well, it is but also so much more. Bread roll diminishes it."

"Why did you bring breakfast? We always go to the pasticium?"

"Because today we work, work, work and study, study, study. We've only got today together, and we need to cram a lot in. Hang on…"

Amelia investigated the washer and under the bed.

"What are you searching for?"

"Who, not what. Statesman Patrick. I'm just checking he went back to his own quarters last night."

Strange, Alice thought, a little while ago, she would have blushed and stammered at such a remark, but now, she found it amusing.

"He's not here. I promise you; he left me here alone last night."

"You must need lessons in kissing, Alice," Amelia said through a mouthful of bagel while taking a seat in front of the registry.

Alice sat beside her.

"You might be right," she shrugged, "but I've only

kissed one other man."

Amelia's jaw dropped in astonishment.

"One. Other. Man? Are you telling me the truth?"

Alice nodded. "Yes, as I remember it but, we can't be sure, can we?"

"Shall I ask who?"

"Not if you won't like the answer."

"Someone from the past we don't believe is yours?"

Alice turned down the corners of her mouth and nodded a yes.

As promised, it was a day to study. Even though Alice recognised almost nothing and uncovered little to jog any memories, they pored over the books, mostly written after her time. Jointly declaring the exercise a failure, they consulted the registry, from where Amelia gave her a crash course in Earth's social structure.

Alice learned most couples have one child, two at most and usually within a year or two of each other. Children attend day school from age five but stay with their parents until they turn fifteen. During that time, parents receive assignments befitting of their professions, but both parents must be available to be with the children, that includes military couples, which are rare. At fifteen, the child leaves home and begins aptitudes.

The first two years of aptitudes are on Earth, with introductions to such areas as agriculture, education and medicine. Science subjects follow. Art and music are initially extracurricular but encouraged. The child spends the last year of aptitudes in space, a few months on a space station and a few on a starship. Few opt-out of the space assignment.

"But it does happen that a child has no desire to go into space," Amelia explained, "and if their interests point in a different direction, the arts or music, for example, the Tabernacle will support their preference. Final year aptitudants, like Drake, will spend a year on a principality vessel like this one only if there is a strong interest in the military, coupled with distinguished achievements in their science studies. Assignment to principality ships will increase the length of aptitudes due to the nature of deep space assignments."

She went on to say that when aptitudes finish, university begins. Graduation is at twenty-two for educators and some agriculturists. A science student doesn't graduate until twenty-five, and afterwards, spends a year as an intern. All science graduates must continue to study in their preferred field with one additional option for a further two years.

"We almost never stop learning, Alice. Educators must complete an upgrade block at year five from graduation if they want to teach older children. I can only teach five to nine-year-olds."

"About my level! So, am I right, Amelia, if you are three years from graduation, you are twenty-five?"

"That's right. Five years younger than you, so when you are old and ugly, I will still be young and beautiful!"

Alice pulled a face at her.

"So how do people end up as stewards? Not good at their jobs?"

Amelia told her no, not the case. Everyone may retire at sixty-five, but some apply for continuation in their profession, and generally, that lasts for another five years, though they can reapply. At sixty-five, if an individual wants a different path, their personal circumstances are evaluated, and their aptitude and desires considered.

"Don't they mind being told to retire?"

"No, they love it, those who do. They can do nothing if they wish. We have people, even ex-military, who make clothes, cook in dining halls and pasticiums, work in construction, breed animals. Many once worked on the ships as science officers or communications specialists and enjoy participation in, and are fulfilled by other, Earth-centred activities. And we have agriculturalists, educators and previously planet-based doctors working on starships. But after sixty-five, even if you are continued or reassigned, you can stop whenever you choose."

"I still don't understand Calamities and Loyalties, Amelia. You are all so used to the idea; it seems I should just accept it as normal."

"We don't have a complicated society, Alice. The basis is respect…"

"I would have thought if your society respected other people, you wouldn't need the Calamities."

"I was about to say respect for the laws and tenets.

Our laws and respect for them form the building blocks of the social order we enjoy. Earth's society is peaceful and its laws, fair."

"Tell me about disabled children."

Amelia had never had to justify her society to anyone. She couldn't remember a time when she had not been filled with gratitude for her world and all it offered. Her childhood had been idyllic, free from care and her aptitude years, inspired by tutors who nurtured and instilled in her a love of teaching. Her days at university were happy, full of laughter and friendship, mingled with the certainty she would receive every support she required to achieve her goals and live a happy, productive life. A far cry, she was sure, from the uncertainties of a life lived by the youth of four centuries earlier.

"We haven't any," she said. "None born with defects, anyway. Naturally, disabilities can happen through illness or accident, but that's a different matter altogether. Doctors monitor a pregnancy for any sign of problems. If an abnormality is detected, one that can't be rectified either before or shortly after birth, the doctor will terminate the pregnancy. It seldom happens."

Alice had seen children and adults strapped in wheelchairs, not knowing what was going on around them, never feeding themselves, unable to speak. Would it have been better for them if they hadn't been born? Marie, the butcher's daughter, had Down syndrome, and Alice knew the little girl from birth, about fourteen now but a happier, friendlier child you couldn't wish to meet. She helped Dan in the shop, attended the local school, and her presence made the world a better place, even if Alice had trouble understanding anything she said.

"You're lost in thought," Amelia took Alice's hand, fearful her comments had upset her friend.

"I knew some disabled people,' Alice stated. "They never hurt anyone."

Amelia smiled and inclined her head to say she understood. Soon Alice would see society for herself, and it would fall into place. She couldn't deny the sense of relief when Alice moved away from the subject of terminations.

"Tell me more about why people get sent to the Calamities?"

"I'll tell you about the scale. It leads on to the answer to your question. We have a scale for marriage. For example, a man from Principality 14, perhaps a scientist, gets assigned to a starship where he meets me, even though educators aren't assigned to starships. If we want to marry, the Tabernacle will apply the scale."

"What would happen?"

"Rejection. 14 and 49 where I'm from, can't marry."

"Why not?"

"Because our ethnic origins are too dissimilar. It would be the first order of rejection."

"We had heaps of mixed marriages in my time. What happened to their descendants?"

"The plague diminished every race, Alice. By the fourth decade of the twenty-second century, around the time the A'khet started to help us rebuild, many people, as their DNA identified them with a specific racial group, trickled back to their original homelands. For many, the historical reasons their ancestors left no longer existed, and the desire to restore their culture and heritage became paramount. With the assistance of the A'khet and the provision of Substance, which Statesman Patrick told you about, we built shuttles that travelled at greater speeds than conventional means. It meant connections were established between the expanding civilisations."

"At a speed of light?"

"No, that came later. In a short time, the trickle back to individual homelands became a full-on flow and marriages between races were a far less common occurrence. The world never became the all-encompassing, loving, multicultural melting pot early social analysts dreamed about, and society came to appreciate that joining two races or cultures was self-defeating and only gave rise to division. With the memory of the plague and its devastation still raw, people of that time became keen to preserve their individual cultures and purity of race, lest they lose it for all time. The government implemented the scale, not to restrict interracial marriage but to preserve cultural dignity and diversity."

Amelia's explanation stunned Alice. "What are the other orders?"

"Skin colour is an absolute," Amelia explained. "The Tabernacle has criteria of the ethnic or racial origin applied to each principality."

"I took a class on phylogeny at university, based on

cultural phenomena," Alice said suddenly, "I should have paid more attention."

"Pardon?" Amelia's voice was shocked to a squeak.

"I didn't say anything," but in truth, Alice felt the moment of absence.

"You said you took a class at university…"

"I don't think so, Amelia. I didn't go to university."

"I thought—I'm sorry Alice, I'm sure you said something…unexpected."

Amelia was her friend, this might happen again, so it was only fair to tell her.

"I do from time to time, Amelia. I never remember what I say. I'm sorry."

"Okay, we'll just carry on." But Alice's words rock Amelia to the core. She had come to know Alice as a friend as well as a student, and what she said was indeed unexpected. She took a deep breath and took up the lesson again.

"These criteria are used in assessing a marriage application. But even choosing someone from your native principality is no guarantee of approval. Even then, the scale is applied. For example, an artist can't marry a scientist. An artist can only marry another artist or someone in an Earth-based occupation."

"Why?"

"Why an artist and a scientist or artist and artist?"

"Both."

"Because they're polar opposites. He's at home, painting, composing, cooking, or whatever branch of art he's an expert in, and she's on a starship or an installation. Even if she isn't military, it's almost certain she will be off-world part of the time. Artists can hang out together wherever they are."

"What if you fall in love and marry regardless of the law? Can 'they', and I don't know who 'they' are, stop you?"

" 'They' are the Tabernacle, and no, they won't stop you, but if you choose not to live loyally to society, then you go to the Calamities. And you can't have children. As a married couple, you still get accommodation assigned according to your requirements."

"They give you a house, but they don't turn off your chip so that you can have a family?"

"That's right. But if it is a male-to-male relationship or female to female, why does it matter? A same-sex couple can't procreate."

"It sounds harsh."

"You need to live in our society to understand it, Alice. I've only given you an overview. You'll find it simpler once you understand the workings of government. My view is it gives us a solid foundation. If two people choose not to conform, the Calamities are a way they can live their lives away from normal people."

Alice found this problematic. *Normal people?* Everyone here was so genuine and kind. She remembered a word Ted liked to use. Bigots. Were they bigots? She thought of Patrick's kindness and Amelia, so gentle and caring, how could either of them have such calm acceptance of these distinctions?

"Are the Calamities like a prison? Dr Grossmith said the people there had rights and privileges."

"They do, Alice; they're the same as everyone. We're not barbarians! But where a loyal couple will often, though not always, be assigned together until they start a family, people who live in the Calamities are not assigned alongside their partner. They can travel on permit outside the Calamities, but it must be alone. They can go anywhere inside the Calamities they like with their partner and can visit other Calamities but must travel singly and meet up at their destination."

"Why not travel together? What could happen?"

"How they've chosen to live is not acceptable in society, Alice. If they commit to those choices, they must accept the consequences. Didn't you have laws?"

"Yes, but not about loving each other. Mainly about criminals, you know, murdering and stealing and things like that."

Amelia knew Alice found these ideas complex.

"Consider your body Alice, your anatomy. It's designed for sexual congress with a male. Do you agree?"

"I suppose."

"How would two women achieve this congress?"

"I'm not sure."

"What about two males?"

Alice had no comment.

"Heterosexual sex is both recreational and an expression of love, Alice, but at least once, the expected outcome of married intercourse is conception. Can two females achieve this?"

"Not on their own."

"What do you mean, not on their own?"

"They could get a man to, you know, do what he has to do, so one of the women has a baby, and the two men could get a woman, I suppose." Alice was out of her depth, but she didn't like what Amelia was saying.

"So, two women in a relationship would still need a man to procreate?"

"Yes."

"Does that sound tidy? Does it make their relationship normal?"

Amelia smiled and patted Alice's arm.

"You might not see it now, but the world is very tolerant. The conflict of your time is a thing of the distant past."

The link distracted them, and Amelia answered. It was Patrick.

"Educator Sebel."

"Statesman Patrick."

"Is Dr Langley with you?"

"She is."

Alice peered over Amelia's shoulder and smiled. Amelia moved to the side, winking at Alice as soon as she had her back to Patrick.

"We arrive in space dock early tomorrow. We'll deliver you to Principal Katya at the Tabernacle. Alice, I know Principal Katya well, and she is looking forward to receiving you."

"Delivered? Receiving?" Alice echoed, not sure about his choice of words.

"Yes, and as you will be in the Tabernacle, I'll see you within the week."

Arrangements neatly made, it would seem.

"Thank you, Statesman. I'll look forward to seeing you."

When he'd gone, Alice turned to Amelia.

"I'm pleased about this, aren't I, Amelia? This Principal Katya and the Tabernacle?"

"You should be. I've never met Principal Katya, but I hear she is a delight."

"That's what Patrick says but being delivered and received, like a parcel. He might have chosen his words a little better."

Amelia hugged Alice. So far, today's lessons had proven to be a little disquieting, and Amelia wanted to reassure Alice she could ask her anything she wished.

"They're trying to do the right thing by you, Alice. Don't read anything into what Patrick said. They do know best."

Alice didn't reply. In a society where protocols and manners were so important, it wouldn't have hurt them to include her in the discussion.

CHAPTER TWENTY-SIX _

It ended up as the longest day of tuition Alice ever had, far longer than any she remembered from her schooldays. Alice listened and questioned and doubted and re-examined and hoped she'd remember it all.

"Can we go for a walk, Amelia?" she begged eventually, her bottom numb from sitting.

"No, get up and make coffee; that'll get your circulation going. Drake will be here in a moment with food."

"We always seem to be eating. Doesn't Tyro Drake have a job," Alice stood and rubbed the base of her spine, "other than to obey your every command?"

"I can distract him from time to time," Amelia gave a vague wave. "He's going back to Earth to university to study cosmology."

Alice sat the coffees in front of them as Tyro Drake arrived. She watched with amusement at a little secret giggling between him and Amelia and, as he left, noted he neither bowed nor addressed Amelia by title. She ignored

Alice's sideways grin as she turned her attention to the registry, making it clear that today was not the day to discuss her relationship with Tyro Drake.

"Back to work. Eat if you want, but we've still got a few hours to go."

Alice believed she learned more in that one day than in ten years of formal education. Amelia's knowledge and energy turned school into a lot of fun.

Eventually, the subject of music came up; Alice had waited all day for the right moment to tell Amelia about the events of the previous night.

"Amelia, can I tell you something—something strange that happened?"

"There's a lot about you that's strange, sweetie. I doubt it'll surprise me."

"Remember Patrick took me to the concert last night?"

"Yes, was it wonderful? I forgot to ask about that. I was more interested in the Patrick kissy bits part."

"Yes, amazing! But after I got ready for bed, a tune kept going around in my head. I don't know many tunes, but they played this one at the concert."

"What happened?"

"Somehow, and I wasn't even aware of it happening, after showering, I got dressed again and went back to the auditorium and played the piano. I didn't even put my shoes on. Apparently, I played well, but I don't remember any of it."

"None of it?"

Alice shook her head. "No, well, kind of, but it's out of reach. A shadow. More an echo. I keep trying to glimpse it, but—it's gone."

"If you can't remember, how do you know you played and played well?"

"Principal Ryan came into the auditorium. He told me."

"Principal *Ryan?*"

Alice nodded, reminded of her fear at being caught out, doing something she didn't recall.

"He said he heard me playing, but I only remember being startled and seeing him standing there and thinking he was cross."

"Cross?"

"Yes, angry, but he wasn't angry, at least I don't think so, but I didn't know what to say. I got nervous and embarrassed and made as polite a getaway as possible."

"Where's that music now?" Amelia asked.

"Gone mostly, just a feeling, a sense. Sometimes, I can't decide if I am Alice Watkins pretending to be Alexis Langley or Alexis Langley hiding somewhere inside Alice Watkins."

"Perhaps, for now, you need to be both until you recover your true memories. One day, the real you will emerge."

"What if I emerge as Alice Watkins?"

"Can Alice Watkins play the piano?"

"No."

"Then I doubt that ultimately it will be Alice

Watkins." Amelia made a legitimate point.

"Anyway, no matter, I like whoever you are!"

Later, when Amelia left for whatever tryst she'd set up with Tyro Drake, Alice flopped face down on the bed, consumed by lack of sleep from the night before and the workout her brain received that day. Closing her eyes, she planned only on dozing, but sleep overwhelmed her. She woke with a start a considerable time later. Night mode was running, and Alice shifted her position to look at the viewport without moving from the bed, watching the grey rock passing underneath. The rock displayed none of the glory it did when viewed from Earth. It didn't shine yellow, just looked like a chunk of bright clay. The moon, she figured but didn't get up to look.

Principal Ryan was in his quarters, still deliberating on the incident involving Dr Langley in the auditorium. He put in a link to Principal Hardy.

"Hardy."

"Ryan. How are things with our Dr Langley? No problems, I hope. Are you keeping her entertained?"

"Patrick seems adequate for the task. Were you aware she plays the piano?"

Principal Hardy's surprise was genuine.

"No, I wasn't aware."

"Well, she does. She plays well."

"Alice isn't one to make a display. How did you find

out?"

"Patrick brought her up to one of the "sleep-inducing" crew recitals, then later, I observed her playing the piano in the auditorium."

"And you say she played well?"

"Yes, very well."

"Thank you for telling me, Ryan. She arrives at the Tabernacle tomorrow. It'll be interesting to see what transpires there."

"It wasn't the playing that struck me as the extraordinary part, Hardy; it was her confusion as to why she was there. She didn't believe me when I told her. She told Patrick earlier she knew nothing about music but then made an observation during the recital which, he claims, refuted that."

"Is it only Patrick who escorts Alice?"

"Alice? That's what Patrick calls Dr Langley."

"Is that so?" Hardy wasn't pleased to learn of Patrick straying from protocol. "We call her Alice, Alexis, without the 'x'. She dislikes being referred to as Dr Langley, and although it's possible she asked Patrick to use her preferred name, I have concerns about him not addressing her formally in company. His conduct is professional, I trust?"

"I assume so; you were the one who suggested him as the best person to put her at ease."

"I'm thinking about his reputation."

"Which reputation? Outstanding officer? Gifted engineer?"

"The other reputation."

"It's not my business, Hardy."

"I'm not suggesting it is, but he is under your command, and she is fragile. Take notes and step in if need be."

Principal Hardy took the slight movement of Ryan's shoulders as a non-committal shrug.

"I thought the piano incident would be of interest. Anything else, well, Ryan out."

As the link ended, Hardy twisted one end of his moustache, deep in thought. Perhaps he should have listened to Grossmith's warning about Patrick, although it was inconceivable to him that Alice might have reached a stage where her sexuality had emerged. She showed no signs of it on Saturn Station, never even noticing the half-dozen or so councilmen who always arranged their mealtimes to coincide with hers.

When Alice woke again, her room was still in darkness. She looked up to the top of her bed to check night mode. Still two hours before daytime. She had been asleep for ten hours or more and felt crumpled and washed out. She got up to look out of the window. The moon hung in its proper place, far from Earth, looking comfortably bright and familiar.

Alice showered and brushed her hair, then pulled on yet another grey shift and grey knickers before slipping into her sandals and Amelia's jacket before making her way to the guest deck observation lounge. The environmentalists from the assembly were there, standing with their backs to her, taking in the view in complete silence.

Alice couldn't feel movement from the ship, but there was plenty of action in space outside, small shuttles buzzed about, and even smaller vehicles followed in their wake.

Space dock. This mighty ship had slipped noiselessly into its berth above the world while she slept. Beyond the busy vessels hung a world, blue and green, haloed in gold.

Unprepared for the beauty of the planet below, Alice took a few steps forward, disturbing the environmentalists, one of whom turned.

"Magnificent," was all he said and didn't wait for Alice to reply before returning to marvel at the scene.

There was nothing to say. Alice held her breath, her joy at returning and awe at the splendour of her homeworld blowing around in her head like leaves in the wind. Only part of the Earth was visible, much of it covered in white clouds. Below those swirling mists, she caught glimpses of continents and geographical features she couldn't name. Here, on the observation deck of a starship, goodness knows how far above the Earth and so many centuries into the future, she felt comfortingly close to home.

Alice blew out her breath. Magnificent? She disagreed. One could describe the Significator as "magnificent", but this…this wondrous sight was beyond the limits of common adjectives, even beyond the beauty and majesty of Saturn.

Amelia found her much later in the same spot, still

captivated.

"Now, how did I know you would be here?" she placed her arm over Alice's shoulder and joined her in admiring their world.

"The moon's behind us, so I supposed Earth would be in front."

"Very logical, but we need to get you packed. The shuttle is leaving soon."

"Leaving?" Alice echoed. Standing here, looking at Earth, she had forgotten that her time on the ship was at an end. There was only ever time to get used to somewhere and make friends, and then she got moved on, only to start the process over again, pushed from pillar to post.

"Yes. We're leaving."

Alice followed Amelia back to her quarters and let her help put the few borrowed possessions in a bag. At the shuttle portal, Tyro Drake passed their bags to the pilot and waited for the signal to board.

"Alice!"

They all turned. Patrick was slowing from a run to a fast walk. He nodded to Drake and Amelia without using their names or titles and then, defying protocols, took Alice's hand and held it gently, just for an instant. Drake shot a look at Amelia, who, trying to stifle her own smile, engaged Tyro Drake in distracting small talk.

"I couldn't let you go without seeing you, Alice. I'm on my way back to engineering, so I took a detour." Patrick lowered his voice, throwing a meaningful glance at Drake and Amelia to encourage them to turn away. Alice blushed a little at the public display of affection and was thankful Amelia had somehow manoeuvred Drake to turn his back to them. She smiled but only managed to summon up a no-nonsense response.

"Then, off you go. I'm not going to keep you from your work."

"Are you happy I came to wave you goodbye?" he treated her to his devastating smile.

"Yes, I am," she gave him a small, shy smile of her own. So much for no-nonsense.

Onboard the shuttle, Amelia stilled her tongue. But not for long.

" 'Off you go? I'm not going to keep you from your work?' " Amelia's eyes were wide with disbelief. "You sound like his mother! Alice, he's gorgeous! What! have you got heaps of others in line?"

Tyro Drake was listening, but Alice knew he was pretending he wasn't.

"What was I supposed to say? He breached a few protocols, not least the one of him even being here."

"He knows what he's doing. No-one will tell on him; they all love him; besides, after Principal Ryan, he's the chief. Anyway," Amelia nudged her, "Were you pleased to see him?"

"Of course."

Alice *had* been pleased to see Patrick. She'd hoped she wouldn't have had to leave without seeing him, but when he arrived, felt awkward and exposed with his show of affection. She hadn't yet learned how to respond to him and just didn't want it so public.

But the Earth proved a perfect diversion. Alice watched as it became larger and larger until it swallowed the entire front viewport. Then larger still until it surrounded them. First, a particle followed by a dot, then a blob, headed toward that huge world.

Amelia had seen all this before, and although she glanced up on occasions, she and Tyro Drake were involved in deep conversation. Alice was too busy with the view to join in and not sure she would be welcome anyway. As the shuttle flew lower, Alice made out fields and farms and an impressive building, white and gold and gleaming. The shuttle came to rest on a lawned area, and the pilot released the door.

For the second time that morning, Alice's first sight of Earth took her breath away. A broad lake opened out before her, clear as glass and reflecting the blue from the sky. Willow trees dipped their branches into the water, sending ripples to a sculpted fountain, with cherubs facing south, east, north and west, and shining white in the morning sun. There were separate, smaller fountains with ducks bobbing up and down. Ducks!! Oh, my goodness, ducks! Immaculate lawns surrounded the lake, and the garden beds held tall flowers which nodded in the breeze. At the far end stood a white summerhouse. To Alice, it was a vision of heaven.

Amelia stood beside her. "Beautiful, isn't it?"

Alice couldn't speak, only moved her head slowly from side-to-side, then she realised her mouth was hanging open in wonderment.

"Well, turn around," Amelia took her hand.

Alice obeyed. She'd seen the Tabernacle as they flew over, but from the ground, she could gaze on it in all its glory. The wide pavilion overlooked the lawns, and broad, sweeping steps extended along the entire width. At intervals, slim, square columns, covered in a blaze of many-coloured bougainvillaea in full bloom, stood like sentries. Above the pavilion, the dome, brilliant and golden in the sunlight, rose to proclaim its importance.

"It's a palace!"

"Well, I suppose the Tabernacle is like a palace, although we no longer have those. This is where our main seat of government resides."

"I'm spending today with my mouth open, Amelia. First, the view of Earth from the ship, then this. Where will it all end?"

"Not until you experience everything Earth offers, Alice. Now, the pilot is waiting for me, but I'll check on you tomorrow. When you're settled, we'll arrange a visit. I'm your new best friend; have I told you that?"

"No, but I'm relieved to hear it."

The two new best friends embraced, and Amelia climbed into the shuttle with a wave, on her way to her principality, Principality 49. France, in Alice's time. Alice didn't have a principality; she only had what and who was in the here and now. And for now, she had the beautiful lake, where the air smelled of flowers and freshness, and the Tabernacle, covered in its cascade of purples and pinks.

As she gazed in admiration at the beautiful palace-like building and the perfectly manicured gardens, she heard a familiar sound coming from the lake, the blessed sound of a quacking duck.

CHAPTER TWENTY-SEVEN _

Its beauty aside, the Tabernacle was the grandest and most imposing building Alice had ever seen. Decisions made within its walls affected the lives of every citizen of Earth; where they should live, whom they could marry, if they should have children, where in space they might be assigned. Almost every aspect of how this society functioned had its foundation in this place.

She didn't know what awaited her here; she was still learning how to communicate with the people she met and overcome her feelings of inadequacy, and faced with the Tabernacle's grandeur, some of her confidence was in danger of slipping away. It was as though her life was playing out as a character in a book, not knowing what happens next until someone turns the page.

A man and a woman appeared on the Tabernacle steps. They spoke briefly, and the man bowed, remaining on the steps while the woman hurried across the lawn towards Alice, waving when she was close enough to be sure Alice had seen her.

Principal Katya. Alice recognised her from the image on the registry. It would appear the age sixty-five retiring rule didn't apply to Principal Katya, not even with extensions. Principal Katya was around seventy-five, dressed in a plain, black ankle-length shift. With short, white hair floating in little wisps around an impish heart-shaped face, her eyes were little half-moons, which curled down as her mouth wrinkled in a smile of welcome. She reached Alice and clasped both her hands, only slightly breathless from the exertion of hurrying.

"Welcome, welcome, Dr Langley, I am Principal Katya, and we were waiting for you, my adviser and I. Watching and waiting then foolishly taking our eyes from the lake so we did not see the shuttle arrive a few minutes early. Oh, how you caught us out! We thought to be here as you arrived. What little we knew!" She turned and took Alice's arm, giving Alice no opportunity to reply or greet her in return.

"Now, to the Tabernacle!"

Principal Katya, a little shorter than Alice and despite a noticeable limp, took off in the same hurry she had been to greet Alice. Alice had to tilt slightly to the side to accommodate the difference in their heights. Principal Katya spoke with an accent, Alice guessed, after meeting different cultures on Saturn Station and in consulting maps, was Northern European—Principality 7 or 8.

"Now, I will not call you 'Dr Langley'. It is too fussy. Dr Grossmith tells me your name is pronounced as Alice, and we do not use the 'x'. Am I correct?"

Alice smiled, sending silent thanks to Dr Grossmith and Kelly for helping her out with this. It would feel awkward at this early stage to explain why she preferred Alice to Alexis.

"Yes, Principal Katya, that's right."

"And Dr Grossmith also tells me your memories are confused, and you believe you are someone else?"

"Oh, well, yes, Principal Katya, I suppose I do." So much for Principal Katya not knowing about the name issue.

"Then you are to have a *vacation*! That is the order of the day! We will not be pestering you to remember anything at all. Do you hear me now, young Alice? You will remember whatever you want, or you will remember nothing at all!"

A vacation! A holiday? Alice never took holidays. Mother thought them a waste of time. Ted thought…well, he thought like mother, so Alice's delight was genuine.

"I would love to, Principal Katya, but I don't know where to go for a vacation."

"*Here,* my dear girl. You will vacation here! With me! It will be splendid!" Principal Katya laughed and rubbed Alice's hand.

Alice laughed too; she was bowled over! A holiday! In a Palace with the Principal of the World. Even her mother would have approved! Principal Katya responded to Alice's delight by squeezing her arm and giving her a beaming smile.

As they reached the building, Principal Katya

stopped and invited the tall, massively built and impeccably dressed man with a goatee beard to step forward.

"Dr Langley, this is Statesman Mellor. He is my most senior adviser and will fill my shoes after I die in my bed."

What? Alice couldn't believe her ears.

Statesman Mellor, unperturbed by the comment, just dipped his head in acknowledgement. Then Alice saw the twinkle in Principal Katya's eye; it would seem the Principal of the World didn't take herself too seriously.

Statesman Mellor then bowed to Alice,

"Dr Langley."

Principal Katya's morbid humour seemed not to have ruffled him, and Alice liked him on sight.

"Statesman Mellor, Dr Langley prefers Alice, don't you, Alice?" Principal Katya didn't pause for any confirmation from Alice before moving on, "And that is how we will address her in private. In official company, observe protocols," then with a wave of her hand to signify the introduction was over, she led Alice up the steps. Statesman Mellor winked at Alice behind Principal Katya's back. Alice smiled at him.

"I saw that Statesman," Principal Katya declared, without stopping. "Winking is not protocol." Statesman Mellor grinned, and together, he and Alice followed Principal Katya into the building.

Furnished with grandeur and opulence from end to end, the vast hall had enormous arches that propped up the ceiling along its length. Against every wall, proper mirrors with frames were placed in such a manner, a person, standing before any one of them, would see countless echoes of their image, reflecting into eternity. Throughout the hall, massive doors, each thrown wide and hewn of real wood and polished to a brilliant sheen, heralded an entrance to other, vast areas. Accustomed to technology in recent months, Alice assumed on Earth ordinary doors would be deemed cumbersome and redundant, so to see such beautiful carving was heartening. The large central doors were the only ones closed, and a red and grey banner hung above.

The furniture, an eclectic mixture of antiques, coexisted comfortably and tastefully alongside modern tables and sofas. The floor, all wood and polished to the same high sheen as the doors, was garnished with large rugs, cleverly scattered about to add colour and design. Where no mirrors hung, paintings of different sizes graced the walls with scenes of the countryside—landscapes, Alice recalled, alongside portraits of noble-looking people.

Despite the immensity of the hall, despite its grandness, Alice felt welcome there. This was a place to congregate, to sit and talk. In small groups or alone, people milled around, entering and leaving rooms and going about their business, all without disrupting the sense of warmth and calm that permeated throughout. None of it struck Alice as official or imposing though she couldn't help noticing the ceilings were rather high and found herself at a loss to imagine a ladder tall enough to climb up to knock down the cobwebs.

Chandeliers dangled from central carvings, and Alice supposed those lights came on at night like sensors. The only source of natural light was the entrance which led out to the steps from where they had entered, but it was still lovely and bright.

Principal Katya told her the two large, bannered and closed doors led to the Tabernacle and Cloisters, the place of governance where only principals and members of the council and invited guests were admitted.

She conducted Alice around the hall, pointing out specific areas and informing Alice of their role and history. Through that door is the library, she said, warning Alice that many of the books were ancient and fragile but that she would have unrestricted access. Principal Katya pointed to another open door, the dining hall.

"But we go to the garden for meals when the weather is nice," Principal Katya made a vague gesture somewhere towards where Alice supposed she would find a garden, then drew Alice to the base of a grand, curving, carpeted staircase.

"The staircase leads to the level in front of the dome, Alice. I occupy a small suite, and I have arranged the same for you."

Alice learned the unmarried statesmen who lived at the Tabernacle also had suites, but there were no children as Principal Katya thought it too solemn a place for little children, who should run and play and laugh and make a noise. It was plain to Alice she didn't need to speak or comment, only listen, or perhaps speak only when questioned. But what use were words anyway, when faced with a place and a person, this remarkable.

"I am an old lady Alice," Principal Katya smiled as Alice turned almost a full circle to view the hall from all angles. "I am used to my routines. At this time, I take tea. Tea with bread and butter. Do you like tea with bread and butter?" Principal Katya had Alice's attention.

"I love it, Principal Katya. I love tea and bread and butter at mid-morning. I've missed it so much!"

"Then there is a little old lady inside you waiting to get out, Alice! We will sit here—"

She showed Alice to a small table, with two chairs, beside an arch which rose from a ledge above the floor and tapered to an elegant point just below the high ceiling. On the other side of the arch, a fernery, interspersed with strange curling flowers and stems that Alice didn't recognise, grew green and lush.

"—and the steward will wait on us and make-believe we are important."

But Alice knew this pleasant, dry humoured lady *was* very important, possibly the most important person on the planet. Even sitting with her made Alice feel special.

The steward brought tea on a hover-trolley. Alice had seen them on the Significator and found them satisfyingly enough like a trolley *with* wheels to make them civilised and homely. The tea, served in a pot, with china cups and saucers and odd-looking, reddish-bread with normal-looking butter arranged neatly on a plate, was placed on the table. Principal Katya checked inside the teapot as Alice always did to see if the tea leaves were still floating.

"My nephew informs me you play the piano. Excuse me if I am 'mother'," she said as she poured the tea.

"Your nephew?" Alice looked up from the tempting spread before her.

"Yes, Principal Ryan."

"Oh, he didn't say he was your nephew."

"Well, he wouldn't. Barely speaks. Never much to say."

This chatty lady was Principal Ryan's *aunt?*

Principal Katya pushed the plate of bread and a dish of jam closer to Alice, and for a moment, she was back at home doing her usual things. She spread the jam on the bread and took a bite. The bread was excellent, and the strawberry jam, divine. Alice turned her eyes heavenward.

Principal Katya grinned. "Good, eh?"

"Heavenly," Alice sighed, rolling her eyes.

"So, does he inform me correctly? Do you play the piano?"

Alice only knew what Principal Ryan had told her.

"So it seems, Principal Katya, I don't remember how it happened. It's hazy now."

"There is a piano here, through there," she aimed her spoon at the library. "You may play it at any time, day or night."

"Thank you, but the truth is, I don't recall playing," she eyed the bread and butter and smiled. "Right now, I'm so grateful to have bread and butter and tea and for it feeling…*so familiar.* Thank you, Principal Katya."

"You are welcome," Principal Katya took her hand and gave it a little shake. "I am delighted you are here. Even though I have promised a vacation, I must mention something that cannot wait, in case other plans need to be made."

Alice waited. What now?

Principal Katya put down her cup.

"When we were certain your new insides were successful, and you showed signs of independence, Principal Hardy suggested we set about searching for your family."

It would seem people didn't become principals by sitting on their hands. It appeared pretty much all contingencies for Alice's reintegration into society had been covered.

"My family? Surely they're long gone?" Alice thought about her mother and her uncle Dave, who she liked, but she didn't know her father, who died soon after her birth.

"Well, your immediate family, of course, but we found DNA matches—we found many, but one, a match to your mother, appeared to have a stronger link than most of the others."

"My mother?"

"Yes, Caroline Watkins. When she married, she became Langley. It seems your uncle, Martin Watkins, raised you following your parent's death in an accident. We have no idea where you lived. There are no records."

It was Alexis Langley's family they'd found, not hers, but *Watkins?* Like Martin Watkins? Alice wondered how she and Alexis were related because evidently, they were.

"Who is it you found, Principal Katya?"

"Her name is Mary Greer. And I believe you will find she is an excellent choice."

"Choice?" Alice echoed.

"As your guardian, only until you grow confident in your new world. It had always been our intention for you to stay here, but I see it would be better for you to have a home and a family, Alice, as you adapt to your new life."

This was difficult information to process. Alice figured her real descendants would come from Michelle's children and Michelle's married name was Campbell, not Watkins. Steven hadn't married, so how did this Caroline become Watkins? Uncle Dave's descendants?

"She lives in the Calamities. In your home country."

"The Calamities?" Alice echoed again. She still hadn't got her head around this concept. "What did she do?"

"She is in an unholy alliance. She has married another woman, a woman of a different race." Principal Katya delivered the news matter-of-factly, casually placing jam on her piece of bread, trying to duplicate the same eye-rolling experience Alice had.

"But you want me to live with her?"

"My wish is for your happiness, and Mary is delightful. She has a charming home, where I spent a few pleasant hours with Mary and her wife, Jane. They will welcome you with open arms. I will send for her after your vacation."

"You seem accepting of their lifestyle, Principal Katya."

Principal Katya raised an eyebrow at the comment.

"Why not? It is their choice. We are all human beings, sometimes frail in our decisions."

Alice was disappointed. She was being sent to the Calamities even though Dr Grossmith had said she wouldn't. Alice had never met a lesbian, her mother told her about them, and she didn't want to become one herself.

"As a loyal citizen," Principal Katya continued, "you will be permitted the freedoms they are not, and while your home will be in the Calamities, you may come and go as you please."

So, the decision had been made, and once more, no one asked Alice but Principal Katya, as though she read Alice's mind, added.

"And that is the last decision we make without you. In the future, you make all your decisions, and we will guide and support you in every way. After tea, I have organised something special for you. We will go to your suite, and we will go shopping. You cannot wear only grey. It does not suit you!!"

Alice glanced down at her grey outfit. She agreed, but...shopping?

"I haven't any money, any currency."

"We don't have currency, Alice. You may choose

whatever you wish. How old are you now?"

"Sixty…um, thirty?"

"Then you have thirty years of shopping. I planned to take you to the city, but my nephew reports you value your privacy. The tailor and purveyor are ordered to attend here."

"Thank you, Principal Katya."

What could she say in the face of such kindness and generosity? Alice had an image of Principal Ryan catching her in the auditorium that night when she had been a stammering wreck. How thoughtful of him to tell his aunt of her shyness.

CHAPTER TWENTY-EIGHT _

Principal Katya was in no rush to finish her tea and bread and butter; in fact, everything and everyone in attendance seemed to accommodate her pace. She smiled often and spoke non-stop about the Tabernacle and the surrounding area, her lively chatter leaving Alice with the opinion she should be related to Patrick rather than the stern Principal Ryan. By the end of morning tea, Alice felt as though she'd known her for years.

Principal Katya personally showed Alice to her suite. Each room assigned to Alice since waking up on Saturn Station stepped up each time in comfort, but this surpassed all her expectations. Tall windows, open wide to the day, provided spectacular views over the gardens and lake. Sheer curtains fluttered in the breeze and outside on the lawn, birdbaths, complete with little birds flitting and splashing about.

Like the great hall, the room was furnished in a mix of styles, many she recognised as coming from her time and which would now be considered antiques; others were more modern and artistic, but all functional and attractive. The bed lay cradled within four turned wood posts, definitely not one of Kelly's "bunks". A communications registry panel sat on a carved desk. Alice noted the absence of the blinking and listening icon.

With all the furnishings so easy on the eye and designed for convenience and comfort, the room exuded luxury.

The washer, which Alice joyously recognised as a proper bathroom, sported more recognisable utilities than on the ship with not a gel pack in sight. She smiled at Principal Katya, who read her expression with uncanny accuracy.

"Dreadful those dry showers. Here we have water, *proper water*—wet water to wash with. When the tailor and purveyor have attended, you will have oils and lotions and perfumes. All the beautiful things a young girl should have."

When Alice was the former Alice and not this privileged version, she sometimes wondered about royalty, how they lived and bathed and slept, and fancied they would have bathrooms and bedrooms like this. Had she been so dissatisfied with her life, she'd created a dream life like this? It occurred to her she'd experienced little joy as a young woman and never had the pleasure of beautiful things. The only happiness she remembered was the time spent with her children and grandchildren.

Alice's steward, Sarah, had once been an educator; she showed the tailor and the purveyor into the suite.

The tailor, a young male with dark hair and an unlined face, nowhere near retirement age and the female purveyor, also on the young side for retirement, made an enormous fuss of Alice. They helped her choose perfumes and products to pamper while the tailor offered her a choice of whichever colour she preferred, provided she chose white, grey, a single shade of green, blue or various shades of red, except pink. The fabric, soft and beautiful to the touch, almost made up for the shortfall in colours.

With the dresses, the tailor only presented varying styles of shifts and, despite Alice considering herself to be a plain dresser, wondered if other, more feminine designs might be available. The tailor expressed surprise at her request but suggested adding a draping collar to the green and perhaps capped sleeves to the white? A more flattering waist on the blue?

The tailor presented slacks and smart white blouses which Alice loved, and boots and sandals with odd little socks that fitted inside the boots. She was measured for hats to protect from the sun, and jackets and other personal items were selected. It was like being a child in a toy store and having unlimited money. Alice was quite overcome until she remembered an essential item of clothing. She'd almost depleted her stash of panties from the station. She hadn't put them in the gel washer for fear of discovery of her periods; instead, she had disposed of them, so her supply was fast running out. She couldn't say anything to Principal Katya, knowing she was related to Principal Ryan and definitely not the tailor. He was a man; how would she say she wanted knickers?

Sarah stood by the door. Alice smiled and sidled over, hoping Principal Katya wouldn't notice.

"Sarah. I need something, and I can't ask the tailor. Where I come from, we don't discuss personal items of clothing."

"Which personal items? I'll ask him as he leaves. Don't worry; I'll be discreet."

"I need—" Alice looked to make sure they weren't being overheard and whispered. Sarah bent her head to hear better. "—I need knickers."

"Knickers?"

"Panties."

Sarah smiled in understanding.

"That's no problem, Dr Langley. The tailor will know about them. Many older women and men wear them, not usually an item for someone as young as you."

"Men?" Alice couldn't fathom it, but no time for that now. "Would you mind asking him? Quietly, like you said. I'd be so grateful."

"Consider it done."

Alice had to trust.

Principal Katya remained with Alice for a few minutes after the tailor and purveyor left.

"Thank you, Principal Katya, that was amazing! Just like Christmas. I must admit, though, I would be rather interested to see a city."

"We no longer have Christmas, Alice, not for centuries. In time, you will see the city. You will see many of the world's cities and many of the wonderful places we have on Earth. I see you get on with Sarah. A kinder, more attentive girl you couldn't wish to meet."

"May I ask, Principal Katya, why the tailor is so young? I understood these positions were only for people over sixty-five when they retire."

"Not in all cases, Alice. The professions that make up the branches of science, education and agriculture are offered to all youngsters. Music and creative arts, across all mediums, are encouraged alongside their studies. Sometimes, children will discover their love of music or textiles or painting exceeds any interest in the professions. That child will become our performer and composer of the future, or our tailor or purveyor or possibly, our chef or baker." She pointed out the paintings in the room.

"The children whose creative ability shines and who wish to follow their hearts are afforded the respect, recognition and entitlements given to any profession."

"Do any of them live in the Calamities?"

"Only those who need to. If there is a need for bakers or chefs or tailors and none is resident, then one will be assigned. Now, no more questions. You are on vacation. What would you like to do?"

Alice looked with longing at the bath.

Principal Katya nodded. "I understand. Enjoy. Sarah will call me if you need me, and if you don't need me, she will find you when it is time for lunch."

Alice watched her leave. Patrick and Dr Grossmith were right about Principal Katya. What a delight! She hadn't met one unpleasant person since waking up on Saturn Station, then adjusted that thought and singled out Dr Clere as the possible exception, even though he grew her a new heart for which she was most appreciative. Now, she was being treated like royalty.

The bath was light blue, deep and wide, with water that flowed with a wave of her hand. There wasn't a tap, only a panel on the inner surface, but the water was real and delivered at the perfect temperature. The purveyor left behind small bottles of all the lotions and bath additives she had chosen to use until her own arrived.

Alice hated showers in her old life; finding her stiff hips made it impossible to reach down to clean her feet, but a bath, a nice, deep bath like this… The water moved in gentle ripples, and she rested her head against a soft pillow Sarah had placed there for her. Alice closed her eyes and drifted off.

She woke, gasping for breath. A burst of geometrical shapes and sharp colours evaporated as her vision cleared. The youthful man with the pure white hair from her earlier dreams had appeared swathed in the colours. He was so real; she was certain he was here, in the washer. She sat bolt upright and looked around, reaching for a towel to protect her modesty, her heart racing. She *had* seen him; she was sure, and he'd smiled but mingled in with that smile, she also saw pity or—or...*concern* in his expression. Alice blew out her breath as her heart slowed to normal, then rechecked the room, making sure no-one was with her.

A soft, sweet humming came from her bedroom. Climbing out of the bath, Alice found a robe folded on a nearby shelf and slipped into it as she peeped into her room. Sarah was there, and she saw Alice peeking round the door.

"Hello, Dr Langley, I thought you might be fast asleep in there."

"I didn't sleep for long; the water's still warm. Did you come into the washer a moment ago?"

"No, I wouldn't do that unless you called for me. The water is still warm because the temperature stays the same for the duration of your bath. You've been there a good hour. Now, I've laid out these clothes for you. I see you only have a few, but that will change when your new wardrobe arrives tomorrow, then you'll have more choice. It's a lovely day. You won't need a jacket."

Alice sat on the bed and watched Sarah being busy. Still unnerved by her experience in the bath, she distracted herself by asking Sarah a question.

"Principal Katya says you're an educator?"

Sarah nodded. "That's right. When I turned sixty-five, I requested stewardship here because it's such a beautiful environment. I can come here for a day or two every few weeks and still pursue my first love."

"Oh, you have a husband?"

Sarah laughed at Alice's misunderstanding. "I do, but I was referring to art. I like to paint. It's how I met my husband, something we had in common outside of educating. He's retired now, but I still enjoy these days here, and we live so close to the Tabernacle, it's ideal."

"So, you're an artist?"

"Yes, I am. I taught creative arts as part of my educator role. I loved it, but when my time to retire came, I decided enough was enough, and it was time to do more for myself. It wasn't too long before I found I missed working outside my home, so I asked for a reassignment."

"But a steward?"

"I like to serve. If the day comes when I stop enjoying my work, I'll walk away. What about you?"

Alice hesitated. It was conceivable, as an educator, Sarah would know of her. She wasn't good at conjuring up stories; besides, Sarah was lovely, and Principal Katya obviously liked and trusted her. In her position, Principal Katya would be an experienced judge of character.

"Do you know anything about me?"

"Should I?" Sarah stopped what she was doing, looking at Alice with curiosity.

"You might. Heaps of people do, most of the world, in fact, but only a few know what I'm doing now."

Sarah, intrigued, had to ask, "Well, who are you?"

"I was in a glass coffin, a sarcophagus," Alice said, abridging a four-centuries-old mystery. "Asleep for hundreds of years. I'm not sure I'm meant to talk about it."

Sarah sat down beside her, her half-folded bundle on her lap.

"You're the Sleeping Beauty?"

"I don't know if anyone actually called me that,"

Alice said, feeling it was not a very accurate description. "That's what they called the project. I woke up, got a new heart and kidneys and now I'm here."

Alice had told no-one any of this; the only people who knew were directly involved with her, so she couldn't gauge what Sarah's reaction might be. She didn't feel important, but she understood Alexis Langley's historical significance.

Sarah stared down at the bundle in her lap. Whether she was shocked or just believing herself to be on the receiving end of a prank, it was difficult to tell. When she spoke again, Alice heard only calm acceptance.

"I learned something about the project at school, but there has been no news of you in many years. I remember the doctor who referred to the project as 'Sleeping Beauty' believed you would wake without help but, when it didn't happen, or we thought it didn't happen, as people do, we turned our attention to other things."

"I hope I can fade into obscurity."

"Your privacy will be respected, Dr Langley," Sarah said. "Anyone who learns of this will have questions, I'm sure, but that's natural. You've no need to fear you'll become a curiosity or be on display. As before, we will in time, find other things to amaze us, though I expect you will be written up in scientific journals forever!!" she laughed. "But to your friends, you'll just be yourself."

"Scientific papers sound awful. And please, call me Alice. Dr Grossmith, on Saturn Station, describes my awakening as a miracle, but after seeing images on the registry, I'm a little afraid of being famous."

"You are already immortalised…Alice. I'm not sure you should be telling me this, either."

"You're the first person I've spoken to who didn't have any idea who I was when I met them, apart from the principal of the ship and his officers and then I believe he was told before I left Saturn Station—so I suppose that doesn't count," Alice shook her head. "I'm not clever enough to invent a history. Everyone I've had any proper conversation with so far has known my origins. So, if people ask me about myself, I don't have anything else to tell them but the truth."

"It must be so strange."

Alice agreed. "Stranger than fiction. I don't believe it myself most of the time."

Sarah sat for a moment longer, pondering the revelation, and Alice wondered if she should have made up a story, but with no background, what else was there to offer but the truth? Sarah had asked her, and as she would be living here in this world, she might have to get used to other people asking the same question. She couldn't hide forever, even if her story did seem far-fetched. She may need to declassify herself and hope people accept her.

Sarah got up and put her hand on Alice's shoulder.

"Well, it's surprising news, but I also believe it's yours to give out as you see fit. I'll keep it as a confidence. Now, get dressed and put some of this on." She handed Alice a delicate bottle, "I'll take you down to Principal Katya. She is a dear but doesn't like to be kept waiting, particularly for her lunch."

CHAPTER TWENTY-NINE _

On board the Significator, Statesman Patrick peeled off his overalls and stood in the shower. He closed his eyes. It had only been a few hours since Alice left, and he wondered what she thought of the sharp-witted and deeply intuitive Principal Katya, a woman for whom he had immeasurable respect.

In his room, the bed beckoned. He'd been on duty for twenty-four hours, and now he was tired, and his body ached. The preparation for the Gravidarum and portage cylinders' modifications was going well but poring over the initial specifications made his head hurt. He often found his attention wandering to the moment he said goodbye to Alice, not precisely the lapse of professionalism young Tyro Drake needed to witness from his superior officer. Patrick pushed the thought away; it was done, no point in overthinking it now. He sighed, rubbed his eyes and pulled on the first shirt and slacks he found. After looking longingly once more at the bed, he decided first and foremost, he needed food.

Statesman Hennessey was seated alone at a table in the officer's dining hall, picking at his meal and reading from his portable registry. Patrick seated himself opposite. They offered each other the usual, single name greeting common among senior personnel.

"Hennessey."

"Patrick."

"When are you going to the surface?" Hennessey closed the registry to give his full attention to his colleague. "That all-nighter ensured you're on schedule, so Ryan could spare you. He's been on the bridge since last night; the way he behaves, anyone would think you're leaving for your next mission next week."

"I need another all-nighter to finish, so I'm back on duty in eight hours. I'll go to the surface in a couple of days. Ryan needs to visit his family at some point, as well. His father is ill, I hear. When do you leave for Earth?"

"Tomorrow."

"You don't seem very happy. I thought you'd be relieved."

"I am happy, Patrick, about going home, but leaving here? Well, mixed emotions, I suppose. Junnot is definitely coming back?"

"Her linguistics are pretty good. What's the problem?"

"Mine are better. It's going to be hard to be based on Earth again."

"You married into an Earth-based profession. You knew the rules."

The conversation gave Patrick an idea, and he signalled to Hennessey to hand over his portable registry. Hennessey obliged without a word, knowing Patrick had a habit of changing tack mid-conversation if the fancy took him.

"Tabernacle," Patrick added his signature to the link. "Statesman Patrick, message to Principal Katya."

Sarah showed Alice to a spacious patio area in the garden where groups of people, statesmen and other dignitaries, sat at tables, eating and conversing, while others, seated alone with portable registries, were enjoying the sunshine. Principal Katya was alone and gave Alice a delighted smile when she caught sight of her.

"Alice, you have had a long soak, I think. Feel better?"

"Yes, thank you, Principal Katya, I loved it, and Sarah is so attentive. I'm being treated like royalty!"

"Good, good. I hear too, from my nephew, that Statesman Patrick took you under his wing on the Significator."

"Yes, he did, Principal Katya. He helped me a lot."

"Patrick is a good man, an eye for the ladies, though. A veritable trail of broken hearts across the galaxy!"

Principal Katya chuckled at her choice of words, an innocent enough remark but one which gave Alice pause. She wouldn't be one in a long line of broken hearts, and it surprised her to learn such a thing about Patrick, but really, she shouldn't; Statesman Patrick was the best-looking man in the universe.

"Patrick comes here the day after tomorrow. He sent word a few minutes ago to say he is arriving that morning and would see you. I have told him you are on vacation and will accept a visit only if it pleases you to do so."

"I'd like that, Principal Katya. I consider him a good friend."

"Then, we will admit him." She sounded stern, but as Alice soon learned, the twinkling in her eyes meant her tone might seem steely, but her words were only meant in fun.

Principal Katya chatted pleasantly throughout lunch on topics ranging from the gardens to the history of the area and allowing Alice to ask one or two questions about the Tabernacle and even about Principal Katya herself.

"That, my child, is the briefest of stories. I chose agriculture as a profession, the same as all my family, from generations back, apart from my sister, who elected to enter the sciences. My nephew, her son, followed her, but his study took him to the stars." She stopped, and Alice wondered if her question was too personal, but Principal Katya sat herself up tall in her chair, contemplating how she should continue. It wasn't a story she often repeated, but this young girl had much to learn about society; her own story was as good a place as any to start.

"One day, forty years ago or thereabouts, I was working in Principality 12, while there, I developed a wasting disease in my leg. The doctors cured the disease, but the experience changed not only my height but my ability to carry out the manual work on the land that I loved and…I was alone—no, Alice, don't you dare look so sad," she laughed and took Alice's hand. "I had no husband, no child. I didn't want to twiddle my thumbs, as they say, so I came here, put my bags on the doorstep and said I would not leave until they gave me work to do!"

"And they made you Principal of the World?"

"Not straight away, my dear girl, but I was admitted to the council, in the capacity of Statesman here at the Tabernacle before being reassigned back to Principality 12 a few years later, to preside as the principal. When Principal Hallam, my predecessor, died, the council recalled me. I have been principal for twenty years, and I will stay principal until I drop to the floor at the feet of my councilmen!" Possessed of such an impish and mischievous smile, Alice found it difficult to believe this friendly, funny lady was related to the dour Principal Ryan.

"If each country, principality, has a principal," Alice asked. "What do you do here?"

"We govern reproduction, removal to the Calamities, marriage applications, regulate space travel and myriad other issues to make the world beautiful and safe and of course, to keep our minds and bodies healthy and us old people busy!"

She was remarkable, wise and intelligent and funny. Alice compared Principal Katya's vitality and enthusiasm to her own previous existence, to her own advancing years. The old Alice possessed none of her qualities.

"What are you looking at, my dear?"

In her reverie, Alice had been staring at Principal Katya's snow-white hair, remembering her blue rinse, which she thought so smart.

"I'm sorry, Principal Katya," she apologised. "I didn't mean to stare, but you have such lovely white hair, I always—I mean, in my time, some ladies liked to rinse blue through the hair. It was considered stylish."

Alice knew blue rinses were very unfashionable, but she had loved hers.

"Blue hair?" Principal Katya's face lit up with interest.

"Not very blue," Alice hastened to explain, "not like the sky, only a hint, yours would be lovely."

"I must try this blue. Steward!"

Within seconds the steward was at their side.

"Let Miss Ling know I wish to see her. Here." Principal Katya pointed at the table then winked at the steward. "Let her know we are going to experiment and have some fun!"

He left with a bow and a large grin.

"Now, what other curious and remarkable pastimes from your time do we need to learn?" she clasped her elegant hands in front of her on the table, waiting for Alice to offer up the mysteries of her life. A life she knew Principal Katya believed existed only in her imagination.

"Well, I can't remember too much that was exciting," she confessed, but in a moment of inspiration, she told Principal Katya about the television soap operas.

She took care not to refer to her own experiences but to say, 'they' and 'some people,' thus avoiding speculation about herself. She mentioned knitting and crochet, and Principal Katya demanded further information on 'this crochet'. Alice found it a challenge to explain as Principal Katya had no concept of yarn. She continued the struggle until Miss Ling arrived, tall and elegant, with expertly applied makeup and perfectly manicured nails, intrigued by the 'experiment' alluded to by the steward.

Principal Katya introduced Alice and told Miss Ling the story of white-haired ladies who rinsed their hair blue. She wished to try this, and could it be done? Miss Ling frowned here and there at places during Alice's explanation.

"Yes, Principal Katya," she said, thinking inwardly how like Principal Katya, to try something so outlandish, but she obediently reached for her portable registry. "We will need to use a few pigments. Just a moment."

Moving her slender fingers across the screen, Miss Ling selected different hues of blue and played with them until she saw one which might suit, then set it against the registry's likeness of Principal Katya's hair. The result was anything but subtle. Both women looked at Alice for her approval, but the colour was ghastly.

"It's too dark," came her tactful response, hoping not to offend Miss Ling. "The intention is to highlight the hair, brighten it, not change the colour to a solid blue. Can you make it less intense, Miss Ling, perhaps take this pigment out, fade it a little?"

She offered Alice the portable registry. Although it was a device she had never used, she shaped the colour palette with confidence, playing it against the white and resulting in a colour Alice considered as close to desirable as possible. She handed the screen back to Miss Ling, wondering for an instant how the registry came to be in her hands in the first place, but she had an idea how the blue rinse might look on Principal Katya, the way Alice's blue rinse looked before she became a carrot head.

Principal Katya, eager to try the hair colour, was already out of her seat, beckoning to Alice and Miss Ling to follow. Miss Ling whispered to Alice.

"Principal Katya loves to try new things and meet new people. She has been so looking forward to your arrival and will want to try everything you do that she has never tried."

"I am not deaf, you girls," Principal Katya called over her shoulder. "I can hear you chattering behind my back as if I were an old lady to be humoured!"

They followed Principal Katya through the great hall to Miss Ling's salon, a surprise to Alice such a place existed within such a grand and hallowed place. There were no hairdryers, no basins, no mirrors around the wall and in many ways, not unlike the room she first remembered on waking, sparse and functional with minimal furnishings. The walls were curved opaque glass and had a proper door through which to enter and exit. There was a single large chair in which Principal Katya sat, like a monarch on her throne.

Miss Ling applied the pigment by reproducing the colour from the registry into a small cylinder and brushing the device through Principal Katya's hair. As she did, she twirled the hair around the cylinder to form soft curls, and as Alice watched, a blue highlight appeared. Miss Ling showed Principal Katya her reflection in an image definer, but Alice still considered it just a shade too blue.

Not so Principal Katya, who turned to Alice with unconcealed delight.

"Alice, this is splendid! I will always have this now. I am renewed. And now, I wish to crochet."

"Well, to crochet, we need yarn and hooks, Principal Katya." Alice had only been here a few hours, but she was worn out! Principal Katya had the energy of a teenager and would take a lot of keeping up with!

Principal Katya petitioned Miss Ling for advice.

"Do you know where we can obtain this yarn and hooks?"

"What is the expected outcome of the exercise, Principal Katya?"

Alice was the only one able to answer this question, and both women looked to her. Outcome? Alice didn't use the word 'outcome' in crochet unless you considered finishing a project, a shawl or a baby jacket an 'outcome'.

"A blanket might be an easy place to start." In the absence of patterns, a blanket would be the best guarantee of an 'outcome.'

"A blanket. As in a cover? Like a blanket of snow?" Principal Katya loved the idea.

"Yes, but more of a blanket to put over your knees or lay across your bed to make it pretty. We start by crocheting squares then joining them together."

Miss Ling understood. "I suggest you try the tailor, Principal Katya. Fabrics are his area of expertise. Perhaps he will understand yarn."

"Indeed, the tailor. Alice, you will go to the city today, after all!"

A short time later, Alice found herself out the front of the Tabernacle with Principal Katya, awaiting the shuttle's arrival.

Principal Katya laughed.

"Here I am, directing things," she prodded Alice gently in the arm. "You should have reminded me; this is your vacation. I confess I get tremendously excited about new things."

"Please don't worry, Principal Katya, I'm happy to go. Remember, I'm new here, and the city will be an experience."

"Then we are both happy. Here is the transport."

The pilot helped Principal Katya into her seat but, apart from a bow of acknowledgement, left Alice to seat herself. She was young now, younger even than he, and of course, he wouldn't have considered her in need of assistance.

"Fly low, please, Pilot." Principal Katya instructed. "Our guest can see the countryside. It is a beautiful time of year, Alice; Spring has only just begun."

Yes, Alice thought, beautiful. Breathtakingly so. Below her, homesteads nestled in lush green gardens the size of smallholdings. Cows and horses grazed undisturbed, and from a few of the dwellings, dogs ran and barked as the shuttle flew above their gardens. Never, anywhere, not even in a magazine at the hairdressers had she seen such a structure as large and impressive as the city.

Built into the side of a mountain, the city rose in sheer proportions from the ground, reaching up and onwards almost as far as Alice could see. The city extended out by more than five kilometres with a central level supported by a single, slender stem.

"The habitation area and infirmary," Principal Katya pointed out. "Over there, we have the Merchants; Providores, pasticiums, dining halls, purveyors, tailors, all those who keep our bellies full and clothes on our backs." She smiled at Alice, evidently a popular and oft-visited destination for Principal Katya.

"Below," she pointed out the lower sections, further into the rock, "is the Industrial Sector, housing small item manufacturing workshops and high above, closer to the clouds, are the entertainment areas and theatres."

Alice was lost for words at the enormity of the place. Like the principality ship, it resembled a small country rather than a man-made structure. Principal Katya astounded her further by telling her Principality One had not just one, but three cities, this being the largest. Alice tried to pay attention to Principal Katya's narrative but was too overawed. The city was staggering in its size—a colossus. Above the city, the top of the mountain rose high, like a crown atop a regal head and where the city was in part formed from the rock and in part built against it, the mountain curved around like a protective shell.

The Merchant sector resembled a Christmas tree ablaze with lights while the lower sections were less visible. The habitat and infirmary arm glistened with clusters of lit areas. The pilot brought the shuttle down to the lower level and came about to present Alice with a panoramic view from all directions. At the base of the stem, many large shuttles, with markings different to the Tabernacle shuttles, took off and landed.

"Those belong to the city," Principal Katya explained. "Anyone can use them to order."

After allowing Alice ample opportunity to be awestruck, the pilot took the shuttle to one of the upper levels, landing on a small platform on the city's broadest part, outside the Merchant area. She dared only guess at what the pilot thought of her astonishment, or even if he knew seeing this was a first for her.

Alice climbed from the shuttle onto the landing pad, at a startling height. Usually afraid of anything above the first rung of a stepladder, Alice felt no fear, merely turned to aid Principal Katya, as though standing this distance above the ground, with a rippling forcefield below, was an everyday occurrence.

CHAPTER THIRTY _

The Merchant sector operated on several levels. Elevators not only travelled up and down but side to side, even spiralling in a slow circle to the more inaccessible areas. It was a busy place, with many people in uniform, some with military insignias, and many families with small children. Alice recognised the light blue uniform worn by several Tyros, who passed them on the walkways.

The various sectors remained open twenty-four hours each day while the habitat arm provided accommodation for single people working here. Principal Katya told her that Tyros taking aptitudes, spent six months assigned to a city, working in each section as part of training to be in service to the world.

Each studio on this level (not 'shop' Principal Katya corrected her) was set back from the walkway and partitioned from its neighbour by simple columns. The studios on this level were solely for the manufacture and production of footwear and apparel. None of the open-fronted studios displayed their wares.

On each level, there was a hub for the elevators to take them wherever they needed to go in the city. A few narrow windows offered restricted glimpses of the outside. Principal Katya told Alice other parts of the city had larger windows and viewports with uninterrupted views of the surrounding countryside, where one could see for miles and miles. Alice would have liked to enjoy those views, but Principal Katya was on a mission for yarn and hooks.

The tailor who visited the Tabernacle earlier appeared flustered by their arrival.

"Principal Katya, Dr Langley," he bowed to them both, his young face flushed and anxious. "I'm afraid your garments won't be ready until tomorrow morning."

Alice had chosen so many outfits; how could they make them all in only one day? But she didn't ask.

Principal Katya held up her hands to calm him.

"Tailor Mitchell, we are not here about the garments, though we might have saved you a journey. We are here on another matter. A conundrum for you, I believe."

"A conundrum, Principal Katya?"

"Yes, Dr Langley has extraordinary knowledge of ancient craftwork, and we need, what is it, Dr Langley? Yarn? Yes, yarn."

Principal Katya waited while Tailor Mitchell gathered his wits. He had never heard of yarn.

"Yarn?"

Alice decided it might be prudent to step in here.

"We wish to make a blanket, Tailor Mitchell," she said, "using squares of fabric like the samples you showed me this morning, but we want to make it ourselves. To do that, we must have long pieces of fabric, only this thick." She tried to show him between her thumb and forefinger, "and it would need winding into a ball or skein. We also require a hook to work the fabric."

Principal Katya nodded her agreement often while Alice explained as though she couldn't have said it better herself.

Tailor Mitchell stroked his chin, pondering Principal Katya's 'conundrum'. He placed a sheet of cloth onto a narrow master plate and activated a second plate, suspended above, with a flick of his finger. He then guided the master plate by manipulating beams of light and, in a few seconds, a length of fabric stripped from the sheet, far too short for their purposes, but he held it up in triumph, convinced he had solved their predicament.

Alice took it from him. It was light to the touch, so might be workable but needed to be thinner and much, much longer. And they still lacked a hook.

"How long can you make one of these strands, Tailor Mitchell?" Alice handed the fabric back.

"As long as you wish, Dr Langley."

"Is it possible to make it thinner? Half as thin?"

"Yes, Dr Langley."

"Can you do it by weight?"

"Yes, I can do that too. Do you have a weight in mind?"

Alice looked around and spotted the odd boot sock thingies the tailor showed her earlier. She picked up a few.

"I don't know how you weigh things here, but each ball of the fabric needs to weigh as much as this and be continuous."

"Would you mind leaving this with me? Let me experiment? May I suggest you have tea at a pasticium, and I will link with you as soon as I come up with a solution? Hopefully, not too long. Would that be agreeable, Principal Katya?"

"Excellent suggestion. We will wait to hear from you."

Outside the tailor's studio, Principal Katya nudged Alice.

"You will learn I need no excuse for a cup of tea, Alice, but first we need to find this hook. Do you know the material used in its manufacture?"

"Metal or plastic, not long, about this length…" and she again held up her fingers, "it's got a little hook on the end to catch the yarn."

Principal Katya understood. "Someone who works with metal can produce such a tool. I am not sure of this plastic, but I think I know where to look."

Principal Katya found a stray Tyro to conduct them to the Industrial Sector, telling the girl what kind of industry she required. The young woman took them in an elevator to the levels below the retail sector, chatting about aptitudes and agricultural options with Principal Katya.

Standing where the Tyro left them in the Industrial Sector, Alice realised these were not simple machine shops, garages, or engineering workrooms. Where she had expected oil or grease and grubby overalls, the entire area was as ordered and tidy as the engine room of the Significator, and the men and women working here were dressed neatly in uniforms. These were more like laboratories.

Principal Katya spoke a few words to a steward who disappeared inside one of the laboratories and returned with an official-looking man. He addressed Principal Katya with the customary bow but paid no attention to Alice.

"We need a hook with which to work fabric. My friend here, Dr Langley—" and at that, the man turned and bowed, "—is to teach me a new craft. She will furnish you with dimensions, and you can fashion the implement."

Principal Katya took a seat, hands in lap, she waited for them to begin their task.

Alice drew a childish line drawing of a crochet hook on the registry notepad, hoping it corresponded with the width of the yarn Tailor Mitchell produced. The engineer noted her sketch and withdrew, promising to return directly.

He returned within ten minutes carrying several prototypes, none perfect or exact, but after a few trials, came up with one Alice was confident would fit the bill. All this kerfuffle to find yarn and hooks made her wonder if the person who invented crochet faced as many problems in getting started. If so, she was surprised it ever survived.

Principal Katya took Alice for tea as suggested by Tailor Mitchell. It was only mid-afternoon, and the third time she had sat down to eat. Had she remembered to eat breakfast, this would have been the fourth. How did everyone look so fit and well?

The cakes and pastries were irresistible, and all the food she'd tried over the months was delicious, except for the rolls and firewater. The steward brought them tea and cake decorated with a large quantity of cream. All these years later and cream still looked and tasted like cream. She could only hope that calories in the future were less than calories in the past.

Tailor Mitchell made several balls of fabric, each with contrasting colours and within the scope of what he thought appropriate. Principal Katya inspected his efforts but first sought Alice's approval before giving the tailor her compliments. The tailor had done a remarkable job in producing a workable, stretchy, almost-yarn. Alice most certainly approved, and he promised he would work on the concept further.

Before starting the homeward trip to the Tabernacle, the pilot took the shuttle high over the city for Alice to view from above. Breathtaking from all angles, and from so high, Alice gained a perspective of the sheer scale of the relationship between the manmade components and natural formation of the mountain. Principal Katya smiled, delighting in the opportunity of being the first to show her these wonders. Alice opened her hands, palms up as if to say, "I cannot believe this!" Principal Katya heard her unspoken wonder loud and clear.

Late in the afternoon, Alice and Principal Katya were sitting together in the garden. Alice closed her eyes. It had been hundreds of years since the sun last warmed her face, that is if she decided to believe all she had been told, but the sun felt so good. It would have been nice to nap, but with a student sitting opposite, impatient to learn the art of crochet, she had no time to sleep or ponder the vagaries of her unexpected situation.

Unfortunately, those intervening hundreds of years since she had last crocheted made their presence felt when, trying to co-ordinate hook and yarn, Alice struggled. The technique was in her head, but her fingers wouldn't co-operate, and the results were rather untidy, an odd experience for someone who used to make jumpers and blankets and baby clothes by the dozen. She put the yarn down with a sigh, wracking her brain for a clue as to what she might be doing wrong. Alice had no choice but to keep trying, reasoning that as a novice, Principal Katya only needed the basics, and if she concentrated, the technique would return.

Happily, it did, but as Alice's ability improved, it became apparent that Principal Katya was not a natural. She fumbled and fiddled and tied her yarn in knots until, after a few false starts and with Alice's help, she gained a degree of mastery in the knack of juggling hook and yarn. Miss Ling joined them, wishing to try her hand, then Statesmen Mellor wandered over, followed by two stewards and Sarah. Miss Ling had the most success in handling the hook, Principal Katya the least, but she would not be dissuaded. At the end of an hour, under Alice's watchful eye and with considerable persistence, she had crocheted a line of work.

"We must all be taught this by Alice," Principal Katya announced. "I think it will be therapeutic. Very relaxing." A few members of the group agreed, while others concluded it might not be for them. Alice took Sarah to one side.

"Why would the male statesmen want to do craftwork? I didn't know any men who did."

Sarah laughed. "Well, we love Principal Katya, and if it gives her pleasure, and assuming we can take the time from our duties, we'll join in with her. Don't let her sense of fun deceive you; she works incredibly hard and takes little leisure time. I know she's cramming in lots of activities, but at any moment, affairs of the world can take her attention away for many days, and she's determined to make you feel welcome. We all enjoy her company, and none of us gets to spend much time with her. Besides, this crochet is intriguing. I'm going to check it out on the registry. By the way, you will find there is no real delineation of roles between the sexes. It's all common territory."

For a moment, Alice screwed up her face in puzzlement. Okay, no specific male and female-dominated roles but *crochet!!* Well, yes, *she* liked it, but why these brainy types would find it rewarding boggled her mind. Crochet was something to do while watching telly, mindless stuff to occupy idle hands, certainly not something to get too excited about. Naturally, you took pride in a project completed well but now, teaching it to the people who ran the world beggared belief.

So, no nanna nap on her first day on Earth, Instead, after Principal Katya excused herself, Alice retreated to her suite and sat in the window seat, looking out to the lake and reflecting on the events of the day. She went through each experience, from waking on the Significator to seeing Patrick as she left, her arrival in the shuttle and saying goodbye to Amelia. Then meeting the amazing Principal Katya, that lovely deep bath, shopping, if one could call that shopping, getting to know Sarah, visiting the city, so much in one day! Only this morning, she stood on the observation deck of a starship. It was all going so *fast*.

The sun was setting, casting a soft glow across the lawns. The garden would be lovely now, so she made her way down the winding staircase and across the almost deserted great hall, unseen apart from one or two stewards who glanced in her direction.

Standing on the steps, the Tabernacle lights reflected over the surface of the lake, shimmering like stars. The lawns spread out before her, inviting her to step out. She glanced behind to make sure she was alone, then kicked off her sandals and wriggled her toes, enjoying the damp softness beneath her feet. How glorious! For months, she had been in the bright, artificial and clinical environment of Saturn Station, and now, standing on Earth, on the grass and watching a beautiful sunset, she didn't want to be anywhere else.

The gardens were peaceful and quiet. Sandals in hand, Alice sauntered down by the lake, intending to walk as far as the summer house at the far end. The ducks had put themselves to bed, and half a dozen rabbits were too busy munching their evening meal on the lawn to care about their visitor. Alice stopped to listen to an early hoot of an owl in the distance, and in the trees around the lake, birds chattered as they found their perches for the night. It surprised Alice to find she was the only person out here in such a beautiful part of the evening, but also glad of the solitude after so many months of having someone supervising her every move.

She found a stone garden seat to sit on and looked up into the evening sky, hoping for a glimpse of Saturn. She didn't know its position in the heavens, and it would be too far away to see anyway, one point two billion kilometres or something Hennessey said. Saturn Station, her first home since waking, was also somewhere above her, amongst those points of light.

Summerhouse forgotten, she watched as one by one, more stars appeared, and the moon rose to take its place, the same moon that shone down on her centuries ago. It's much prettier from here, she thought, remembering how much like clay it looked close to.

Out there, in the peace of the garden, bathed in the glow from the great hall, Alice permitted herself to dwell on the complexities of her new life, her rebirth. Perhaps one day, she might be able to explain the events that brought her to this place, learn which universal force played a part in taking her from one life and placing her in another. And when that time comes, she might understand the reason why.

CHAPTER THIRTY-ONE _

Statesman Mellor, silhouetted in the lights, called to her from the steps of the great hall. Alice stood and signalled to let him know she'd seen him and hurried towards the Tabernacle. He bowed but didn't say, "Dr Langley," instead, he addressed her as "Alice".

"Principal Katya has arrived for dinner," he said, inviting Alice to fall into step beside him. "She enquires after you and hopes you will join her. We dine late here," he grinned. "Has she run you ragged today?"

"She's so kind, Statesman Mellor, you all are. I enjoyed her company. Just now, out at the lake, I was thinking about all the things we did today; I didn't realise the time!"

Statesman Mellor escorted Alice to the garden where Principal Katya waited with Miss Ling, giving Alice a quick smile, he withdrew back to the great hall.

"Alice, there you are."

Principal Katya pointed to a covered dish in the centre of the table. "Do you like potatoes with butter? We have potatoes with butter." She lifted the lid.

But Alice didn't feel hungry. Where on earth did these people put all the food they ate? She was starting to appreciate the controlled portions on the station and starship.

"Yes, I do, Principal Katya, but I'm not terribly..."

Principal Katya wasn't listening.

"We have researched the diets of your time and asked the chef to create something familiar. Are we not clever?"

"You're very thoughtful," Alice accepted a plate from Principal Katya.

Alice recognised potatoes and butter. Although she had never seen potatoes of such a vivid yellow before, she decided to try them, glad to see the other vegetables, like carrots and broccoli, seemed familiar. Chef had prepared a brown sauce which Alice supposed was gravy, but only after pouring it on the vegetables did she realise it was caramel. To her horror, Principal Katya and Miss Ling followed suit.

Not unexpectedly, neither was impressed.

"I'm so sorry, Principal Katya. I didn't realise the sauce was sweet," Alice apologised, even the error wasn't of her making. Clearly, their research needed tweaking.

"This is not how you ate?" Principal Katya looked down at her caramel covered supper.

"It's a good sauce," Alice lied. She hated caramel sauce. "But we would have had the potatoes and vegetables with a pork chop or a chicken leg."

"A pork chop? Steward," Principal Katya called out. "Bring Chef!"

The steward was dispatched, and the chef summoned. He sat down, and Alice questioned him on pork chops and chicken legs. They seldom ate chickens, he said, only for celebrations, but eggs, yes, and they had pig meat. The chef had never heard of chops, and Alice couldn't tell him what part of the pig they originated from, so they deliberated together on the different pieces of pig meat on the registry. None were recognisable as chops. Alice wasn't sure and shook her head.

"Do you have beef?" she asked in the hope Chef might show her something more recognisable.

She was advised, yes, beef is used in many meals.

Alice asked if they had sausages because she loved sausages, but her questions were answered with blank looks and mystified shrugs. Hamburgers proved to be a mystery too, so Alice gave Chef the recipe for meat patties, forgetting to explain hamburgers were the finished dish and meat patties only one component. Principal Katya said they would wait.

"Now, Alice, what do we do with this sweet sauce?"

"Usually, you have it with pudding."

"Pudding. Yes, after your meal?"

"That's right, sometimes we called it dessert, but you would have a savoury sauce with the dinner. We called it gravy."

"Fruit is pudding, I understand from the registry?"

"Yes, fruit can be pudding, but pudding is a kind of

dense cake."

"Hmmm." Principal Katya peered at the registry. Alice saw all this confused her dinner companions.

"Can you tell Chef how to make dense pudding?"

"Possibly." Alice supposed just a plain cake might suffice if they had the ingredients.

Then Principal Katya held up her hand.

"But you are on holiday, and I am taking up too much of your time!"

And even though Alice had never crammed so much into one day, she meant it when she answered,

"To be honest, Principal Katya, this is a perfect holiday."

The meat patties needed work. Chef missed the point about seasoning, and they had the appearance of being cooked with a blowtorch, but they still tasted raw. Alice knew she hadn't explained it well, so with the promise of further instruction in hamburgers and much to Alice's relief, they instead dined on cheese and fruit, which meant she could nibble, and no-one would be any the wiser.

Much later, in the washer, Alice found a small cubicle tucked away and inside, a regular, running water shower. Fancier than any shower she had ever seen, Alice had to do a bit of hand waving to discover where the water came from because there didn't appear to be a showerhead. In all other ways, it was just a regular shower, and she discovered scented wafers to use as soap.

Sarah had put a nightgown on the pillow, but she was so worn out, she slid into bed without paying it much mind. Tomorrow, she expected she would teach crochet and give Chef instructions on making a pudding, and she would walk in the garden again at sunset. A simply perfect and perfectly simple day to look forward to. Patrick was due the day after, and she was happy she would see him again so soon.

"Knock, knock!" Sarah's cheerful voice startled her awake.

Alice blinked, her eyes taking a moment to adjust to the natural light. The blinds were up, and daylight poured in the windows.

"Only me." Sarah came in with a hover-trolley, and Alice pushed herself up, bleary-eyed, into a sitting position, before remembering she'd gone to bed naked. She looked down, ready to pull the sheet over her, but to her surprise, she was wearing the nightdress she saw folded up on the pillow the previous night.

"Principal Katya has a council meeting," Sarah told her, bringing the trolley to the side of the bed and pouring coffee. "When you didn't come for breakfast, she thought you might be enjoying a nice sleep and suggested I serve you something here in your suite."

"I'd like the coffee, thank you, Sarah. My head feels like it's stuffed with cotton wool. I'm still tired."

Sarah grinned. "I'm glad to see you wearing your nightwear, Alice."

"I don't remember putting it on," Alice plumped her pillows up and sat back. Never in her life had anyone brought her coffee or breakfast in bed before, and she was going to enjoy it.

"Statesman Mellor says you spent most of the night in the library."

"The library? What was I doing?" Alice was puzzled; she didn't remember going to the library. Statesman Mellor must be mistaken.

"Playing the piano," Sarah said. "Statesman Mellor was sitting in the great hall. He said you played for almost two hours, and you were still playing when he retired to his suite."

"Oh, no!" Alice's eyes widened in horror. "Sarah, I got into bed naked. I was so tired!" Having no memory of playing the piano again was one thing but to do it *in the nude!* Alice pulled the sheet over her head to hide her shame. Sarah chuckled as she sat on the bed and pulled the sheet away. It appeared to be no big deal at all to her.

"Alice, Statesman Mellor wouldn't continue listening to you play the piano had you been naked, I can assure you," she lifted the collar of Alice's nightdress. "From the look of it, you put this on before you went downstairs. Statesman Mellor didn't realise you were sleepwalking; if he had, and particularly if you were naked, he would have called for Principal Katya."

"Sarah, I can't remember," Alice blushed even at the possibility of wandering around the Tabernacle in her nightie.

"Modesty is ingrained. Remember you were even too shy to ask about panties? You might have gone to bed naked, but you took the time to put something on before you left your room."

"No wonder I'm half-asleep."

Alice rubbed her eyes and sipped the coffee, trying to recall the events of the previous night, but it was useless. Her mind was a complete blank.

"Statesman Mellor told me he spoke to you and asked your consent to listen," Sarah said. "You even discussed with him the pieces you played. He thought nothing untoward, even the fact you were in your nightwear. It's odd you don't recall being there."

Alice sighed. "I don't know, Sarah. I played the piano on the Significator. At least that's what I was told. But I don't remember any of that either, only the experience of finding myself standing by the piano when Principal Ryan found me. The music's vague," Alice shrugged, "like a feeling I can't hold onto."

"Maybe part of you is recovering memories. I expect it's a good thing." Sarah stood. "Now, have your coffee, have a nibble at what you fancy and go and do something, anything you wish. Principal Katya advises the shuttles are at your disposal, provided the pilot stays with you at all times. She doesn't want you getting lost!"

"I wouldn't know where to go."

"Well, just tell the pilot to take you on a tour of the principality."

"What a good idea. Yes, thank you, I will, though

Principal Katya expected to do more crochet today."

"She does, and she has sent to the city for more yarn and hooks, but she won't press you if you want to do other things."

"I wouldn't dream of saying no to her, she's lovely, and as she's enjoying crochet so much, I would like to do another class."

An hour later, as Alice stood outside the Tabernacle waiting for the pilot to collect her for the tour, she recognised the distinctive markings of a principality ship shuttle as it descended nearby. She prepared her most welcoming smile, ready for Patrick just in case he arrived early, but it was Hennessey who climbed down, reaching out to help a slim girl with a ponytail. A sling was tied to the front of her body. Hennessey saw Alice and waved, indicating to the girl by his side that he knew Alice and should go across to say hello.

"Dr Langley," he looked happy. "This is my wife, Sylvia." Hennessey introduced the lovely, fair-haired girl at his side. She stepped forward and inclined her head in greeting.

"Dr Langley."

Alice noticed Sylvia was introduced only as 'wife' with no professional title. She hadn't come across that before. Alice noticed the sling was moving, the little cherub inside was wide awake, and he was a darling!

"And who's this little sweetheart?" Alice peeked

inside, then smiled up at the parents.

"This is Lester. He's almost four months," Sylvia said, thrilled to show off her new baby.

"Lester?" Alice glanced at Hennessey, too puffed up with pride to notice the hint of a query in her voice. "That's a good solid name," she said, recollecting how Patrick told her Hennessey hated his Christian name.

"He's gorgeous. Congratulations!"

Such a beautiful family. It must have been a wrench for Hennessey to leave his wife and go into space for a year.

"Thank you, Dr Langley. Will you be coming to the cotillion?" Sylvia asked.

"Cotillion?"

"The Spring Ball," Statesman Hennessey added. "It will be held in another six weeks. Everyone attached to the Tabernacle attends, and Dr Langley, as you are now part of everyone, I presume you will be there." He placed his arm around his wife and grinned at Alice.

Alice thought him unwelcoming when she first met him and was glad now of these opportunities to change her opinions. He was entitled to be a little short-tempered at the dinner; he probably just wanted to get home to his lovely family and not have unnecessary distractions. His wife was lovely and, Alice speculated, a fair bit younger than him.

"Then Statesmen Hennessey, if that's the case, I'll be there."

Alice thought she might be making a huge assumption; no-one else had mentioned it. A Spring Ball—

a Cotillion, sounded formal, and she might not be important enough. "I will be spending time in Principality 19, visiting family, but I will come back for the ball if I receive an invitation."

Hennessey bowed.

"We are also returning to our principality. My wife has just had a tour of the Significator, and now, the council is waiting. If you'll excuse us?"

Alice sighed as she watched them walk away, arms around each other. A happy little family, a place to go, a home to return to. As they disappeared into the great hall, she turned towards the lake. Her home had another name now. Principality 19. Not Australia. Principality 19 is where she would be 'visiting' family. The Calamities, where Tasmania used to be. Not so bad maybe, she had always wanted to go to Tasmania. Seeing Statesman Hennessey's little boy made Alice wonder if Michelle's new baby had arrived yet.

The pilot arrived in a similar shuttle to the one which transported them to the city. Alice recognised the Tabernacle markings of two circles, one light green and a darker green in an eclipse against a silver background. This made the shuttle easily identifiable as a Tabernacle vehicle and altogether different from the bold blue and gold chevrons, set within a red braided circle which distinguished a military shuttle.

Pilot Marks, mid-twenties and with an easy manner,

showed Alice the boundaries of Principality One on the shuttle registry, World Government Territory. The boundaries are not physical, he assured her; people moved with freedom between principalities unless they are consigned to the Calamities. Alice had no desire to discuss Calamities, so she told Pilot Marks this area was once called America.

Principal Katya herself had directed Pilot Marks that his passenger had been ill and sometimes, may say odd things. If she did, he must imagine himself as showing the principality to someone who had never visited Earth and to answer as accurately as possible. If he didn't know an answer or how to respond, he must say so. This was one of those times.

"I don't know this area as America, Dr Langley, but old maps exist where this region is referred to as Washington. That was centuries ago, but I'm not sure if this entire continent was called America. There is a place called the Americas, but it's not a principality. All the principalities had names, but not in living memory. History isn't my strong point, but I can research a more accurate and reliable answer if you wish?"

Washington, America. The place of government and where the President lived. For Alice to have travelled there, in her small world, would have been like going to the moon. Now, she had got to do both, visit Washington *and* fly over the moon.

Pilot Marks explained the continent was divided into five principalities. Alice hoped they might travel to them all today, but he informed her, no, it would take too long to visit each one, and their clearance was only within this principality.

As the shuttle lifted into the air, Alice wondered how these vehicles exhibited so little sensation of movement or vibration. Still, she was sure if she enquired, the answer would be technical in the extreme. Hence, she contented herself with using Pilot Marks as a tour guide, asking questions about agriculture, education and the animals she had seen on the smallholdings on the way to the city the previous day.

"All the buildings you see to your right are places of learning, Dr Langley," he banked the shuttle for her to get a good look. "All children in the world will pass through institutions such as these. Most of the animals are owned privately in assigned housing; other animals you see roaming about belong to the science and agricultural schools."

"Did you attend the schools here?"

"I still do. I've almost completed my engineering studies, I graduate in a month, and I'm due to begin my assignment on the Significator when it leaves." Pilot Marks grinned from ear to ear. Alice knew assignment to any principality ship was a huge achievement.

"I've been on the Significator. It's enormous!"

"It is. A city in space and a society all its own."

Alice agreed. It was that.

The sweep of the principality took them a little over two hours. Alice would have liked to spent time walking around the farms and seeing the animals, but the pilot only took the shuttle low enough for a glimpse, reminding her people lived in the houses. Alice understood how rude it would be to land in someone's garden uninvited, but at one property, he dropped low and told her Sarah lived there.

"My steward?"

"Yes, and my mother!"

"Oh, how lovely. Sarah is wonderful!"

Alice looked down on the homestead. White, red-roofed and sitting prettily in the middle of a lawn surrounded by flowers and animals and trees. A beautiful place for an artist to live, with views of the hills and the gleaming dome of the Tabernacle in the far distance.

The university buildings were impressive, with people hurrying around, set on their tasks and oblivious to their humming about overhead. Pilot Marks asked for permission to land the shuttle, and Alice took the opportunity to wander and explore. The buildings were similar in style and possibly as old as the Tabernacle, with the same wide terraces and columns. In contrast to the Tabernacle, these halls had grand, arched windows, with much of the glass stained in reds and greens and reflecting the morning sunshine. To Alice, the colours were so brilliant and glorious; she imagined they might be encrusted with real gemstones.

No-one paid Alice and her pilot any mind. Regardless of whether they were wearing long or short sleeves, each student sported a coloured cuff on their wrist, showing both the training they were undertaking and their education level. Alice saw a few with maroon cuffs and guessed they were learning to be educators.

All the students were in their late teens or early twenties; some men and women were much older. Pilot Marks told her these would be the Lecturers and Professors, drawing her attention again to the different cuff colours. Alice had assumed correctly, maroon for the educators, just like Amelia. Everyone seemed content to be here, unlike Alice's schooldays, when everyone longed for the bell to ring at the end of the day.

The buildings had a majesty to rival the Tabernacle, and Pilot Marks didn't hurry her while she marvelled at the architecture and explored the halls. He knew many of the students, all happy to share with Alice their pride in this beautiful university and their excitement in beginning their prospective careers.

Alice hadn't paid attention to architecture before, but the buildings she'd seen in the past twenty-four hours, the Tabernacle, the city and the university were so impressive; graceful and elegant and unbelievably splendid, it was a subject worthy of further study.

On their return, Pilot Marks left Alice by the lake. It occurred to her that, in all her life, she had never pleased herself and now, it pleased her to walk around the lake and watch the ducks quack and bob up and down, just as they had centuries ago.

This time, Alice made it to the summer house at the far end and sat on the steps. The Tabernacle, its dome of gleaming gold, shone brightly in the midday sun. The lake lay sparkling clear and blue between the summer house and the Tabernacle. Its beauty and clarity made Alice compare it to the small lake near the house she had lived in when she was married to Ted. Such a dirty lake, shopping trolleys and rubbish littered through it with nothing for the poor ducks to eat. It was so polluted; nothing survived in its depths. She used to take the children down there with scraps of bread to feed the ducks. Those poor ducks, soaking the bread in the dirty water before they swallowed. These ducks, here at the Tabernacle, are very lucky ducks.

CHAPTER THIRTY-TWO _

"Alice!!"

She heard her name and looked up to see Sarah hurrying around the perimeter of the lake. Alice stood, meaning to walk to meet her but surprised herself by breaking into a jog. Alice had never run or jogged, ever.

"Sarah! I met your son. He was the pilot who flew me around the principality."

"That was Peter. He's going to the Significator on its next mission,"

"He told me. You must be so proud! How exciting! He took me to his university. I loved it, the buildings were so grand, and he was very informative."

"We'll miss him. He'll be gone for two years, but we've been fortunate to have him close to home this last year."

"Oh, Sarah, sorry, I'm chattering like a monkey. Did you need me for something? Am I late for crochet class?"

"Of course not, it's scheduled for after lunch, but we need to go back to the Tabernacle because Principal Katya has someone she wishes you to meet."

Alice fell into step beside Sarah.

"Meet someone? Who?"

Sarah slowed a little, and Alice got the distinct feeling she was trying to prepare her. She stopped walking, and Sarah turned to her.

"Alice, I assume you have heard of the A'khet?"

A small knot of anxiety formed deep in Alice's stomach. A'khet were aliens.

"A'khet has come to visit Principal Katya. They are close friends. Some people go their entire lives without ever seeing them, but as you are a special guest of the Tabernacle, A'khet wishes to meet you."

"How many are there?"

"Only one."

"Sarah, I'm not sure I want to meet a being from another world. I'm still getting used to beings from this world."

There was no ready answer. Sarah was carrying out Principal Katya's wishes to find Alice and escort her to the library. She now had to appeal to Alice to be brave and sensible.

"Well, you are a being from another time, and we accept you!"

Alice understood and appreciated Sarah's attempt to lighten her apprehension.

"Sarah, on Saturn Station, I was sent to a dinner, on my own with the Significators Principal and his officers. I'd never met them, and I was petrified, but I had no choice. I made a fool of myself in front of them."

"Principal Katya has asked you to come, Alice."

"And in this, I have no choice?"

No-one ever refused a meeting with A'khet. Sarah didn't want to be the one to take a refusal to Principal Katya.

"You can do this with A'khet. I promise. They're good people."

Principal Katya had treated her so well since she'd arrived, but she'd also said no more decisions would be made on her behalf. Would this be the last, or should she expect more? It would be unthinkable to refuse, but the thought terrified her more than the dinner. She trailed along behind Sarah, her throat constricted and her heart bouncing against her ribs, undecided whether to steel herself and summon up courage or run from the scene, screaming. She did neither.

The figure standing beside Principal Katya in the library was around Alice's height. She couldn't make out if the figure were a he or she, but he or she was clad in a long orange and brown robe and around the head, a braided purple and orange band. There were no ears Alice could see, and the small amount of grey hair upon the head was wispy and sparse.

What would be the proper reaction to seeing an alien for the first time? Whether it was from wide-eyed, heart-stopping fear or horrified fascination, Alice's insides flip-flopped and turned somersaults. Her legs turned to jelly as she briefly thought how useful one of Saturn Station's callipers would be right at this moment. Of all the fantastic, odd, frightening and wonderful things to happen to her over the past months, to meet an alien took it all to another dimension.

In a vain struggle to calm her nerves, she inhaled sharply and noisily, causing Principal Katya to turn towards the library entrance. With a squeeze of Alice's arm to encourage her, Sarah took her leave, and Principal Katya beckoned Alice to join them.

As A'khet studied her halting, nervous approach, Alice felt an unspoken command to raise her eyes, and when she obeyed, A'khet's gaze held hers. A sense of calm and serenity trickled from Alice's head down to her toes, and the fear which engulfed her only moments before melted like snow.

"Alice," Principal Katya drew her near. "This is A'khet, here to visit an old lady and to meet you."

Calmed and confident now, Alice's legs grew strong again. Close up, A'khet's large, brown eyes had no eyelashes but, as the being continued to hold her in its gaze, a third eyelid moved across the eyes at regular intervals. A'khet's skin was dark and weathered and reminded Alice of her favourite brown leather handbag, the one with the small creases she kept for best. A'khet's nose and mouth were petite and perfect. Regular, five-fingered hands peeped out from under a cloak.

With the softest and sweetest smile forming on the A'khet's lips, one hand lifted and reached towards Alice to touch her lightly on the arm. At the contact, a pleasant pulsating tingle traversed her arm and shoulder, a tingling that remained even as A'khet pulled its hand back with a suddenness that drew a look of concern from Principal Katya. A'khet's hand remained raised, but the fingers folded over the palm. The tingling continued to make gentle tracks sideways through Alice's chest before moving up through her head to disappear somewhere beyond where she stood.

Principal Katya's concern at A'khet's apparent recoil was partly dispelled when she saw, far from being unsettled, A'khet assumed an expression of recognition and knowing. In her ignorance, Alice didn't realise the significance of this reaction. A'khet nodded slightly, and for a moment, all attention turned inwards, then with eyes lifted again to Alice, A'khet spoke softly.

"Alice?"

There was sadness in A'khet's voice as if in touching Alice, something was learned and accepted. It seemed that using her name framed a sorrowful question—a question that floated between them in the ensuing silence, during which A'khet again gazed deep into Alice's eyes, searching.

"A'khet are gratified to see this temple," A'khet said at length, elegantly sweeping a hand towards Alice's body, "is restored."

Alice didn't answer, only smiled and tilted her head, unable to perceive the meaning behind A'khet's words but recognising no harm would come to her from this gentle person.

For a few seconds more—trancelike, Alice and

A'khet stood opposite one another. In a slow, involuntary movement, Alice lifted her hand. Her fingers opened to press just below her throat, her palm over her chest and there followed an indescribable and overwhelming sense of peace.

A'khet turned her gaze to Principal Katya and, with a tiny gesture, wordlessly expressed the audience be concluded.

Surprised and somewhat troubled by the meeting but losing none of her usual briskness and composure, Principal Katya took Alice's hand.

"So, my dear, you have met A'khet. The first meeting is always brief. This is their way." A'khet made a sideways dip of the head to acknowledge Principal Katya's words. "Now, run along," Principal Katya ushered her out as if speaking to a small child. "There is a surprise for you in your suite."

Not reading anything into the way Principal Katya dismissed her, Alice withdrew, acknowledging both Principal Katya and A'khet with a smile. It occurred to her as she left; she had not uttered a word during the entire interview. Still, there had been an expression, a conveyancing or extraction of information Alice couldn't comprehend. There'd been no reason to fear this meeting; she was such a silly goose.

Principal Katya and her guest watched as Alice disappeared through the wooden doors and headed for the staircase. As soon as she was out of sight, Principal Katya frowned.

"What happened? I have never seen A'khet recoil in this manner."

A'khet held Principal Katya's hand and answered without words.

"A'khet did not recoil, Katya. *She* is A'khet Umru. She is fluid, like the tides, she moves towards, she moves away, but uneven, irregular."

"Umru? I will not pretend to know this word, but does she know this? Does she hide a truth from us?" Principal Katya followed the progress of the Sleeping Beauty phenomenon for decades, and now, having known this lovely girl for only a day, she had made an indelible mark on her life. It would be profoundly disturbing to learn things were not as they seemed.

"She conceals nothing from you, dear sister," A'khet knew her thoughts and reassured her with a touch. "But deeper, too deep even for A'khet, there is…a shadow—a silhouette."

"Evil?"

"Not evil, natural—but not according to nature."

"A'khet makes no sense. Must we fear her? Could it be her awakening is an error that will have consequences for both our species?"

A'khet considered her question and looked back towards the open doorway. Principal Katya felt palpable relief as A'khet communicated the much hoped for reassurance.

"You may love her, Katya, with all your heart, as others will. The young woman will bring immeasurable happiness to you. Do not feel fear; only rejoice she is among you."

Alice walked calmly up the stairs, then paused at the top of the staircase, turning to look down at the great hall. An alien had touched her, man or woman, she couldn't tell, but the strange, reassuring peace A'khet bestowed upon her still tingled around her heart.

CHAPTER THIRTY-THREE _

In her suite, Alice's new clothing had arrived. The tailor had laid out dresses and blouses across the bed, slacks, and other items were folded neatly on the chairs. Alice didn't know where to start. Most of what she wore during her married life came from charity shops and jumble sales, and she only ever bought the cheapest brands of shoes. These beautiful garments, all delivered for her personal use, made her sit and weep with joy and gratitude.

Alice wiped her eyes, sniffed inelegantly and looked around. Next to her lay a large, framed portrait. She lifted the picture to get a better view, supporting the bottom of the frame on the bed.

The artist had cleverly captured the woman's simplicity through a modest line drawing, with touches of colour added to reflect the copper glints of her hair, laid loosely over the left shoulder, her face inclined towards an area below the lower right-hand corner of the frame. Her startling green eyes, looking up from under dark-lashed eyelids, held the secret of an age-old riddle. Her lips curved gently in a childlike smile.

The subject's neck and shoulders were bare, save for one arm crossed over her breast to lay against the opposite shoulder in a protective pose. The fingers were slender, devoid of jewellery and clasped a small spray of lavender between her finger and thumb. The delicate floral pattern on the garment she wore caught the colour of the lavender on a background of white linen and lace.

It was superbly drawn—a portrait of her. For the first time since waking, she experienced a real connection to this body, not just an appreciation of its youth and form, but the freedom to see herself as another sees her, instead of through her own disbelieving eyes in an image definer or mirror.

"Do you like it?"

Sarah stood in the doorway.

"I love it. I—I don't know what to say. It's the most beautiful thing I've ever seen." Alice realised she might sound prideful. "Oh, does that sound terrible?"

Sarah laughed.

"No! I sketched it for you to see how you appear to me. I stayed up all night to get it finished! Alice, you are such a mixture of happiness and sadness, of hope, joy and fear and wonder. I couldn't resist you as a subject. And," she gestured to the clothes lying about the room. "while it's lovely to have all these things; everyone has them, but not everyone has this," she picked up the portrait. "It's something individual, like you, for you to own and to take with you to your new home."

Alice, touched by both Sarah's kindness and the sincerity of the gift, struggled to find the words to express her thanks.

"This is the most wonderful gift I've ever received, Sarah. I will treasure it."

"I know. I won't see you after today as my duties are finished now for a few weeks, but I will see you when you come back to visit. Now, we need to check out these new clothes! What do you think?"

To Alice's delight, Sarah turned to the chair and held up the blouse from the portrait. She explained how it came about.

"Tailor Mitchell and I occasionally design textile patterns together. Principal Katya favours the plain colours, that was why you had little choice. When I spoke to him about your panties, I also asked him to select printed fabrics for the coordinates and design a garment he considered you exclusively. Hence, the blouse."

Alice always wanted to wear something off the shoulder. It had been a long-cherished dream, but in her old life, she'd grown too old to indulge in such a fashion, but now, the floral blouse with the deep frill was a fulfilment of that dream, and to her surprise, everything fitted perfectly.

"My friend, Statesman Patrick, arrives tomorrow. I'll wear the blouse then."

"I know Statesman Patrick. He's a lovely person."

"Yes, he's been so kind. You all have."

"How did your meeting with A'khet go?" It had

been on Sarah's mind after witnessing Alice's uneasiness at the prospect.

"I'm not sure; I assume it went well," Alice hedged a little with her reply. She didn't know how to answer. In hindsight, it hadn't seemed momentous; over it seemed even before it began, the calm and peace she felt for those few minutes afterwards had passed, leaving her puzzled. She thought she would see what Sarah made of it.

"A'khet put her hand on my arm and then took it away as if something had stung her. I think it bothered Principal Katya. We stood looking at each other, it felt pleasant and peaceful, but I believe there was a lot more to it than I understood. Then Principal Katya told me to come up here and that the first meeting is always quick."

"A'khet communicate via touch and telepathy. Verbal communication is selective."

"This one spoke out loud. I didn't get any sense of words in my head; she told me A'khet was happy I was recovered, and then she smiled. She called me a temple."

Sarah laughed. "Not she, not he either. There is no gender with the A'khet."

"Really? How do they have babies?"

"Alice, like you, that has been a mystery for centuries."

"Oh." Alice wasn't sure she aspired to be a mystery alongside aliens.

"Now," Sarah said, sorting through the piles of new clothes. "Choose something nice to wear to show off to Principal Katya, and I'll see you at crochet.

Alice did as she was told. *Something* she didn't fully grasp passed between her and A'khet. Like music, it fluttered around outside the frame of remembrance. Alice shook her head to clear away the feeling, and as soon as she was dressed, went out to the garden in search of Principal Katya. She didn't know whether to hope A'khet was there or not, but she couldn't deny a sense of relief when she found Principal Katya alone.

"Principal Katya, has your visitor left already?" Alice looked around, just in case.

"Always brief visits, my dear. A'khet do not tarry long. They are impatient for the companionship of their own kind. This time, A'khet was interested in meeting you. I find them restful, gentle beings, so they are always welcome here."

Principal Katya made no further mention of the A'khet's visit and though Alice had a few questions, decided she would wait until she saw Patrick the next day and ask him, knowing he knew about them. Meanwhile, one statesman formulated a pattern based on Alice's teachings and wished to present it to the afternoon's crochet class.

Alice was surprised at how interest in the group had grown in a single day. Several male statesmen and councilmen also attended plus Chef, although most were female stewards and female statesmen. The statesman presented the new pattern and method to the class. The design incorporated beads and gemstones and looked to be beyond anything Alice had ever attempted, but on closer examination, she saw it was based only on the few stitches she had shown them. The pattern's designer, a pleasant older lady and former engineer, took a scientific approach, which appeared to sit well with the class's intellect. There were new yarns delivered too; the tailor had taken the time to research crochet and, gaining an understanding of the yarn' purpose, refined the fabric from his first attempt to provide a more supple and workable material.

The progress from the single lesson the day before was impressive. Despite minor fumbling and frustration with co-ordination, Alice noted with interest—and she realised this was a silly old prejudice—even the men were as good at crochet as the women. Most men from her old existence wouldn't be seen dead with a crochet hook in hand!

Between helping and instructing and answering crochet-related questions, Alice noticed everyone chatting and laughing together. Crochet, such a commonplace craft in her time, but here, the greatest minds on the planet were enjoying the simple task of hooking yarn and shaping it into patterns, all the while creating a happy social group of which she was glad to be a part.

Later, alone in her beautiful suite, with her new clothes stored and the portrait hung on the wall, Alice was sorting through and opening the elegant bottles and scents laid out for her exclusive use. It would be an impossible task to choose between each luxurious and indulgent lotion, so she ran the bath and made extravagant with them all.

As on the previous evening, Alice ate so much during the day, when it came to dinner, she felt no desire to eat, but knowing how much Principal Katya liked food, she was concerned not joining her for dinner might cause disappointment. She could make no excuses and decided a walk in the garden might work up an appetite, stopping as she passed the library. The piano stood in the window, polished bright and gleaming. A tune wafted through her head, and although she tried to catch it, it proved too elusive.

The library, where today she met A'khet and last night, according to Statesman Mellor, she played the piano and discussed with him the merits of Mozart and Brahms. He mentioned it to her during crochet, astounded she remembered none of it. She'd played so beautifully, he said, trying to jog her memory but in the end, allowed her assurances she had no recollection of either being in the library or speaking with him. He had not pressed his point further, assuming it must be a side effect of her amnesia.

Books of all sizes covered the library shelves. A few councilmen and statesmen sat on sofas and at registry tables, engrossed in study. There was even a tall, thin robot to locate and fetch the massive tomes from the highest shelf, but it reminded Alice of the blinking, listening light on the ship's registry, so she steered herself as far away as possible.

On a lower shelf, at the opposite end of the library,

Alice found other, simpler and less grand-looking books. Novels maybe? Bending down, she looked through, one title caught her eye, and she took the book from the shelf, wandering over to sit in a window seat. The cover only gave its title, The Element, but nothing inside revealed the subject, or even who wrote it. Still, she began to read anyway and in no time, was swept up in a romantic tale of pirates and wenches, old taverns and hidden treasure, though it struck her at one stage the contents of the book had little to do with its title.

As the evening drew in, the sensor lights responded to her presence. She didn't notice she had now become the sole occupant of the library, and as she hadn't taken the walk, hunger didn't send her to the dining hall or garden.

Principal Katya found her much later after Alice had read almost the entire story.

She sat beside her and peered at the book. "This is a good book, Alice. I have also read it, but *I* did not miss dinner. *I* did not miss hamburgers."

"Principal Katya," Alice closed the book. "I'm so sorry!"

"I am teasing, Alice. You are on vacation. You have given us of your time to teach us crochet. We can surely forgive you for missing dinner, but are you hungry? A young girl should eat. It isn't good to go without food. Would you like hamburgers?"

Alice knew they'd gone to trouble to produce the hamburgers, so she didn't protest. Principal Katya took her hand.

"We will proceed to the kitchen, and Chef will prepare them for you. He followed your instructions to the letter. I liked them. Statesman Mellor did not and pulled a face."

The chef was a little disconcerted with having Principal Katya in the kitchen but found stools for them both to sit up at the counter where he served Alice the hamburger.

Although the lonely, circular creation served in the centre of a plate tasted like a meat pattie, it appeared Chef had only half-listened to Alice's instructions because the meal was again devoid of any accompaniments, suggesting a need to explain the whole thing again, but Principal Katya, keen for a verdict, watched as Alice finished the meat pattie.

"It's good, Principal Katya," Alice smiled to acknowledge the chef's achievement.

Alice's smile did not persuade Principal Katya.

"But you have more to say, I think." She folded her arms, waiting.

"The patties are never served alone," Alice pointed to her empty plate, "usually, we put them with bread and salad and onions and ketchup. That's what makes it a hamburger."

"We can do this, can't we, Chef?" Principal Katya turned to Chef.

"Principal Katya," he raised his hands. "I will have to research ketchup. My aim is to provide a balanced diet for those in the Tabernacle. I would need to investigate to make sure this combination is healthy."

"Chef's right, Principal Katya, all things in moderation."

Chef was grateful for Alice's support. Principal Katya penchant for trying new things was legendary, particularly regarding food.

"You could serve the meat pattie with veggies and leave out the bread," Alice suggested.

"What are these veggies?"

"Vegetables, then have a savoury sauce as an accompaniment," Alice said, hoping this hamburger fixation of Principal Katya's would not become a minor juggernaut.

"Ah. I liked the hamburgers very much, Alice, but we will have them with veggies next time for the balance. Happy Chef?"

He bowed. "Very happy, Principal Katya."

"Then we will try again tomorrow, Chef. Hamburgers and *veggies* with savoury sauce! We will all have this but put another dish on standby for Statesman Mellor, then next day, we will try with bread and lettuce, and Alice will show you how to make ketchup."

Chef bowed to them both, smiling a secret smile at Alice, so much for all things in moderation.

Alice wondered if she should stop telling Principal Katya about the cuisine in the twenty-first century. Her interest in food was unmistakable, and she had many rituals that revolved around mealtimes. Alice was amazed she stayed so slim, but now, thankfully, she didn't insist on Alice eating anything else, walking instead with her to her suite.

"So, you like the new clothing?" she asked.

"Yes, I love them, Principal Katya. You've been unbelievably kind."

"Not at all. Beautiful things make us feel special. You must feel you belong with us."

Alice chose loose yellow slacks and a white blouse as the first items to wear. She felt glamorous and elegant, and when she met with Principal Katya earlier, even though she hadn't commented, Alice had seen her smile of approval.

"In my time, Principal Katya, we went to a shop—a studio—and paid for clothes that were already made. The same for shoes." Alice decided not to mention charity shops.

"Did this clothing fit?"

"Not always, no," Alice admitted. "Or they fitted mostly, and sometimes, the shoes rubbed until you wore them in."

"Then I am glad we have moved on from this practice. This outfit you wear today looks superb. You have splendid taste."

The compliment thrilled Alice because after seeing Sarah's portrait, she now took a different view of her appearance. Good taste? Yes, she looked good in the clothes she'd selected; she didn't care her mother would have been mortified at such a display of pride.

"Sarah made me a gift too."

"Did she? She is wonderfully kind."

"She drew me, Principal Katya, and put the picture in a frame under glass. I love it. May I show it to you?"

"Yes, Alice, thank you. Sarah is an excellent artist."

Alice held the door of her suite open for Principal Katya. The portrait hung in such a way to become the focal point in the room. Principal Katya approached and stood, admiring and appreciative.

"Sarah has captured all we see in you, child. Your sadness, your innocence, your sweetness and the hope of happiness."

She reached across and patted Alice's face, then took her hands and held them in hers, making no attempt to hide her growing affection. "You will have happiness, Alice. Great happiness."

Alice responded with a small smile, and tears welled in her eyes. It was easy to believe what Principal Katya said, for in such a short time, Alice found she admired and liked her perceptive new friend and most importantly, she trusted her.

After Principal Katya left, Alice got ready for bed, searching for the most modest of her new nightgowns to slip into. Unlike the Alice of old, she now preferred to sleep without nightclothes, but if she went sleepwalking in search of the piano again, she would be doubly sure she wouldn't be naked!

As she drifted off to sleep, a tune came into her head. An apt theme for a place like this. Pom, pom... Yes, that's the one, Pomp and Circumstance. Elgar. Yes, Elgar.

She snuggled down in bed, too sleepy to consider she had never heard of anyone called Elgar.

CHAPTER THIRTY-FOUR _

The following morning, Alice's primary task involved checking her nightie was still in place and had the appearance of having been slept in. Much to her relief, it was crumpled and ridden up almost to her armpits. The blinds were already open to herald the day, and Alice hopped out of bed to go over to the window to look out over the lake—her favourite view. Less tired this morning, she took it as a sign she hadn't been on any nocturnal quest to the library.

Over the last couple of days, since arriving back on Earth, she stopped wishing she would wake up in her old life. She wanted to stay here. She still didn't believe she was Alexis Langley, and although her memory of her life as Alice Watkins had become a kind of postscript, she couldn't yet discard those memories because sometimes, they still resonated too loudly to ignore. In many ways, and despite her progress with learning and making friends, she was just as simple as she'd always been.

The morning air was crisp and fresh, her new body

bursting with energy and, enjoying feeling young and free, Alice twirled around, laughing in celebration of the day, only stopping when she caught sight of her portrait. She tilted her head to one side.

"People see sadness in your face?" she asked the redheaded girl in the frame. "That will change."

Alice took great care in dressing that morning. Among her new clothes, she found a pair of below-knee slacks that fitted easily on her slim waist. Alice loved them; she hadn't been this slender in her other life, ever. She pulled on the lavender and white top, adjusted it around her shoulders, and then looked at herself in the image definer. The purveyor had selected a few items of jewellery and, among them, a gold bracelet. Alice liked the effect but also found a delicate chain to place around her neck to lessen the bareness of her neck and shoulders. Perfume was the next mystery. She had never, ever owned perfume, and now she had about ten bottles of varying scents, from floral to spicy. Less is more, someone once said, so she applied it sparingly before taking one last look at the image definer. It was as though she had been called upon to appraise the appearance of someone she was only just getting to know. It didn't take long because, yes, she approved.

Alice's happiness at seeing Patrick again made it difficult for her to focus on breakfast. Her excitement wasn't lost on Principal Katya.

"It is clear to me you can't wait," she stood and

beckoned for Alice to follow her. "Come, we will go and see if he has arrived."

They walked arm in arm out to the great hall. The shuttle was leaving with Patrick already heading for the Tabernacle. As soon as he spotted them, he broke into a run and caught Alice in a bear hug, leaving her speechless and breathless. She hadn't even said hello, and what about protocols?

"You have never greeted your Principal with such enthusiasm, young Patrick," Principal Katya sniffed.

"I'm sorry, Principal Katya," he said, laughing and kissing her on both cheeks before executing the usual bow. These two were close, that much was obvious, close enough for Patrick to have no worries about showing his affection towards Alice in her presence.

"That is alright, Patrick. I am happy you are here. A year is too long, and we miss having a Patrick in the Tabernacle."

"I'm glad to be here," he replied, sending a dazzling smile Alice's way. Principal Katya, keen-eyed, didn't miss it.

"Yes, I can imagine. Now, Patrick, I have told you, Alice is on vacation. She will do only what she wishes. You do not give her orders. Her time is her own."

"Yes, Principal Katya."

Principal Katya smiled at Alice.

"Go and enjoy yourselves. Alice, don't let him bully you and don't forget crochet class this afternoon."

She left them standing out on the lawn.

Patrick put his arm around Alice's shoulder and pulled her close.

"Crochet class?"

"It's a craft we practised in my time," Alice told him. "Principal Katya is quite taken with it. A few of the statesmen and councilmen have joined in too."

"Can I come to the class? Principal Katya has instructed that I'm not to intrude upon your time. Obviously, that excludes *her* taking up your time. But if it's the only way I can spend time with you…"

"I liked showing them how to crochet, Patrick, although I must admit, I'm surprised it's so popular. They don't really need me there; they've already turned it into a science."

"Are you responsible for her hair too?"

"Afraid so."

"Well, creating quite a stir, aren't you?"

Alice didn't know about creating a stir, but as they walked down to the lake, she enjoyed telling him all the things she'd done in her short time there.

He drew her into the shade of one of the giant willows and encircled her in his arms.

"Did you miss me, Alice?" he murmured against her hair.

Alice lifted her head and looked up at him. How handsome he looked this morning, running across the lawn, white shirt open, curly hair unconfined and falling to his shoulders, like a scene from a film. He waited for her to answer, blue eyes twinkling, and his mouth lifted into that achingly attractive lop-sided smile. This man, confident, attractive, accomplished, had left the bridge of a mighty starship to be here with her. She leaned her face against him, her hands resting on his chest as she listened to the beating of his heart.

"Yes, Patrick," she said, wondering why she hesitated after her earlier excitement. "I did miss you."

They sat together on the grass, in idle conversation, watching the ducks and birds and insects go about their daily business.

"How long are you here for?" she asked.

"Only till the morning," he kissed her on her shoulder. "I need to visit my mother before I go back to space dock."

"I'm leaving to be with my new family soon. I'll be living in the Calamities."

Alice thought she could become used to the idea of a family, but the concept of the Calamities still troubled her. Patrick, however, was delighted with the news.

"Which relatives and which Calamities?"

"I'm not sure exactly, Patrick, and the Calamities are in my homeland, apparently."

"That's wonderful, Alice," he hugged her close. "I spent a year at university in Principality 19, close to the Calamities. It's pleasant there; you'll love it. I can take time off, so I'll visit. As I said, I tend to come and go while we're in space dock."

Alice had decided not to research the Calamities on the registry. She was nervous enough without facing the prison-like landscape from her dream. Dr Grossmith had told her it was lovely, and now Patrick was saying the same, but she wouldn't believe it till she saw it for herself.

"I would like it if you came to see me, Patrick. It's kind of you to make time."

"Not kind at all Alice, I enjoy being with you."

Her head was resting against his shoulder, so he used his free hand to lift her face, and she closed her eyes. His lips were soft on her cheek, moving down to the side of her neck, and she felt his warm breath on her skin. Laying her down gently in the grass, he placed his mouth over hers. Instead of being lost in the moment, it occurred to Alice that Patrick was doubtless exceedingly skilled at kissing, given Principal Katya's remark about a trail of broken hearts across the galaxy. Alice wondered whether he would put his tongue inside her top lip again; he was placing a fair amount of pressure on her lips, so he probably would have to pull back or start again.

Her eyes snapped open, but she quickly closed them again, sure he hadn't seen that instead of enjoying the kiss, she was performing an analysis! Perhaps, starting a romance at this stage, regardless of Patrick's dazzling good looks, might be a mistake, especially when her emotions were in such turmoil. Even so, to not hurt his feelings when he let her go, Alice tried to behave in a manner she thought someone who liked to be kissed would behave.

"You seem to know this place well," she said, sitting

up and hoping to divert him. "What do you like to do when you are here?"

"My father became second Statesman to Principal Hallam after he was injured in an accident. I lived over there." He leaned upon his elbow and pointed through the trees to a house on a hill. Neat and well-kept, like the others she had seen, and set within lovely gardens.

"Does anyone live there now?"

"I expect so; I don't know who, but you asked what I like doing here. First thing? I go swimming."

"Swimming?" she echoed. It wasn't the answer Alice expected. "I can't swim."

"That's okay, it's not deep and not serious swimming. I'll show you."

She could complain about cold or something, but on such a warm day, it would have sounded like an excuse. He took her hand and pulled her to her feet. Alice was going swimming, like it or not.

CHAPTER THIRTY-FIVE _

The pool lay tucked away at the garden's furthermost edge, in a clearing close to the rear of the Tabernacle and down a grassy bank. A narrow waterfall skipped over the top of a low cliff, dropping down into the clear water and making little splashlings spray up and sparkle like diamonds in the morning sun.

Alice fell in love instantly with this extraordinary haven for waterbirds and wildlife, the variety of willows and water grasses, more ducks, and the sounds of birds in the trees. She wondered why she hadn't discovered it when she explored the gardens.

Patrick sprinted on ahead.

"This is one of my favourite places on the planet," he shouted back to her. "*Any* planet!"

As he ran, he shed his clothes. By the time he reached the water, he was stark naked. Alice stopped, shocked, shutting her eyes too late to miss the sight of his bare bottom as he plunged laughing into the pool.

The excited splashing stopped, and she could tell he

was watching, but still, she kept her eyes closed.

"What's wrong?" Patrick's voice came from somewhere up ahead.

"*You haven't got any clothes on*," she whispered, but he heard her.

"Why would I?" he called back. "I'm in the water. It's lovely. Come in."

When she didn't move or open her eyes, it was easy for Patrick to work out the reason why she had suddenly become bashful.

"Don't worry, Alice. I'm pretty much covered."

"Patrick, I don't have a cozzie."

"What's a cozzie?"

"A swimming costume. To wear when you go swimming."

She took a deep breath and opened one eye. Sure enough, he was waist-deep—the only problem? The water was like glass. She looked away.

"Is it like clothes?"

"Yes."

"Why wear clothes when you're going to get wet?"

"Where I come from, we don't swim naked." Alice thought it wasn't strictly true; she knew people swam and sunbathed in the nude.

"Oh, well, you can come in as you are." He held out his arms to her.

Alice took a few faltering steps forward, then looked down at her new slacks and top and decided she wouldn't. She knew she was a party-pooper.

"If you must wear a swimming costume, Alice, wear one that hides those thighs. And you are lily-white. A moon tan. That's what you've got."- Alice's mother.

An uncommon trait in women of his time, Alice's shyness amused Patrick, but it wasn't his intention to see her struggle.

"It's okay, Alice, put my shirt on; it'll be fine."

She looked at Patrick's shirt, lying where he discarded it and large enough to cover her up so only her lower legs would show. She picked it up and slipped out of her top, but he was still watching.

"Patrick!"

He laughed and ducked down under the water.

Alice had never stripped so fast; she dragged his shirt over her head, feeling an uncomfortable intimacy wearing his clothes. It was enormous on her, so she rolled up the sleeves and tied the hem around her thighs to stop it flapping. He bobbed up again just in time to see her pulling the shirt tight to hide her panties.

Of course, he'd peeked; it was in his nature. Patrick had never seen a woman in panties. He knew of their existence but thought they were a garment only for the elderly. Alice was a source of never-ending surprise, and standing there on the grass, dipping her toe in the pool, wearing his shirt with those little panties underneath, she was also very desirable. He'd expected her to undress and jump in with him; in this culture, everyone swam naked. It wasn't an invitation to ogle, although he often did. Again, it was in his nature.

He bit his lip at his frank self-appraisal. He'd never met a woman like Alice. She didn't wear her beauty to seduce or beguile, nor use her appeal to further ambition. New to this world, she was an innocent. And she had charmed him.

She saw him watching her and jumped, gasping as she hit the cold water, he caught her in his arms and splashed her, and she splashed right back. Thankfully, standing on tiptoe, she just touched the bottom of the pool so she could get away from him when he chased her. They played together like children until exhausted, he helped her up onto a boulder behind the waterfall. When he put his arms around her, she leaned against him, making sure she positioned herself so as not to come eye to eye with his lower half.

Her wet hair was draped across her chest and dripping onto her legs. Looking down, she saw her breasts outlined through the damp shirt and moved to cover them, hoping Patrick hadn't noticed.

His arm tightened around her, his body cool against her back. He kissed the back of her neck, then trailed gentle kisses down toward her shoulder. She sat up.

"What's wrong?" he asked, allowing her out of his embrace but keeping his hand on her back. She felt its warmth through the shirt.

"Nothing."

Pulling up her knees in a hug, she turned her head towards him, smiling, so he wouldn't think she was rejecting him, although that was precisely what she was doing. She just didn't know why.

"I wanted to ask you about the A'khet."

"Principal Katya told me that any education was out of the question. You are supposed to be relaxing." He stroked her back.

"She also said I could do what I wanted," she reminded him.

"That's true," he grinned. "Okay, ask away."

"Well, I know you know the A'khet well. This Knowledge you received from them; can you tell me more?"

"I'm sorry, I can't," he said. "Knowledge comes directly from the A'khet, but as I told you on the Significator, without it, we wouldn't have such advanced space travel or shuttles or automatrans and definitely, no household utilities. A'khet helped the world recover from the effects of the plague. Mankind had so much work ahead in repairing society on this planet. A'khet, in their wisdom, did not offer us the means of space exploration until we made substantial inroads into rebuilding and reformation. When the space programs resumed at the end of the twenty-second century, we were no further along than say, unmanned probes to Mars."

"You've come a long way. And only a few receive this Knowledge?"

"That's right," Patrick sat up and leaned forward, adopting a similar pose to Alice. She was glad of it because his knees were hiding his you-know-what.

"An ancestor of mine lived among them for a

while." He ran his finger down her arm, then folded his arms over his knees and rested his chin comfortably, looking out at the water sprinkling down from the waterfall. "She was the first to receive Knowledge, and since then, any member of the Patrick family who takes up the same branch of engineering may receive it, but as I said, it can only be given by the A'khet. My sister doesn't have it, and that may be because she is an educator. You might get to meet A'khet one day. Principal Katya is close to them. I sometimes think Principal Katya has Knowledge of some kind."

"I met one, Patrick, yesterday, Principal Katya introduced us, but it was all over in seconds. I thought I had offended her or him. I'm not sure. Sarah, my steward, said there is no he or she, only they, or just A'khet."

He was genuinely surprised.

"A'khet are reclusive, and for one of them to leave their community is an unusual move. You are honoured, Alice, and Sarah is correct, they're genderless, and there are no children. My ancestor has written papers recounting her time with them and mentions there seems to be no reproductive process. No-one can explain it, and the A'khet aren't telling."

"But they told you about the engines."

"They told us about Substance and how to align it, but we had to do our work as well."

Alice hadn't been behind a waterfall, and it was nice just to sit here and chat. It would be perfect if she and Patrick could simply be friends.

"May I ask you a question now?"

She rested her cheek on her knees, hugging herself tightly and smiling an unspoken 'of course'.

Patrick thought back to a few days before, in the engine room. He hadn't mentioned the incident to anyone, even Ryan. It might have been a random and unimportant memory, but he thought he would still ask.

"When we were at the Gravidarum, you pointed to the Substance housings and said, 'I know these'. Had you seen them on the registry?"

She shook her head. "No. I don't understand engines. The only ones I have ever seen are in cars and motorbikes. I certainly don't remember seeing the ones on the ship anywhere before that day. Are you sure that's what I said?"

"Positive. Hmm, car and motorbike? I know of these—combustion engines of the twentieth and twenty-first centuries. Pollutants powered them. I thought it odd for you to comment on the technology."

"Patrick, I say and do many things I either don't remember or that make no sense to me. Don't read too much into it. I have a lot of memories to recover, and occasionally, the water gets a bit muddied."

He had to be satisfied with her answer; there was no other explanation, so he reached out and gently pulled her back against his chest. She had to close her eyes as he moved his body to hold her close. His bottom was already more of his anatomy than she needed to see.

"You know, you have me thinking about you all the

time," his voice was low. "Your hair, your eyes, the things you say, your sweetness. And now I know about crochet and blue hair and panties."

"Panties!?"

She squirmed away to glare at him, accusing, forgetting to avert her eyes. He had seen her *panties!?*

"Well," he flashed her a crooked smile and kissed her hand. "I haven't ever actually seen anyone wearing them, but on you, they're quite sexy!"

"Patrick, you are shocking!" Wriggling free of his grasp, she scaled down the boulder back into the water, Patrick in pursuit.

Scrambling out of the pool, she didn't look at him as he flopped onto the grass, insisting she would only lie next to him if he lay on his stomach, laughing, he rolled over, and Alice closed her eyes so as not to see his bottom as she laid down beside him. They spent a pleasant hour, letting the sun dry them off, Patrick's arm draped lazily across her back and occasionally, brushing away a little insect or pointing out the native wildlife that turned up to investigate.

"I'm dry now," Alice said, in danger of dozing off in the warmth and peace. "What other things do you like to do when you are here?"

"I'll show you."

He reached over and handed Alice her blouse. "I'm not much into sports, but there is one pastime I do enjoy. You might too, but I'll need my shirt back."

Alice stood and held up her blouse and slacks. This

time, he took the hint and turned his back, but she heard him having a little, hardly suppressed chuckle to himself. Once dressed, she handed him back his still-damp shirt, and it was her turn to turn away, only opening her eyes when he took her hand to lead her away from the pool.

They clambered up the grassy slope, leading to the side of the stream that fed the waterfall. From the top, they had a good view of the house Patrick had lived in as a child. He stopped to look.

"You have happy memories of this place?"

"Yes, I do, but I didn't live here until I was five. My parents were both in the military, working on the starships. They met, married and had my sister all within a year. Mother had short assignments on Saturn Station. She was a geologist with a special interest in Saturn's moons, but my father's assignments were always that bit longer, mainly because of the importance of his work and the fact he had A'khet knowledge. From the beginning, they decided only to have one child, with the idea that when Eileen went to aptitudes at fifteen, they would return to work in space."

"What happened?"

"Me!" he laughed. "I happened. Mother became pregnant when Eileen was ten. It's rare and usually a result of a chip malfunction. It was a surprise when I came along; it meant they never returned to long-term space assignments."

"Were they upset?" She thought how angry Ted had been when she became pregnant with Steven when Michelle was ten as if it were all her fault.

"Not at all! They were great parents, and Eileen and I had great childhoods, but my father was injured in an explosion on the space dock. He recovered, but even after extensive investigations, no-one ever discovered the cause. The injuries kept him earthbound, and Principal Hallam, the World Principal at the time, requested he come here to Principality One to become an adviser to the Space Program Engineering Division at the Tabernacle. Hence, that house and this…" he gestured all around and towards the pool, "my playground."

They were standing by the stream, the pool below them.

"That way is a shortcut to the Tabernacle," he pointed towards a narrow crossing. "There are stepping-stones over there."

Placed short distances apart, the stones were large and flat enough for Alice to negotiate with ease.

"Did you put these stones here?" she imagined he played here often in his childhood. To her amazement, Patrick told her no, Ryan had placed the stones there when Patrick hadn't been big enough to lift them but wanted to go back and forth whenever he needed to go from the house to the Tabernacle.

"I was six or seven, a scrawny little thing," he smiled at the memory. "Ryan about thirteen or so. He and his sisters were here for recess."

Alice couldn't imagine Principal Ryan ever being a child. He was too large.

"Where are your parents now?"

"My father died a few years ago, Mother lives back in our home principality, and Eileen lives there too. She's married and has a son, Edmund; he's fourteen.

"Your mother will be thrilled to see you, Patrick. Mothers are important," and briefly, a shadow dulled the brilliance of her eyes. On instinct, he softened his voice to match the sudden change in her mood.

"Yes, they are, and my mother is wonderful. I'll take you to meet her one day."

He lifted her hands to his lips and held them there. Patrick couldn't possibly have known, but speaking of his mother reminded Alice of Michelle.

"Don't be silly, mum; you aren't a nuisance. I'll pop over when I've finished feeding the twins"- Michelle, Alice's daughter.

And then she would forget to come.

"Mums need their kids, Patrick," Alice said, removing her hands from his and turning to walk down the hill towards the Tabernacle, leaving him to stand and reflect on the meaning of her last, somewhat mournful remark.

CHAPTER THIRTY-SIX _

It did not surprise Alice that Patrick, with his years of being the only child who lived at the Tabernacle, knew every single hidden path and back entrance to the building. Naturally, one led to the kitchen, where he was eager to try the hamburgers he'd heard about from Principal Katya. Chef, fed up with the sight of meat patties, showed Alice how to use cooking plates and heating beams to make them herself, then left her to assemble the burger using a bun that wasn't real bread and ketchup that only gave a nod to ketchup. It all made little difference to Patrick, who, impressed by the fact Alice could cook, finished the whole thing in three bites; he took longer to finish praising her "invention."

In the afternoon, he took her to another of his favourite pastimes. Archery. Alice smacked herself in the face several times before shooting any arrows, and she missed every target. Most of the arrows she fired disappeared into bushes or the sky, never to be seen again or, as Patrick teased, for collection from space dock after being plucked out of some unsuspecting, passing starship. By the end of the afternoon, her only compensation was a sore arm which Patrick massaged until the stiffness eased, but in no way did it spoil her mood. For too many years, Alice had been a stranger to laughter and play, and today, she experienced all those things, mostly, she thought, thanks to Patrick. Apart from his romantic overtures, which she didn't know how to handle, he might be just what the doctor ordered.

Now there's a thought. Dr Grossmith wouldn't have *ordered*...?

She knew it was foolish. Patrick's importance to the Significator couldn't be underestimated. That he took time away from his work to be with her should be assurance enough, his affection was genuine.

So, between archery, happy conversation and visiting one of the city's pasticiums, the afternoon flew by, and as foreseen by Principal Katya, crochet class went ahead without Alice.

Just before sunset, Patrick left her at her suite to bathe and change her clothes before dinner. She stripped off, wrinkling up her nose as she picked bits of grass off her skin and from inside her blouse, even finding a daisy stuck to her tummy. Waving her hand over the water controls, Alice watched the bath fill, idly contemplating the bubbles arising from too liberal a dose of the lavender-scented gel she discovered in the toiletries. Looking up, she saw herself in the image definer.

"You," she said out loud to her flushed and vibrant reflection, "look like the cat that got the cream."

Setting the image definer to full length, she surveyed her body. Her breasts were firm and round, with rosy pink nipples. Her skin glowed with health, and her belly, smooth and flat. A faint line was just visible between her breasts, and she ran her finger down to where it finished above her navel. Where they put in the new cells for her heart and other things, she supposed. She twisted around to search for scars on her back, but besides two tiny indentations above her kidneys, it was unblemished—a nice body, far nicer than the one she had in her old life.

Later, Patrick stood with Principal Katya, waiting for Alice to arrive for dinner.

"So, Patrick, a conquest?"

"No, Principal Katya," he replied, clasping his hands behind his back and glancing towards the door where he expected Alice any moment. "She's a mystery, I know she has a fondness for me, but as soon as I get close, she pulls away. I'm at a loss."

Principal Katya gave much thought during the day to Patrick's unrestrained delight at seeing Alice. Many women fell under his spell, and it would indeed bewilder him to meet a woman who did not succumb at once to his charm, but never, had she seen, as she had that morning, Patrick make such a show of public affection towards one woman.

"No, she has conquered you, is what I mean."

His face broke into a broad smile, and he shrugged a little.

"Well, you must admit, she's exceptional. Beautiful, sweet…" he drifted off, lost in thoughts romantic.

Principal Katya considered telling him of A'khet's solemn disclosure,

"She is A'khet Umru."

Perhaps attempting to speak of it would invoke a paralysis of speech, the temporary stilling of the tongue placed on all Knowledge holders by the A'khet, lest their most precious secrets fall into the wrong hands. When A'khet communicated with her, even though the word was unknown to Principal Katya, she became conscious of the extraordinary sanctity of Umru, but the meaning was withheld. Principal Katya had been close to A'khet for many years and had received necessary snippets of Knowledge in that time, but none carried the weight of Umru.

Patrick was falling for Alice, so, in this matter, she would keep her own counsel and only tell him that A'khet requested Alice to visit them at their sanctuary. They may then inform him of Alice's special significance themselves.

"A'khet came to see her."

There would be no other ground-shaking revelations tonight, she decided.

"Yes, she told me. Interesting."

"They want her to go to them."

"They do?" he turned to her, his perfect forehead creasing into a frown. He waited for her to explain, scanning her face for the answer to the unspoken question of "why?" But Principal Katya wisely allowed the question to hang between them.

Alice's arrival at the dining hall distracted him. Wearing a simple and elegant ankle-length white dress, her hair swept over her shoulder; she saw they were waiting for her but took the time to greet statesmen and councilmen who acknowledged her as she made her way across the room.

"I'll return as soon as I'm able, Principal Katya," Patrick kept Alice in his sights, "and take her to A'khet then. Right now, she's enjoying the Tabernacle." He glanced down and gave Principal Katya a conspiratorial wink, "and me, I hope."

She put her arm through his and smiled.

"I hoped you would take her, Patrick. She deserves to know who she is."

Dinner turned out to be a pleasant affair, one shared with Statesman Mellor, who enjoyed the company without contributing too much to the conversation and a somewhat dour and serious Statesman Evesham, who Alice had met only once. Statesman Evesham succeeded Patrick's father in the Space Engineering Division. His wife, Karla, a stunning ebony-skinned woman in her fifties, possessed a wit to rival even Patrick's. Alice, the two statesmen and

Principal Katya spent much of the evening watching the amusing repartee between Karla and Patrick, an animated display of one-upmanship which Patrick was at risk of losing. Alice had never laughed so hard and the evening such fun, everyone forgot the time, ending up late to their beds.

Patrick escorted Alice back to her suite. The sensor lights only offered a dim response to their presence in the deserted corridor. She opened her door and turned to him.

"I wish you weren't leaving tomorrow, Patrick. I had a lovely time today," she said.

In reply, he gathered her into his arms, stepped inside the room and buried his face in her neck. It was so sudden, Alice gasped. She heard a soft click as he pushed the door closed with his foot.

"I won't be gone for long, and I'm here now," he whispered, his lips moving over her neck and her shoulder.

What was she supposed to do? His embrace was urgent, persuasive, but did she want this? Are her hormones meant to get triggered about now? Would she even know if they did? Her only information had been gleaned from silly romantic stories in magazines and novels, so she copied the heroines and slid her arms around his waist and over his back. Encouraged, his mouth moved to hers, and she tried to kiss him back as best she knew how, but when his tongue probed deeper than the inside of her top lip, Alice found it startling and intrusive and had to steel herself not to pull away.

"You only get back what you put in."-Alice's mother.

Mother probably hadn't specifically meant something like this. Ted had always maintained she was frigid. Perhaps if she tried harder with Patrick, she would feel something more than…appreciation? Friendship? *Companionship?*

She closed her eyes, trying to focus on any positive feelings. How nice he smelled, his back hard and muscular beneath his shirt. He pushed her hair from her shoulder and kissed the other side of her neck. Well, that's a pleasant enough sensation, she decided after a moment, reminding herself to be positive and stop analysing. She tried jogging a response by evoking an image of seeing him naked that day at the pool. He had muscles and a smooth, hairless chest, and he looked nice, she reasoned. What if she tried moving her hands around his chest and up to the back of his neck?

She got it right, for him at least. Once more, his mouth came down on hers, harder this time, and he slid his hands down to grip her bottom, pulling her against him. For the first time since Ted, Alice felt the full length of a man against her, and it was too much. She took a deep breath and reached behind to take his hands away, old guilt rushing up, mixed with appalling shame she had let it get this far.

"Is that a no?" Patrick stepped back, surprised, his breathing ragged.

"Yes, no. I mean, yes, it's a no."

She shouldn't have led him on. She gazed at the floor, embarrassed, but he lifted her face, perhaps to find out why the apparent change of heart, but she pulled away and stood, miserable and returned her gaze downwards. He placed both his hands on her shoulders and bent down a little to peer at her face, prompting her to look at him. But she remained silent.

"For a moment, I thought it was a yes," he spoke gently. He'd been too eager; the last thing he wanted was to scare her away.

"Patrick," Alice said, fidgeting with her hands and ignoring his efforts to get her to look at him. "You are the most handsome and confident man I have ever met, and I am so confused. Where I come from, people don't do these things unless they're married."

He smoothed out a strand of her hair.

"That can be arranged."

"Patrick!"

Her surprise made her look up. Unbelievably, he was serious.

"We've only known each other for *two weeks!!* Ted and I were engaged for a whole year!!"

He took his hand away.

"Who's Ted?"

There, she had spoken without thinking and not told the truth about having to be married to have sex; it was just a lame excuse. So now she must explain herself if she could.

"Are you aware—did Dr Grossmith tell you I believe I'm Alice Watkins and not Alexis Langley?"

"His report speaks of a transitional personality confusion disorder, he isn't dismissive, but he doesn't think it will be permanent either. The name Alice Watkins isn't mentioned at all, so I would have to say, no, I'm not aware."

"Well, Alice Watkins—me, I have been married, I—she, had children, Patrick I'm sorry, I'm in a muddle, it's hard to explain," she put her hands to her face and closed her eyes. "I remember my husband dying and every detail of that life, even the grandchildren, birthdays, anniversaries. It's so clear; I can hardly believe it's not my history. Alexis Langley…she's a stranger to me. I know nothing of science or spaceships or the world. In fact, I know very little about anything at all. In many ways, I still think like Alice Watkins."

"But there's no doubt you are Alexis Langley," Patrick could be a pragmatist when needed, "and before you were preserved, you were a biochemist. These memories of this other woman can't be explained. Dr Grossmith believes they will fade."

"They haven't faded yet, not completely anyway," Alice mumbled.

Well, Patrick thought, serve him right for not reading the full report. If he had, he would have been better prepared, though her story explains why she prefers being called Alice to Alexis. Maybe speaking of this Alice Watkins might give them both some perspective.

"Did Alice Watkins love her husband?" he risked a question.

"As it happened, Patrick, I hated him," Alice decided under the circumstances, honesty would be the best policy. "I've only come to realise that fact lately. I had a miserable existence with him. The children were the only good things to have come from the marriage."

"Why did she marry him?" *And children?* It was difficult to imagine her in such a situation.

"Because her mother—my mother, told me to."

"You aren't old enough to have had children and grandchildren, and if you're widowed, you are free to marry again."

"That's the point, Patrick. I don't even look like Alice Watkins; part of me thinks as Principal Hardy and Dr Grossmith, that I can't possibly be her. She's sixty-four, white-haired and wrinkled," she pointed to the image definer. "That tells a different story."

He thinks I'm batty, she thought, and her misery increased with each passing moment.

"Your physical appearance proves this theory of yours to be wrong, Alice."

He took her hand, intertwining their fingers. She welcomed the gesture, for she couldn't bear to part on bad terms.

"I know," she sighed. "Like everyone, you're right, but I have her memories and morals somehow instilled in me, and they are hard to dismiss." Alice had to concede that on her appearance alone, all notions about being Alice Watkins should be thrown out the window. "Outwardly, I'm Alexis Langley, even I accept that, but looking like one person and experiencing the feelings of another has its crippling moments."

"How do you know you're not experiencing Alexis Langley? Perhaps what you perceive as the moral stance of Alice Watkins belongs, in fact, to her? It may be that your mind has created a history for itself until the amnesia passes. You may be behaving exactly as Alexis Langley behaves." Patrick remembered his father grappling with memory issues for a few months following his accident.

"I'm trying to accept all assurances that in time, things will become clear, but Patrick, you must see I'm not ready to have a relationship. I haven't even got a relationship with myself yet."

Patrick stood in silence. Alice half expected him to turn on his heel and slam the door shut behind him. It would have been understandable, but she misjudged him, giving her another reason to feel ashamed because instead of walking out, he smiled and tenderly stroked her face.

"You are wise, Alice. Wiser than I have been, but I'm not planning on giving up. If I rushed you, I'm sorry. In a few months, I'll be leaving Earth, and I'll be away for two years. Would that be long enough to learn who you are, so you can teach me about yourself when I get back? We can spend time together before I leave."

He pulled her close again, and she let him kiss her to make things alright.

Alone again, Alice sat on the bed, her emotions in a

complete jumble over what had passed between them. No-one had ever made a pass at her, well not at Alice Watkins. It never entered her head that such a momentous event would ever occur, and now it had, with someone she liked and respected, she'd said no, not willing yet to experiment with this body.

The window was wide open, the moon high in the sky and its reflection bobbed about in the lake like a giant gold ball, but her thoughts stayed with Patrick. So kind and attentive and such a dear. She touched her mouth, the sensation of his tongue against hers; had she truly not liked it? And, her shyness aside, seeing his beautiful body as he ran into the pool, surely something should have stirred? But she couldn't deny the truth that each time he kissed her, she felt *nothing*.

CHAPTER THIRTY-SEVEN _

The exchange with Alice left Patrick restless, compounded by the inescapable memory of her in those tiny grey panties. He never imagined old women's underwear would be so erotic. And his shirt, several sizes too large, tied around her thighs and then later, in her suite, feeling her so close to him, her body responding to his for those brief moments before she called a halt. Even the serious nature of the conversation when she rejected him hadn't diminished his desire for her.

He got out of bed, pulled his shirt over his head, hopped into his slacks and went in search of a drink. At this hour, he knew where to find one.

Statesman Mellor was sitting in the big hall. Glasses and a bottle of the finest Scotch on a table at his side, he motioned for Patrick to join him.

"Drink?"

"Yes, thank you, Mellor."

"I saw you leave the suites earlier," Mellor said. "Teaching our little fledgeling how to fly?"

"Hardly."

Patrick took the drink and took the seat opposite Statesman Mellor.

"As she points out, we've only known each other for a couple of weeks."

"That makes a difference to her?"

"It does, and I will respect that, seeing as I got roundly rejected. She says in her time, sexual freedom is bound up in commitment, marriage, namely. To cap it all, she's unsure about who she is and her place in our society."

"Well, she's important to you, and she's made many friends here in such a short time. Alice is a likeable girl."

"That's true, Mellor, but there are times when she makes comments, then doesn't remember what she said, or she may remember events from the past that can't possibly be the way things happened. It all only adds up to a sentence here and there, but I find it perplexing."

"Well, I can testify to that."

"Testify to what?"

"Her memory of events. The other night as is my usual practice, I was seated here. Alice came down those stairs and, without a word," he pointed to the main staircase, "entered the library and played the piano; at first, I thought nothing of it."

"Played the piano? I don't understand. She claims she knows nothing about music. Wait—she *made* that claim and then commented on a piece played at a chamber concert on the ship. I thought it odd at the time."

"Well," Statesman Mellor continued, "after an hour

of listening to a precise and well-executed performance, I went in and there she was, in her nightclothes."

"*Night clothes?* That doesn't sound like Alice."

"Nevertheless, in her nightclothes and barefoot, I may add, playing Rachmaninov, followed by Beethoven, then Chopin and a fine rendition of To a Wild Rose. I am a pianist myself. I know well-played when I hear it."

"I can't believe it."

"You're not alone there; she doesn't believe it either. When I saw her the next day, she had no recollection. I told her I spoke to her at length about the pieces she played and how very well-exercised she was in the classical composers. She was utterly at a loss to explain herself and marginally uncomfortable I even mentioned it."

"Surely, music would be intrinsic, Mellor, like artistic ability. How can she not remember?"

"I can't answer that, Patrick. I've not been briefed on the full details of her revival."

Statesman Mellor leaned forward; there were times even intrepid young principality ship officers need fatherly counsel.

"Patrick, do yourself a favour. Let her take her time. She's right; two weeks isn't long, and let's be realistic, where women are concerned, you have a short attention span."

Statesman Mellor had known Patrick since he and his family arrived at the Tabernacle following his father's accident and had always felt a special affinity to the younger Patrick, but faced with a thoughtful silence, wondered if his opinion had been unwelcome. Patrick merely shook his head slowly.

"Not this time, Statesman. Not this time." He stood. "Thank you for the drink, Statesman Mellor, I'm leaving to visit my family in the morning, but I'll be back at the Tabernacle for the cotillion."

Mellor grinned and saluted him with his glass. He'd heard it all, many times. Patrick was a wolf. A likeable wolf, but a wolf nonetheless.

Patrick ordered a one-person shuttle and, jumping into the pilot's seat, placed a call to his mother, then sped towards the city. He'd planned to give Alice something to remember him by tonight, but it wasn't meant to be. So, he'd thought of something else to give her instead.

As usual, when the blinds rose, Alice checked her nightclothes to establish that if she had gone walkabout during the night, she had not gone naked. Assured of her decency, she wandered into the bathroom. Bath or shower, she said to herself. Decisions, decisions, then stepped into the shower. Patrick had to leave first thing, and she didn't want to miss him, wanting to be sure their conversation the night before hadn't diminished their friendship. Still damp from the shower and pulling on her bathrobe, she barely covered herself when Patrick stuck his head around the door unannounced.

"Patrick. You could have knocked."

"I know that, but if you had been naked, you

wouldn't have let me in."

He closed the door behind him, not waiting for an invitation to enter.

"Of course I wouldn't. I still haven't; you invited yourself."

"Exactly. Alice, I'm about to leave. The shuttle will be here at any moment. I wanted to be sure that our conversation last night hadn't made any difference to, well, us."

She smiled. Only moments ago, she was thinking the same thing.

"No, Patrick, we're still friends."

He put his arms around her, and she heard him sigh.

"Well, you know I'd like more, but I've promised not to rush you. I wanted you to have this before I left." He let her go and held out a slender, white, silken case, tied with a red ribbon.

She took it and looked up at him.

"Patrick, I..."

"Open it." He brushed the back of his fingers over her cheek. "It reminded me of you."

Alice pulled the ribbon away and opened the case. Nestled against a background of rich crimson velvet lay strands of the most delicate and tiniest pearls Alice had ever seen. Patrick turned her to face the image definer and took the necklace from its box to fasten it around her neck. He kissed her shoulder as he fastened the clasp, then stepped back, assured of the reception of his gift.

Alice had never received a gift so exquisite. Three

strands of tiny pearls hung from the clasp, their lustre matched only by the brilliance of the teardrop-shaped emerald, suspended in a frame of diamonds.

What can anyone say when they receive a gift such as this? Alice touched the emerald and turned to look up at Patrick. She couldn't speak, and tears pricked behind her eyes.

"I—I don't know what to say," her voice wavered. "I want to say beautiful, but it doesn't go far enough."

Patrick brushed her hair away from her neck, exposing more of the pearls.

"Alice, a pearl is the most natural and perfect creation of nature, but even pearls and emeralds cannot express how lovely you are or how precious."

He took her hand in his and held it against him, smoothing her cheek with his other hand. Overcome, she stood and allowed him to draw her into his embrace. She saw their reflection in the image definer. They looked like the perfect couple.

"I'll return soon and visit you at…" his voice trailed off when he caught sight of the portrait on the wall behind her.

"That's you."

"Sarah, the steward, did it for me," Alice looked up at the picture.

"She's caught you exactly. I love the mouth and chin. Proud. Hopeful and determined."

"You see things others don't."

"Do I? Maybe, I'm closer to you than the others."

And after brushing her lips with his, he was gone.

Alice sat at her dressing table and ran her fingers lightly over the necklace. Patrick had chosen well. The pendant cleverly brought out the subtleties of her skin and eyes, and for him to bring her such a wonderful gift after her refusal last night only highlighted his sincerity and affection. Perhaps her feelings for him would change over time, and though she did not intend to hurt him, she'd spent her whole life pleasing other people, doing what they insisted.

Alice unclasped the necklace and placed it carefully in its box. Patrick was special, and he was dear to her, but wishing she loved him wouldn't make it happen.

Alice found Principal Katya at breakfast, and she sat down with a courteous, "Good morning, Principal Katya," before picking up the teapot and pouring them both tea.

"Good morning, Alice. Patrick left to visit his family, I hear. He didn't wake me to say goodbye."

"I saw him; he stopped by on his way to the shuttle."

Principal Katya eyed her young companion, trying to detect any shadow of disappointment because she seemed different this morning.

"He is taken with you."

Alice felt a flush of shyness. She finished her task of pouring tea and tried to speak casually of her relationship with Patrick.

"He thinks he is too, Principal Katya, he's a dear

friend, but we scarcely know each other."

Principal Katya agreed and let the matter drop.

"Are you ready to meet your new family, Alice?" she asked. "Mary will arrive in two days, and you will start your new life."

Alice mustered a confidence to her voice she didn't altogether feel. It had been enough, just saying goodbye to Patrick. All these emotions. All these new beginnings. Her 'vacation' had been such a whirlwind of new experiences; she barely had time to catch her breath. Principal Katya, so kind and generous, needed an answer Alice hoped would be sufficiently convincing.

"Yes, I'm looking forward to meeting her. I think it will be nice to have a home."

Principal Katya watched her over the rim of her teacup. There was bravado in that reply. Alice looked out over the gardens, chiefly to avoid meeting Principal Katya's unblinking gaze, a gaze which had become a time-honoured skill, developed solely to read a person's reactions.

"If you find you are not happy, Alice. Please contact me. You may come back here, and we will see what will make you happy." Principal Katya reached over and took Alice's hand to reassure her she may belong here if she chose.

"That's very kind, Principal Katya, thank you, but I'm sure Mary is as nervous about meeting me as I am of her."

"Well, you have two days of your vacation left to do

as you please." Principal Katya, back in cheerful mode, patted her hands on the table. "After breakfast, you do what you wish. No crochet today. Just go and play. If you need a shuttle, speak to a steward, and one will be ordered for you."

———

Alice asked Chef for bread to take down to the ducks at the lake, much to Statesman Mellor's amusement, who joined her on her walk in the garden, engaging her in a discussion about plants and flowers. At least it distracted her thoughts from all the goodbyes she had to endure and the reality that soon, there would be more.

Throughout the afternoon, Alice enjoyed links from both Principal Hardy and Dr Grossmith and later, after she dressed for dinner, took a call from Amelia, who, true to her word, had left a message each day.

"You look fabulous. New clothes?"

"Yes, Principal Katya and I went shopping. Well, shopping here in my suite."

"Suite? My goodness! That sounds grand."

"It is Amelia. It's beautiful here, and they treat me like a queen. I have clothes and things of my own now, and the day after tomorrow, I meet my new family."

"Wow, how come?

"They did some sort of profile, genetics, DNA. There were thousands of matches, but one matched me in a way most of the others didn't. She's coming here and has agreed I can stay with her if I like."

"That's brilliant. Where does she live?"

"In the Calamities."

"Which ones?"

Again, not a hint of judgement.

"Principality 19. It's my home country. Australia."

Amelia nodded. Alice still thought of her home country by name.

"A proper home and being established may be just what you need."

Alice agreed. "I'm tired of saying goodbye to people. Dr Grossmith, Kelly, you, Patrick this morning and soon, Principal Katya…"

"Whoa, back up. Statesman Patrick?"

"Yes. We spent the day together yesterday, swimming at a pool in the Tabernacle grounds, then we archered, played archery, um, I'm not sure what they call it, but it was good fun. He's very sweet."

"I see. Good fun? Sweet?"

"I can't imagine what you mean, Amelia. He's just a friend. Talking of friends, I haven't heard from Kelly."

Amelia shook her head and pulled one of her many faces. This one was her puzzled face.

"Did you expect to?"

"Well, yes, she said she would try to keep in touch."

"Ah, yes," Amelia realised what had happened. "Kelly had your cells. Once they're removed, she forgets everything about you. KELA is designed like that. You were a bit special; perhaps she thought the truth might upset you."

"Have you heard from her?"

Amelia reluctantly admitted she had. "But she didn't have a KELA procedure with me. My surgery was more routine. I was born with three kidneys."

"Three kidneys?"

"Yes, I know, bizarre, but they all worked until two of them failed, both at the same time, then the third one got lonely and started failing as well. Dr Clere grew two replacements, and Principal Hardy removed the extra kidney. I had to stay on the station longer because my body was used to functioning with three kidneys, and they had to be sure it was okay with one less. Kelly Ann stayed with me for a few days because I only needed observation. You had KELA carers before Kelly Ann; you were her assignment after she left me."

"According to Kelly, hearts can take up to three years to grow, but kidneys only take a month. I learned a lot from her."

"You still have me, Alice. And Patrick and Principal Katya. You've only been back in the land of the living for a few years and only a few months with walking and talking properly. There are other friends out there waiting for you to find them."

"It's disappointing about Kelly. I never had friends before, and I suppose I don't want to part with even one."

"Well, I'm being reassigned later this week. Recuperation officially over, I'm glad to say."

"Will you be on Earth?"

"Of course. Not sure where yet, I can list

preferences, but I haven't decided."

"How is Tyro Drake?"

Amelia grinned. "He's gone home. He's six years younger than me, Alice; people will talk!"

Amelia promised a visit when she settled into her new assignment, and hearing from her cheered Alice. It was sad about Kelly, but it wasn't in Alice's power to change the workings of this world.

CHAPTER THIRTY-EIGHT _

Principal Ryan stepped from the elevator onto the senior officer's deck early after spending the night in stellar mapping. He never kept track of the hours he spent there, but he was tired enough to realise he'd probably overdone it. Thankfully, there was plenty of time to shower and sleep before he was due back on the bridge. Patrick was back on board, so there was no need to rush.

Principal Ryan's presence on the officers' deck coincided with that of a young woman, evidently hurrying to leave Patrick's quarters, jacket undone and fruitlessly striving to pin up her hair as she stepped through the portal. Principal Ryan recognised her as a member of the engineering crew, but she didn't see him. He stood still, almost causing her to collide with him. She recovered herself with the selfsame look of horror he witnessed when encountering Dr Langley in the auditorium.

"Engineer McIntyre."

He kept his chin level with the floor, his eyes fixed downwards at her, his face stern.

Upon finding him barring her escape, she dropped her arms to her sides, her hair sliding down in an untidy knot to her shoulder. Principal Ryan appraised her dishevelled appearance with a disparaging up and down movement of his eyes. She knew he permitted no-one to be out of uniform anywhere on the ship other than their assigned deck and at leisure in designated areas. She took a deep breath to calm herself but, faced with him grim and unsmiling, stammered out whatever came into her head.

"Principal Ryan, I'm so sorry I…" and she glanced toward Patrick's quarters. Then quickly zipped up her jacket. "I'm late for duty, I…"

He kept her there a moment longer, just for sport, she thought accusingly, allowing her to act pathetic, disregarding her attempts to explain and allowing her to squirm her way through a blush. Then he stood aside and watched her scamper past with a mumbled,

"Thank you, Principal Ryan."

He started back towards his quarters. McIntyre was just Patrick's type. Tall, athletic, long dark hair, though he wouldn't have considered her rather quiet nature to have appealed to Patrick. This wasn't an isolated incident. Female crewmembers were relatively frequent visitors to Patrick's quarters, but at least the others had the decency and respect for protocol to adjust their uniforms properly when they left. He would mention McIntyre's transgression to Patrick later.

Later in the day, he and Patrick stood together, observing the proceedings out on the space dock.

"I see you spent yesterday in engineering, Patrick."

"I didn't get back until the afternoon. I intended coming up to the bridge, but I made the mistake of checking in on engineering first and, I'm afraid, there I stayed."

"You didn't spend long with your family."

"Most of the day, Ryan. I'll see them again. Mother will hound me if I don't, but she'll come up to the ship as she usually does, anyway. She sends her regards to you and said she saw your parents at the Tabernacle during winter. Is your father still ill?"

Ryan never discussed his personal life.

"Yes, recovering though, my mother tells me."

The short answer as predicted.

"Are you going to the surface, Ryan?"

"Yes, soon. I'll stay with my parents until the cotillion. I can't leave here until Statesman Junnot arrives."

"She has big shoes to fill. Hennessey was an incredible asset."

"Agreed, but it was Junnot's posting until she mangled herself, and Hennessey knew it was temporary. On another matter," Ryan swung briefly towards Patrick before returning to his previous position. "I saw Engineer McIntyre leaving your quarters this morning, half in and half out of her uniform."

"I was still asleep when she left. I didn't see her."

"She seemed uncomfortable about meeting me in the corridor. You may need to remind her of protocol, Patrick."

"McIntyre's scared of you, Ryan!" Patrick laughed. "Anyway, she's reassigned to the Magellan for her next tour of duty."

"I'd like to go and look over the Magellan myself," Ryan said, McIntyre's uniform breach requiring no further discussion.

"It's only a shell. Half of it's in space dock; the other half is still in the shipyard."

"Even so. It would be interesting. Where is McIntyre assigned?"

"Shipyard for now, on the engineering team."

"She won't have uniform concerns there."

Patrick grinned to himself. Ryan was such a stuffed shirt.

Alice stilled the anxious little worm wriggling around inside her and busied herself with getting ready to meet Mary Greer. When the register announced a message, she thought it would be Principal Katya to tell her to come to the great hall, but it was Patrick.

"Good morning, Alice. I just wanted to wish you luck for today, not that you'll need it. You seem to be wowing everyone wherever you go! Even Principal Katya's picked up a few of your sayings."

"Hello, Patrick. It's lovely to hear from you. Which sayings has she picked up?"

"I heard her say, 'I love it,' often. You say that."

"I didn't realise."

"Well, you do. I find it endearing."

"I didn't realise that, either."

"You're gorgeous! Don't ever change. Alice, I must go; this was just a quick call. I can't wait to see you again."

The registry flickered off, but that Patrick cared enough to call gave Alice's spirits a much-needed lift.

Alice saw the automatrans from the window, a different vehicle entirely from a shuttle and only big enough for two people. She knew these ships were high altitude and flew incredibly fast. This one had Tabernacle markings and came to rest a little out of her view. It was time to meet her new family.

Principal Katya stood with Alice on the steps of the Tabernacle. The grey-haired woman who alighted from the automatrans stood in much the same way as Alice had on her first day here, her back to the Tabernacle and looking out over the lake. Like most people here, she was taller than Alice. She wore khaki-coloured pants with a white blouse, her jacket thrown casually over her shoulder, presenting the air of someone comfortable in their surroundings. Alice stepped down and made her way towards her, checking that Principal Katya was walking alongside. Seeing her apprehension, Principal Katya took her arm.

As they drew near, Mary Greer turned and smiled broadly at Alice. Possibly seventy years old, perhaps a little more, with a youngish, unlined face. Her eyes, the same green as Alice's, were misty with unshed tears.

Alice felt a baffling connection to her, so when Mary

raised her arms, Alice went into them with hesitating, as though this moment, this belonging, had waited for her all her life.

"Alice? Alice, I am so happy to meet you. I'm Mary Greer," she said, laughing through her tears. Her voice, educated and pleasant, had a familiar accent. Wiping away her tears with the back of her hand, she apologised, "I'm sorry for blubbering, I'm an old softie, it's just that since I knew about you; since Principal Katya asked me to come here, that you might be part of my family, I have so longed for this day."

Any fears Alice had about meeting Mary and moving to the Calamities were dispelled in those first few seconds. Mary Greer was family; of that, there could be no doubt. Alice's face set into a smile she was sure would be permanent.

Principal Katya kept her distance while Alice and Mary embraced, looking for all the world like a family reunion. She silently praised Principal Hardy's vision of a family for Alice and her cleverness at bringing these two people together.

"A happy meeting, I think," she said finally, her face lit with the happiest of smiles. "Alice, you have an Aunt Mary."

"Aunt?" Alice looked at Principal Katya.

"From what we can tell, Alice, and we are not exactly certain, Mary's line matches with the Watkins line. As your uncle was Martin Watkins, I thought she might be best suited as an aunt."

Mary laughed. "Well, I am never going to be anyone's mother. Aunt will do nicely." Then she looked at Alice for her agreement. "Mary is fine if you prefer."

Alice was speechless, lost somewhere between sheer happiness at meeting her family and bewilderment at the connection to Mary. Principal Katya waved away the worry about titles as a thing that would happen naturally, but Alice loved the idea.

"Aunt would be wonderful," she found herself babbling, "though we never said 'aunt', it was always auntie. An aunt was someone to be feared. Someone strict!" Alice brought her excitement under control. This aunt would be neither fearful nor strict.

"Auntie, it is. I love it," her choice of words catching Alice by surprise. "Or Mary. Or both!"

Principal Katya positioned herself between the two women and linked arms.

"We will have tea. You two have much to talk about. Mary?"

"Yes, Principal Katya?"

"If you and Alice wish to stay for a few days before you return home, you are most welcome."

"That's kind of you, but I've left Jane alone, and she is longing to meet Alice, our new niece." Mary looked over to Alice, making sure she knew that she now belonged with her and Jane.

Alice felt like a child, to be handheld as she walked through a new place. She had been offered a family of her own, people to love who wanted and welcomed her. She felt no fear at being led because she didn't know the way, and this time, she held no resentment.

As Mary and Principal Katya chatted, looking over crochet designs and discussing hamburgers and pudding, Alice speculated, without a trace of her natural caution, about her new life with an Auntie Mary and Auntie Jane of her own to love.

Principal Katya decided they would return to Auntie Mary's farm in the automatrans, making the flight above the ocean faster and less dull. To say goodbye to Principal Katya and Statesman Mellor was hard for Alice, but knowing she had only to say the word and she may visit anytime made the parting so much easier. Principal Katya kissed Mary and Alice both and waved until the automatrans rose so high, she became a little speck on the grass.

Alice expected awkwardness when she first met Mary, but it was as though they had known each other for years. Although the journey to Principality 19 was relatively short, she had so many questions, she wasn't aware of time passing. Mary told her all about the location of her new home, and Alice listened with interest.

"We used to call that area Tasmania," she said. "But I've never been there."

"It's beautiful, trust me."

Alice did trust her.

"Tell me about Auntie Jane."

"Well, she and I are both medical doctors, or rather we were, we're the same age, seventy-three and retired for many years. As we live in the Calamities, we didn't like to spend too much time apart, so we didn't apply for extensions."

"Principal Katya said that was why Jane couldn't travel with you today. I know that people from the Calamities, or couples, have to travel separately."

"That's right, but we seldom go anywhere anyway," Mary said with a smile. "We're happy and comfortable where we are. Jane and I have been together for forty years. She has a problem with her voice; she doesn't speak so much, but she listens well!"

"Where does Jane come from?"

"Principality 19, descended from the original inhabitants."

"She's aboriginal?"

"Why yes, Alice, that is the old term. Of course, there must have been many in your time. The last wave of plague took a terrible toll on her race, as it did on many."

It hadn't occurred to Alice that Jane was aboriginal.

"In the 1800s," Alice's words came tumbling out, dispossessed of her control over her voice, "the settlers drove all the indigenous tribes from Tasmania. There was such racism and mistrust of the native people; the settlers took all their lands and completely displaced them, driving them off Tasmania and onto the islands. Never to return."

Mary was horrified. "That's barbaric. I didn't know that."

No, Alice said to herself, as her thoughts once more became her own, *neither did I.*

They'd left Principality One in the early evening, just as the sun set. When the automatrans came to a smooth stop, Alice was amazed to see that same sun rising over the Earth. She had lost an entire night in less than an hour. Mary saw her looking at the sky

"Time difference, Alice. You get used to it when you travel."

Alice jumped down, her heart beating hard with anticipation and possibly, just a smidgeon unprepared to be convinced about the Calamities. Still, the automatrans set them down on a green lawn where several tall trees towered above them, and Alice caught the scent of lemon-scented gum trees. They smelled divine. The house, a single storey dwelling with a verandah skirting three sides, was achingly familiar to the houses from her old life. Set up high on a clifftop with breathtaking views of the ocean. From the verandah at the back, wide steps led down to neat gardens and beyond, pastures, green and glorious. The house was painted white, with the large windows reflecting the morning sunlight. This was not small, not dilapidated, not prison-like. To Alice, the whole property was more like a prize, a reward, rather than a punishment for being different.

Two large, boisterous dogs ran barking from the house, followed by a woman, hurrying as fast as she could. She was of a similar build and height to Auntie Mary, her skin was dark, and her curly, greying hair was tied back in a bun. She pushed the dogs away as they tried to include her in their excitement at having Mary home.

Giving up trying to hurry the woman along, the dogs dashed off towards Mary, smothering her with wet kisses of greeting. They then turned their attention to Alice for the same treatment, unmindful of almost knocking her to the ground. Once Alice was sufficiently slobbered on, they dashed back to Jane to encourage her along. Mary greeted the other woman, embracing her as if their separation had been weeks instead of just a few hours.

Alice stopped walking; this place was idyllic. She took a deep breath, sea air, mingled with the lemon-scented gum, infused her with a sense of beginning. She had been blessed to be brought here, and her ridiculous inherited prejudices and fear of lesbians, along with her dread of the Calamities, were completely erased.

Mary held Jane's hand and drew her close to Alice. Jane was smiling and weeping and shaking her head and wiping her eyes. She held Alice's face in her hands and then embraced her fondly; Alice had to wipe the tears from her own eyes. Jane's voice was soft, and although Alice found it difficult to hear, the emotion and love were unmistakable.

"Principal Katya messaged that you were on your way. Alice, I'm Jane Greer, and I am proud to be your Auntie."

Mary joined in with the hugging, and the dogs, not to be excluded, bounded around with excitement. The three women laughed, putting their arms around each other as they walked together across the grass to the house. Alice glanced back as the automatrans lifted, and for a second, fancied she saw a tiny explosion of colour and a glimpse of the youthful figure she had seen before. The vision was so fleeting; she decided it was simply her mind playing tricks. She wouldn't think about it now, not in the moment of such happiness. This was Alice's, or perhaps Alexis's as well—final homecoming.

END BOOK ONE

ACKNOWLEDGEMENTS

Thank you for reading The Afterlife of Alice Watkins: Book One. If you enjoyed the first part of Alice's story, I would love you to hop over to your orders page on Amazon and leave a review. Good reviews are the lifeblood of Indie Authors and we all thank you for your support.

I would also like to thank my editors, Amy and Jo for their patience and diligence. I am so lucky to have them on the team!

If you would like to keep updated with new releases, you can sign up for my (occasional) newsletter on my website: https://matildascotneybooks.com/

Or connect with me on Facebook:
https://www.facebook.com/Offtheplanetbooks

OTHER BOOKS BY MATILDA SCOTNEY

The Afterlife of Alice Watkins: Book Two
The Soul Monger: Book One
Revelations: The Soul Monger Book Two
Testimony: The Soul Monger Book Three
Joy in Four Parts: A Quirky Sci Fi Novella
Myth of Origin: A Sci Fi Adventure
Foresight: A Science Fiction short story

ABOUT THE AUTHOR _

When I'm not on off on some galactic quest of the imagination with my trusty chihuahua sidekick Oggie, I can be found in Australia collecting teapots and nerding about all things Star Wars.